MAD JONES, HERO

THE ACCIDENTAL PROPHET

— BOOK 2 —

BY

QUIN HILLYER

A LIBERTY ISLAND BOOK
ISBN: 978-1-947942-46-2

Liberty Island
libertyislandmag.com

Published in the United States of America

In loving memory of Haywood H. Hillyer III
and Haywood H. Hillyer IV

CONTENTS

PROLOGUE

In *Mad Jones, Heretic,* young high school history teacher Madison Lee Jones of Mobile, Alabama, already having lost both parents at a young age, suffers as his grandfather, his wife, his unborn child, and his mother-in-law all die tragically in rapid succession. Grief-stricken and angry, Jones vents by penning 59 religious theses (see appendix) and pinning them to church doors in Mobile and in New Orleans. With his theses unexpectedly (and unintentionally) attracting a national social media following, and spurred on by an odd collection of entrepreneurial friends, Jones—an only intermittently churchgoing Episcopalian—begins a writing and public-speaking "ministry" to elucidate his theme that anger at God can lead to deeper faith. His inaugural public speech/homily, at a Good Friday service at a "charismatic" church in a New Orleans suburb, begins as a fiasco and a comedy of errors—yet somehow ends in triumph, as Jones leaves the church "experiencing a boundless optimism.... He felt that he was leaving a wilderness, and that a Promised Land awaited."

BOOK THREE: CHRONICLES

CHAPTER ONE

Radiating enthusiasm, the Heberts had prevailed upon Mad to stay for dinner with some of the congregation's leaders after the triumphal Good Friday service. (The same invitation had not been extended to Becky, who couldn't help radiating a disdain for the brand of religion they practiced.) Mad hadn't been there long before he realized that the dinner was matchmaker Angelina's setup for him to meet Tonya and Rhonda, two of the most devout young adults at the church. Both wore sequined, body-hugging outfits; both had highly styled, shoulder-length hair, Tonya's jet black and Rhonda's bleached blonde. Rhonda, a 20-year-old waitress, seemed genuinely sweet and demure. But Tonya, 21, a student at the University of New Orleans, kept finding ways to put her hand on Mad's butt, and kept licking her lips at him and winking when she thought nobody else could see. Mad had been relieved to finally escape, and made the drive back to Mobile in just over two hours.

He found Becky waiting for him on his front porch. She was in a foul mood. She said the video taken that day would be a disaster if shown to any Catholic or mainline Protestant audience; she said she was surprised Mad hadn't stayed overnight with "one of those little holy-roller tarts" (apparently referring to Tonya and Rhonda); she said Mad's tardiness was inexcusably unprofessional; and she said she had put too much work into the new venture to see Mad screw it all up—"especially when I'm not getting laid while I'm at it." She was some kind of ticked off. Mad felt thoroughly chastened.

Two days later, Mad repaired immediately from Easter services to join the headmaster's family for dinner. The headmaster wanted Mad to know that even though his teaching job was lost for now, he still was considered part of the school family and still was afforded everybody's love and sympathy. Mad appreciated the gesture.

By Monday night, Becky's attitude had changed entirely. The office phone had rung all day, with charismatic churches all across the country

3

calling to schedule Mad. Word had gone out all weekend from Apostles of the Word that Mad was the real deal, despite what the highly respected Rev. Rob Patterson had thought and said. But except for a few Gulf Coast–area engagements (at which Becky agreed to let Mad speak for less than what would behis usual fee), Mad's first real speaking tour would not begin for about another month. (It was being set up quite carefully to best use the board members' strengths and to appeal to carefully targeted demographics.)

Also on Monday, Mad's first daily, self-syndicated, spiritual-advice newspaper column—called "Madison Avenue"—had run in 11 morning papers ranging from Florida to Oregon. It was packaged to run only 300 words each day, letter writer's question included. The first question had been picked by Mad from submissions to the web site: "Dear Madison: I want to be devout, but I can't stand my pastor, and I can't leave my church because my family has gone to the same church for three generations and it would break my mother's heart if I did. What should I do? Sincerely, Stuck in Wrong Flock."

"Dear Stuck," answered Mad. "Your note didn't say why you are not happy with your pastor, but the way I see it, faith isn't for the faint-hearted. Only the faint-hearted would let a poor pastor be an obstacle for a spiritual life.

"Even though the Bible says that the way to God the Father is through the Son, it still leaves open the possibility that there are many ways to the Son. A church is more than its pastor or priest. A church is made up of a whole community of believers. Find people in your church with whom you share interests or values, and work with them to house the homeless or feed the hungry, or to start a spiritual discussion group, or whatever else floats your religious boat so it can sail toward Jesus. Christ did not say (Thesis 56) 'come unto thy pastor…and he will refresh you.' He said to go unto Him, unto Jesus. Meanwhile, though, try to get to know your pastor more deeply. Maybe you are missing something good in him. We're all flawed, and the important thing is to look past what you see as flaws and find the good in someone. That's how it is with approaching God, as well. Even if God seems to have acquiesced to something that seems unfair to us, we need to keep going back to Him and back to Him and back to Him. That's what faith is all about."

4

Mad meant every word of it but, frankly, he thought it nevertheless was pablum. "What the heck do I know about this stuff?" he kept saying to Becky and Justin. "I've never been profound about anything, so why should anyone take me seriously?"

"Oh, just shut up and write, loverboy," was Becky's invariable answer, once adding that "there's gold in your lack of profundity."

Mad reacted angrily to that; he didn't care about gold but about helping people find faith.

Amazingly to him, it seemed that lots and lots of people wanted Mad to help them find it. In addition to the strong demand for Mad to take speaking engagements (usually at $1,000, plus bare-minimum travel expenses, per appearance), letters were flooding in to "Madison Avenue"—and the Mad Religion website was already attracting a fair number of advertisers and loads of web-surfer "hits." Part of the appeal was that Mad promised to write at least one entry each day for the chat room. (Becky had set up a special electronic identifier, triggered only by Mad's special password, that let other chat participants know that it was indeed Mad, not some impostor from Timbuktu or somewhere.)

By week's end, six more papers had signed up to start running Mad's advice column within the month. Arrangements had been made, too, by an aggressive young New York book publisher to send down a ghostwriter in the near future who would spend hours talking to and taping Mad, so the writer and publisher could start figuring out how best to present Mad's ideas in a marketable book format.

Mad didn't really know what to make of all this. He just followed whatever schedule Becky gave him each day. He did as much as he could from home, so as to avoid Becky's unceasing sexual innuendoes whenever he joined her and the new (grandmotherly) part-time secretary at the office. Staying away from the office also meant he was blessedly able to see less of Justin, who kept finding excuses between physical training sessions to drop in at the office unannounced. Justin's motive was as obvious as it was seemingly hopeless: He desperately wanted a romance with Becky. To discourage him, Becky still insisted on calling him Mr. Luke, even though they were contemporaries.

("Mad," Becky complained late that first week, "if that little fruitcake doesn't find somebody else to dream about humping, and find her soon,

I'm gonna personally castrate his little things and throw them to the fishes in Mobile Bay!" Then, as an afterthought: "On the other hand, Mad, if *you* do not *start* humping me, I'll castrate you, too, and make you the modern world's first gelded prophet.")

Despite all her inexplicable crassness, Mad had to admit to himself that Becky was enormously talented at the business side. He had doubted that Mad, Mad World, Inc. could attract enough money to pay the salaries and fees for Mad, Becky, Justin, Mary, Buzz, Don, and the part-time secretary, much less generate a cash flow big enough to have some left over for charity. But Becky was a whiz. He had no clue how it all worked; he knew only that Becky announced four days after Easter that he should already start thinking about which charitable causes he wanted to support with MMW's first grant.

In the chat room, FD Thom, Affirmed, and Perdicaris had become the most frequent participants, along with a new, bitter critic calling himself Defender of the Faith (later shortened to just Defender). M. Magdalene, oddly, had dropped completely from the picture.

Late in the week, Mad was happy to see Jezebel? finally show up again, even for only one quick comment. It was in response to a particularly venomous entry from Defender, part of which said that Mad ought to "stop polluting his family name with his idiotic blatherings."

"Hey, Defender, lay off," wrote Jezebel?. "I knew Mad's father, and I think he'd be proud that his son is inspiring atheists like me to consider whether there really might be a God after all. You may think you have all the answers, but I don't think you even understand the questions some of us have. Mad does, and I thank him for it."

Mad was dying to know who Jezebel? was. He figured that if she had known Ben, she must be somebody from Mobile. Maybe one of those liberal English or sociology professors from Spring Hill, he thought. Maybe one of those intelligent women who always wished that Ben would let go of Mel's memory and begin dating again.

"Hello, Jezebel?," Mad wrote, his entry highlighted on the screen with the purple border Becky had created. "Thanks for being so nice. I really wish I knew who you were. Please let me know. If not on the chat room, then call my office."

But Jezebel? neither answered nor called, and Affirmed and Perdicaris picked up the cudgel against Defender for several more hours of sometimes vitriolic debate. Affirmed, thought Mad when reviewing the messages later that night, was starting to go a little overboard, at one point writing that Mad might even be "a new Moses."

The lines that Mad liked best, however, came from Cowardly Lion, who was apparently a new participant. "I can't believe how intense and angry all you folks are getting," he wrote. "Some of you Mad-vocates sound like you have no brains, and Defender, sounds like you have no heart. If I had enough courage, I'd tell the whole lot of you to get off this yellow-brick Internet and go get high in the poppy fields. Every one of you needs to just chill out, dudes, or else the great Wizard will never let you reach the Emerald City in the sky."

It was a bizarre entry, thought Mad, but something about it really tickled him.

MMW kept growing, and Mad actually became somewhat accustomed to the routine of monitoring the web site, writing his newspaper column, reading a host of books on theology and spirituality, exercising nearly daily, and writing notes to himself for things he wanted to include in future discussions with his book ghostwriter. He also wrote and re-wrote notes for his upcoming lecture tour, and repeatedly practiced his delivery in front of a mirror. He still had trouble ginning up consistent enthusiasm for the whole enterprise, but figured that he darn well ought to live up to the responsibilities he had assumed. He told himself that, in a roundabout way, he was doing it to honor Claire's memory—and also because he knew Daddy Lee would be disappointed if he ever failed to deliver on an obligation.

Fortunately, ever since his post-press conference plea to the demonstrators for them to vacate his block for the sake of his neighbors—which, amazingly, they honored—Mad no longer felt under siege. The mime and a small, hardy band of enthusiasts did occasionally show up outside the charmless office building that MMW shared with a small realty firm and a three-person law partnership, almost always with some new, clever chant or posterboard sign, but they never stayed more than an hour or so and never really got in anybody's way. Mad once had tried to approach the mime to express appreciation (feigned) for the mime's support, but the mime arched his back, hissed, and ran away like a skittish kitten.

Toward the end of April, Steve Matheson had the Rev. Patterson as a guest on *Gut Check*. Patterson was railing against President Clinton about the Lewinsky situation. With a few minutes left in the show, Matheson deftly switched gears.

"Okay, Rob, lemme move on to a slightly different topic. You know, I've been fascinated by this guy Madison Jones, down in Mobile, who wrote up 59 religious propositions where he says God isn't always perfect, but in the long run God does offer salvation and should therefore still be worshipped. That's not exactly it, but as I see it, that's the gist of what Jones is saying. What I love about this young guy—and he's only 25, I think—what I love is that he doesn't take any guff from anybody. He held a press conference a few weeks back, and one of those arrogant network reporters asked a question that seemed to belittle Christian faith as a fairy tale or something, and this Jones guy just ripped him to shreds. It was beautiful, just beautiful."

Patterson, anticipating where Matheson's monologue was going, tried to interrupt, but Matheson's word flow was like a river too big to dam.

"Anyway," continued Matheson, "I've watched re-runs of a feature on Jones that the *Acute Vision* show did, and in it Jones was asked about the Lewinsky situation, and he was critical of the president just like you are, although really not very stridently. Still, he's on your side on this, Reverend. But you have been very critical of this young man. You've called him a 'false prophet' and a 'pretty boy,' and you said he is 'a blasphemer, a heretic, and a profiteer of the rankest New Age variety.' That's really harsh, Rob, really harsh. What I want to know is, if this young man is inspiring skeptics to become Christians, and if he's on your side of the culture wars, or at least of the Clinton wars, then why are you blasting him from here to kingdom come?"

Finally, Patterson spoke up, voice oozing with Georgia peachiness. "Well, Steve, I'm just not sure you unduh-sta-uhnd. Anybody with a lick of clev-uh-ness can position himself against the lies and moral de-PRAV-uh-tee of Bill Clinton, especially if he's in the South where such de-PRAV-uh-tee is especially detested. The boy is trying to fool devout God-fearing people into buying his snake oil to make him rich. But the Scripture says…"

Matheson interrupted: "But Rob, here's a guy who took on the demon 'elite media' that you are always warning against! And he says that even if we interpret God as having done us wrong, we should still remain faithful! And he says Clinton's lying! Isn't this Jones guy a horse out of your own barn?"

"Steve, this Jones guy even goes by the name of Mad. That's what he truly is; he's mad. I think the young man is unstable. He says God is a jerk, and…"

"And he says," broke in Matheson, looking down at some notes, "be strong and of good courage, uh…da-dum-da-dum-da-dum, some other stuff along those lines, quote, 'because God's love has been poured into our hearts through the Holy Spirit which has been given to us.' That's right up your alley, Reverend, and then, this is what I love about this guy, just a real gut-check kinda guy, he closes by writing, 'Here I shout; I cannot do otherwise.'"

"But Steve…"

"He's paraphrasing your Protestant founder, Reverend. He's paraphrasing Martin Luther, who of course all urban Catholics like me were taught was almost akin to Lucifer, but he's your idol, and Luther said, 'Here I stand,' and now this Jones guy says, 'Here I shout!' Nothing reticent about this guy, Reverend, and he's right from your Protestant tradition. You should love him! Anyway, time's run out; we gotta go. I thank the Rev. Patterson and my other guests; this has been *Gut Check*, and we'll have more gut checks same time tomorrow night. G'bye!"

Laura Green's life had become a whirlwind. Her work on *Acute Vision*, which had boosted the ratings enough to earn the show a renewal for next fall, had so impressed the network majordomos that they had twice again requested she be pulled from her new duties at the New Orleans station to do special assignments for them. Rumor had it, they were considering a full-time contract offer for her as the ace reporter, second only to the show's hostess. The honchos had always liked a male-female balance; but their market research showed that tabloidish news magazine

9

shows were seen as more believable, and drew larger audiences, when the reports were made by women. So the new schtick for *Acute Vision*, to distinguish it from all the other similar shows, would be for women to do almost all the on-camera work. And Laura supposedly was at the top of their list.

Not only that, but a New York–based network reporter, a fast-rising young star, had shown some major extracurricular interest in Laura. He had flown her up to the Big Apple each of the last three weekends of April, wined and diner her and, by the third weekend, bedded her as well. (Obviously, she knew how and when to use sex for her benefit. Besides, this guy *really* was a hunk, even if a little shallow and vain for her tastes.)

Still, she couldn't get Mad out of her mind. On that first weekend visiting the New York hunk, her flight out of New Orleans had left on Friday evening. She knew that Mad's first speaking engagement would be that afternoon at Apostles of the Word, which wasn't too far from the airport. The timing was just right. Out of sheer curiosity (so she told herself), she had attended. Within two minutes of her arrival, she had felt like Charlton Heston on the Planet of the Apes, visiting territory that looked familiar but that had a distinctly alien feel. Everything seemed off-kilter. This wasn't Uptown or even Mid-City New Orleans, or even the Jefferson Parish suburbs that she knew. Surrounded by enthusiasts quickly enraptured by every mention of the Lord or Jesus, her senses assaulted by loud, repetitive music, Laura had had no idea how to behave. And she couldn't understand why, during the first half hour, Mad was nowhere to be seen. On either side of her, people had begun speaking in tongues. But she had stood there, toward the back of the far-right row, stiff-legged and uncomfortable.

When Mad made his dramatic entrance and tried to explain his lateness, only to have his whole story treated as a parable by the Rev. Hebert, Laura had first been offended by Hebert's interruptions and then amazed that everybody around her accepted it as part of the normal order of things. "Poor, poor Mad," she had thought. "He's become a one-man freak show, and this is all my fault."

Yet just as she felt the most out of place and out of sorts, she had glimpsed a few rows away one other young woman, a buxom and slightly thick-hipped blonde maybe 30 years old, who looked as uncomfortable as she, Laura, felt. Ms. Buxom had not spoken in tongues, had not joined the chants, had not participated at all. She had just stared way up to where Mad stood in front of the congregation, looked decidedly perplexed and troubled, and occasionally wiped her eyes. Like Laura, she was dressed in a slightly more muted, more classic blouse and skirt, unlike the gaudier clothes of most of the female Apostles worshippers. Laura had felt the blonde was a kindred spirit, and had determined to speak with her when the service concluded. But when it finally did end, the blonde disappeared quickly from the crush of people, and Laura missed her.

Now, three weeks later, some wild hair had led Laura to watch *Gut Check*, and there she had seen host Steve Matheson take the unctuous Rev. Patterson to task. And out of the blue, a picture of the buxom blonde flashed across her mind again. Whoever she was, she had seemed moved by Mad in a similar way to Laura.

And it was only in thinking *that*, that Laura first acknowledged to herself that she indeed had been moved. It wasn't the sex; it was the faith. Something about Mad's earnestness had moved her. Something about his pain-deepened courage. Somehow, it radiated. *He* radiated. Or, rather, something radiated that was both from within him and yet greater than he and working through him, taking on Mad's essence as it did.

Laura shook her head to clear it. Damn, what was she thinking? What was all of this esoteric crap?

From the Mad Religion chat room:

"Hey, did you all see the way Steve Matheson blew away Rob Patterson last night?" wrote FD Thom. "Matheson made a monkey of him!"

From Cowardly Lion: "Yeah, but some monkeys can fly, and they'll swoop down and snatch you from the Yellow Brick Road and put you in the witch's castle!"

To which somebody writing anonymously said: "Hey Coward, your act is getting old and it always was pointless. Why don't you just shut up already with your Oz sh**?"

On April 30, a few days before he was to begin his first extensive speaking tour, Mad pulled out of his large stack of mail a hand-addressed envelope with a Spring Hill College logo. Inside was a multi-page, hand-written letter:

Dear Madison,

I don't know if you would remember meeting me, although we have met once or twice, but through my prayers I have felt an increasing impulse to contact you. I can't seem to reach you by phone, because your home number is unlisted and the messages I've left at your office are probably lost among who knows how many others. Anyway, we have a number of connections, you and I. I am semi-retiring next month after 36 years on the Theology faculty here at Spring Hill. Your father, Ben, over in the history department, was a younger colleague of mine whom I respected and liked although age and differing interests played a role in keeping us from a true friendship. But my uncle was the chairman of the history department who hired Ben. In fact, Ben was his very last hire before my uncle retired. Also, you and I share another kinship: I also attended Georgetown (nearly 40 years or so before you), where Father Joe Durkin, my uncle's very good friend, was probably my most important mentor, just as he had been a mentor for Ben's wife, your late mother, Mel. And, from what dear Claire told me, old Father Durkin still was active enough when you two both attended the Hilltop that he had been important to her experience there as well—and indeed, she told me, Father D. was the one who arranged for her to go on some excursion down Virginia-way somewhere, which provided her the opportunity to meet you.

Ah, Claire. I was not really her boss, but I was one of those Jesuits she performed work for here at the college. She was a lovely young woman, bright and kind and devout and true, and I mourn her passing very greatly, and I send my deepest condolences to you for her loss.

All this is prologue, Madison, for the real point of my letter. When I attended the memorial services for Claire and for the child who surely would have graced both your lives, I was so very disheartened to find that you were not there—that you were apparently too distraught to receive the hundreds of condolences that might have been of comfort to you. Ever since then, I have followed your saga closely.

It might surprise you to know that although I am as orthodox a Catholic as you will meet, I nevertheless find much of value in your theses. (As a Catholic, and an ordained Jesuit at that, the very idea of theses on church doors, with their evocation of Luther's crusade that split the church, might have been enough, when I was younger, to dangerously raise my blood pressure—but age has a way of mellowing a person.) I think that you have touched on an age-old, almost insoluble paradox of the Christian faith, namely the problem of evil and of wholly undeserved bad fortune, in a way that is so fresh and raw that it piques my interest. A very Jesuitical thing, it is, this desire to welcome and be challenged by fresh ideas, even if only to respond by exposing the errors therein. Not that all of your ideas are wrong. In fact, I find them worthy of discussion, of intellectual inquiry, of serious philosophical and theological discourse.

But more than that, I have been emphatically moved by your saga, by your struggle to come to grips with, to articulate, and to hold true to, your innermost emotions, in a way that is both intellectually honest and that somehow finds a path back to faith in Our Heavenly Father. I watch you, and I ache with you, and, though you are ever so much younger than I am, I admire you. And, as a man facing retirement and thus obviously on the verge of leaving "middle-aged" for "old" (how hard that is to admit!), I have the aging man's egotistical notion that I have accumulated enough wisdom and discernment and maybe empathetic abilities as well so that what I say and do may be of service or of succor to you. In short, Madison, I am offering myself as a sounding board, a confidant, a spiritual adviser if needed (although I certainly do not want to infer that your own priest—I understand you are Episcopalian—is unsuited for that task), or just as an older friend, if you should ever find yourself feeling lost or overwhelmed by this new task you have taken on. I will certainly not be offended should you decline my offer, but just keep it at hand in case you feel the need for the counsel of a rather cranky Jesuit who doesn't really know what he's going to do with his time now that he is leaving full-time professorship duties. (I'll still teach a seminar or two.)

All my best to you, and for your new endeavors.

In the Lord's name, yours truly,
Peter Vignelli, S.J.

Mad read and re-read the letter several times. The words anchored themselves in his heart. He thought he knew which one Vignelli was—balding, mid-60s, but still very athletic-looking. If it were indeed Vignelli he was picturing in his mind's eye, the Jesuit had the look and air of somebody solid and strong and admirable. Yes, Mad would call him. Soon. Take him to lunch, maybe. This was a man he should know.

Two days later, just before midnight on a Saturday, Becky Matthews lay in her bed in the small unit she rented in a West Mobile apartment complex. Her head rested in the narrow, partial valley between two pillows. Her knees hugged another pillow, and her arms were tightly wrapped around yet a fourth. Silent tears streamed down her face.

Becky had now lived in Mobile for more than a month, and she was miserable. Soul-black miserable. She had left her promising (though boring) job at the Houston oil company, left the environs near to her family members (who had made clear their strong disagreement with her unconventional career choice), left the fun and familiar social life surrounding so many of her high school friends who had moved back to Houston after college, left all the big-city offerings, not just because she had always longed for an entrepreneurial enterprise, but also because she really believed in Mad. Not in his message (such as it was), actually, but in Mad himself. She believed there was something special about him. In fact, she thought she loved him. She loved him for the ease with which he seemed to move through life, and for his utter lack of meanness—

and, of course, for the way, when they were together, that he made her nerve endings jump and her mind and heart float in an ecstatic trance-like state. She had loved him ever since their first night together during their all-too-stunningly-brief romance at Georgetown. Unlike most of the other girls who seemed oddly contented to enjoy Mad's attentions for just a little while and not overly upset (just sort of happily wistful) when he moved on, Becky had taken the "breakup" hard. Not that she showed it, of course. But it had eaten at her for months, and she had never understood why he had not wanted to continue the relationship. And she didn't understand now why he wouldn't renew it.

Becky knew she was hot-looking. All the guys told her that. Guys tried to hit on her all the time. She had a body well-endowed by nature and well-maintained through her own hard work at staying in shape. She had a pretty face and luscious hair that was a natural strawberry blonde with no artificial coloring required. And she didn't play games about sex: She liked sex and made it known she liked it—and after all, wasn't that what men wanted, anyway? No games, no hassle, just honest enjoyment of mutual attraction.

Yet with all Becky had to offer him, Mad acted as if she were part of the furniture. She had come to this godforsaken town that the rednecks and social elite alike in Alabama actually considered a big city, and she knew nobody except Mad. She had found nothing fun to do and not enough people she considered intelligent, and she had done a remarkable job in creating MMW from scratch…and yet Mad seemed, if anything, annoyed by her labors and perhaps by her very presence. His attitude broke her heart.

And it was a real heart she had, a heart as tender as everybody else's, even though she did her best to hide it behind her unhidden sexuality and her unyielding, modern-woman toughness.

Then, tonight, she had found herself so mind-numbingly, godforsakingly bored that she had finally consented to join Justin for a night out at what she considered those two-bit bars and dance clubs that made up a few-block strip on Lower Dauphin Street in downtown Mobile. The whole situation sucked. Justin kept insisting on dancing, even though he looked as goofy as Dudley Moore's character in that old Goldie Hawn movie *Foul Play*. Idiot rednecky guys or sophomoric college guys kept trying to hit on her when Justin either wasn't looking or had excused himself to the restroom. Then, the only time all night when she saw two young men who had the look and air of Becky's type, Justin noticed their interest and moved in close to her as if he owned her. Those two guys had turned away, laughing at some private joke that Becky was sure must have expressed contempt for her own taste or self-worth on the basis that she allowed herself to be seen with such a runt.

Appalled that she had sunk to such a low, all in service of a guy named Mad—MAD, indeed!—who paid her no respect, she had pleaded a headache long before Justin was ready to call it a night.

But Justin's disappointment was so palpable as he drove her home that she felt a twinge of remorse, for the first time, at treating him so shabbily.

"Holy mother of God!" her brain had screamed. On top of all the rest of it, on top of being a total loser who had given up a good life for a dumb pursuit in a town that (compared to Houston) was just Podunksville, USA, "you're also a bitch of the first order," she told herself contemptuously. "Who the hell are you to look down on that well-meaning little twerp?"

In bed now, Becky squeezed her pillows even more tightly, and cried still harder. Tomorrow was supposed to be a triumphant day for her, and instead it promised nothing but disaster.

The next day, Sunday, Mad would embark on his first real mini-tour as a speaker. Becky had arranged the whole thing, using her hometown of Houston as a point of embarkation. They would fly to Houston, meet Don the PR guy from Washington (his resignation from the staff of the California congressman had become official on Friday), have a late lunch with her wealthy parents (at *their* insistence; she feared it would be a disaster), and then have Mad speak at the Sunday-night service of a large Methodist church. The next morning they would drive down to Galveston for the breakfast meeting of a prominent civic club, back up to Houston for a luncheon sponsored by a major women's auxiliary, and then all the way over to San Antonio for the monthly Monday-night forum of a large young professionals' group. The next day would feature another luncheon, this one in Austin, followed by a flight home (plane change in Dallas) to Mobile that evening.

Mad was as nervous as a caged blue jay in a cat kennel. He could barely sleep that night, and when he did sleep (fitfully) he kept having variations of one particular dream.

It always started the same. Mad was in a bumper boat, a fountain splashing down on his head, the boat turning lazy circles in a weak whirlpool beneath it. But the whole situation was wonderfully funny and lighthearted. Claire drove her little boat 30 yards away, pointing at him and laughing merrily. Even at that distance, her laughter was so infectious that Mad had to laugh too, almost entirely unembarrassed by the jeers of bystanders at the boat pool's edge.

But then the dream always started going wrong. The gentle whirlpool became stronger and then stronger still. Rather than holding his bumper boat in a lazy circular pattern under the gusher, the whirlpool started spinning him faster and faster. Soon Mad spun around like a passenger on an amusement park ride before being sucked into the whirlpool's vortex. He no longer was in the boat, but instead in the insane clutches of Becky and Justin and Buzz and Mary. And it wasn't Claire laughing merrily whom he heard, but a green-clad Laura Green talking into a microphone like a play-by-play announcer, describing Mad's whirlpool plight as if he were the athlete in a spectator sport. Then Laura turned into Rob Patterson telling Mad that the whirlpool would carry him straight down to Hell, and then Patterson turned into the kind Rev. Hebert yelling helplessly that Mad had left his blackberries at the side of the pool. And just as Mad seemed about to be sucked under for good, he awoke.

When Mad finally fell into the next sleep, he had the dream again, and this time it was the mime and the iguana lady and the tall white Mobile TV reporter guy who had him in their clutches. And another time as he sank into the vortex, he grabbed for a lifeline somebody had thrown him—only to have it yanked away by Officer Williams on account of Mad's being a "nigger lover." Still another time Mad actually grabbed the lifeline and pulled himself to apparent safety—only to be so startled, as he finally stood poolside, by the feel of black-haired Tonya's hand on his buttocks that he fell back into the water and began to be sucked under...

This time, before drowning, Mad awoke to see his clock showing a bit past 6 a.m., and he decided he might as well get up and start prepping for his 9 a.m. flight. The only thing that kept his jitters from being unbearable for the rest of that morning was that when he checked the web site, he found a late-night entry from M. Magdalene. Unless he had missed one somewhere along the way, this was her first appearance on the site since the night before MMW's opening press conference. Just as on that earlier night, her message here was as brief as could be.

"Hey, Mad," she wrote. "Good luck with your Texas speeches."

That was it—but it was enough, somehow, to calm Mad down. Calmed him enough, in fact, to allow him to notice that when he picked Becky up on the way to the airport, she looked unusually pale and drawn and uncharacteristically despondent. She was surprised, pleasantly, when he gave her shoulders a reassuring squeeze before she got into his car.

"I know you've put a lot of work into this, Becky," he said. "I appreciate it, and I won't let you down."

Becky sighed and managed a wan half smile.

CHAPTER TWO

If Mad had been familiar with Washington's Capitol Hill, he might have recognized Don the PR guy as a typical representative of one of the Hill's several sub-species: blow-dried and buffed and too immaculately dressed, blandly well-meaning and with an intelligence just enough above average for him to excel at conventional wisdom but to shrink from original thought, Don was trim, proper, and dark-haired handsome. Still, when he met Mad and Becky's plane at the Houston airport, Mad *still* didn't remember him from his Georgetown days. Maybe Don had been one of those boring sorts who always told the professor exactly what Don thought the professor wanted to hear. Mad had never paid attention to those people. But Don greeted him like a long-lost friend from the cradle. And he kept flashing toward Becky those knowing, sideways glances that Mad assumed meant they had, at least once, "hooked up" on campus.

For whatever reason, Becky perked up to about four-fifths of her normal energy level. Four-fifths, Mad thought, was just about right: Rather than being loud and attention-hogging, and refinedly crass in the way some debutantes are to try to show they aren't porcelain princesses, Becky at four-fifths energy was vibrant and attention-earning and just edgy enough to be exciting. For the first time since she had shown up uninvited at his door some seven weeks earlier, she evoked in Mad the libidinous sensations that had briefly attracted him at Georgetown.

Mad's focus was re-directed quickly, though, by Don, who had morphed seamlessly from old-friend pleasantries to what could only be described as an aide's briefing to a boss. Such and such a number of people were expected that night in Houston, compared to X number in Galveston the next morning. Podiums were set up at all locations, but the PA system could be switched to a portable microphone if Mad wanted. The press probably would be at a few of the events, but he didn't have to take their questions if he didn't want to, and it was best to limit media access at least somewhat. Don hadn't done press releases because Mad had not been ready to tell Don what he planned to say.

And so mind-numbingly they moved on, down to baggage claim (past two people who recognized Mad and asked for an autograph), over to the rental car, and onto the highway, with Becky driving, toward the home of Becky's parents. Finally, mainly to put an end to Don's officious chatter, Mad changed the subject.

"Hey, Don, are any of those congressmen decent people, or are they all just a bunch of self-important jackasses?"

"You got all types, Mad, all types. My boss was a raging tyrant— the stories I could tell you about him! A lot of them are basically well-meaning but a little aloof. Staffers know which ones are which. And some of 'em are real great guys. For instance, Bob Livingston from Louisiana, all his staffers think he's terrific. And everybody was bummed when Sonny Bono died; he was nice to everybody. And…"

Mad listened with half an ear. With the rest of his brain, he again tried to remember what class or activity at Georgetown had been the one he and Don had in common. It was like trying to remember what the campus cafeteria had served the day the Hoyas lost to U. Mass in the Elite Eight round of the NCAA tourney. Don had made no impression at all.

What soon *did* make an impression on Mad was the neighborhood into which Becky had turned. Huge mansions, widely spaced, lined the streets. Large, grassy medians dotted with small trees divided the sides of a boulevard. Ancient and majestic trees shaded the mansions themselves. Front yards were spacious, driveways and garages decidedly ample, and front porticos semi-tastefully ornate.

"Here we are, homey-home-home of the parental magnates," said Becky, rather sneeringly, as she pulled onto a brick drive encircling a stone fountain, a good seven feet in diameter, with a stone Cupid and two small stone nymphs adorning its center. "The place where black gold and greenbacks turn into cold white marble. The finest place money can buy, except of course for the chalet in the Alps and the 5,000-square-foot 'cottage' on Monterey. The place where Daddy Dearest hangs his slippers and the Mommy with the Mostest hosts her ring of amazing gossip! Welcome, welcome, and try not to run away too soon!"

Mad was taken aback by Becky's bitterness. But Don entirely missed her sarcasm.

"Oh, is your mom a good conversationalist?" he asked with an almost creepy earnestness. "I can't wait to meet her."

By the time all three of them climbed out of the rental car, a Hispanic maid in a perfectly starched white uniform had emerged from a wooden door so thick and heavy, it looked like the entrance to a church crypt. "Miss Becky, Miss Becky, you still looking bue-tee-foll, just as bue-tee-foll as ever!!!"

"Yeah, whatever," Becky mumbled, sidestepping her impatiently... and then, as if suddenly stricken with a conscience, she stopped and turned back to face the maid. "Oh, Gloria," she said, giving the woman a semi-formal half hug, "you're always so sweet to me. It's good to see you. Gloria, this is Madison and this is Don; you all, this is Gloria. She's my fave, my heart. Now c'mon inside to face the firing squad!"

Back in Mobile, Justin sat in his upscale condo, fidgeting and nervously punching the TV remote control. The final round of a golf tournament was on, and a tennis match, and an NBA game, and a Braves game with Greg Maddux pitching. None of them meant much to him, although later in the season he would pay more attention to the Braves. For now, though, he just didn't know what to do with himself. He really had wanted to travel to Houston with Becky and Mad, but he had to admit there was no role for him there. He just hated that Becky had been feeling ill last night; he knew that her headache probably had been a tension headache, and as a trainer he knew exactly the right pressure points to relieve tension headaches.

And what bad luck! Just when Becky had finally agreed to come out with him and was obviously having a good time, that headache of hers had to strike! He knew she wasn't overwhelmed by him, but he was sure there was at least a little spark somewhere; just give him a chance and he'd show her! Yes indeed he would!

But then she had gotten that headache, and now she was in Houston with Mad, whom she obviously had a crush on, and one of these days Mad would wake up and grab her and then he, Justin, would be out of luck. And with all the attention he had paid to Becky, he had tried less

21

often to reach that girl in Pensacola who had seemed so promising, and whenever he *did* try, he got her answering machine—but he didn't think it worked right, because she never called him back.

Then those thoughts, those thoughts that he hated, started creeping into his mind. Those thoughts told him that Becky wasn't even the slightest bit interested. And that the machine in Pensacola did work, but that the girl had no desire to call back. And that all those 40-somethings at the gym who were so impressed by his knowledge and approach as a trainer were the only women who would ever pay him any heed—and that while they all liked him, not a single one had any romantic inclinations toward him of the Mrs. Robinson–to–Dustin Hoffman variety. Maybe all they saw was the inches of air above his five-foot-three-inch height, those inches where the men they wanted had strong faces to look up to rather than a clever little face like his that was at their own eye level or even below.

Justin didn't want to admit, not even to himself, how lonely he was. Heck, if it weren't for his good buddy Mad, he would have hardly any social life at all. And now Mad was on the road with that exquisitely sexy and intelligent creature Becky, and Justin was stuck at home watching the Braves lose and feeling like a total loser himself. He knew he wasn't a loser, he told himself, but sometimes he sure as hell felt like one.

Damn, if only Becky could see the real him!

Becky led Mad and Don through an ornate hallway and a very unlived-in living room full of antique furniture and porcelain figurines, to a cold and spacious room dominated by a huge ebony table five paces long. Rising from a stiff chair at one end, a hearty-looking rock of a man, maybe 50-ish, was welcoming them all, extending a hand of introduction to Mad and Don, and then trying awkwardly to hug a resentful-looking Becky. Chet Matthews was a third-generation oil magnate who had shown a solid ability to take a minor fortune and turn it into a sextupled one. He exuded an aura of somebody trying desperately and sincerely to come across with warmth, but succeeding only in projecting a heightened territoriality.

At the other end of the table, a perfectly coiffed, tight-skinned, thin-boned woman sat frigidly in a cushioned armchair. She had a once-natural prettiness now marred by a store-bought beauty and a mouth whose smile muscles seemed to have atrophied.

"Becky, dear, are you going to present these two young gentlemen to your mother?" Ginger Matthews spoke without even shifting in her armchair. Don walked toward her with the practiced ease of a trained courtier. "Mrs. Matthews, I'm honored," he said, taking her limply extended hand as if it were silk-lined taffeta. "So gracious of you to invite us to your home."

Ginger Matthews nodded assent.

"And you," she said, turning to Mad, "you're the young man who has taken Becky on this fool's errand. Tell me, is my lovely daughter shacking up with you yet?"

There was an awkward silence. Chet chewed sternly on his lower lip while his eyes shot angry lasers at his wife. Ginger paid him no heed but stared stonily at Mad. Don smiled nervously. Becky shut her eyes tightly and clenched her teeth. Mad looked down at his feet, shifting his weight uneasily back and forth.

"Oh, come now," Ginger said, now half smiling. "I *do* have a lovely and talented daughter of whom I'm very proud, I'm sure. I figured it would take a young man like you, who looks like Robert Redford, to snare her. You should be proud of your looks, young Madison. With the right kind of training, you could put them to worthwhile use. I know some divorcees my age who could really use a good boy toy."

That was enough for Chet.

"Don't mind my wife," he interrupted, looking at Mad with what he hoped was male camaraderie. "She's just upset that her daughter moved away."

Then an odd thing happened. Becky sprung to her mother's defense. Here was her father trying (if not entirely successfully) to be friendly, and yet it was at her father that Becky flashed her fury—as if, Mad thought, it was a subconscious transference of her rage from the offending object, her mother, to the one, her father, who had been inoffensive. "Well at least Mother shows some concern about my pursuits, Daddy Dearest," she said, voice icy enough to sink the *Titanic*. "Whatever I do is just fine with you, since nothing a little girlie can do will amount to a hill o' beans anyway, compared to what a mythical son of yours could have done if he had played for the Longhorns."

Becky's inflections and accents, while never losing their chill, alternated oddly between Texas cowboy and Houston debutante, with a touch of oil bidnessman thrown in for a word or two. And Chet, looking as if he had been winged by a sniper but wanted to tough out the pain, turned on his heel toward the kitchen mumbling something about "making sure Buster knows when to baste the prime rib." Mad and Don, each struggling with discomfort, silently found a tableside seat.

The rest of their visit—a hearty four-course lunch, with apparently mandatory Heinekens for the men and a 1977 white wine for the women, followed by three quick games of pool in the billiards room (Mad and Chet versus Don and Becky, with Ginger having excused herself)—was less awkward only in comparison to that rocky beginning. As most women did, Ginger warmed (or at least thawed) toward Mad, even to the point of flirting. She continued to treat Becky almost disdainfully, but when she did acknowledge Becky's existence without an unambiguous insult, Becky hung upon each word as if it were the tender cooing of a long-lost true love. Conversely, on the repeated occasions when Chet inexpertly and almost desperately tried to show a real fondness for his daughter, Becky reacted as if he had spoken to her like an ogre to a captive young duchess. The psychology of it all was rather strange.

"No, Daddy Dearest," she said sarcastically at one point, as she connected on a 2-ball-to-6-ball combination to a corner pocket, "I haven't found a nice neighborhood yet where your little girlie can be safey-wafey; I'm in a little condo where I can hear the upstairs neighbors boink each other at 3 a.m. every other night."

When she excused herself once to go to the restroom, and Don went to return his beer glass to the kitchen in order to save the maid the trouble, Chet looked at Mad with an expression as pained as could be from a man of such otherwise aggressive solidity.

"Mad," he said in a muted tone, "my daughter doesn't like me, and I don't know why. And while I was dead set against her leaving her job here and going to Mobile to run your preachin' bidness, I've changed my mind today. I like you, son. Somethin' tells me you got integrity and prob'ly some goodness as well. Maybe you can rub off on her. Becky's

24

not a happy person. And I'd do anything I could to make her happy. She doesn't understand that I respect her, much less that I love her. But if you can help her find somethin' inside herself that makes her more content, then I say more power to you. I want my daughter back, Mad, I want her back in this big, dumb old father's heart of mine. You help bring her back to me, son, and I'll be forever in your debt."

Becky and Don both re-entered the room from different doorways, and Chet lined up and perfectly executed three shots in a row.

"Game, set, and match, kids," he said as the 8-ball disappeared in the appropriate pocket. "Nobody beats Chet Matthews in my own damn house."

At six that evening, Buzz met TV host Steve Matheson for dinner at the Tombs in Georgetown. The two had hit it off well when Buzz served as a stand-in guest on Mad's behalf. Matheson had told Buzz he would call soon to grab a bite, and now several weeks later proved true to his word. Matheson was not only a political junkie but an amateur military history buff, and he thought that a meal with a military history professor would be a pretty interesting way to spend an evening, since his wife was out of town visiting relatives. And Buzz, who liked Matheson's take-no-prisoners on-air persona, was flattered that a big TV guy was paying attention to him.

All Buzz's life, he had played the sturdy second fiddle. In high school football in south-central Pennsylvania, he had been an all-district guard, a basically anonymous position, at a mid-sized school. But that still left him nowhere near good enough to play college football except at a small school that didn't give scholarships, and he opted instead for an ROTC partial scholarship to the University of Maryland. There he avoided the student protests, kept his nose clean except for drinking lots of beer, and through sheer hard work earned grades high enough to make him a candidate for a decent grad school—but just six one-hundredths of a point too low to be *cum laude*. The University of Virginia at first indicated he would not be admitted to its master's history program, and Buzz was all ready to serve his ROTC obligation in 'Nam when UVA accepted him as a replacement for another graduate candidate (who had deferred admission at the last moment for family reasons).

At Virginia he made a fast friend in Ben Jones, but always came off a bit dull in comparison to Ben's quiet panache.

After graduate school and his rotation in Vietnam (away from the front lines, thank goodness), Buzz came home eager to settle down with a sweet all-American girl. Instead he lost his heart to Suzy Wilson, a vivacious little sprite who looked far sweeter than she turned out to be. They divorced after just two years when he caught her in an affair with a rich Chevy Chase doctor. For the next two decades, he had put on the public face of one of those beefy he-men who chose bachelorhood because it gave him more options to play the field. But the truth was that nothing much ever really clicked for him on that front.

Professionally, his reputation as a professor was that of an unremarkable workman who neither bored his students nor greatly inspired them, and whose scholarship was steady but far from original.

So, having a recognizable TV guy like Matheson take a liking to him was a highly welcome development.

"So, Buzz," Matheson was saying between swallows of Killian's Red, "what's the over-under on how long your godson keeps this religious thing going? Eight months? Year and a half?"

Buzz didn't really want to talk about Mad. When he was around Mad or even on the phone with him, it was true, he did for some reason fall into the habit of deferring to the younger man. The second-fiddle role was just too ingrained. But he didn't want to waste a meal with Matheson on Mad's stuff, when he could be talking politics or the military or women or something fun. (Not that he wasn't enthusiastic about MMW; he truly did want Mad to succeed. Mad was a good kid; besides, he felt a duty to his late friend Ben to be there for Ben's son.) But Buzz wanted to talk to Matheson, who was about Buzz's age, as a peer—not as a shill for somebody else.

"Well, Steve, I'd say Mad will still get attention at least as long as this Lewinsky mess continues, if only because I think the whole scandal brings values issues to the core, so there's a market for people talking about subjects like religion. Speaking of which"—and it was here that he tried to segue away from the subject of Mad—"how do you see this Lewinsky stuff playing in the elections six months from now? Do Clinton's troubles mean death to the Democrats or what?"

26

Since Matheson could never resist a conversation about politics, even when he was not working, Buzz's segue had the desired effect. And politics morphed into foreign policy, and from there into military affairs and then (over dessert and even more libations) into military history, and the subject of Mad's endeavors was pushed well aside. Matheson eventually cabbed it home thinking that this Buzz guy was a pretty decent "average Joe," not at all like most of the highfalutin pointy-heads usually associated with academia.

One time zone behind Buzz and Matheson, 537 people packed the Methodist church for an evening service that usually drew only 125. Two TV cameras stood watch outside the building, but the minister and ushers had refused them admittance to the service itself. A newspaper guy and a radio lady, however, both smuggled tape recorders into pews near the front.

The service proceeded in its normal manner until it was time for the sermon. The lead minister took the pulpit as he ordinarily would, but said: "Tonight, as you all know, we will not have a sermon by me or another ordained minister, but a homily instead, by a new lay leader whose thoughtful Christian theses have challenged both the faith and the intellect of a rapidly growing number of adherents and critics alike. Tonight we welcome him to our pulpit neither to endorse his views nor to dispute them, but instead to be provoked and prodded into reflections on our own faith. He quite rightly claims no particular authority to interpret Scripture, but after reading his work and speaking to him on the phone and meeting with him for a half hour before this service, I'm convinced he possesses a heart honestly engaged in the struggle and the duty to know God and to love Him. Tonight we welcome Mr. Madison Lee Jones. Mr. Jones, the pulpit is yours."

Mad was quite nervous as he took the pulpit. Something had gone very wrong. He had pulled out his Episcopal prayer book weeks earlier, in anticipation of this event, and looked up the readings for this Sunday. His whole homily was based on those readings. But the readings—the two lessons and the Gospel—that they had just finished hearing were *not* the same ones he had prepared for. Maybe the Methodists used a different lectionary than Episcopalians did. He hadn't thought of that.

He licked his lips. He cleared his throat. He licked his lips again. He took a deep breath. Finally, he managed to begin.

"To you good people of this vibrant church, I thank you for your hospitality. I pray that nothing I say makes you regret it. I come not to offend, nor to teach, for I have no formal authority on matters of faith. I come only to facilitate discussion by speaking from the heart, from a wounded heart and its particular point of view that is concerned not with being orthodox or with overthrowing orthodoxy, but only with being heard and understood on that particular heart's own terms.

"But, good people, be forewarned: That heart's terms, *my* heart's terms, are the terms of a heart that is hurt and angry and frightened. As most of you may have heard, I have had an odd and ugly relationship with childbirth and with death. My mother died while birthing me. My father died when I was young. My grandfather, who was my friend and mentor and larger than life, fell off his horse earlier this year and died. And two months ago my young wife and unborn child both died, as had my mother, of a massive hemorrhage. And my wife's mother, who had become like a mother to me, died in a car wreck while rushing to join me in mutual commiseration.

"Good people: I have never been good at dealing with pain. I have never been good at dealing with deep feelings. And when all this happened, I was not only *not* good; I was very bad. I wrote my theses to channel my grief. No more reason than that, and no less. Yet today I find myself giving you a homily, from the pulpit, as if I'm an expert or a man of God. I am neither. In fact, so limited is my knowledge in most areas that I somehow prepared for different lessons and a different Gospel than the ones we have heard tonight. I thought all mainline Protestants used the same lectionary, but I am obviously mistaken. I prepared for the Episcopal readings today. So please bear with me."

There was a nervous fidgeting from some of the pews. Mad continued:

"Regardless of the proper readings, the problem of spiritual pain will not go away, especially from a layman too confused to focus on the correct Gospel passage for your lovely church. All I am is a young man to whom much of the teaching of the modern churches does not make sense. It does not square with the reality I've experienced. And, if you are honest with yourself, I dare say that it might not square with your experience either.

"Take today's psalm. By sheer coincidence of the calendars of both the Episcopal Church and the Methodist one, today's psalm for both denominations is the most famous and comforting one in the whole Bible. At one point children learned it by heart by the time they were five or six years old; even today, it is part of the warp and woof of our most spiritual hearts. You all know the 23rd psalm; we just recited it: 'The Lord is my shepherd, I shall not want, etc., etc.... Even though I walk through the valley of the shadows of death, I shall fear no evil; for thou art with me, etc.... Surely goodness and mercy shall follow me all the days of my life.'

"To all of which, good people, I say this: 'Yada yada yada, BS, and yada some more.'"

From multiple places in the congregation arose an audible intake of breath, followed by a disturbed and perhaps angry buzz. Mad continued:

"People, this is baby food; this is a comforting fairy tale to tell us that all will be right with the world because nice, kind Daddy in heaven will protect us. *Yeah, right.* Some protection.

"The first lesson that I prepared for today is from Acts. It is the story of Stephen, the pure and devoted disciple, a man described as being, quote, 'full of faith and of the Holy Spirit.' And for his troubles, what kind of mercy did Stephen receive? He was stoned to death for preaching the Gospel.

"And then, in what I thought was supposed to be today's second lesson, there is the First Letter of Peter. Peter, or the anonymous author writing in Peter's name, recognizes how often those who do right are nevertheless forced to suffer, or at least allowed to suffer. 'For one is approved,' Peter writes, 'if, mindful of God, he endures pain while suffering unjustly.... But if when you do right and suffer for it you take it patiently, you have God's approval. For to this you have been called, because Christ also suffered for you, leaving you an example, that you should follow in his steps.' And so on and so forth, until Peter writes that by Christ's wounds 'you have been healed.'

"Well, good people, I don't know about healing. I don't know when the magic moment occurs when somebody unjustly victimized becomes

29

more healed than he is suffering. But I do know this: The Bible is full of unmerited suffering. So are the stories of the Christian saints. And the Old Testament especially is full of stories of suffering not just allowed by God—which would be bad enough—but caused directly by God. God caused Job to suffer merely so He, God, could prove a point to his evil counterpart. God demanded of Abraham that Abe be willing to sacrifice his own son, the pride and love of his life, just to prove Abraham's own obedience to God. And God did not lift a finger when I lost my mother and my father and my grandfather and my wife and my child and my mother-in-law, each of them well before their time.

"And God allows innocent children in sub-Saharan Africa to suffer and starve and bloat and die. He allows innocent children in our inner cities to be terrorized by crack-addicted parents. And this suffering is so very unwarranted.

"And you out there in the fourth pew: Yes, you in the navy blue dress. Have you never suffered, not from your own mistakes nor from the cruelty of other people, but from seemingly random acts of fate? I bet you have. And you two rows further back, in the tan suit with the flowered tie: Haven't you at times felt like the world, God's world, did you harm you did not deserve?

"Conversely, to all of you, I ask: Do you really fear no evil when you walk or hobble or even crawl through the valley? Do you have a table prepared for you in the sight of your enemies?

"Of course not. Not if you are honest. More likely, there have been times in all your lives, dark times, when as in the Letter to the Romans—in a passage that became my 18th thesis, from the King James version—'We know that the whole creation groaneth and travaileth in pain together until now.' And later in Romans, also quoted in my theses, for God's sake 'we are killed all the day long; we are accounted as sheep for the slaughter.'

"Yes, people, this is the God that we worship. Does He sound much like one worth worshipping?"

One couple about three-quarters of the way back in the congregation gathered up their three young children and ostentatiously walked out of the church. A clearly unhappy murmur spread through many of the other pews. Mad could feel a nervous sweat trickling down the back of his neck. But he knew he was ready to turn the theme around, and so he pressed forward.

"And yet…and yet and yet and yet. Yet in all this pain and all this suffering, suffering that an all-powerful God surely could alleviate if he chose, still we believers have an ace in the hole. Still we believers have hope, and still we believers have life. Our faiths, our hopes, our very lives, find their redemption in the Gospel. They find their redemption in the person of Jesus of Nazareth, whom we call the Christ. In what I thought was today's Gospel, John chapter 10 a few verses before our own readings today actually begin, Jesus says it concisely. 'I am the door of the sheep,' he says. 'I am the door; if any one enters by me, he will be saved, and will go in and out and find pasture.… I came that they may have life, and have it abundantly.'

"Yes, suffering does occur. God allows or sometimes forces suffering to occur. And some of that suffering is decidedly undeserved. Some of us, probably all of us at times, are victims, pure and simple. But the same God who so messed up his own creation, and who still so messes it up, has sent us a Christ to represent God's own ultimate will: His ultimate will that, in the end, regardless of our own many many egregious mistakes and of God's own failings as well, we will all be reconciled together, we and God, if we have faith, through the mediation of the Christ who is God's only perfect creation. Our suffering will continue, but with Christ we now have everlasting life, with the 23rd psalm's clear still waters, to look forward to. That everlasting life in Christ's love may be exceedingly small comfort now, but it is all the comfort we have and it might just be enough comfort for us, to know that sometime in what seems the far-too-distant future, sometime when life is done, a better and more comforting and more loving life awaits. Christ is our door to that life, and it is toward that door we must always aim our steps.

"Finally, I dare say that our steps will lead us to that door more readily, more surely and unambiguously, if we walk in love with the world around us, with the people around us, each one of us lending a shoulder, each one of us there to pick another off the ground if one falls.

"This is the message of the Gospel; this is the message of our hope. And while it may sometimes seem paltry indeed in times of pain and trouble, it may still be message enough if we trust enough and believe enough and pray enough to let it be so.

"Therefore, in all our anger and all our pain and all our weak humanity, let us nevertheless praise the Father for giving us his Son, and praise the Son for giving us our hope, world without end, Amen."

As Mad walked back to his seat, the church was engulfed in utter silence that lasted a good 15 seconds. But when the celebrant audibly gulped and then began the prayer that continued the service, the two reporters clicked off their tape recorders, grabbed their notebooks, and walked purposefully down the aisles to the church entrance and thence back to their respective haunts. Both had latched onto the same segment of Mad's homily that they were sure would get their reports decent attention...

After the service, a number of the congregation members exited quickly, many with pursed lips and angry glares. The cameras outside caught their expressions. But a couple of hundred stayed for a reception with Mad in the church's meeting hall, and dozens crowded around him excitedly, wanting to shake his hand and thank him for inspiring them. Even though both Don and especially Becky tried to stay right by Mad's side, three women in their 20s each managed to slip phone numbers into Mad's pockets. An intense 17-year-old boy tried to argue with Mad, but his mother pulled him away. An older man, who could only be described as elegant, briefly monopolized Mad's attention; he kept calling Mad "my dear boy" and alternately praising and refuting some of Mad's various preachings. And the lead minister stood fairly close by, perfectly gracious but with a decidedly uncomfortable smile painted, with great effort, on his face.

At 9 p.m. Central time, the Rev. Bill White opened his nationally broadcast radio program with a sorrowful warning against "a new, sinful voice of anger." He meant Mad. The Rev. White was a nominal Southern Baptist, both an ally and a rival of the Rev. Rob Patterson and a onetime lieutenant of the Rev. Larry Falstaff before branching off and making a name for himself. Pudgy and wholly unimpressive in person, he had a perfect voice for radio and a knack for using deliberate understatement in a kind of reverse-psychology way that made his points all the stronger for sounding so reasonable. The radio reporter in the Methodist church was White's top assistant.

"I don't want to unduly prejudice the opinions of you, my faithful listeners, against this poor, confused young man who calls himself Mad," White said. "I'll let you decide for yourselves. Here's what Mad Jones, speaking right here in Houston less than three miles from my ministry office, had to say about our beloved 23rd psalm."

A tape of Mad's voice began to roll: "You all know the 23rd psalm; we just recited it: 'The Lord is my shepherd, I shall not want, etc., etc.... Even though I walk through the valley of the shadows of death, I shall fear no evil; for thou art with me, etc.... Surely goodness and mercy shall follow me all the days of my life.'

"To all of which, good people, I say this: 'Yada yada yada, BS, and yada some more.' People, this is baby food; this is a comforting fairy tale to tell us that all will be right with the world because nice, kind Daddy in heaven will protect us. *Yeah, right.* Some protection."

The Rev. White continued: "But that's not all this poor, deluded boy had to say. Later in his sermonette, he continued his—shall we say unique?—version of witnessing to the Lord's works."

Tape again: "More likely, there have been times in all your lives, dark times, when as in the Letter to the Romans—in a passage that became my 18th thesis, quoting from the King James version—'We know that the whole creation groaneth and travaileth in pain together until now.' And later in Romans, also quoted in my theses, for God's sake 'we are killed all the day long; we are accounted as sheep for the slaughter.'

"Yes, people, this is the God that we worship. Does He sound much like one worth worshipping?"

Again the Rev. White: "Okay, listeners, you have heard the words of Mr. Jones. Some would say they sound immoderate. Some would say they sound impudent. Some would say they even sound blasphemous. Yes, I daresay many would say they sound blasphemous, but who am I to judge? Let he who has not sinned cast the first stone. But I myself, I the sinner, feel confident in saying at least this much. I say that Madison Jones is not spreading a message that godly people will agree with. I say that the pain of some devastating losses—and yes, people, you should all know in this young man's defense that he has suffered the untimely death of a number of loved ones—I say the pain of his losses has led him at least a little bit astray.

"I am not angered by his words. Who am I, a sinner, to be angry? But some of you listeners may be angry. And if you are, it is undoubtedly a righteous anger. There is sinful anger, the anger of improperly challenging God, the anger displayed so prominently by Madison Jones. And then there is righteous anger, the anger of those who proclaim the Gospel and those who seek the truth, the anger of the elect company of believers. And I know many of you fall into that company, and I will not dissuade you from your anger. God may indeed forgive this boy, but forgiveness is God's to grant; forgiveness of egregious sin is not our province. Our province—or rather, *your* province, dear godly listeners who are not guilty of my own sins of false pride—yes, I say, your province is to decide for yourselves whether the words of Madison Jones will go uncontested, or instead whether you will warn your flocks against what you know in your hearts is the dangerous and heretical notion that God is not to be worshipped and loved and praised.

"The choice is up to you. You can stand up for God, or you can stand silently by and let sinfully angry words go unchallenged. I am not one to say what is sinful, for I am a sinner. But if you yourselves recognize sin, then call a spade a spade and identify the sin for what it is, and go ahead and denounce it.

"In sum, Madison Jones makes me sorrowful at the same time he seems to insult those of you who have been born again in the Spirit. May God show mercy upon his sinful soul…. Now, I'll be back after these brief commercial messages."

Mad's web site was sleepy on Sunday night; not many of the true regulars listened to the Rev. White's show, so they were unaware of his commentary. But Defender was a White devotee, and he blistered Mad in three lengthy entries. In addition to ripping Mad on substance, he also noted that not only had Mad used the Episcopal lectionary instead of the Methodist one, but that he had also used the readings from the wrong year in the three-year Episcopal cycle. "Not only is he obnoxious," Defender wrote of Mad in his final comment of the night, "but he doesn't know enough about his faith to fill a chalice even halfway. Somebody needs to muzzle this guy, and soon."

Also that night, Shiloh Jones paced back and forth across his bedroom floor, quite upset, while LaShauna sat propped up in bed with a romance novel. Shiloh often listened to the Rev. White, and tonight he had been stunned by what he had heard.

"I just can't believe Mad said that!" Shiloh repeated for about the fifth time. "I mean, that's just wrong, calling the Lord's word 'yada yada and BS.' And especially in the 23rd psalm! My mother always made me recite that one when I was growing up. Mad just *couldn't* have meant it! There must be more to what he said!"

LaShauna put down her book. "Honey, I got two things to say," she said, with some exasperation. "First, I think he's got a point. That psalm sounds all pretty, but it ain't reality. Reality ain't so pretty. That ain't God's word; that psalm is the words of some Hebrew way back then who wanted his world to seem nicer than it was."

Shiloh hated when LaShauna got like this, so he pretended he hadn't heard it. If he really had to acknowledge to himself that that was how she saw the world, it would have upset him too much.

"Mad *must* have said more than that," he continued. "I've seen it happen for weeks now: The press only reports part of what he says, the part that sounds most controversial, and they don't do justice to the whole man. I don't agree with everything he says, but his heart is in the right place—and now even Rev. White isn't giving the whole picture!"

"Honey, you're getting too upset, especially over a white man." Now LaShauna was going places Shiloh really couldn't abide. "That's the second thing I wanted to say. He might've been nice to you, made you think your opinion's important or something. But you know damn well that when it really comes down to it, Mad Jones just thinks of your opinion as an interesting little sideshow. He still sees you as a *black* man; ain't no white guy gonna put your opinion above what white power says to him."

"That's *enough*, LaShauna! That's just not true! This man is a friend of mine."

"Ain't no white man really your friend, honey, not even one who I think makes lotsa sense. You just be careful now."

Her tone was less sympathetic than it was hectoring. Shiloh didn't answer. He clenched his fists and walked out of the bedroom and out his front door. He sat on the curbside for nearly an hour, staring into the night.

The next morning, Houstonians who turned to the first page of the local-news section of the Houston paper were greeted by a headline just below the fold: "Homilist pans 23rd psalm." The longer subhead read: "Jones calls psalm 'baby food,' 'fairy tale'—says God allows too much suffering."

A sleepy Mad read it en route to Galveston, as Becky chauffeured in icy silence and Don, in the back seat, dutifully made a list of the benefits and drawbacks of the coverage thus far. Mad was pleased to see that one member of the congregation, a woman identified as Diana Evans, was quoted saying, "You had to listen to his whole homily to get his message, which was that Christ makes everything right and offers us hope. I thought Jones was inspiring."

But another man, who wouldn't give his name, said he was "greatly offended, not only by Jones' message, but also because he didn't even do his homework. He based his whole offensive homily on the wrong Gospel passage and the wrong lessons. It showed a great disrespect for our congregation, and it shows he's too uninformed to pay any attention to at all. He doesn't need to preach; he just needs therapy."

"Help me, Claire," Mad silently said to the heavens. "If you can hear me, please help me."

A vision flashed into his mind. A green-eyed brunette looked down at him, laughingly, from the lap of a statue of a priest, patriot, and prelate, and he began to clamber up after her, knowing that a first kiss would be his prize.

Outside the civic club meeting in Galveston, a bearded man with wild eyes shouted epithets as he ran up, shaking his fist angrily, to where Mad was climbing out of the rental car. A security guard intercepted him and led him away.

Mad's speech there followed the same lines as his homily the evening before, but today Mad somehow found the grace and humor to make fun of himself for having used the Episcopal reading schedule instead of the Methodist one. He added an awful pun: "I guess my preparations weren't Method-ical, or maybe not Methodistical, enough."

Also, at Don's suggestion, "yada yada yada BS" became "and so on and so on," and "fairy tale" became "a reassuring story."

In short, Mad took some of the edge off. And unlike in the church, today's breakfast meeting allowed about 10 minutes for a post-speech Q&A. Somehow Mad had touched the good side of most of the audience, so the Q&A actually produced some lighthearted banter.

"Mad, I understand that last night you called the 23rd psalm a fairy tale," said one 40-ish businessman, obviously the club's resident wag, trying ineffectually to be funny. "Are you talking Brothers Grimm here, or more like Mother Goose?"

Mad said the first thing that popped into his head. "Well, the psalm talks about a shepherd, so maybe it's more along the lines of Little Bo Peep," he said. Some people chuckled at the inanity of the exchange, but others looked offended, so Mad quickly added: "Seriously, the psalm is lovely poetry. I'm not trying to put down the people who build their faiths around its imagery. It just doesn't work for me, at least not now." Then, not wanting to lose the lighthearted mood that had developed, he added: "Maybe that makes me a 'baa baa black sheep' for questioning the psalm at all, but last I checked, God still offers forgiveness even to black sheep, so maybe there's hope for me yet."

In the ride back to Houston, Becky showed at least a smidgen of life and decent humor for the first time this entire trip.

"Hey, loverboy, maybe I won't murder you after all," she said. "You actually charmed some of those people."

"Charmed" became an understatement at the next meeting—the women's auxiliary meeting in Houston. Most of the women were old enough to be his mother, a few old enough to be his grandmother— and Mad flirted shamelessly with them all. Before, during, and after his speech, he made lots of eye contact, winked a few times, smiled a lot, and made wry, ever-so-slightly risqué comments every chance he could. He didn't really know why, but he was on a roll.

Also, even more than in Galveston, the bitter edges fell from his speech, the angry tone softened to a mere sorrowful one, and the redemptive elements took on more life and more power.

"So therefore, in all our anger and all our pain and all our weak humanity," Mad began to sum up, "let us all nevertheless praise the Father for giving us his Son, and praise the Son for giving us our hope—and praise our mothers and sisters and wives and daughters for keeping us civilized enough and loved enough and inspired enough to latch onto the hope for everything we're worth, world without end, Amen."

"Madison, can I adopt you?" asked the first woman, age 60 or so, to reach the microphone after his speech.

"Forget adoption; will you marry me?" shouted another one, in her early 40s, to peals of laughter.

"Hell, Marge, forgit marriage!" yelled still a third. "How 'bout just a nice little torrid affair?"

The room broke up.

Only problem was, TV cameras and microphones, attracted by that morning's headlines, were there recording the whole thing. The mood in the banquet hall was warm and light, but the electronic media couldn't capture the atmosphere. What the newscasts would show that night was cropped footage full of seeming non sequiturs, with a young man saying that God allows innocent children to suffer, and then clearly winking at an unseen audience member, and then laughing as a clearly fading former beauty yelled out that she wanted to marry him—all punctuated by the shallow narration of hair-sprayed news anchors reading scripts written by uncomprehending producers. The impression created was that of a bizarre cult-like gathering.

Leaving the banquet hall, Mad and Becky were startled to see the mime waiting for them, with yet another camera recording the scene. This time he was dressed to impressively detailed effect as a rampant lion, fully maned, holding aloft a banner saying, "Hear God's Mad roar!"

"That guy's *everywhere!*" whispered Mad to Becky as they walked out of earshot. "New Orleans, Mobile, and now all the way over here in Houston!"

"Geez, doesn't he have a *life?*" Becky responded.

By the time they reached San Antonio after an afternoon's drive, the Internet, radio, and news wires had all ginned up further interest in Mad's appearance. Word was out that the guy who had called God a jerk was now saying that the 23rd psalm was baby food and a fairy tale; yet somehow, he was attracting a bigger and bigger following that included women so devoted, they were calling out marriage proposals to him. Further, Mad's disciples included a mime most recently dressed up as a lion, while national conservative religious leaders took highly public shots at him and a heated web site debate raged between characters known as Formerly Doubting Thomas, Defender, and Cowardly Lion, the latter of whom was clearly a loose cannon. This was a freak show, soap opera, and religious dispute all wrapped up into one, and it made for great theater.

More media, protesters, supporters, and curious onlookers greeted Mad, Becky, and Don as they arrived at the hotel where the young professionals club had rented a meeting room. Don tried to run interference with the reporters and cameramen, but the rest of the crowd, maybe 50 strong, was unwieldy, and security was either non-existent or so weak as to be wholly ineffective. Pushing through the crowd, even through the friendly component, was a decidedly unpleasant experience, and Becky was sure that some moisture she felt on one of her arms was the result of somebody's spitting on them.

Mad was already tired from the long day. Public speaking, especially with lots of travel involved, can be exhausting. As a new experience, it can be downright draining. Now, with the added element of an unruly crowd, Mad felt shaken and very off his game.

Also, even though the day's two meetings had gone fairly well, Don had strongly advised him to alter his approach to the Yuppies and make it less sermon-like, less overtly religious, somehow more of a generic exhortation to experience personal growth and hope through self-sufficiency. The instructions, and what he thought was an implicit criticism of his approach, perplexed him. How could he make a religious topic less religious?

Being tired, frazzled, and confused also made Mad nervous. As he hobnobbed with Yuppie strangers sipping wine and beer at the pre-meeting reception, he felt a fiasco brewing. Then, when the official program started, the club president introduced him in a sort of smirking fashion (although, on the surface, entirely politely), as if this month's meeting represented a break from serious topics in favor of what amounted to a curiosity piece just for fun. One of those super-serious, break-the-glass-ceiling types of young women, the president seemed oblivious to any reason why Mad's message should prove attractive.

On the other hand, Becky's fine looks were attracting serious attention from some of the young men, including three with wedding rings on their fingers who appeared to be imbibing heavily. The ring-wearers she tried to ignore, but two others were very handsome, confident, and quite obviously successful. They were just the type she would like to disappear with for a while, if she hadn't felt the need to nursemaid Mad for the sake of her nascent business venture. The result was that when an out-of-sorts Mad tried to catch her eye for a reassuring glance, she greeted him instead with a kind of resentful indifference before returning her focus to the Yuppies.

So, by the time Mad took the microphone, he felt utterly lost.

"Hello, everybody, and thank you for having me here," he began, uninspiringly. "I come tonight as a rather befuddled participant in a growing enterprise that I began without intending to do so. I'm a high school history teacher at heart, not a preacher or a theologian.

"But I bet my kind of story isn't new to many of you. I bet many of you left college certain you were on track for a particular job, only to find that you have not only changed jobs but entire careers for reasons you never would have imagined even a few short years before. The old orthodoxy of climbing the corporate ladder, rung by rung, just doesn't apply anymore. Similarly, I've found in the past few months that a religious orthodoxy I had neither questioned nor particularly thought much about has turned out not to fit my life or my experiences or my heart."

Then Mad segued into lines from his sermon of the night before.

"*My* heart's terms, I must admit, are now the terms of a heart that is hurt and angry and frightened. As most of you may have heard, I have had an odd and ugly relationship with childbirth and with death." Mad went into his litany of woe. But this time, his delivery was flat.

He sounded not at all compelling but whiny. No decent response, no positive energy, came his way from the audience. Mad began to sweat.

"Anyway, you all probably know the story. As a way to cope, I wrote a bunch of religious propositions, more to work through my own grief than for any other reason. Then, in an almost catatonic state of grief, I posted them at a bunch of churches, and that caused a bunch of trouble, and now here I am making a bunch of speeches."

Mad had little idea where he was going with this, and his whole demeanor showed it. He saw a number of people fidgeting in their chairs as if trying to force themselves to pay attention, perhaps even to keep from dozing off. The room was a little too warm.

Still, he went on: "And I guess there is a point to what I've been saying, but some TV and media reports would make you think my whole point is that God's a jerk or that the 23rd psalm is nonsense or that, I don't know, maybe even that we're better than God Himself is. People hear me complaining about how I've suffered or how Job suffered in the Bible or how life is unfair or whatever, and…and…and, well, they miss the point, or at least what I think my point is…when I'm thinking at all, which some people may say I'm not doing."

Mad was trying vaguely to be self-deprecatingly funny, trying vaguely to find the thread of a message, and trying haphazardly to give his audience a reason to show some life. He was floundering badly, and he knew it. Desperate, he threw up a Hail Mary pass.

"So let's cut to the chase," he said, still not knowing exactly what his next sentence would be. Stalling, he interjected: "I love saying that: 'Cut to the chase.' It makes me think of Meg Ryan saying that line; I think it was in that movie *The Presidio*. Let's cut to the chase. Here's what the chase is.… The chase is this…"

Something, something angry, frustrated, wild, and irrepressible clicked in Mad's brain, and he just let it fly:

"The chase is the quest to make some sense of our lives by getting ahead in business, or getting laid, or getting some notoriety, or by doing any number of things to make ourselves feel important.

"And you know what? It's all crap. It's all a bunch of self-aggrandizing, onanistic crap!

"Because you know what really matters? What really matters is the integrity that shows itself in doing good for its own sake, whether anybody notices or not and whether there is a God to reward us or not. What matters is the wholeness that comes from loving people and loving this world for the sake of those people and the sake of this world.

"And what does God have to do with any of this? Why is it that what I've said and written has anything to do with God? Because that's how I believe God loves us and loves this world. Just as, even with the best of intentions, we make others suffer; and just as our own actions or failure to act can force or allow suffering to happen in a way that, we tell ourselves, we have no control over, so too I think that a not-quite-perfect God allows suffering and even causes it, but in His heart of hearts He would rather that we not suffer. In my own view, Jesus is His emissary to tell us and show us that suffering is not necessarily eternal and that redemption is always possible.

"And our petty, onanistic concerns can get in the way of recognizing and grabbing hold of those redemptive possibilities. Our striving to get ahead for any reason other than to improve our deepest selves, to improve our wholeness and integrity...that kind of striving, for reasons other than these, is just crap!

"So go out and love somebody today. Go out and love the world today. And while you're at it, go out and love God today, because in the course of loving we find small but wonderful redemptions all along the way."

Mad paused and considered whether to say more. He couldn't think of anything else. He was spent.

"Anyway, that's all I have to say right now. I don't know if it made any sense to you all, and if it didn't, then I guess I'm outta luck. Thanks for listening to me rant."

With that, he turned from the podium. He felt claustrophobic and dizzy, and he had to leave. With applause, angry shouts, questions, reverent compliments, and offended glances all surrounding him in a great big jumble, Mad hurried from the meeting room without another word. He and Becky and Don were all staying in separate rooms at that very hotel, and he hustled to the elevator and up to his room without waiting for Becky and Don to catch up. Pushing through his door, he roughly slung the Do Not Disturb sign onto the outer doorknob, and fell into a bed and waited for his heart to slow down and his head to stop spinning. What in the Lord's name had he gotten himself into?

In the crowd at the young professionals meeting, some were clearly inspired by Mad's sudden intensity and by his challenge to them to seek redemptive possibilities. Others, perhaps the majority, were deeply angered by his message and his attitude, and furious at his abrupt departure. Don dutifully went to work trying to spin the media and soothe the fury of the club president. Becky decided Mad was so maddening that he wasn't even worth worrying about, at least not for that night. Of the two young men she was most interested in that evening, she made a hard choice and slowly (and expertly) blew one off while signaling the other that she was open to his company. Even if it just led to a nice one-night stand, well... she was a *Sex and the City* aficionado. She had been working hard and deserved a chance to play.

The guy she chose, Brad, was stereotypically tall, dark, and handsome. He sold her on a jazz club on San Antonio's famous riverfront called Jim Cullum's Landing. Nice place. Great photographs of old-time jazz musicians graced the walls. Lots of people having fun, enjoying the music. But Becky had anticipated that the music would be Charlie Parker–like, or Miles Davis, and this was something she wasn't used to; it was the *really* old stuff, the stuff that had come out of New Orleans in, like, the 1920s or something. She could vaguely understand its appeal, but it just wasn't her thing. As it turned out, neither was Brad. She had been attracted by his obvious physical attributes and by his apparent wealth. She thought he might be a good lay. But as they sat in the jazz club, his vanity overwhelmed her. He was interested in Brad, Bradself, and Bradley, and secondarily interested in how lucky Becky would feel if she gave herself to Brad, Bradself, and Bradley. As frustrated as Becky was, as much in need of a little diversion to work out her frustrations from these past few months and from her uncomfortable visit back home the day before, Bradley wasn't the answer by a long shot. By 10:30 p.m., she convinced him to escort her back to the hotel, where she left him in the lobby without a backward glance. Once finally in bed, she wanted to cry, but mercifully and quickly fell asleep instead.

Her sleep was a good thing, too. As was Mad's. Both of them needed it to face the newspaper and radio stories the next morning. The newspaper helpfully pointed out that "onanistic" meant "masturbatory," and a regional radio talk show was having a field day with Mad's remarks. Phone-in lines at the station were so busy that the technician thought the system might crash. Some callers were thrilled that Mad had "told it like it was," and seemed to revel in the idea of somebody's speaking bluntly to a bunch of stuffed shirts. Many others were offended beyond belief that a speaker on a religious topic had used language as coarse as "onanistic crap."

Not only that, but word was also out, even in areas whose daily papers did not carry Mad's advice column, that his column that morning had dealt with sex. In answer to a writer's question, Mad had written that, as far as he could tell, pre-marital sex among never-married people did not qualify as "adultery," and that it was not his role to either encourage or discourage it for consenting adults. His point was that "this is a matter of morality and ethics to be determined within and through the web of relationships that may include family and priest, pastor or rabbi. The potentially important faith considerations make it a question that should, in theory at least, be considered prayerfully. No one knows with certainty what God thinks about this issue (or any other), but it is a certainty that sins of the flesh have the potential to put up barriers between man and God."

At one of the 17 papers carrying the column, a headline writer who was either less than careful or else a deliberate muck-stirrer had titled that column thusly: "God may not frown on pre-marital sex." The radio talk show host, alerted via e-mail, was naturally all over that one.

By the time the now sullen MMW threesome reached Austin for their luncheon, all Hades seemed ready to break as loose as a runaway barge down the mighty Mississippi.

Amazingly, the mime had somehow managed to make his way to Austin, still in his lion suit, and he was using hand signals to lead a group of maybe 60 or 70 supporters in cheers of "Mad is good! Mad is good!" A number of the supporters looked college age or else very recently graduated bohemian types.

But even in the hip town of Austin, they were mostly drowned out by unhappy protesters, some business-suited, some conservative-at-home-mom-attired, some grandmotherly, and some of the righteously-well-groomed-but-intensely-angry-young-man variety. One hundred strong had gathered to denounce Mad's dangerously libertine and profane messages. Security was reasonably tight, but nevertheless someone managed, unseen by officers, to hurl over the crowd several stones, one of which missed Becky's forehead by inches and another of which actually grazed the shoulder of Mad's suit jacket. So it was a frightened Becky and an angrily befuddled Mad who entered the country club restaurant. Even Don, whose whole persona and professional conceit relied on an air of unflappability, seemed for once not only flappable but positively flapped.

The country clubbers in attendance had signed up for what had been marketed as an interesting talk on religion by a nice but galvanizing young man who was becoming all the rage for in-the-know people to talk about if they wanted a "serious" topic other than Lewinsky. What they got instead was this rabble outside, and a speaker whose mood was better suited for a fight than a speech.

Unintroduced, Mad took the microphone even before the waiters had finished filling the water and iced tea glasses.

"Hello, everybody, I'm obviously Madison Jones," he said. "Look, every time I give a speech or write something down or give an interview, some media muckraker takes my points out of context and turns what I hope are nuanced thoughts into a controversial caricature. So today I'm scrapping the nuance, and I'm scrapping any set speech. All I'm gonna say is that life can be something other than a beach, and that I think an omnipotent God who is also all-loving could, if He wanted to, and probably should, ease some of the suffering—but that even with all the suffering that God unreasonably allows, we are still better off, still better people, still more whole, and still more fully human in the best sense and, yes, still more blessed, if we are in relationship with God than we are without Him. That's it. Pretty simple, really. Any questions?"

The floodgates opened. Questions flowed in from front, left, back, and right. Some were approving, some comforting in tone, some angry, some challenging, some searching, some excited, some flustered, some confused. With no holds barred, Mad answered everyone with penetrating directness. *Take it or leave it*, his whole demeanor said. *This is how I think, and for some odd reason people are paying attention to what and how I think, so let 'er rip.* Love, sex, death, time, God, redemption, intellectual and spiritual rebellion, subservience to greater goods and higher understandings, and the ceaseless human quest—quoting Tennyson—"to strive, to seek, to find, and not to yield": All of these and more were topics over and through which Mad roamed for the next solid hour and a half. Whether people agreed or disagreed with what he said, or even whether they were able or unable to follow the logic (or, arguably, lack thereof), it was a tour de force. At the end, the enraged and the enthused alike gave Mad a roaring and vociferous ovation more fit for a union hall than a country club ballroom.

The MMW threesome flew home that evening as if in the thrall of an epiphany. And the buzz about Mad, that he was a young man to behold, grew and grew and spread and spread. Among the many dozens of participants that night in a web site debate that raged on past midnight, it was an exchange between the Cowardly Lion, Perdicaris, and some new guys called The Scot and Ever Faithful that caught the mood the best.

"I think Mad is showing great courage," wrote Cowardly Lion. "And as you know, I'm an expert on the need for courage, since it took the Wizard to help me find my own. If he keeps his courage up, he'll be able to overcome the flying monkeys. If he doesn't—watch out!"

"Aye, but ye'll soon be in trouble beyond your ken if ye have nought but courage without some sense of how the world works and how ye need to pick your spots," wrote The Scot. "I'm all for what the young man is saying, but there's a time to charge like William Wallace and a time to plan and plot your moves. 'Hidden bunkers' aren't hidden if ye walk the course beforehand to plan your approach. That's what Jones must do if he's to survive and keep doing good work."

Ever Faithful shot back: "I think my man Defender has gone to bed, so I'm carrying this argument alone right now, but I have enough of that idiot lion's courage to say that you all are a bunch of fools. Jones isn't avoiding bunkers; he IS a bunker. The only way to God's green is to follow the way, the truth and the light, and what this nincompoop Jones is preaching is nothing but a hazard. Follow Christ, my friends, and sin no more."

Perdicaris responded: "Sin, schmin. You worry about sin, I'll take redemption any day. Mad helps make me feel able to be redeemed. That's good enough for me."

(Cowardly Lion, offended, also made a retort. "I resent being called an idiot. It wasn't me without a brain; that was the scarecrow. Get your story straight!")

CHAPTER THREE

"Young Alabama preacher causes stir," read the headline of a small story buried on page B-7 of the next morning's *New Orleans Times-Picayune*. The story identified Mad as the young man who had first come to prominence by posting his theses at the Crescent City's St. Louis Cathedral, and then briefly summarized the controversy he had fomented during his Texas stops and in the previous day's spiritual advice column. Grace rarely got that far into the morning paper before taking her kids to school, but she saw the headline when that particular page fell out in the course of her using the paper to swat at a mosquito that had found its way into her Uptown house. Taken from an Associated Press wire account that ran in dozens of papers across the country, the article described the growing unruliness of the crowds that greeted Mad's appearances. It reported Mad's dismissal of the 23rd psalm, his use of the words "crap" and "onanism," and his refusal to condemn premarital sex. Then, as if he had used "sex" and "love" interchangeably, it quoted the penultimate lines from his "onanism speech" in San Antonio: "Go out and love somebody today. Go out and love the world today. And while you're at it, go out and love God today, because in the course of loving we find small but wonderful redemptions all along the way." The effect made him sound like a late-1960s "free love" enthusiast.

But for Grace, the apparent sexual context was background noise. Something in those lines struck her the way Mad had meant them, in a way that spoke of attitudes of the spirit. As she hustled her ever squabbling kids off to school and, later, herself to work, the last two phrases reverberated in her consciousness. "Go out and love God today, because in the course of loving we find small but wonderful redemptions along the way." Grace felt again what she had lately begun to realize, namely that she had never developed a full understanding of what love is. She had thought she loved her ex-husband, but in retrospect, something vital had always been missing. She knew she loved her kids, unruly as they were, with a love that ached and consumed her. But even that wasn't what Mad seemed to be talking about; her love for her kids was like loving two extensions of herself that she could advise and direct but could not control.

Somehow, though, she sensed from those few short newspaper lines that Mad was talking about something different. Something so different it both unnerved her and inspired her simultaneously.

But how could someone love an amorphous entity like God, especially one for which, unicorn-like, there was no empirical evidence of existence? Grace had major difficulties with the whole God concept.

And what did "redemption" really mean? What events, what occurrences, qualified as redemptions? And why did these questions nag at her so insistently? Why were they so compelling? Her occasional childhood visits to a synagogue had meant almost nothing to her; no majesty or mystery had impressed itself upon her psyche. And her visit the previous month to Apostles of the Word was like being beamed onto an alien planet. People writhing and speaking in tongues, and a loud-voiced preacher interpreting Mad's blackberry story as if it were a wise and thoughtful parable: Was this what the Christian religion was all about?

Thanks, but no thanks.

And yet...and yet. Every single time during these past few months that she had seen reports of Mad's doings, something about his words or his actions had moved her. And she was sure that it wasn't exclusively Mad himself, but rather his message. If Mad had stood before a crowd and extolled the majesty of the game of baseball, Grace was sure she would *not* have been so moved.

God...redemption...love.... Why did these considerations, these ill-defined concepts, bother her so much? Grace just could not let go of them.

As she entered the elevator of the downtown office building where she worked, she shuddered to see that the only person inside was the recently divorced partner in her boss' firm who was always making suggestive remarks to her—remarks that were just barely on the safe side of legally actionable as sexual harassment. *Sleazebag.* If she could invent a God, she thought, He would give this lawyer a severe case of excruciatingly itchy hives every time he even thought about a woman.

For Mad, the next several months roared by like a Gulf-fed squall, with unpredictable elements so stark and sudden they were frightening—yet, at the same time, strangely invigorating. Mad and Don were traveling four or five days of every other week, with Mad making speeches or homilies to a variety of cultural and civic groups, faith-based charities, and Christian churches of virtually every denomination. (Becky always stayed back in the Mobile office; she had accompanied them on the first trip only because it was based out of her hometown of Houston.) Each trip was a roller coaster of highs and lows, of support and rejection, of well-crafted remarks that sometimes soared and sometimes fell utterly flat and also of off-the-cuff rants that sometimes enraged the audience but more often won its awestruck allegiance by virtue of Mad's raw honesty and passion. Everywhere they went, Mad unintentionally found some new way to generate controversy. Everywhere they went, at least some people in the crowd were angry enough to seem scary. Everywhere they went, a few of the media accounts were fair and accurate but more were sensationalized or hopelessly out of context. To believe some of the articles, Mad was a stereotypical Southern white guy in unfocused revolt against a world he could not control; by other accounts he was the voice of a radical assault against traditional virtues.

He repeatedly earned the opprobrium either of the Rev. Rob Patterson or of the Rev. Bill White or, less caustically, of the Rev. Larry Falstaff. A number of charismatic churches organized noisy protests against his appearances. But Mad also found that among his heartiest admirers were ministers in still other charismatic churches who were thrilled, as the Rev. Hebert had been, by Mad's emphasis on redemption and ultimate reconciliation with God. At the four appearances Mad made at such churches in the next two months, he found that many of the worshippers were among the most warm and genuine he had encountered anywhere, and also among the least cynical. And they certainly were generous: Three of the four insisted that as part of his visit, he devote some time or attention to one of the vast social service ministries the churches oversaw. As for the Rev. Hebert, he repeatedly and politely pestered Becky to schedule a return visit by Mad, and won assurances that one would be arranged soon.

As for Don, Mad never was exactly sure what he did, because the press' agenda always seemed impervious to Don's influence. But Becky insisted that Don was an integral part of the operation, and his personality was so generic and studiously inoffensive as to make him an acceptable traveling companion.

Don joined Becky (and Justin and, by phone, Buzz and Mary) in growing concern over the unruliness and near violence of some of the mobs that greeted Mad on the road, but Mad learned to tune out most of it. Amazingly, the mime managed to show up for at least one stop of each bi-weekly excursion, once in San Diego, once in Columbus, Ohio, and once in Jacksonville, Florida.

Mad's daily column picked up seven more papers as subscribers as of June 1—for a total now of 24—and Steve Matheson took to quoting from it on *Gut Check* at least once a week. "And before I leave the air tonight," he'd say after a whole hour of Lewinsky talk, "my favorite young social commentator has done it again, with the kind of straight talk that I wish our politicians would emulate. This is a line from his column this morning, this one in response to one of those whiny letter writers who wants spiritual cover for having committed some unspecified indiscretion. I quote: 'God's not to blame, and neither is anybody else but you, if your suffering is self-inflicted.' Isn't that great? I mean, Mad Jones wasn't talking about anything having to do with politics, but I'd like to leave that as a parting thought for Bill Clinton tonight. The president's troubles right now are self-inflicted, and I say he needs to stop whining. That's *Gut Check* for tonight. G'bye!"

Mad got a kick out of Matheson's enthusiastic support but was far less enthused by the attention he began receiving from renegade Catholic priests and sex-crazed, left-wing, mainline Protestant ministers. Just as the likes of Patterson, White, and sometimes Falstaff were demonizing Mad for their own purposes, so too were these leftist yahoos using random sentences from Mad to push their radical re-creation of Christianity in their own image. One said, quite approvingly, that Mad's ultimate message was that Jesus was a homosexual activist. Another, equally approvingly, somehow found in Mad's speeches support for the argument that Christ was a Marxist feminist vegetarian. A third interpreted a Mad column as a theologically sound call to arms against American hegemony.

Mad, of course, had said and written nothing of the sort. Don dutifully put out press releases denouncing these misrepresentations, but few media outlets paid attention to them.

Meanwhile, a nationally renowned black activist, commonly referred to simply as The Rev, ran with some otherwise forgettable, passing remark Mad had made in criticism of white racism.

"Here's a white mouth of the South," said The Rev, "who sees through the trees. Here's a man of the hour who speaks truth to power. The first Madison wrote the Constitution; today's Madison offers a solution. Follow the logic of his declaration, and it leads to reparations. America, the home of the brave, must do justice to the descendants of the slaves. The Lord is like a mighty river, and it's time for His people to deliver. Justice for African Americans! Homage paid to African Americans! Reparations for African Americans! Justice now! Justice now! Justice now!"

It was enough to make Mad nauseous.

What sustained him were the times he spent, when not on the road, with friends back in Mobile. When he could escape Justin, he hung out and went for runs or played golf with his friend Jason, a math teacher and soccer coach. When Becky wasn't riding him to prepare speeches and his newspaper columns, he sometimes vegged out in front of the TV tuned to ESPN. And he made time at least once a week to grab cups of coffee, always at Carpe Diem, while engaging in long discussions either with Shiloh Jones (with whom a genuine friendship had developed despite LaShauna's warnings) or with the semi-retired Jesuit Peter Vignelli. Yes, Mad had called Vignelli the day after returning from his Texas tour, and found in the priest the mentor he desperately needed.

One Saturday afternoon, Mad managed to get Shiloh and Father Vignelli to Carpe Diem at the same time.

"Look, Mad," Shiloh was saying, "I just watched *The Poseidon Adventure* on cable last night. And the way I see it, Gene Hackman's character made the same mistake you make in your theses. At the beginning of the movie he's there preaching on the deck of the boat, and he goes on and on about how God loves winners and God wants you to be strong and self-reliant, and stuff about how we need to worship the part of God that is in ourselves, not the God up in heaven. And then the whole way up to where they're gonna get rescued, Hackman is yelling at God and acting like he, Hackman, is the one saving everybody while God tries to put roadblocks in their path. Well, look who dies: It's Hackman. Mr. Self-Reliant, Mr. God Inside Myself, is the one who dies. And where does he die? He falls into the fire, like he's falling into Hell. That's what worries me, Mad—I think you're a good man, but you're always talking about challenging God rather than obeying him, just like Gene Hackman did, and that's a sure way to let the devil pull you down into Hell. I don't want that to happen to you, Mad. And I think Father here probably agrees with me."

Mad started to protest, but Father Vignelli responded first:

"Shiloh's basically right, Mad. One of the most major sins, a sin of the spirit more serious than many sins of the flesh, is pride so overblown that it puts ourselves above God and says, in effect, that we are responsible for our own salvation. You're right in your theses when you say that God wants us to try to be strong—to 'be lions,' as you put it—but that comes only after we acknowledge the far more difficult thing for us prideful humans to admit, which is that we are creatures who are very, very weak, especially spiritually weak. We lean on God to forgive our weakness and make us strong, and then with God's help we lend our own effort to living life.

"Maybe that wasn't clear enough. What I mean, and what the church has always taught, is that if we just give up then we won't be able to draw upon the strength that God gives us. So there is a sense that how we live depends on our own will and our own effort. But even with our own will and effort, our strength doesn't come from within ourselves; our strength comes from God, and our choice is whether to accept that strength and do something good with it, or to reject God's strength and live a life devoid of effort and meaning."

"But what if God is working against us?" Mad asked. "That's what Gene Hackman said at the end, that God was working against them. That's why Hackman had to die, as one more sacrifice that God either demanded or else sat back and let fate demand from the group Hackman was leading."

"God doesn't work against us," said Shiloh. "Satan does. Hackman was wrong to blame God for the work of Satan."

"Look, let's forget fiction for a moment," said Vignelli. "Mad, if this gets too uncomfortable, please stop me, and I'll use another example. But we've talked several times in the past few weeks about what happened in your life, and Shiloh here knows your basic story. Can I talk about Claire?"

Mad felt a chill and a shudder pass through him. But he nodded for the Jesuit to continue.

"I've told you how fond I was of Claire," said Vignelli. "Although you haven't explicitly said so, your logic in your theses seems to say you believe that God either caused what happened to Claire or else that he was at least indifferent to it—indifferent to her extreme sudden suffering and indifferent to the suffering that her death caused you to experience. Now I've grown fond of you, just as I was fond of Claire, and I wouldn't worship a God who was indifferent to the suffering of a lovely girl like Claire or of a good and decent young man like you. The God I believe in is not indifferent to that suffering. He suffers with you, and…"

"But then you've got to say He's not omnipotent, then," Mad broke in. "Either He is omnipotent, in which case He can stop the suffering if the suffering is not part of His will, or else he's not all-powerful after all."

"That's the classic argument and the classic dilemma," the priest said. "But can't you see a third way? Can't you see that a God who neither desires our suffering nor is indifferent to it, nevertheless must allow it to occur, while He suffers along with us, if He is going to deal honestly with this world He has created?"

"Honestly?!?" Mad was perplexed and a little angry at Vignelli's words. "What does honesty have to do with it? Are you saying that God sort of sets the rules in advance, and that it wouldn't be right for Him to change them mid-course—that it would somehow break the rules for Him to step in every time or at least some of the time in order to stop sinless suffering from occurring? If God wanted to, couldn't He have created a world where He didn't face that kind of choice? Couldn't He have created a world where unmerited suffering didn't happen at all? And if He could have done so but didn't do so, then in some sense He is the original cause of the suffering and is responsible for it."

"But you're forgetting Satan," Shiloh broke in. "What if Satan is the one who introduced suffering into the world, and what if Satan is nearly as powerful as God is that God can't help but lose a lot of individual battles to Satan, little battles of suffering, even if God by the very nature of good over evil is destined to win out in the end because love is more powerful than hate? Am I making any sense to you?"

Round and round the three of them went, on the selfsame topic that millions have debated, over dinner and over wine and in prisons and in churches and in other places of both horror and beauty, over the course of thousands of years. After a while their conversation went off on tangents, and at one point strong Shiloh got teary-eyed when recounting something unintentionally hurtful that LaShauna had said to him that week, and at another point Peter Vignelli felt a deep ache when telling of the young woman whose love he had to abjure some four decades ago when he entered Catholic seminary and took a vow to wed himself to God and the church.

After well more than two hours, the conversation hit a lull and a silence intruded in a way that begged its own removal.

"So..." Mad said, looking for relief from the weight of their discussion, "how 'bout that Mike Ditka? D' y'all think he's really got the Saints going in the right direction this year?"

Fifteen minutes later, all three were on their respective ways back home.

Becky wasn't able to enjoy any such interpersonal communion. She was working too hard running MMW, the work broken only by daily trips to a health club at odd hours that didn't afford her the chance to meet anybody interesting. Mad took her to lunch a couple of times a week but otherwise left her to her own devices—and managed to evade being around her in any circumstances, especially at night, that might suggest any romantic possibilities.

Justin constantly found new excuses to ask her out, new "can't miss" events around Mobile or at the Gulf Shores beach an hour away—but she usually found excuses of her own for why she couldn't join him. To her big-city mind, "can't miss" in Mobile was usually very missable indeed, especially when a companion got on her nerves the way Justin did. One time, though, she did consent to joining Justin for a dinner with one of his potential clients for his MMW/physical training spinoff business, and Becky actually found the evening enjoyable. They and the client's husband went to dinner at a little place in West Mobile called Guido's that was carved out of a small wood-frame house, and she was surprised to find the meal to be of admirably high quality. For quite a reasonable price, Becky had a broiled fish smothered in some luscious lemon sauce, with a nice salad and fresh vegetables and two glasses of an exquisite white wine. The client, a 42-year-old trying hard, but only partially successfully, to maintain her figure, and her husband, a balding lawyer, both turned out to be excellent conversationalists. But what was most amazing was that Justin somehow managed not only to contain his usual goofiness but to contribute a few wry, perfectly timed lines that were actually quite funny. And she was touched when he said to the other couple, in all earnestness and without any sense of false flattery, that Mobile should feel lucky Becky had moved there, because she brought with her a "radiance that can enlighten us all."

Sweet, goofy, annoying little Justin: He truly had a good heart.

For his part, Justin too was consumed with work. Using the lionhearted themes from Mad's theses, Justin was trying to market (first regionally and then, hopefully, nationally) a body-and-spirit training regimen that he hoped would earn a fortune while spreading health and happiness to its adherents.

Not that he himself was really happy, if he allowed himself to assess his own state of mind. Something was missing in his life. Something important. He missed, profoundly, the sense of being in relationship with anybody else—romantic or friendly—who cared about him in any deep or meaningful way. Sure, there was his "good buddy" Mad, who had never pushed Justin away like so many others (for some reason) seemed to do. But Mad these days was distracted, only intermittently present in the everyday world. When Mad wasn't on the road or working on MMW tasks, he would disappear to points unknown (unknown at least to Justin). In any case, Mad certainly wasn't available for the kind of social bonding that Justin profoundly needed.

But that was okay, Justin kept telling himself. He, Justin Luke, knew that he was a winner. He knew he had a lionhearted attitude. And he knew that lovely, sexy Becky would eventually see and be impressed by that attitude. He knew it, he told himself. He just knew it.

On June 26, a front-page story in *The New York Times* proclaimed, "Vatican Settles a Historic Issue With Lutherans." The story went to the heart of Mad's main area of expertise as a historian, namely the dispute that had led Martin Luther to begin splitting from the Catholic Church in 1517. Mad's focus had always been less on the theology of the dispute (that was Claire's big interest) than on the societal and political changes that had exploded out of Luther's challenge. Still, he considered the apparent new accord a momentous development—and, as one who, like Luther, had posted theses on church doors, he was immediately besieged by the media for a response.

The argument, 481 years old, concerned the route to salvation. Luther's careful study of the Bible, especially the letters of Paul, led him to believe that salvation came not as a result of any works of man—not something earned, like brownie points—but only through grace from a God of mercy. Those who had faith in God's grace were saved *in spite of* the inevitable failure of their attempts to live sinless lives.

The Catholic Church, on the other hand, believed that although grace was the foremost cause of man's salvation, the grace became manifest only through good works, without which the grace almost always lay dormant and unredeemed. The Catholic Church feared that Luther's way would lead to a wholesale abandonment of good works, making society less orderly, more brutish and, what was worse, more licentious.

Luther, in increasingly intemperate language, insisted that the church was mistaken: that good works would not only continue but be of purer motivation, if they were undertaken not in hopes of "earning" salvation but, instead, as a response to the salvation that had already been offered. Righteous lives and selfless actions, said Luther, would multiply among men and women in gratitude for the grace they had received.

Luther also objected to the church's practice, growing from the theological idea of "works righteousness," of encouraging even its poorer adherents to buy indulgences (official pardons for their sins). In effect, Luther thought, the church profited from the poor while also harming their souls by leading them to believe that the act of paying money for indulgences could itself represent a good work that would help them find salvation.

And so the matter stood until 1965, when the Vatican and the Lutheran World Federation began allowing groups of scholars to re-study the issue and try to reach an accommodation. In 1983, the 500th anniversary of Luther's birth, the scholars achieved an initial consensus. But it took another 15 years for the two denominations to announce they had achieved (tentatively) an agreement. While reserving the right to differ on emphases and other peripheral issues of some import, reported the *Times*, the churches agreed on a carefully worded 44-point statement.

The statement's most important passage was elegant: "Together we confess: By grace alone, in faith in Christ's saving work and not by any merit on our part, we are accepted by God and receive the Holy Spirit, who renews our hearts while equipping us and calling us to good works."

When fully parsed, the statement certainly looked to Mad as if it were, effectively, a victory for Luther's interpretation of Scripture.

The first person to call Mad for his reaction to the story was an enterprising reporter for *The Metropolitan Daily* (motto: The Newspaper of Record). His full-time news beat was religion. "You imitated Luther when you posted your theses on all those church doors," the reporter said to Mad, as Don listened in on a phone extension. "You must have some reaction to this development."

"Well, I'm not in total agreement with Luther's take on everything—in fact, I think some of Luther's ideas ought to be turned on their heads—but as far as this new accord goes, I think Luther's position pretty much kicked butt."

From his perch on the other line, Don cringed and covered his eyes. Mad continued: "What I mean is that anybody who reads the letters of Paul with an open mind has to admit that, objectively speaking, Luther interpreted Paul correctly. If Paul is the authority, then the Papists were clearly wrong. This accord looks to me like a dignified way for the Catholic Church to yield on this one very important point: that salvation occurs not because of our actions but through faith alone."

The reporter was a real pro, with an excellent grasp of his subject. He immediately homed in on the three focal points of Mad's answer.

"Okay, from what I can see, you've raised three different issues," he said. "I'll throw all three out right now, and we can then take them one at a time if you want.

"First, why is this such a victory for Luther? All of the official statements and all the expert analysis I've seen so far indicates that this is a pretty darn good 50-50 compromise. Why do you think differently?

"Second, what is it about Luther's teachings that you personally disagree with? How is it that his ideas should be turned on their heads?

"And third, you included a qualifier in your answer. You said *if* Paul is the authority. That's a pretty big 'if.' Are you suggesting that Paul should *not* be the authority?"

After all his experiences with clueless journalists, Mad was delighted to be confronted with a reporter who really knew his stuff. Mad dropped all his defenses and launched into a broad intellectual discussion of the issues involved.

"Well, let me pull out my Luther book.... Yes, that's where I thought this was. You obviously don't have this right in front of you, but after I saw today's story I was in the process of pulling this out when you called. I'm looking at Luther's theses for the Heidelberg Disputation, thesis number 25. It says, quote, 'The one who does much "work" is not the righteous one, but the one who, without "work," has much faith in Christ.' The new Catholic–Lutheran accord uses almost the exact same words: 'In faith in Christ's saving work and not by any merit on our part, we are accepted by God and receive the Holy Spirit.' And lemme see, I've got a note cross-referenced here in my book. Gimme a second to look it up.... Yeah, here's from Luther's preface to the New Testament: 'It is not by our own works, but by His work, His passion and death, that He makes us righteous, and gives us life and salvation.'

"That's why I say Luther kicked butt: because this accord tracks Luther's position almost exactly.

"Now, let me take your questions out of order. I think it was your third question that asked whether Paul was the correct authority. I mean, Luther identified explicitly with Paul, and his writings clearly track Paul's own. The Catholic Church was spitting in the wind by trying to deny that. But what made Paul the be-all and end-all, anyway? Paul spread the Gospel, but does that mean that the words of Paul himself should be taken as Gospel? The way I see it, the Gospel is the Gospel, and Paul's epistles are Paul's epistles, his letters—and the two should not be confused with each other. The ultimate authority shouldn't be Paul; the ultimate authority is Jesus Christ. Who's to say that Paul didn't misinterpret Jesus? I mean, Luther could have been right about Paul, but that doesn't mean that Paul was always right about Christ."

The reporter was intrigued. "Well, is there any example you can give where you think Paul and Jesus were at odds?"

Mad thought a moment. "Hmmmm.... Okay, try this. Now this is sorta off the top of my head; I mean, I've thought of this before but haven't really thought it all the way through, but just use this for the sake of argument of what I mean *could* be an example..."

"Okay, okay," said the reporter. "Enough of the disclaimers. I get it; I get it: We're talking hypothetically. Go ahead and spill the beans already."

"Okay, think about probably the most famous parable of all, the one about the Good Samaritan," Mad said. "In the verses just before the parable itself, what was the question the guy asked, the one that Jesus' parable responded to? I'll tell you what the question was; the question was precisely the one at issue in this dispute between the Catholic Church and Luther. The question was, 'Teacher, what shall I do to inherit eternal life?'

"Now look closely at Jesus' answer. He said there were two things the man could do. First, he should love the Lord, etc. Basically, that's faith. That could be taken to support Luther's position of salvation through faith alone. But then there's the second thing: Love thy neighbor. The man specifically was told to love his neighbor—and then Jesus went on to explain what it meant to love a neighbor. That's when He told this parable about the Samaritan, and the Samaritan's good works to help the injured man along the roadside..."

"Yeah, yeah, I know the story," said the reporter impatiently. His willingness to explore the issues did not translate into a desire to sit around for the equivalent of a dorm room bull session. He had work to do. "What's the point?"

"Okay, I'm getting there," said Mad, a little taken aback by the reporter's East Coast brusqueness. "Don't you see? Jesus was talking about reaching salvation by loving one's neighbor, and he specifically equated loving one's neighbor with doing the kinds of acts that demonstrate love. The man asked Jesus what to do to inherit eternal life; Jesus answered, in effect, by telling him to go do works of love. And that's the centuries-old Catholic position, that through our good works we can earn, or at least help ourselves earn, salvation. But it's not Paul's position: Luther was right that Paul said we are 'justified,' or saved, by grace alone, not by our own works. So Paul and Jesus seem to be at odds, and while Luther was right on the scholarship, it might make more sense to use Jesus as the authority, not Paul—dontcha think?"

The reporter's head was spinning a little, but he was able to get the gist of Mad's logic, such as it was.

"Okay, then, what you're saying is," the reporter summarized, "that this week's accord is a capitulation by the Catholics to the effect that Luther was right about what Paul said, and therefore that Luther was right about the way to salvation—but that even though the Catholics are admitting defeat, as well they should if the answer is to be based solely on a correct interpretation of Paul, the Catholics might actually be correct on the larger issue of salvation; because Paul himself is wrong, because *his* teachings don't track Jesus'. Is that what you're saying?"

Now it was Mad's turn to try to follow the other person's logic. In this case, Mad had to think a few seconds to try to figure out the reporter's logic in the reporter's effort to follow Mad's own logic on a set of abstract concepts. It had the potential to degenerate into one of those vaudeville routines where one guy says to the other that he said that the second one said that the first one said that the second one said that…ad infinitum.

"Well," Mad said, tentatively. "Yes, that sounds like what I'm saying."

"So, in a nutshell," the reporter said, now trying for something more concise that he could use in his story, "you say the accord shows that the Catholics were wrong even though the Catholics are actually right."

"Yes," said Mad. "More or less. Maybe."

"Okay, now that we've got *that* settled," said the reporter, stifling a chuckle that showed he actually did have a sense of humor, "there's the third question I asked, or actually the second question, but you've left it as the third one to answer. What is it about Luther's teachings that you personally disagree with? How is it that his ideas should be turned on their heads? Is it just that Luther was wrong to give primacy to Paul when we should actually all give primacy to Jesus' own teachings, or is there something more?"

"Well, there's that, yes, but there's also more. The whole upshot of Luther's message was that only God is good and that man is never truly good, and that God is by his very nature nothing *but* good, all the time, world without end, Amen. Here, since I've got Luther's Heidelberg Disputation theses open, here's thesis number four, in Luther's own words. Luther said, quote, 'The works of God may always appear to be unattractive and seemingly bad. They are nevertheless truly immortal merits.' End quote. But that's the opposite of what I wrote in my 59 theses that landed me into this whole public mess that makes people like you act as if I'm worth asking about any of this. I wrote that God Himself is imperfect, and that He sent Jesus to reconcile His own, God the Father's, imperfections with man's own imperfections, to mediate and achieve an ultimate perfection or state of grace from the mire of two separate sets of imperfection.

"Luther wrote that everything God does is actually an immortal merit, while I wrote that 'God is jealous and wrathful and unfair, and arrogant and prone to going mad with his own power, and that he punishes mankind overly harshly.' That's the polar opposite of Luther's message. In the short run at least, I guess it turns Luther on his head— even though, in the end, we both come back to the goodness of God's ultimate will and the need to have faith in God's grace even when faith is severely tested."

Something in what Mad said struck the reporter in a way that for some reason seemed sort of funny. Stupid funny but funny nonetheless.

"You said you wrote 59 theses?" he asked. "Somehow that number never registered with me before now. You posted 59 theses on church doors, and Luther posted 95 theses on the church door at Wittenberg. And now you say you are turning Luther on his head. Luther, 95; you, 59—95-59. On his head. Get it? Turn 95 over, you get 59. I don't know why, but that seems really funny to me. What a riot: '*On his head.*' That's just too rich."

Mad had never thought of this before, and it struck him, too, as being funny. For some reason the numerical pun put him in a good mood. He ended the interview and hung up the phone feeling certain he finally had found a reporter (in addition to the kind-faced young woman in Mobile) who would neither twist nor sensationalize what he said. This guy was really conversant with the issues, such as they were, and so his story could help Mad avoid another round of bitter controversy.

Don wasn't so sure. Don, trained media ear that he was, thought he recognized a host of potential pitfalls—a bevy of fires lit by Mad that MMW Corp. might have to douse.

Don was correct.

It was the Sunday *Metropolitan Daily*, invariably a top seller nationwide, that ran the reporter's story as a lengthy, in-depth feature. The article itself was a remarkably well-crafted piece on the tentative accord, with a thorough and readily understandable history of the centuries-old dispute and a nuanced explanation of the issues, combined with a broad range of reactions from experts across the theological spectrum. Mad's responses, appropriately enough, were afforded just five paragraphs halfway through a 75-paragraph story. The text itself was unexceptional:

> *One commentator, a historian and scholar and imitator of Luther, took issue with the prevailing opinion that the accord's central statement represented equal concessions from both sides. Madison Jones, the young man from Mobile, Alabama, who in the past few months has launched a growing nationwide ministry, said that Catholic theologians gave far more ground because they acknowledged for the first time the undisputed primacy of "faith" over "works" in the quest for eternal salvation.*
>
> *"I think Luther pretty much kicked butt," Jones said, before launching into a lengthy and far more measured explanation. "The Papists were clearly wrong."*
>
> *To support his contention, Jones quoted the following passage from Luther's writings: "It is not by our own works, but by His work, His passion and death, that He makes us righteous, and gives us life and salvation." Jones compared that to the new accord's passage that salvation comes "in faith in Christ's saving work and not because of any merit on our part."*
>
> *But Jones, who has quickly established a reputation for unconventional interpretations, said that despite his own*

Protestantism he thinks the former Catholic position might actually be the stronger one. He said that the new accord more accurately represents the views expressed in the letters of the apostle Paul, but that the question shouldn't end there.

"The ultimate authority shouldn't be Paul," Jones said. "The ultimate authority is Jesus Christ. Who's to say that Paul didn't misinterpret Jesus?"

And Jesus, Jones said, consistently preached a message that emphasized the necessity of good works.

Leaders of other mainline Protestant denominations, meanwhile...

Fair and accurate as the article was, however, it was the sub-*sub*-headline that raised a ruckus. The story was headlined "Harmonic convergence?" with a slightly smaller-type sub-head saying, "Faith accord strikes 'grace' notes." But then came the kicker sub-head: "But one observer says 'Luther...kicked butt.'"

It was enough to send some Catholics into apoplexy. A national hyper-traditionalist Catholic organization, Pulchra Maria (Beautiful Mary), denounced both the accord and Mad in scathing terms. "The reaction of Mr. Jones is evidence of a disrespect, bordering on dangerous bias, against the Catholic faithful," said its press release. "Triumphalist reactions like his also show the folly of any efforts by Rome to yield, even on semantics, to any psychological need for 'validation' on the part of Protestants in expiation for their mistake of abandoning the One True Faith. We urge the Holy See to reject this tentative accord rather than signing it, as scheduled, this fall. Protestants should always be welcome to return to the fold, but it is they, not Catholics, who must undertake the journey."

A few archbishops also responded negatively, albeit in gentler and more politic language, to Mad's "kicked butt" line.

And then there was the legendary conservative Catholic political activist out of Chicago, Gladys Phillpott. Mrs. Phillpott, now well into her 70s, had wielded a conservative cudgel in national politics since the days of Robert Taft's battles against Thomas Dewey for Republican supremacy in the mid-1940s. Feminists despised her and ridiculed her as an embittered but cowering housewife. During the abortion battles of the 1970s and 1980s, they even made a pun from her name for a silly chant with which they greeted each of her public appearances: "Fill pots and fill pans, and kiss the feet of your man!"

But for all that, Mrs. Phillpott was a formidable and indefatigable trench fighter. And nothing, no Reagan or Helms or Buchanan, was more important to her than her faith. Through her national conservative woman's organization, The "Old Glory" Chorus, she released the following personal statement:

"I usually would not deign to respond to an upstart young man who enjoys neither ecclesiastical authority from any church nor any elective office. But the remarks of Madison Jones (if reported accurately by the liberal *Metropolitan Daily*) bear careful scrutiny. Like many other committed Catholics, I was insulted by Mr. Jones' comment that Martin Luther has now effectively 'kicked butt' against the Catholic Church. But a closer reading caused me a momentary double take. It is important that, in other remarks, Mr. Jones acknowledged the primacy of Our Lord Jesus Christ whenever the Lord's own words seem in apparent contradiction with other parts of the Bible—and that he credited Catholics, in passing at least, for our fealty to Christ's words. Clearly, Mr. Jones is a young man able to recognize, at least on an intellectual level, the nuances of our faith.

"Nevertheless, I must in the end denounce Mr. Jones in the strongest terms—not because he is a danger to a faith too strong to be easily wounded, but because he is a danger to our politics. The danger was buried in the text of yesterday's feature article. What he said was, and I quote, that 'the Papists were clearly wrong' about how the letters of Paul should be interpreted. The problem is in the word 'Papists.' I'm not usually one for political correctness based on hurt feelings over word use. But the term 'Papist' long has been used as a pejorative, especially in the South, to indicate a wholly unjustified fear that Catholics were loyal to the pope rather than to our nation, even on matters of purely secular authority. In short, it questions our patriotism. And it gives voice to the anti-Catholic prejudices that ruled this nation's politics for some 175 years.

"For conservative and patriotic Catholic Americans such as myself, therefore, this indication of hostility to our faith, no matter how well disguised by other, purely intellectual concessions, represents a serious threat if it goes unchallenged. I call on all the media of this country, therefore, to no longer provide a forum for Madison Jones—who, after all, has no church authority, no Ph.D., no elective office and, in short, no legitimacy other than a talent for self-promotion."

Mad was stunned. He had meant no slur against Catholics. "Papists" was a word Luther himself often used, in his debates with Erasmus and others, to distinguish those who backed the pope on central issues from those who agreed with Luther's interpretation of Scripture. Mad had used the term as an academician would, in effect paying homage to his subject by using his subject's own language.

Mad therefore asked MMW's grandmotherly secretary to track down Mrs. Phillpott's phone number, and he placed a call to the conservative movement's doyenne. He wanted to apologize and to explain his word choice. Gladys Phillpott, though, was brusque and skeptical.

"You're a very cheeky young man," she finally said. "If this call is sincere, then I appreciate it. But I'll be watching you. You're playing in the big leagues now, and I've seen plenty of ambitious youngsters like you over the last half century who caused harm to our society before being deservedly hoisted on their own petards. So you be careful. You don't want to make an enemy out of me."

Somehow, the lady's harshness did not make Mad angry, but rather made him feel chastened. It was like being lectured to by a venerable great-aunt, too mean to truly love but who nevertheless had lived a life of such unbending principle that she commanded respect.

"Mrs. Phillpott," he responded. "Please don't judge me too soon or too harshly. In more ways than not, I'm basically on your side."

Mrs. Phillpott harrumphed. "We'll see about that. Goodbye."

Two hours later, Mad was rocked from both sides of the religio-political spectrum for his challenge to the authority of St. Paul. From the Rev. Larry Falstaff: "Jones denigrates the Word of God, which cannot contradict itself. Paul's letters may have been physically penned by Paul's hand, but the words are the Lord's, which is why they are Scripture. And Scripture is infallible. Mad Jones is therefore as wrong as he can be, and he risks mightily the just and majestic wrath of God."

And he also came under attack from The Rev, part of whose shtick in his preachings to black congregations was that he, like St. Paul, had experienced a similar white-light-and-booming-voice conversion experience. Not only did The Rev identify with St. Paul, but he also fancied himself a diplomat of the first order who claimed a special ability to negotiate with Syria.

Referring to Mad, The Rev had this to say: "He should come and ask us who have been to Damascus. St. Paul's words are strong and can never be wrong. Jones is picking a fight, but he can't see the light. His nice comments on race have made him my brother, but on Scriptural word there can be no other—no other than me, The Rev, because like Paul I know, what it's like when God's favor sets me aglow. Praise the Lord—The Rev will lead you! Praise the Lord—The Rev will lead you! Praise the Lord!"

"I *say*, I say, I mean I say," said the booming Southern voice of The Colonel, through the phone line to Mad's house late at night. "Every time I turn around, son, you are causing another tempest in a teapot, and your teapots keep getting bigger and bigger. I say, son, don't you realize you're embarrassing yourself?"

The phone call had woken Mad from the first stages of REM sleep. His mind was foggy and a little scrambled. "I'm not trying to be an embassment...a barament...I mean, sir, I'm not trying to be an em-barr-assment. Everything I say just gets all twusted, ip, uhh, twisted up."

"Sounds to me like your brain's all twisted up, son. I say, have you been drinking? Don't you know how to hold your bourbon, son?"

"No, sir. I'm sorry, sir; I just woke up."

"Well, son, I say, speaking of sorry, you've got $80,000 of our money, son, and some of us are feeling mighty sorry that we gave it to you. You're not doing us proud, son. I say, you're not doing us proud at all."

The phone line went dead.

While it seemed to Mad as if all kinds of people he had never meant to offend were furious at him, his advocates in the chat room were now more than ever in his corner, one of them to an extent that actually had become uncomfortable.

From Affirmed: "Let all the false idolators [sic] fulminate! I still say Mad is our new Moses and Luther all wrapped into one! You know the man speaks truth when the harpies of the right and the demagogues of the left both criticize him. GO MAD GO! GO MAD GO! GO MAD GO!"

To which Defender acidly responded: "Straight to perdition, you doofus, straight to perdition."

CHAPTER FOUR

In late July, Mad received in the mail an announcement from the St. Louis law firm of Zimlich, Shanahan and Woods to the effect that recent Washington University (of St. Louis) law school graduate Mary McWyre would be joining the firm. Mad had not spoken much with Mary in the past few months; he knew she was finishing school and studying for the bar exam, and Becky had been diligent in relaying the few messages Mary sent his way. Mad also knew that, a week hence, Mary and Buzz were both to fly down to Mobile from their respective cities for the first official MMW board meeting. But the mailed announcement somehow made Mad especially proud of his soft-spoken friend, so he decided not to wait until the following week to congratulate her.

"Hey Mary, this is Mad," he said into the phone. "I got the announcement from the Zimlich law firm. Many congrats!"

Mary was more than a little surprised to hear from him. Mad had broken her heart back in college, abandoning her almost cavalierly, and now all these years later he had seemed utterly ungrateful for her work (or Becky's or anybody else's) in launching MMW. And, of course, he had again shown no interest whatsoever in resuming any kind of romantic relationship—not that she had made an obvious play for one, unlike Becky.

Mary was from a huge family, the sixth of 10 kids, seven of whom were girls. Plain and quiet and shy and earnest, she was accustomed to being lost in the shuffle. But that didn't mean she liked it. By two one-hundredths of a point, she had finished third in her class at her Catholic high school, and thus had missed being recognized as either the valedictorian or the salutatorian. She had been decent but not spectacular at field hockey, for which she received an all-district honorable mention—but the local paper did not print the honorable mentions. She tried her hand at high school theater, for which she once had been named the lead's understudy (and never made it onstage) and three times been given "fifth business" parts for which her dialogue consisted of "straight" lines that provided material for the other actors to play off for either laughs or high drama.

Accepted to Georgetown off its wait list, she missed Phi Beta Kappa solely because of a disputed C in an economics elective, and otherwise floated through her four years while causing nary a ripple. Sure, she made some decent friends, two of whom would likely be friends for life. And she'd had one other boyfriend, who actually lasted most of her senior year, but neither was truly enamored of the other, and they just sort of drifted apart. And she took a Capitol Hill internship one semester, and she spent half her junior year abroad at the University of Limerick in Ireland, and she was always dutiful and kind, and people referred to her (when they referred to her at all) as "good ol' Mary."

Law school was more of the same: hard work, good grades, one more blah boyfriend for five months during the three-year school ride, and little notice from most of her professors or classmates.

And for some reason a few months ago she had found herself driving all night from St. Louis to Mobile to comfort a guy who had treated her like a short-term fling, and then worked feverishly (using her developing legal knowledge in the process) to help set up a nationwide enterprise for him. Yet until this phone call, she hadn't even been sure that the guy ever thought of her or valued her in the slightest.

"Oh, well, thanks a lot, Mad. It's good to hear from you."

"Well, I'm not as good as I should be about keeping in touch, but I wanted you to know I'm impressed. I'm told that Zimlich, Shanahan is one of the most respected firms in all of Missouri."

"They're okay," said Mary.

"Hey, listen, I've also got to apologize. All along I thought your name was spelled M-c-G-u-i-r-e, but I see from this announcement that it's spelled with a 'w' and a 'y.' I've never seen it spelled that way."

"Nothing to apologize for. I just changed it from McGuire-with-a-'g' last month. When I spent my junior year in Ireland, I started researching my genealogy, and I've kept up with the research sporadically since then. I found that my ancestors had actually lived in Wales in the 1100s, and the 'wy' is a more accurate rendition of their name than 'gui' is. I figured it was distinctive, too, and might help me stand out in the legal profession—so I went ahead and had the spelling legally changed. How's that for an example of thorough research? I'm actually sorta hoping the story gets out, because it might impress potential clients with the quality and persistence of my researching abilities. If I can find some Welsh-Irish peasants back in the 12th century, maybe my potential clients will think I'll be able to find the buried legal clause or piece of evidence that wins their case for them."

Mad had to laugh. Mary was so quiet, but she never, ever missed her mark. She was pretty damned sharp.

"That's damned good, Mary, damn good. Hey, look, anyway, Becky's after me to get my column for three weeks from now written and transmitted off to the syndicate that distributes it, so I gotta run. But I just wanted to congratulate you. I'll see you next week, and we can catch up more then."

At noon on Saturday, August 1, all six of MMW's principals gathered in Mad's living room. It was the first time that Buzz had actually met Becky and Mary in person. Becky had insisted that a summer Saturday in Mobile was too hot, even with air conditioning available, for anything but casual clothes, and she arrived wearing shorts and a sleeveless chemise that well highlighted her physical assets. Even though her attitude was all business, Buzz had a hard time trying not to leer at her. Mary, meanwhile, in shapeless shorts and T-shirt, seemed at first to fade into the background. Don was as efficient and colorless as always, and Justin, of course, couldn't shut up. Mad, for his part, just wanted to get the whole thing over with.

Becky reported that MMW's balance sheet was already getting very close to, yes, balance. She explained that an operating deficit so small after such a short time was a very impressive performance. She also explained that the unique deal she had worked out with the book publisher in New York called for a two-part advance: a smaller sum at the beginning of the interview process by the ghostwriter—a process now complete—and a larger sum once Mad signed off on the final version of the book, which was supposed to be by mid-October so the publisher could rush it into print for the official day-after-Thanksgiving start to the Christmas season. Her point was that with the larger part of the advance still coming— and, if things went very well, with a royalty-escalator clause that would begin to kick in if more than 20,000 of the books were sold—there was a chance for MMW to reach or even surpass break-even by year's end. And if the company was turning a profit by the next regularly scheduled board meeting in February of 1999, it would be time for Mad (with the board's input) to begin deciding which charities would get the proceeds.

Justin reported that his spinoff business was growing, too. In fact, he reported it in great detail (despite its having no legal connection with MMW) and with such a super-abundance of enthusiasm that Buzz tuned out completely in favor of daydreaming about disrobing Becky, who of course was young enough to be his daughter.

But it was Mary who, by incremental degrees, took over the meeting without anybody's being aware that she was doing so. She kept asking probing questions, usually involving legal angles, that showed deep insights of a mind both analytic and creative. After a while, even Buzz was impressed enough to stop sneaking glances at Becky's cleavage. Mary was plain-looking, but as Buzz became ever more impressed by the acuity of her intelligence, he began to look at her more than he stared at Becky.

Mad, for his part, was struck by how lucky he was to have talented friends like these who had re-arranged their own lives out of a fondness for him and a belief in his potential.

Then Becky and Don brought them all up short. They reported there was still one serious problem that was not being addressed. Mad's propensity to shoot from the hip, his talent for creating unintended controversy, was engendering an increasingly volatile atmosphere at his public appearances. Don reported a situation that Mad had become somewhat oblivious to, namely that some protesters seemed ripe for violence. In addition to the occasion on the Texas trip, there had been two other incidents of rock-throwing, and almost every appearance was now marred by at least some fairly aggressive pushing and shoving. Then Becky lowered the boom: In the past 10 days, MMW's offices had received two anonymous threats of violence to Mad's person, one by letter and the other by phone, the latter of which sounded like a thinly veiled death threat. She had reported the threats to the Mobile police department, which put her in touch with the FBI, which was now investigating. Both agencies were sympathetic, Becky said, but indicated there was little to offer Mad for his physical protection.

"We'll keep investigating, and we hope to track down these cowards," they had told her, "but meanwhile, your company might want to hire a bodyguard for Mr. Jones."

"Now, Mad, I know you're not going to like this," Becky said, "but I totally agree. There are obviously some real nutcases out there. I think you are in danger. I think you need protection."

"Aw, hell, Becky, I'm just some two-bit history teacher," Mad said. "Nobody would seriously want to hurt me."

Don broke in: "Those rocks weren't aimed at thin air, Mad; they were aimed at you. It's not just that some people are so offended by you and so crazy that they *want* to hurt you; it's that some have already *tried* to hurt you. And frankly, since I'm always right by you on the road, I'm just as unsafe as you are, and *I* demand protection."

"Yes, Mad, I demand it too, for both your sakes," said Becky, to general agreement from all the others assembled. "The only problem is that a bodyguard will cost us a whole other salary, plus raise our travel expenses substantially, and that will throw off the numbers of the rosy financial scenario I've laid out."

Back and forth, around and around they went, but it eventually became clear to Mad that this was an argument he would not win.

Just as Mad began to bow to the inevitable, his phone rang. It was Shiloh, saying that both LaShauna and their baby were taking a nap and that therefore he wanted to get out of the house—and would Mad be interested in meeting him at Carpe Diem, or maybe even going somewhere to throw around a football for the heck of it?

Shiloh! Bingo! That was it!

"Hey, Shiloh, talk about timing! How would you like to be my bodyguard?"

Long story short, Shiloh eventually agreed. But it took some doing, and the details weren't all worked out for nearly a month. Shiloh still had more than three months to go to reach five years on the Mobile police force and thus become vested in its retirement plan. Until then, he would travel with Mad and Don as his police force schedule permitted—moonlighting, as it were. (For other times until Shiloh could come on board full-time, Becky would insist that their hosts provide heightened security.)

As it turned out, the police department was so high on Shiloh that it set up a part-time schedule for him even after he joined MMW full-time. The brass thought he had major leadership potential; they also figured MMW was a flash in the pan and that Shiloh would soon want to come back on board full-time with the force.

As further inducement (other than friendship) for Shiloh to join MMW for a salary only slightly higher than the one from the Mobile force, Mad offered him a side-deal bonus that Shiloh thought (mistakenly) was coming from MMW funds. Mad took $20,000 from his remaining Crazy Eights money and put it in a high-yield investment fund from which Shiloh could eventually draw, for one purpose and one purpose only: college tuition. In a few years, Mad told him, Shiloh could finally achieve his dream of attending college.

MMW Corp., meanwhile, would partially recoup the cost of Shiloh's salary by raising the fees it charged for Mad's appearances (demand was high enough by now to support that anyway), and its principals would have to accept the fact that earning a surplus for charities might not happen as early as next February.

When the board meeting ended, Justin took everybody down to his health club for a workout, sauna session, and free massage by the club's in-house specialist. (He charged it all to the corporate account of his spinoff business.) From there, after a rest and some showers, all six, joined (at Mad's insistence) by Father Vignelli, went to dinner at The Pillars, a fine-dining establishment in a grand old mansion on Mobile's historic Government Street. Becky again was sleeveless, this time in pink satin that would otherwise have been modest except for a teardrop opening at the very top of her bustline. But the real revelation was Mary, who had for once used makeup judiciously, even expertly, to go along with a shimmery light blue dress so well cut that it provided excellent lines for her otherwise unremarkable figure. All the others (except for the collared Father Vignelli) wore sharp business suits, though Justin's bright purple tie was far too loud, especially when contrasted with his shock of mis-cut orange hair.

Problem was, Becky proceeded to drink far too much white wine. She had for months been so stressed and unhappy that, with the board meeting over, she was letting go for the first time since she had moved to Mobile. Father Vignelli, a marvelous storyteller, was in the midst of a sweetly humorous tale about Eugene Walter (the recently late Mobile literary personality and bon vivant) when Becky interrupted.

"You say he was wearing a pnurp, I mean a purple, striped shirt at this formal event?" she repeated in reference to a passing detail in Vignelli's story. "Was it as bwight as Justin's gwow-in-da-dark tie?" Justin looked hurt and nobody else laughed, but Becky didn't notice. She was having trouble not laughing at her own (what she thought was) humor. "Was it a purpowe-peopo-eater shirt, or was this guy fat enuff to be a purpowe-cow?"

Even Buzz, who rarely turned down an opportunity to imbibe, was embarrassed for her. Here was this incredibly sexy and intelligent woman who had done such a good job launching a company and running today's board meeting, and now she was an embarrassing drunk. Mary, sitting next to Buzz, leaned over and whispered in his ear. "Now's your chance, Buzz," she said, teasingly. Buzz turned and looked at Mary in mock confusion.

"I saw her this way one night during senior week at Georgetown," Mary continued, "and she started running a dice game to see which of 10 guys would get to go to bed with her. But Mad won't touch her, and she won't touch Justin, and Father Vignelli is a Catholic priest. Tonight, honey, she's all yours." (She didn't even think to mention Don, who was so bland that he had disappeared into the background.)

Buzz rolled his eyes as if pained. He leaned over and whispered back: "Sorry, but I prefer that my women be at least semi-conscious."

Mary just smiled. The truth was that she had seen no such thing during senior week, although she *had* once seen a drunken Becky ostentatiously grab a then boyfriend's butt. But after all, what was a little exaggeration among friendly business associates?

Soon enough, Becky's drunken voice, spewing inanities, became embarrassing for all assembled. It was not a good closing note for what otherwise had been a fairly upbeat day. Justin, hurt as he was (Becky had by this time referred to his tie in jest more than a dozen times), gallantly insisted on being the one who hustled her out of The Pillars and drove her home to her condo. There, she quickly stumbled to the bathroom, became violently ill, and soon passed out on the linoleum floor.

As she had not closed the door, Justin eventually tiptoed in there to check on her. He found a clean towel and, without her stirring at all, he gently cleaned her mouth and chin. He lifted her head enough to slip underneath it another clean towel, carefully folded into a soft makeshift pillow. She didn't wake.

Justin noticed the bathroom was cold. Exiting the bathroom again temporarily, he looked for a thermostat but didn't find one. So he entered her bedroom, pulled the blanket and bedspread from her bed, pulled out a quilt that he noticed peeking out from underneath the bed, and brought all three back to the bathroom. Draping the first two of those covers over Becky's prone body, Justin then sat back against the side of the bathtub and wrapped the quilt around himself. He then just sat staring at her. Even in a crumpled heap, she was beautiful. Her features were exquisite.

After about an hour, he drifted off to sleep. At around six the next morning, Becky's head throbbing unbearably and her mouth so cottony dry that it hurt even to part her lips, she opened her eyes to see the little guy slumped over, half sitting, half leaning sideways against the tub. Bless his little heart.

Just over two weeks later, on Monday, August 17, President Bill Clinton went before independent counsel Kenneth Starr and admitted, for the first time, that he had had intimate sexual contact with intern Monica Lewinsky. And in a fit of pique that night, the president went on national TV with a disastrously defiant attack on Starr's team. Three days earlier, a local Mobile columnist had already written that the president should resign, not just because of the Lewinsky mess but because of a litany of "abuses of power so great that the precedents he has set are not just disturbing but dangerous." The column ran in many papers, including the *Atlanta Constitution* and the *Houston Chronicle*. Flying back to New Orleans from another three-day-weekend tryst in New York, Laura Green picked up a *Constitution* during her plane's stopover in Atlanta. Seeing the Mobilian's byline gave her an idea.

"Mad, you've just *got* to do this," she said to Mad when he finally (reluctantly and only at Becky's urging) agreed to accept a phone call from Laura. "This is a great opportunity for you. There's nothing in it for me; I'm just trying to be helpful."

Laura suggested that she use her newfound contacts at the network to get Mad included among the list of religious leaders asked to comment on camera about the president's predicament. Southern Baptists were already on record blasting Clinton; some liberal Protestants (including the president's personal "spiritual advisor," named Tony Campolo) were noisily demanding that the nation afford Clinton full forgiveness; and the other usual religio-political suspects were taking their own predictable positions. But the network, which noticed ratings improvements whenever it reported on religious matters, planned to go beyond the Bible-waving professional talking heads and ask influential but less famous religious experts about the spiritual aspects of the scandal. Laura thought this was yet another opportunity for Mad to boost his own profile, and Becky agreed.

"I don't do politics," Mad responded. "Sorry, but I just don't do politics."

Mad's tone of voice was more than a little edgy. He still didn't know how to feel about Laura. Frankly, he thought she had used him, and misrepresented and more than slightly sensationalized his positions, in order to climb the network-star ladder. And he was still ticked off at her nasty phone comment berating him for mourning his wife. Yes, she had apologized on the web site, but he just couldn't be sure she meant it. And now his mind was whirring, trying to figure out what her angle was this time.

"Dammit, Mad, I just don't understand you!" said Laura. "All I've ever wanted to do is help you, and you act like I'm some sort of Jezebel. I really worked hard on the 'Acute Vision' feature on you, and you turned around and cursed me for it. Now you're not only acting suspicious of me, but your tone of voice says I'm just some piece of shit. Damn you! Damn you! Just God-freakin'-damn you to hell."

She hung up the phone.

Mad was stunned. Laura had sounded genuinely hurt. It sounded like she had no ulterior motive. She sounded like she really cared.

But more than all that, a revelation came to him like a flash. Laura had said he was treating her like a Jezebel. Could she be the Jezebel? from the chat room? It made sense. Her own professed ignorance of religious matters, her strong and kind good wishes for him, her use of the question mark in the chat room name to indicate that she might or might not be internally conflicted by ulterior motives: Everything seemed to fit together nicely. And wasn't Jezebel in the Bible a seductress, possibly a seductress and a betrayer at the same time? Mad was no expert on the Old Testament. He'd have to look up the story and check all the details. But Laura certainly had seduced him—and until now, he felt she had betrayed him as well.

Yes, Laura just had to be Jezebel?. And Jezebel?'s chat room comments about him had been so full of feeling, so kind, they had moved him greatly.

But hadn't Jezebel? written that she had known him for a long time, and that she had known his father, too? He wouldn't put it past Laura to have thrown those details in as false clues, as red herrings. Yes, that was certainly it. Laura and Jezebel? were obviously the same.

Mad dialed Laura's phone number. Dadgummed voice mail. Mad wasn't ready for that, so he hung up. Five minutes later, he called again. Voice mail again. But this time Mad was ready.

"Laura, this is Mad. Look, this time it's *my* turn to give *you* an apology. I'm really sorry if I hurt you. Maybe I've misjudged you. In person you've never been anything but extremely sweet to me. I feel like a jerk. Anyway, I still think it's a bad idea for me to comment on Clinton; it's true I just don't want to get involved in politics, cuz all it does is get me more unwanted controversy. So I'm still not gonna accept your offer, your suggestion. But after thinking about it all, I really, truly, absolutely appreciate your thinking of me. I am touched you are still trying to help me. I think maybe we should be friends. And I wish you luck with the fall TV season. You deserve all the success in the world. Okay, that's it, I guess. Sorry for such a long message. Again, thanks, and please forgive me."

She didn't call back.

The Mad Religion chat room was humming. Mad himself may not have wanted to discuss the Lewinsky mess, but the cyberspace aficionados certainly did. While Mad was quietly disdainful of President Clinton, some of his strongest supporters were jumping to the president's defense.

From Perdicaris: "I feel sure that Mad is probably with me on this. Mad's all about forgiveness and moving on with our lives, and that's what we need to do as a nation. Clinton might have acted like a scumbag, but he's got all these ministers saying that he truly repents. Heck, if even God can screw up—which is what Mad says—then certainly we can forgive Bill C. for screwing up, too."

From Cowardly Lion: "Damn, Perd, pay attention: He wasn't screwing up, or screwing down; he wasn't screwing at all; he was just getting some big BJs from an intern chick who saw the president as her personal yellow-brick road. But except for you having your facts wrong on the screwing part, you're probably right. Mad is sure to come to the president's defense. Don't forget that Mad himself wrote that sex can be 'heap big comfort.' Which reminds me: I've always wondered if the Tin Man was oiling up Dorothy when the rest of us weren't paying attention. Anybody have any thoughts on that?"

From FD Thom: "Stupid Lion's act is getting way way way way old but, yeah, I say stick it to all those hypocritical moralists like Patterson and Falstaff. Both of them are calling for Clinton to resign. They're both persecuting Clinton just like they've persecuted Mad. But I say that if those two are against Clinton, then I'm damn well for him, and I bet Mad is, too!"

Defender, of course, disagreed. "This is all typical relativistic bullhockey from all you moronic liberal excuse-makers. Slick Willie's been committing adultery with a girl less than half his age who, as an intern, was supposed to be under his protection. And he committed perjury and obstruction of justice, sure as can be. And that's not all; he's a liar and cheater and scam artist from all the way back to his draft-dodging days, and he's abused all kinds of laws with the FBI files and Travelgate and all the rest. In fact, the only thing Mad has said that I've ever liked was when he criticized Clinton during that TV feature on him by that dumb news magazine show. He's been awfully silent on the subject in recent months, but I bet even Mad, who is your hero, disagrees with you still. I bet he thinks Clinton should go. As for you guys, if you don't like the rule of law, go found an anarchy somewhere and leave us good Americans alone."

And Affirmed broke ranks with his fellow Mad supporters. "I hate to say it," he wrote, "but for once I agree with Defender. Clinton is denigrating the presidency, and he really needs to resign."

Finally, this comment came from Jezebel?, in her first entry in many months: "Look, I don't care for Clinton either way. But I do care about Monica. She's the one really getting a raw deal out of this. She's the one who gave her heart the only way she knew how, which was by giving her body. If that's all she knows, you can't blame her. And now this Ken Starr guy keeps dragging her name all through the mud. The way I see it, Mad is always for the victim, and Monica's the victim here. I'm still not straight with all the God stuff, but I feel sure that if there is a God, then He's gotta be trying to make this poor girl feel better about herself. There are a whole lot of us women out here who have made sexual mistakes but aren't bad people, and who sure as hell are glad we don't have our behavior scrutinized by hundreds of millions of people like Monica's has been. Clinton can go to Hell, and when he does, he'll find some of those prosecutors already roasting there!

"P.S. to Mad if he's reading this: I'm glad you liked my earlier messages. Thanks for being a great guy!"

Reading this around 10 at night, Mad became even more certain that Jezebel? was Laura. It sounded just like her, and this was probably her way of acknowledging his apology without having to call him back. The "sexual mistakes" line also was probably intended for him, Mad thought, as a reference to and an apology for seducing him when he was grieving so desperately for Claire.

The phone rang. It was Shiloh, speaking quietly so as not to wake his wife or baby.

"Mad, I've just gotta know, because I feel strongly about this. Now that Clinton has admitted that he and Lewinsky had sexual contact, what do you think should happen?"

"Well, Shiloh, what do *you* think?"

"The man's gotta go, Mad. He obviously lied under oath, and it's pretty clear he got others to lie as well. That's obstruction of justice, Mad. I'm law enforcement, Mad. I take the law seriously. That's my life, making sure that the laws are followed so that everybody can have their rights protected. We can't have one set of laws for the rest of us and another easier set of laws for a president. Clinton's gotta resign. Or else impeach him. He's bad for this country, Mad."

"Well, Shiloh, I'm staying out of this in public. But I'll tell you the truth: I'm inclined to agree with you. Yes, I do. I agree."

CHAPTER FIVE

"Hey, pretty boy, you been messing where I told you not to mess."

It was Officer Williams, on the Saturday of Labor Day weekend. Off duty and in civilian clothes, he had driven to Mad's house and rung the doorbell. He was mad as a hornet that was far too fat to fly. He had just found out about Mad's deal with Shiloh. Shiloh had arranged some vacation days so he could take a first-time trip as Mad's bodyguard beginning the next morning and running through Wednesday. That's how Officer Williams found out that Shiloh would later that year be leaving the full-time employ of the police department.

Officer Williams turned his head and unleashed a huge wad of spit onto Mad's lawn. "Way back all those months ago, pretty boy, I told you not to mess with my partner Jonesy. Didn't I tell you not to go messing with his head? Didn't I tell you I was watching you? He's just a dumb nigger, but he's a good nigger and he has a good future in front of him in the police—and now you've filled his head with all this bodyguard crap for a dumb-ass fake-religious business that ain't gonna last, and you told him you'll put money aside for him for college, as if a nigger like that who can't no longer play football has any business in college anyway."

Officer Williams' words, drawled as they were, nevertheless were coming in a torrent. "You know as well as I know, pretty boy, that you just using my partner for your own reasons. You're messing with his head, pretty boy, and I don't like it!"

Mad had been watching college football on TV, and the two teams were within a few points of each other late in the fourth quarter. He didn't have time for this racist garbage. He slammed the door in the officer's face.

Early the next morning, at about the same time that Mad, Shiloh, and Don were leaving Mobile via rental car, Pierre and Angelina Hebert sat at their breakfast counter in Kenner, Louisiana. Pierre, as was his custom on Sundays so he would be well fortified for his energetic preaching, was working his way through a feast. Scrambled eggs. Three large whole wheat and apple muffins. A grapefruit. Whole milk. A 32-ounce mega-glass of orange juice. Two oxymoronically "low-fat" sausage patties. A barely ripe banana. This was a meal that was supposed to last him until dinner.

"My good woman, do you realize what an honor this is?" Pierre asked. "Of all the churches in this country, Madison Jones has picked ours to be the site of his first repeat appearance! What an endorsement! It shows this congregation is full of the welcoming Holy Spirit!"

What he didn't say, but of course Angelina knew, was that he had hounded Becky with phone call after phone call, letter after letter, begging for this "honor." Frankly, he was peeved that his indirect spiritual mentor, the Rev. Rob Patterson, was continually and harshly criticizing such a nice young man as Madison Jones. Mad's return visit would serve to show that not all churches loosely affiliated with the Rev. Patterson marched in lockstep to his drumbeat.

Angelina responded with only a small smile. She liked Mad, too, and she appreciated her husband's enthusiasm. But she had been disappointed that Mad had not cottoned to either of the two young women, Tonya and Rhonda, whom she had taken under her wing. She also was fairly certain her husband had misinterpreted Mad's story about picking blackberries. She didn't think Mad had meant to tell a parable. She thought he was just trying to be polite by making a sincere apology for being late.

"And the congregation is so excited, too!" Pierre continued. "What a powerful preacher this young man is!"

"Dearheart," said Angelina, softly. "You know what I think would be a good idea?"

"I always want your input, good woman," he said. "You're full of good ideas."

"Well, Dearheart, I think the young man is such a good speaker that he's one of those rare preachers who doesn't even need a translator. I think you should let him preach on his own, rather than in tandem with you. I think you can wait until he's finished for you to sum up what he has said, if that's even needed."

Seeing her husband's dubious facial expression, one perhaps tinged with hurt on the grounds that his own preaching was being gently criticized, Angelina hurriedly went for a rescue. "Two preachers as powerful as the two of you," she said, "are probably more than our congregation can absorb. If Madison gets their spirits aloft, your passion will probably send them deep into the galaxy, so far that they won't come down to earth again. And I don't think the good Lord wants his flock to leave this earth yet; I don't think he wants a Rapture before its time."

"You are such a good woman," said the appeased husband. "You have so much common sense. Of course you're right. What would I do without you to keep me focused?" He scooched his chair partway around the counter, leaned over while still sitting, and gave Angelina's shoulders a grateful squeeze.

So it was that, three hours later, Mad was surprised to find that the Rev. Hebert was *not* interrupting his homily. Mad had worked hard at crafting a message specifically for Apostles of the Word that was so clear and direct that it lent itself to only one interpretation—so that Hebert's expected running commentary would lend itself to the point Mad was trying to make, not confuse it. In fact, Mad was so expecting Hebert's amplifications that he deliberately kept his own words low-key.

Too low-key. He sensed the audience fidgeting, their minds wandering.

"…And so, on this weekend that we celebrate the good honest labor that the Lord has commanded us to undertake…" Mad paused. He looked over at the Rev. Hebert, who himself was looking pleadingly at his wife with the appearance of a not-fully-broken horse champing at the bit, ready to explode into action. But Angelina was looking not at her husband but at Mad. He wasn't firing on all cylinders today, she thought, but what a nice young man. She wished she had a son like him.

Mad liked the Heberts. Their style of worship wasn't his own, but they clearly meant well. He wanted to please them. He didn't know why Pierre Hebert was being so reticent, but Mad felt compelled to do something grand so as to wake up the congregation and redeem the faith the Heberts had put in his preaching ability. Not only that, but by now, more than three months into his full-time "ministry," Mad had developed a performer's urgent need to please his audience. The worshippers had come in eager anticipation of a boffo homily, and by God, he wasn't going to let them down. He saw Shiloh out of the corner of his eye and remembered their conversation from a few weeks back.

Mad began raising the tempo and volume of his words, and began to ad-lib.

"...As I said, on this weekend of celebrating labor, let us not be unwilling to bear the even heavier yoke that is being put on this country by the scandals that are paralyzing our nation's capital. Let us not allow ourselves to become mere voyeurs looking into the brothel that our elected leader has turned the Oval Office into. Let us not forget that his own adultery and lies and perjury and obstruction of justice, and"—as Mad paused to find words to end the sentence, he felt an approving, excited stir spread through the congregation—"and his venality and false pride and his unseemly anger against law enforcement officials who are just doing their jobs—let us not forget that all of these failings of Bill Clinton *not only* do *not* excuse our own failings, but they require that we ourselves labor even harder to keep this country from being paralyzed by voyeurism. They require that we make our economy continue to hum so as to keep poverty away from God's people. We are too strong to be paralyzed! We are better than that! We're worthier than that! We're more lionhearted than that! In fact, we just won't put up with that!"

"Praise the Lord!" yelled somebody from the congregation. Then several more: "Praise the Lord!"

"Yes, praise the Lord!" shouted Mad, playing thoroughly to his audience. "Praise the Lord for making us a better people than to be brought down by one man turning our Oval Office into an oral office! Praise the Lord! Praise the Lord for giving us the sense to go about our lives! Praise the Lord!"

The congregation, aroused almost to a frenzy, began chanting, again and again: "PRAISE...THE...LORD! PRAISE...THE LORD!!!

Angelina had a mile-wide smile across her face, and Pierre was lifting his hands heavenward while yelling the same chant into his microphone. But in the very back row of the congregation, an unobtrusive Don buried his head in his hands. Earlier, he had seen a reporter with a microphone, trying to find a front-row seat. Don knew this meant more controversy coming his way.

Meanwhile, nobody had noticed the mime standing just inside the back doors of the great hall. He had snuck in late, wearing an extremely baggy but spiffy-clean sweat suit. Now a look of extreme triumph covered his countenance. He had guessed right! The mime pulled off his sweat suit to reveal, underneath, a navy blue cocktail dress with an ugly, blotchy white stain (created with Campbell's clam chowder), low cut to reveal an illusion of cleavage created with different shades of skin-toned body paint. Somehow he also produced a wig of thick, semi-long black hair and, to top it all off, a stylish woman's beret. In the midst of the chanting, worshipping congregation members, the mime ran, leaping, down one aisle and up the next, down another, across the platform up front, and right up to the microphone stand where a stunned Mad watched in horror. Throwing himself to his knees a few feet in front of Mad's waist, the mime proceeded, without actually touching Mad, to perform a perfect thin-air rendition of fellatio.

Many in the congregation thought this was part of Mad's planned act, and they howled with laughter until Mad, horrified, yelled to Shiloh for assistance. But as Shiloh reached the platform, looking ready to manhandle the mime, the mime looked up at the bodyguard, smiled and winked, and then hopped up and sprinted out a side door before Shiloh could catch him.

Angelina, seeing all hell ready to take over the aroused and confused congregation, took to the electric organ and began playing a loud and insistent version of "Amazing Grace." And as the congregation ever so slowly settled down, nobody much noticed a curious little man, with a hidden mini-camera stashed inside what looked like a large Bible, as he eased his way out of the church.

That afternoon, Mad and his traveling companions arrived a bit ahead of schedule for a huge outdoor worship service and picnic that was the annual Labor Sunday tradition of the Holy Pentecostal Methodist American Church of Our Lord and Savior (known colloquially as the American Savior church)—a 100 percent black congregation outside of Canton, Mississippi, a little north of Jackson. There had been some confusion about the fees involved for this appearance. Becky usually demanded Mad's speaking fee up front, but she was eager for Mad to make inroads into the super-active black congregations of the South. And the American Savior church, run by the legendary Preacher McGee, was the top of the line of Southern black churches. That's why, when negotiation with Preacher McGee kept going around in non-concentric circles, Becky didn't pull the plug on the whole deal. For some reason, Preacher wanted to write a check from one account for twice Mad's usual fee, then have Becky send with Mad a check for half that amount from MMW Corp., made payable to "HPMA Church, c/o P. McGee." Preacher, who on the phone sounded warm and wonderful and gracious and big-hearted, said something about how the ceremony of a check from a guest preacher spurred the generosity of the congregation when it came time to pass the offering plate. He said that generosity was the linchpin with which the American Savior church carried out its unparalleled abundance of rural social services.

The account Preacher wanted to write his check on, payable to MMW Corp., had run out of checks, and Preacher expected the new checkbooks to arrive from the bank a few days before Labor Day weekend. "I'll just give your man his check then, little lady," Preacher said with a reassuring warmth.

"Aw, what the hell," Becky had finally said to MMW's part-time secretary. "It's pretty much a shell game with the money, but we'll end up with the same amount either way, so what do I care?"

Anyway, none of that seemed to matter when Mad, Don, and Shiloh arrived at the huge fallow farm field, bordered by and dotted with pecan trees and adorned on one side with a massive fan-cooled tent, which served as the picnic grounds. Preacher, a strapping, smiling man in his mid-50s, welcomed them with a delight and effervescence that put all three immediately at ease. The only discordant notes were the diamond rings that Preacher wore on each pinky finger, and what looked like a ruby set in what was certainly a sterling silver belt buckle attached to a braided-rope belt around Preacher's contentedly ample girth.

After some pleasantries and a quick male-bonding radio checkup on the latest NFL scores, Preacher excused himself. "We'll have plenty of time to visit and to go over our plan for the service," he said. "It's just 4 p.m. now, and we don't start until 5:30—so why don't y'all go mingle and get to know my wonderful people and fill your bellies with good barbecue, and come back to this corner of the tent at, say, 5:15 or maybe a few minutes before that, and we'll get all our plans straight then?"

That was more than fine with Shiloh. Except that it was so rural, this was his kind of crowd, 3,000 strong. Kids in cutoffs ran around playing tag and throwing footballs and climbing trees and splashing through the tiny brook that ran along one edge of the picnic grounds. Men lounged around and drank RC Colas while happily debating the merits of Jackson State football, the size of the coming harvest, and the worthiness of their respective women's backsides. Women congregated on picnic blankets, gossiped, and ladled out cold lemonade to their kids when the young ones ran, panting, back from their play.

Despite the rampant goodwill, Don nervously kept to himself. He had never been around so many black people in one place in his life. But Mad wandered happily through the crowd and joined every bit of merriment and jaunty argument that he could find. Everybody treated him like a longtime member of the community, as if he, too, were black, semi-rural, and a Mississippian. Kids threw balls to him; women of all ages flirted with him with mock propositions; men invited him to share their off-color jokes. These were good people.

The only sign of tension was a heated debate raging throughout the grounds about the Lewinsky scandal. A clear majority backed the president to the hilt, but a fairly sizable minority felt he had disgraced the office and lost all the moral authority needed to govern.

Mad managed to wander off to another group whenever the subject came up.

At 5:15, the three white visitors met up with Preacher and Mrs. McGee, a surprisingly meek little woman who said next to nothing. Lickety-split, Preacher explained the format of the upcoming prayer service. "And don't think I've forgotten the money," he said. "I've got everything all ready."

Deftly, Preacher made a show of producing the check from his church account, for the agreed-upon amount, and even more deftly took possession of the check made out to his care from the MMW Corp. account. Then the checks were handed back and forth one more time for some reason—some kind of dual-endorsement procedure that Mad didn't really understand. And then a fat teenager was blowing a bugle and a loud-voiced man was yelling through a jury-rigged microphone for everybody to gather at the worship tent, which had magically been cleared of the many tables.

Soon enough the service started, and the singing was heartfelt and spirited and loud and heavenly and moving, and Preacher's introduction of Mad was warm and generous and inspiring. When Mad took the portable microphone, he felt so moved that he began ad-libbing in a way, but it was so on target and backed by so much energy, with Mad pacing back and forth like a leopard, that the crowd responded and responded and responded some more with a genuine and deep love for their Creator, their God Jehovah. And when Preacher produced the check Mad had given him and announced how generous it was, the love that flowed from the 3,000 in attendance enveloped Mad like a warm cocoon. Rarely in his adult life, except on his wedding day, had Mad's very soul felt so triumphant.

It was well past dark when Mad, Don, and Shiloh exchanged their final hugs and handshakes with Preacher McGee and the remaining elders of the American Savior church. Driving happily back toward Jackson, where motel rooms awaited, Shiloh remembered something he had promised to do.

"Hey, Mad, Becky told me to be sure to get that check that Preacher gave you. She said you're so absent-minded that you'd lose it somewhere along the roadside."

Mad absent-mindedly replied that he didn't have the check; Preacher surely had given the check to Shiloh, hadn't he?

But nobody in the car had the check. They didn't know it, but the check had been torn into about 60 pieces that rested at the bottom of a huge barbecued-ribs-filled garbage barrel back at the picnic grounds. But on Tuesday, the check from MMW Corp., made payable to "HPMA Church, c/o P. McGee," was cleared and deposited into the McGee bank account, which was rapidly growing large enough to cover the cost of another ruby-encrusted belt.

The reporter at the Heberts' church was with one of the big wire services, and his account ran the next day in many dozens of papers, including the one in Jackson. Obviously, he thought the mime was a planned part of Mad's act, and the article reflected that misperception. Making matters worse, the reporter had misheard Mad's line about the White House's now having an "oral office." Read one headline: "Oval Office now an 'Oral Orifice'?" Another paper wrote: "Lay preacher mimics Clinton's sex act." And so the headlines went, most of them accurately reflecting that same mistaken report. The story described Mad's words as "perhaps the harshest comments yet by an American religious leader." The third paragraph quoted Mad's remark about "the brothel that our elected leader has turned the Oval Office into." He also quoted Mad accusing the president of "venality and false pride" and of "adultery and lies and perjury and obstruction of justice." And then came the misquotation of Mad supposedly saying, "Praise the Lord for making us a better people than to be brought down by one man turning our Oval Office into an oral orifice!" juxtaposed with a description of the mime dressed as Lewinsky pretending to perform oral sex on Mad.

Somehow a Jackson TV station had gotten word that Mad was staying at a motel in town, and Mad was greeted aggressively by its camera when he walked out of his room that morning. Shiloh, trying to interpose himself between Mad and the camera, made matters worse— not because he made any contact with the latter, or even betrayed any anger, but because the camera angle, combined with the picture jiggling as the cameraman retreated, made it appear as if Mad had a big black goon who assaulted the reporter. Hard up for any solid stories on Labor Day, the station ran with the footage on its noon newscast.

Mad's schedule that day began with a private brunch (unpaid) that his church rector in Mobile had asked him to set up, outside of which another unruly mob scene greeted the travelers. From there, the drive north was mostly silent. For Mad and Shiloh, too much was happening, too quickly. They both just cogitated.

Don sat in the back seat, wearing out his cell phone with soft but hectic conversations with contacts all over the country reporting how their local papers were playing the story of this young "religious leader" who had so crudely taken President Clinton to task. He desperately wanted to put out a press release clarifying Mad's remarks from the day before, but Becky was back home in Houston for the long weekend and there was nobody else in Mobile he trusted with the job. Finally, Don found a buddy on Capitol Hill who owed him a favor, and convinced the guy to sneak into his Hill office and put together a press release on plain white paper and distribute it by blast e-mail from a nearby Kinko's. Don was nothing if not diligent. For his efforts, the wire service put out a brief one-line correction noting that Mad had said "oral office," not "oral orifice." (As if it made much difference.) Exactly three papers bothered with the correction the next day.

The next stop on Mad's speaking tour was Oxford, Mississippi. It was the home of Ole Miss University, of William Faulkner's house, and of Square Books, which (along with Maple Street Book Shop in New Orleans) was certainly one of the two most personality-filled bookstores in the South. Oxford also was the hometown, as Becky's research had discovered, of a man named Mark Mariasson, who had first set up the Mad Religion website. (MMW Corp. had bought the web site from Mariasson for $5,000.)

Mad was expected for a courtesy call at Square Books at 4:30 that afternoon. The New York publisher had arranged it. Square Books was a must-stop on the national book-signing circuit; the publisher wanted Mad to charm the store owners. That way, they'd be eager to invite him for a signing that fall or winter, when Mad's book was due out.

First, though, Mad was dying to see Rowan Oak, the home of famed author William Faulkner. They arrived in Oxford at 2:30, so he had plenty of time to spare.

Rowan Oak's front walkway, a gently winding footpath under a canopy of cedar trees, was peaceful and lovely. It was a perfect welcome to a stately white antebellum-looking mini-mansion. It had the look, if not the size, of an old plantation house. Mad wasn't a particularly visual person, certainly not an architecture buff, but he was impressed with the writerly aura that oozed from every nook and cranny. Most fascinating was the back room in which Faulkner had written the outline for his last novel in a sequence on the walls themselves. On Monday, in the novel, such and such was to happen; and then the next wall space listed Tuesday's events, and so on, alongside the adjoining wall, through the book's climax on Sunday. Something about Faulkner's wall scribblings, covering one week's time, reminded Mad of his own weeklong sojourn in the psychiatric ward writing his theses.

"Hey, Shiloh," Mad said as he finished the house tour, "you and Don take a break and go explore the campus or something. I need to do some thinking, and I'd like to hike through Faulkner's woods. Would you just come back and pick me up at 4:15?"

The suggestion was agreeable to them, so Mad wandered onto the path through a wooded area adjoining the house. The path was maintained, and kept open to the public, by the university. This was nice. Summer's heat still lay heavy on Labor Day, but the shade of the woods provided ample relief. Spots of sunlight danced across the leaf-strewn ground the same way as in the woods at the golf course where he'd napped while looking for his errant ball. Mad's mind recalled looking-glass memories of that weird week in the psych ward, the fruits of which had somehow transformed him from a high school history teacher into a nationally controversial religious theorist.

As Mad walked—bearing right over a little bridge, circling even farther right up a hill, still on a narrow sun-dappled footpath through the peaceful woods—he kept searching his memory. Faulkner's room, Faulkner's walls, and now Faulkner's woods were talking to him, urging him to remember something important from the psych ward, something he now had forgotten.

The path split. Mad chose the upper, leftward option. Before long, however, it led out of the woods, onto a semi-ugly hillside overlooking cement tennis courts and towered over by massive power lines. This was not what he wanted. He wandered back down to the fork, tried the other direction, and found that the path faded out into an underbrush too thick for walking. The path had a lovely beginning but no such end; it was not a loop but an enticingly blind alley. Back at the split, Mad sat down on his haunches. He *knew* there was something else he was supposed to remember.

He pulled his legs up to his chest, wrapped his arms around them tightly, and rocked back and forth. It was like the fetal position, but sitting upright rather than lying on his side. He recalled curling into the fetal position several times during the psych-ward week. He remembered how much pain he had felt. Oddly, the agony came back now very rarely, and far less searingly. He remembered when it had been the worst, when he had yelled out and cursed God and...and then had felt folded up like an accordion, and then had felt wracked not with sobs but with a laughter he could not control.

That was it! God had laughed through him. He was sure of it: God had laughed! In the midst of his pain, along with the gritty endurance, there had been an actual laugh burst of joy!

That's what had been missing from Mad's message! Joy! At its best, Mad's message was life-affirming and unwilling to yield to harsh circumstance, insistent that a winning attitude and a willful love for even a flawed God would eventually produce rich rewards. But the message contained no joy. Endurance, but no joy. Hope, but no joy. Life, but no joy.

But God had laughed! *Laughed!* Through him, through Mad, God had laughed.

Mad's revelation was overpowering. He needed to add joy and laughter to his message. Adrenaline suddenly pumping through his veins, Mad leapt up and ran back along the path to its source. A few minutes later, he emerged from the forest, panting happily. Though it was not quite 4:15 yet, Don and Shiloh already were there waiting for him.

Square Books is located on one corner of, yes, the town square of Oxford. Two stories high, with a tiny coffee bar upstairs and a nice long balcony overlooking the shops and restaurants and traffic circle of a truly bustling little town, the shop is such an Oxford landmark that, three years after Mad's visit, its owner would be elected mayor of the town. A few doors down, the same owner ran another shop for used and otherwise discounted books, with room enough to host lectures or book readings for crowds well upward of 100. In order to get Mad invited back there in a few months' time for a reading, Mad's publisher just wanted him to schmooze.

But with all the press coverage of Mad's new controversies, word had gotten around town that he was coming to the bookshop. About a dozen curious Ole Miss students pretended to browse casually through the stacks but obviously were there to see Mad. All of them, guys and gals alike, pointed, whispered, and giggled, with the former doing so dismissively while the girls seemed a little starstruck. A few diffident professor types managed to screw up the courage to address Mad, three from the political left and two from the right. Mad, radiating joy, managed in 10 minutes of conversation to leave all of them feeling as if their shy but deeply held opinions were valuable.

One of the co-eds left the radius of her giggling friends and approached Mad while twirling the ends of her long, blonde hair around a ballpoint pen. "You're Mad Jones, aren't you?" she asked, although she already knew the answer. "My name's Mindy and…well, my girlfriends over there and I, we all think you're cute."

Mindy was slightly heavyset but still shapely and sort of cute. Something about her gave Mad a rush below his beltline of the kind he had consciously tried to avoid in the months since his nighttime encounter with Laura. Against his better judgment, he flashed a warm and wicked smile her way. He was saved, though, by the appearance at his elbow of a pushy, late-middle-aged matron on a mission to save Mad's soul.

As if Mindy weren't even there, the matron started right in with a voice one part honey to five parts Brillo pad. "Madison, I'm Lola Jennings, and I've been reading about you for months now. You've got some potential, young man, but you've also got a penchant for real outlandish behavior. You need to calm down, young man, and get rid of your anger. What you need is a spiritual mentor who can channel your energy toward the good rather than toward some of the imbecilic places your mouth wants to take you. You're fortunate to come to Oxford, though, because we have just the man for you here. He's the rector at the church just two blocks from here—a nice young minister who's probably goin' to be bishop of this state one day…"

Mrs. Jennings was obviously just warming up for what could turn into a Castro-length diatribe that she had been waiting for months to unleash. But Mindy wasn't to be deterred so easily by some old battle-axe.

"Oh, Mrs. Jenkins here"—carelessly getting the name wrong—"is just so right about our rector," Mindy said, touching Mad's arm to draw his attention back to her. "He is just such a sweetheart of a man. But really, Mad"—segueing back to the point of her initial approach—"I think you need to concentrate, like, on people just a little younger than you are, like me and my friends, like, because I think your message can really, uh, influence us, you know?"

Mrs. Jennings' eyes shot switchblades at Mindy. As if Mindy were a fly to be waved at but not worth swatting, Mrs. Jennings picked up her monologue right where she left off.

"You can learn something from a good priest, one who has a real spiritual center that I think you lack…"

Mindy had a competitive nature. She brushed Mad's arm again, jumping right back in. "Yeah, Mad, Mrs. Jenkins is very very wise in telling you to go see our priest; he gives great sermons that really speak to young people like me. But you can reach us even better, because you're almost exactly our generation, you know, and it's like you can just, like, talk to us where we really live. That's why I think you should come to get a pizza with us right down the street, 'cuz your calling really is with college people, you know?"

"I didn't catch your name, miss, but I can see that you might be better off dining with Miss Manners than with confused young Mr. Jones here." As she spoke, Mrs. Jennings told herself she was not to be easily out-gunned by some little college tart. "I think both of you young people should keep your traps shut a little more often and really listen to what our clergy have to say and learn from it."

Mad felt like a mouse in the midst of a closed-arena catfight. But still riding high on his re-discovery of joyfulness, he forced himself to show a broad smile and an expansively welcoming dual-arm gesture. "Ladies, it sounds like both of you agree that I should meet this local minister, and I think that sounds like a good idea. I've already got a dinner engagement for tonight, Mindy, but how 'bout I give you a rain check and promise that the next time I'm in Oxford, I'll set up a function with this minister that *both* of you ladies can come to?"

Mad's charisma level had risen just high enough for him to pull it off. Leaving both Mindy and Mrs. Jennings a little nonplussed, he managed to escape the premises. But only after Mindy had succeeded in pressing into his hand a scrap of paper with her phone number scrawled thereon. (He put it in his pocket.)

"I don't know if I'll ever get to meet this minister," he said to Shiloh and Don back in the car, "but whoever he is, I want to learn his secret. How any one human being can be spoken of so highly by two such different women is beyond me! All I seem to do is divide people and cause controversy; I need to find a way to bring people together instead."

"Amen to that," said the risk-averse Don under his breath.

Dinner was scheduled with Mark Mariasson, the web site creator. Mariasson was a 40-year-old divorced math professor who six months earlier had been spending a random weekend in New Orleans when he noticed, just before dawn, a young man affixing a sheaf of papers to the front of the St. Louis Cathedral. (Mariasson had been returning to his French Quarter bed-and-breakfast from an all-nighter capped by a sober-up visit to Café du Monde for beignets and café au lait.) Something about the theses, or maybe something about all the Pat O'Brien's hurricanes sloshing through his veins, had moved him so greatly that he had returned to his B&B room to grab his portable laptop and bring it back with him to the cathedral. With a few intrigued passers-by also taking a look, Mariasson had typed in all 59 theses, lurched again back to the B&B, and e-mailed them to some friends around the country. He had then tried to sleep but, with so much coffee and chicory in his system, had been unable to do so. Bleary-eyed but caffeinated, partly hungover and partly still drunk, Mariasson had then gone about setting up a crude web site just for the hell of it.

After a short afternoon nap that finally, blessedly came, he had begun the four-plus-hour drive back to Oxford. His body wasn't really up for it. With frequent stops for dizziness, it took him more than six hours, until nearly midnight. Still in recovery the day after that, he had asked his department to post a note on his door canceling classes, and in the early afternoon, bored, he finished enough work on the web site to launch it into cyberspace. He called it Mad Religion, and he did it as a lark. Instead, it helped create a ministry.

Now, six months later, Mad's visit to Mark's house was nothing more than a casual courtesy call over takeout pizza and beer. Mad wanted to know this guy who had started his web site, and Mark wanted to meet the guy whose writings had inspired his site. Truth was, Mark had been going through quite a transformation in his life. When his wife had left him just over a year before, he found himself bereft in a universe of numbers and postulates, devoid of meaning, full of a randomness that probability theory made only starker and more fearsome. He thought Einstein's famous assertion that "God does not play dice with the universe" was true, not because there *was* actually order or meaning in the universe (he thought there wasn't), but because no God existed at all. If God didn't exist, He couldn't play dice. If <not A>, then <not B>.

But in the midst of a black hole labeled "depression," while desperately hoping to find a wrinkle in time that would help him speed more quickly through his miserable existence so that to Earth's elements he could return, Mark had somehow stumbled across the writings of one Arthur Peacocke. Peacocke had a dual Ph.D., first having established a superb international reputation as a physical biochemist and then, while trying to unlock the mysteries of DNA, coming to be so convinced that God was in the sub-atomic details that he earned a doctorate in theology as well and was eventually ordained an Anglican priest. Mark had wondered how this could be. How could an eminent scientist, especially one in the math-physico-chemical realm, where randomness was so conspicuous, possibly buy into the myth called God?

And Peacocke wasn't alone. As Mark Mariasson discovered when he did more research, Peacocke was part of a growing movement of eminent scientists, especially highly theoretical physicists, who were awed by the *improbability* of having random chance combine all the elements and atoms and quarks in just the right way to create the universe as we know it. Behind the randomness, they had come to believe, lay intelligent design. Others of influence, he discovered, included physicist Freeman J. Dyson and physicist-theologian Ian Barbour.

Through Mark's explorations of Peacocke, he found an Internet cross-reference to a Georgetown theology professor named John Haught, who approached the same subject from the other side of the science/religion divide and ended up on similar ground as Peacocke. From there Mark had been off on a journey through the works of 1920s Harvard professor Alfred North Whitehead and of the naturalist-anthropologist-poet Loren Eiseley, and of the Jesuit anthropologist Pierre Teilhard de Chardin, among others, toward a growing realization that distinguished thinkers for decades had been reconciling science and religion, the immanent and the transcendent, the physical and the spiritual.

Mark had not been long on this journey on that morning when he stumbled upon Mad posting his theses at the St. Louis Cathedral. Mark saw Mad as another man who had lost his wife (although, unlike Mariasson, Mad had not been cuckolded), who was dealing with grief— and who in his grief found not the absence of God, not the randomness of sub-atomic particles bouncing hither and yon for no good reason, but instead the absolute presence and ultimate love of a God who Himself wanted a reconciliation with mankind. It was his astonishment at such a discovery that led Mark first to create the web site, then to maintain it for months even while almost never himself joining the chat room discussions—and those few times only anonymously. It had taken some clever sleuthing on Becky's part to track him down so she could buy the site from him, but then he became so flattered by her interest that he begged almost pitifully for a visit sometime by Mad. So it was that Becky had effectively built an entire trip for Mad around a pizza dinner from which MMW (and, eventually, its charitable beneficiaries) would reap exactly zero dollars. (Don, seeing no media potential in the visit, had begged off in favor of trolling the local bars for co-eds.)

Mark lived in a small two-bedroom house on an attractive dead-end street near both the town square and the campus, and less than two blocks from Rowan Oak. It wasn't long after Mad and Shiloh arrived that Mad was struck by the overwhelming fact of Mark's loneliness. This was a man with such a combination of introversion and a wounded heart, Mad sensed, that easy laughter would seem so foreign to Mark as to frighten him. It was almost as if Mark the mathematician had searched so hard to find the non-existent square root of negative one that he himself had subconsciously tried to shrivel up into $-i$. Immediately upon opening the door to his visitors, for instance, Mark had shrunk back into his living room like a lame stray puppy cornered by two alley cats.

"Yer-awf'ly-kind-ter-come-here," he mumbled as he retreated. "Pizza's-commin'-beer-in-fridge."

Mad and Shiloh, exchanging glances that bespoke great sympathy for their meek-souled host, helped themselves to a couple of Michelobs.

"So you must be a real computer whiz, to have set up the web site in just one day," Mad said, trying to break the ice. "I'm impressed."

"Really-nuthin'-to-it. Not-much-brains-needed. Ennybody-coulda-dunnnit."

It took some serious effort by Mad and Shiloh to make Mark feel at home in his own house. But Mad had been so energized by the day's revelation, by his rediscovery of the principle of joyfulness, that he felt especially commissioned for the task of helping Mariasson find his Mark. So open was Mad, so at ease, so kind, that he slowly began producing the desired effect. Shiloh was a big help, too, his solidity and palpable decency so reassuring that Mark started feeling, well, *safe* in the company of others.

An hour later, then, pizza delivered and mostly consumed, with each man into his third lager, Mark was coaxed into enthusiastic discussion of his newfound passion.

"Look, here's a favorite passage of mine from the writings of Albert Einstein," Mark said, thumbing through one of a dozen books he had laid out on his dining room table. "It's from something called 'Religion and Science,' in 1930. Listen. Quote:

"'His religious feeling'—meaning a scientist's—'takes the form of a rapturous amazement at the harmony of natural law, which reveals an intelligence of such superiority that, compared with it, all the systematic thinking and acting of human beings is an utterly insignificant reflection.' And in another essay he wrote for *The New York Times Magazine* in 1930, he said that 'in this materialistic age of ours the serious scientific workers are the only profoundly religious people.' And here, from an address at Princeton in 1939, he famously said that 'science without religion is lame, religion without science is blind.'

"And then there's this guy John Polkinghorne, a professor of mathematical physics so distinguished that he was actually once president of Queens College, Cambridge. He's also an ordained priest in the Church of England and was knighted by the queen last year. Anyway, he says that 'a universe capable of evolving carbon-based life is a very particular universe indeed, *finely tuned* in the character of its basic physical processes, one might say.' And then he takes a while to get to the point, but he pretty much says—here, let me quote again—he says that to understand how everything works so perfectly, it is almost an absolute necessity to, quote, 'look beyond science to some other ground of belief in order to provide an explanation.'"

Like many introverts whose defenses are finally overcome, Mark was so encouraged by finding that he was actually being listened to, and that he actually was in communion with other people, that now his words couldn't be stopped. They gushed forth like a (controlled) nuclear chain reaction, both creating and feeding off their own unleashed energy.

"You see what I'm getting at?" he asked. "Do you get it? God is in the atom. God is in the workings of pi. All of which was a revelation to me, until I realized that if God was in everything, it means that God is in evil as well. And that's exactly the point I had reached when I saw you put up those theorems that said, 'God is a jerk'—but that in the end, He doesn't really mean to be a jerk. He's got all these semi-random scientific processes going on all the time, and He's trying to catch up with all of them, because He's set things up a little cockeyed so that some things get out of hand, so then He sends Christ as His mediator to reconcile all the good with the bad, the weak with the spiritually strong, etc. etc.—and it all ends up fitting together, the way you've explained it combined with the way all these pro-religious scientists explain it, to describe a God I can finally relate to. Not only that, but a God I *want* to relate to.

"I mean, it's just all so cool."

Mad was no scientist, and he was having a little trouble following all the quantum leaps in Mark's logic. But he at least understood the gist of it.

"So you're saying that science is actually proving, or at least giving strong credence, to the fact that God exists?" Mad asked.

"Well, it's the kind of thing that's not provable, but what quantum physics is suggesting is that arriving at the likelihood that God exists isn't too big an ontological leap."

(Neither Mad nor Shiloh was quite sure what "ontological" meant, but both let it pass.)

And so the discussion went (with, of course, a host of digressions), through another beer or two and then some semi-decaf coffee, for more than two more hours. At one point Shiloh made perhaps the most sensible point of the evening.

"But see here," he said, "what it boils down to is that we each find a different way, all based on how our particular minds work, to reach an understanding of God. But no matter how we get there, we all end up with a God who ultimately loves us. Well, I say that that's an incredibly powerful and incredibly *good* God who can take all of our weird minds and find a way to lead them all to Him."

"Praise the Lord!" said Mad, laughing. "And pass some more of that quantum coffee!"

That night, Mark Mariasson went to bed feeling like a man re-born, with the new confidence that comes from having one's ideas validated by others. Meanwhile, the Michelob and coffee both were working just enough on Mad's mind that he arrived at his motel still raring to go. And it really wasn't that late, just 10:30 or so. Emptying his pockets, he came across the phone number Mindy had pressed into his hand at the bookshop. A vision of a cute, blonde-hair-framed smile and shapely chest flashed into his mind. A charge again ran below his beltline. It had been months since he had succumbed to Laura. Temptation was running so high it was barely bearable. It would be so easy to call Mindy now. It wouldn't be too late; all college girls were still up at 10:30, weren't they?

Mad picked up the phone. He started to dial her number. But after just three digits, the phone rang and Shiloh, of all people, answered.

Mad had forgotten to dial 9 to exit the motel's internal phone system. By pure coincidence, the first three digits of Mindy's number were the same as Shiloh's room number. (More proof, perhaps, Mad thought, of intelligent causation behind seemingly random chance?)

"Oh, God, Shiloh, you've got to save me from myself. Remember that blonde college girl at the bookshop? She gave me her number, and I was just about to call her and go get myself laid."

Suddenly Shiloh was formal again, for the first time in months.

"Mr. Jones," he said, "that ain't any of my business. Telling you whether to go around fornicating or not ain't in my job description. And the Bible ain't a hundred percent clear on what a man is supposed to do if his wife up and dies on him. I know what I think are the right morals for your situation, but that's just not for me to say to you."

"Aw, Shiloh, cut out this 'Mr. Jones' crap. It's just that…"

Mad had been instantly annoyed by Shiloh's formality, but as he responded to his new friend, Mad's brain began parsing Shiloh's words. The phrase "wife up and dies on him" brought Mad short. In mid-sentence, a vision of Claire filled his head. The vision overwhelmed his male desires and his pre-Claire habit of easily taking advantage of what was freely offered to him.

Mad's voice trailed off, but Shiloh didn't break the silence.

"Oh, never mind," Mad said, while trying to figure out his own emotions. He sighed, stuffed the paper back into his pants pocket, mumbled "good night," and hung up the phone. Not too much later, he fell asleep—a sleep full of disturbing dreams.

Tuesday was again an early morning. They had to be in Memphis, more than an hour north, for a major 8 a.m. breakfast meeting. About 200 people were expected. But the *Memphis Commercial Appeal* had carried a story about Mad's Sunday comments on the Lewinsky scandal (and the mime's lewd antics), and mentioned that he was making a stop in Memphis. More than 200 outsiders, wholly unconnected with the convention, showed up and demanded admission. Noting that their rented meeting room was plenty big enough, and seeing a way to recoup some of their costs, the convention organizers on the spur of the moment decided to let in anyone from the general public who was willing to pay $10 for the privilege. More than a few reporters squeezed in, too.

Some 400 people, therefore, crowded into the convention room, all wanting to hear, and either applaud or contest, Mad's explanation for why both God and Bill Clinton were jerks.

Again jettisoning his prepared notes, Mad spoke about neither.

"One of the very next books on my reading list is called *Surprised by Joy*, by C.S. Lewis," he told them. "I haven't read it yet, but I love the title, and now I can't wait to get started. You see, yesterday I myself was surprised by joy. And the experience reminded me that God intends, in his deepest and truest longings, to provide for each of us a joy that surpasseth human understanding. Let me tell you about that experience, and about other tastes of joy I've experienced in my life, and about how the promise of the joy of God's love is the precisely desired end result of the process described in the Letter to the Romans, in the passage that ends—and with which my own infamous theses end—with the certainty that, quote, 'God's love has been poured into our hearts through the Holy Spirit which has been given to us…'"

And Mad was off on a happy and rambunctious tour of memories of Faulkner's woods, and of kisses garnered on the lap of Jesuit statues, and of scampering to home plate just ahead of a catcher's tag. And somehow he pulled numerous strands together in a way that inspired the vast bulk of his audience to a standing ovation. And when, in the Q&A session afterward, several people asked about the Lewinsky scandal, Mad repeatedly declined to answer—and by the fourth time he declined, the vast majority of the audience gave him rousing applause. There were huge smiles on faces and rich psychic warmth throughout most of the room, and Mad felt for the first time as if he knew exactly what his mission was and exactly why he had been called into the life of a traveling preacher.

His job was not only to explain why God's jerkiness was *not* the end of the story, but also to proactively spread the news that the rest of the story was joy.

From Memphis it was more than a five-hour drive straight up I-55 to St. Louis. (Don spent almost the whole time on his cell phone, because interest in Mad had continued to snowball since his harsh words and the mime's performance at Apostles of the Word church on Sunday.) Events at the "Gateway to the West" were to be Mary's production, first to last. Because her law firm saw great potential in the business she was bringing its way from MMW, the firm had avoided dumping (yet) the huge new associate's load on her that it otherwise would have, instead giving her a bit more leeway to drum up interest in Mad's appearances. And what Mary did had at first seemed a bit of a risk from the standpoints of both public relations and finance: There was no guaranteed fee for Mad's big lecture that night. Mary had rented a hall that could hold up to 2,000 people, and she was charging $5 admission to the lecture. Up-front costs, for the hall and for publicity, etc., ran around $1,000, so 200 people would have to show just to break even (not even counting travel expenses for Mad, Shiloh, and Don, nor counting the usual fee that MMW charged for each of Mad's appearances).

Mary already had been confident her event would succeed, but with Mad's remarks vis-à-vis Clinton, anticipation had surged. When Mad walked onstage at 6:30 that evening, he was met by an almost raucous crowd that not only filled every seat but also featured perhaps 250 more people standing in the back and in parts of the aisles, and even spilling a bit into the rear foyer. The throng was probably large enough to violate the fire code.

Mad was raring to go. He had spent much of the ride from Memphis completely re-writing his prepared text, and once in St. Louis had had time for a two-hour nap. So it was with neither hesitation nor any pleasing introductory niceties that he leapt right into his speech.

"'God does not play dice with the universe.'

"That's what Albert Einstein once said. And although Einstein's theology was not exactly conventional, he was nevertheless a deeply religious man. So if the world's greatest genius says, first, that there is indeed a God, and, second, that God does not leave his creation to random chance, then I think we all at least ought to take those opinions seriously.

"Don't you?

"Of course, a little background is in order. What Einstein was talking about, and what a whole host of advanced physicists and other scientists are also now saying, is that the odds against life's having developed, and indeed this universe's having developed, exactly as it has, are positively astronomical—literally astronomical, because it all began with the energy of a gazillion stars. So astronomical, in fact, that pure randomness just cannot account for it all. One little change in one little atom at one specific time, and maybe the Big Bang would have been a Big Fizzle instead.

"Or something like that. I'm not only not a scientist, I'm an absolute techno-tard, so don't take my scientific terminology as, well, *Gospel*."

Mad's timing and inflection were right on target, and he was rewarded with an appreciative chuckle from a number of audience members.

"But anyway, here's the deal: If order was unlikely to arise from chaos due to random chance, then—many scientists believe—something must have *caused* the atoms to line up the way they did, and for the quarks to line up inside the atoms the way they did, and so on and so on. In short, some outside agency loaded Einstein's cosmic dice so that they would add up to something rather than crap-out into nothingness. However you or I or anybody understands that outside agency, that cosmic dice-loader, the entity to which we refer is known commonly by the name of God.

"And out of disorder, God created a universe of meaning—just as all the atoms and molecules in the ink in today's newspaper have no intrinsic meaning, but nevertheless are imbued with meaning by the writer, for the reader. In the ink, and in the universe, there is an order and an intelligence and a thoughtfulness that is provided not by the ink itself but by the outside agent, in this case the human, who puts the ink on the paper—and in the universe there is a meaning assigned to it by the God who lined up the atoms in just the way they were lined up.

"Are you following me so far? I see a lot of heads nodding; that's a good sign. Okay, here's where all this gets both more interesting and more challenging—and even more than that, more maddening.

"Here's the problem: If God loaded the dice in order to create order of out chaos, then He is responsible for the form the order has taken. And if what we call God is the sole source of the order, then He is as responsible for the problems in the order as He is for the good parts of the order. He is just as responsible for the pain as He is for the happiness.

"And this holds true whether you are a deist like Thomas Jefferson was, who basically thought of God as a cosmic watchmaker who set things going at the beginning and then stood back for eternity to watch, never again interfering with His own creation; or it holds true if you believe that God acts within history at specific times, through miracles and through answers to prayers and through any number of other means. Either way, God set things up in such a way that some things go wrong. Either way, God is therefore either cruel or else less than perfectly skilled.

"And even if there is an agent of evil, a Satan loose in the world, then that is God's own fault, too. For if God is indeed the Alpha and the Omega, the first cause and the end result of all first causes and end results, then God Himself created Satan *him*self.

"It's like the Snickers bar where no matter how you slice it, it comes up peanuts. In this case, no matter how you slice it, it comes up God's ultimate fault and God's ultimate glory all at the same time, and forever and forever and world without end. And if the world seems nutty, then no matter how you slice it, it comes up that God is the original nut."

By now, Mad's listeners were demonstrating a number of different reactions. A small minority looked bored, and some looked intrigued but puzzled—but most were beginning to show signs of significant reactions to what Mad was saying. Many were chuckling, a few were nodding strong assent. But some were frowning, a few looking angry and a subset of those muttering their objections aloud.

Mad took a sip of water and plunged ahead: "That's sort of where I came in. My world very quickly turned nutty, and horrifyingly painful. Having lost both parents when I was young, my life was horrendously uprooted this year. I lost the grandfather I idolized earlier this year and then, just weeks later, my wife and unborn child died; and then, later that same day, my wife's mother, who had become my surrogate mother as well, died in a car crash. It was pain I didn't know how to deal with, even though it was perhaps less pain even than many others in the world deal with every day. I mean, toddlers with distended bellies or whose mothers are dying of AIDS—those kids have known nothing but a pain that puts my own to shame.

"So I got mad at God. I got mad at the Alpha nut, the first cause, the universe's dice-loader, the one who created the particular order we know out of chaos, the one who created atoms and waves and particles and who created a mind like Einstein's to find sense and meaning in those atoms and waves. What He gave me, what God gave me, seemed to be nothing but pain. And so I wrote that God is a flawed SOB, and that God is a jerk. And I meant it then, and in some ways I still mean it today, still believe today that it is true. If we feel pain, then God's a jerk, because God is the original author of that pain. It's that simple. God's a jerk."

By now, the audience was showing all the signs of a Sybil-like multiple-personality disorder. Mad's whole manner went beyond engaging; it was galvanizing. But the listeners were moved, quite predictably, in different directions. Unlike with previous speeches and homilies over the past six months, though, Mad this time was *not* perfectly happy to see people react angrily, so long as they reacted at all. This time his goal was to bring everybody together, to bring them along with him to a more fulfilling spiritual place. He did not want to leave even a single sheep behind.

So he hurried on:

"But that is *not* the end of the story. In fact, as Winston Churchill said in another context, it is not even the beginning of the end. Instead, the true story about God being a jerk is only the end of the beginning.

"You must understand that what I'm referring to as the beginning is in the *Old* Testament. In many parts of the Old Testament, God is a jerk. I'll be the first to admit that I'm glad I wasn't a Jew during all those times when God was alternately rewarding them for goodness and then punishing them in an absolutely Draconian fashion when they strayed. I mean, yes, they strayed, if you are to take the Bible literally—but God's response to their sins makes the current criminal justice system in Singapore look utterly wimpy by comparison. Floods! Capture! Torture and banishment! Death and destruction! And even the thoroughly innocent Job was treated horrendously for years until God finally repented of God's own cruelty.

"But then...*but then*.... Hear me out, people. BUT THEN, we Christians believe, God sent Christ, His very son, the living Word, to make things right. He sent Jesus Christ to teach, and to live the example of, the *new* Covenant. And the New Covenant was and is and evermore shalt be that our God is ultimately a God less of judgment than of mercy, less a God jealous over our obedience than a God solicitous of our love. Our God is now a God who, despite all His mistakes and despite His own tendencies toward jerkiness, and despite our own manifold wickedness, still and always offers us redemption if we are courageous enough to have faith enough to accept the immeasurable grace that is the wondrous means of that redemption.

"God calls us to be strong—not solely because we need that strength to overcome His own jerkiness, but because He wants us to delight in the strength He gave us as a free gift.

"God calls us to be brave—not solely to overcome the pain that God forces or allows us to suffer, but because He gave us our bravery as part and parcel of our better selves.

"Mostly, God calls us to joy. Yes, joy.

"I'll get back to joy in a minute. But first, please understand what is my favorite passage in the Bible. It's the passage I ended my theses with, the passage that represents the goal toward which we can turn all our pain and sorrow and transform it. It's from St. Paul's Letter to the Romans, chapter five. It says that 'suffering produces endurance, and endurance produces character, and character produces hope, and hope does not disappoint us, because God's love has been poured into our hearts through the Holy Spirit which has been given to us.'

"Until yesterday, I thought that with that passage I had come not just to the end of the beginning, but the be-all and end-all of faith. Until yesterday, that's where my message stopped.

"But now there's more. Now I recognize that passage not as the end of the end, but only as the beginning of the end. Because that passage leaves unanswered, leaves undescribed and un-fleshed-out, the nature of God's love that has been poured into our hearts.

"As of yesterday, I think I now have an inkling of the nature of that love of God's. That love has a name, and its name is *joy*. And joy is so wonderful that it's a wonder that I ever forgot it.

"I was reminded of that joy yesterday, in Oxford, Mississippi, as I sat in the woods on land once owned by the great writer William Faulkner. Faulkner, bless his heart, was in his writings a celebrant of many types of unexpected revelations. And so I found a revelation in Faulkner's woods, on what I thought was a dead-end path. And so you, too, can find revelations in unfamiliar places, even on a path that seems to have petered out.

"And the revelation I had was a memory…a memory of the time when I was in my deepest pain. It was a memory of the time I was in hiding, in the week after my tragedies struck. It was a time when I was literally cursing God, cursing Him aloud, cursing Him for being a jerk— and 'jerk' is a much milder word than I was using.

"And as I was yelling at God, God laughed. I still can't find the right words to describe it, but God *laughed*.

"And He didn't laugh at me; God laughed *through* me and with me, and He turned all my anger into laughter and somehow made me laugh, too. The laugh made no sense, and the laugh had no reason. But it was a laugh of pure, unmitigated, unadulterated joy. In the midst of pain, there suddenly was joy, and the joy made no sense and the joy had no reason, other than the only reason joy ever needs, which is that joy is sent from God. And if the joy is sent by God, then that's all the reason you will ever need. God sends joy. That's what God does. Joy is God's will. And since God's will created everything, God's will *is* everything, and God's will is joy. And our task is merely to rejoice—to *re*joice, to make the joice, or joys, *re*verberate as many times as we can.

"You've had joy. All of you. I know you have. Some of you have known joy in holding the hands of your children. Some of you have known joy in a glance from your spouse. Some have known joy in physical achievement, in an expression of your art, your music, your writing. Some have known joy in the company of a friend, and sometimes even in the company of strangers who turn out not to be so strange after all.

"And yes, we know that God planned this joy. He sent this joy by way of Christ, and His sending of Christ was long in the planning. This may be a little abstruse, but bear with me. Remember how I said that the God of the Old Testament was often the God who was most noticeably a jerk? But even by the end of the Old Testament period, God was beginning to turn. God was beginning to make the way for the Christ of hope and redemption and joy.

"There's a book in the Bible, from the part of the Bible known as the Apocrypha, which contains writings that some officially accept as part of God's word and others don't. Many of those writings were produced after the final, fully accepted part of the Old Testament—far closer to the birth of Christ. And one of those books, called Baruch, may be the book written most closely to the time before God sent His Son, His joy, to Bethlehem. Baruch supposedly lived 500 years before Jesus did, but scholars say the book itself took final form much later, perhaps as late as 60 B.C. So for those reasons, I choose to read Baruch as God's final words before Christ. Baruch showed where God was going.

"And here is how Baruch begins to end. It says to Jerusalem, quote, 'See the joy that is coming to you from God! Behold, your sons are coming, whom you sent away; they are coming, gathered from east and west, at the word of the Holy One, rejoicing in the glory of God. Take off the garment of your sorrow and affliction, O Jerusalem, and put on forever the beauty of the glory from God.'

"And then a few verses later comes the very end of the book of Baruch, the end of what perhaps was the last word from God before He sent His Son. Hear the word, and I quote: 'God has ordered...to make

112

level ground, so that Israel may walk safely in the glory of God. The woods and every fragrant tree have shaded Israel at God's command. For God will lead Israel with joy, in the light of his glory, with the mercy and righteousness that come from him.'

"End quote.

"Again, it says that God will lead Israel with joy—*with joy!*—and that mercy and righteousness come from God. God is a God of mercy and love, even when he began as a God who seemed to be a jerk…and God's love has been poured into our hearts through the Holy Spirit that he has given us, just as mercy and righteousness have been given us, just as joy has been given us.

"Endure, and you will find joy! Show character, and you will find joy! Hold on to hope, and hope will find joy! God's joy through Christ is the Alpha and Omega, world without end. God's joy is our everlasting Amen!"

And then, after a pause, and much much softer, and all the more powerful because it was, Mad said simply: "The dice are loaded in your favor, so joy and Amen to you all."

Applause and cheers washed over him like an updraft from the wings of angels. People were crying and stomping and sobbing and clapping and just flat-out being joyful. Mad's words might have fallen flat, might have sounded trite and syrupy and sickly sweet, if he had not possessed a charisma surpassing most men. But Mad had that charisma, had always had that charisma, and it gave his words the power to move minds and hearts. And so they were moved, minds 2,200 strong and hearts 2,200 strong. Minds and hearts full of joy.

CHAPTER SIX

Mad was spent. But this was Mary's show as much as Houston had been Becky's show, and Mary had arranged for a fancy-restaurant post-forum dinner (sans Don and Shiloh, insensitively) with the managing partner of the Zimlich, Shanahan firm and his wife, and a high school friend of Mary's named Julie who now was a computer graphic artist—and, in a big surprise, with Buzz. It seemed as if Buzz had long been promising to visit an old college buddy of his who now lived in St. Louis, and had decided to turn the visit into a 4½-day weekend so he could see Mad in action.

All five of the other diners said that Mad's address that evening had been spectacular. The Zimlich partner opined that Mad had a persuasive ability that would have served him well in a courtroom if he had gone into law. His wife said Mad should go into politics. (Mad winced.) Mary didn't say much at all, but somehow seemed to be the unseen force guiding the conversation's entire direction. And Julie kept insisting that Mad ought to go into acting, both on Broadway and in Hollywood, because, speaking purely objectively (of course), he had the right sex appeal to be a big star. She said it very matter-of-factly, but did so only while modestly avoiding eye contact with Mad as she twirled and untwirled the ends of her shoulder-length hair around her right index finger.

But it was Buzz who was the most effusive, reiterating in a number of different ways how his "young buddy" had "done the memory of his old man proud."

"You shoulda known Mad's old man," Buzz said at one point very intently, from across the table, to Mary. "A great man, ol' Ben was, a great great friend to have. Of course ol' Buzz here, yours truly, had to teach him a few things about the ways of women, but ol' Ben was just the kind of good and decent man to have such a good and decent son."

Mary smiled, but she was most interested in how the confusing handling of checks at Preacher McGee's gathering would have left MMW

Corp. in arrears on this trip if it had not been for the huge turnout at that night's fee-for-admission speech.

"Sounds to me like you guys got snookered by Preacher McGee," she said. "You know, I think there's a legal way to protect against con artists by instituting a kind of dual-signature requirement for company checks." Turning to the managing partner, she asked, "Isn't that right, Augustus? Isn't there some way to require a counter-signature for certain corporate checks?"

Mad was too tired, and too little interested in the money, to pay much attention, but he gathered that Augustus Whatshisname agreed and that Mary would follow up on the subject with Becky.

"Looks like Mary here has all the bases covered," Buzz said approvingly at one point. "And speaking of covering all the bases, that reminds me of what my good pal Steve Matheson, the TV guy, said over a beer the other night. Steve said that…"

Gab, gab, gab: It was all a blur to Mad. He just kept nodding politely while secretly pining for his hotel bed and, on the morrow, a return flight to Mobile and a day of rest.

But the next day brought no rest. First came a cancelled flight out of St. Louis, then a big layover at the Atlanta airport once the replacement flight deposited the three travelers there. It was already fairly late in the afternoon when the pre-boarding announcements began. Just as the voice on the loudspeakers was saying something about "medallion-level customers," Don jumped up like a jack-in-the-box.

"Geez, Don, cool it," Mad said lightly. "We won't be called for a while; we're in row 14."

But Don was already out of earshot—and he wasn't moving toward the boarding line. Instead, he was running across the way to a newsstand where a deliveryman was dropping off a new load of some magazine or another. Mad couldn't see from his angle what the fuss was about, but he saw Don grab the very first publication off the top of the new stack, before it was even off the man's hand truck. Mad had never seen Don so agitated. He saw Don pull out some money and virtually throw it across the counter and then, thumbing quickly through the pages, slowly stagger back across the concourse. He had the stunned, blank look of somebody stumbling through the immediate wreckage from a tornado in a trailer park. But Mad still couldn't see what periodical it was that Don was holding.

Still more oddly, Don tucked the publication under his arm when he neared the boarding line. The loudspeaker voice was still looking for "rows 20 and above," but Don got in line anyway while determinedly looking away from Mad and Shiloh. The ticket-taker didn't check his seat number closely, so Don was also able to board earlier than his two traveling companions. So it was still another six or seven minutes before Mad finally sat down next to Don in row 14 and said, "So, man, what's up? Why so glum?"

"Mad, I'm sorry; it's all my fault. I'm supposed to know these things are coming out, and I just hadn't heard a word about this. I'm responsible for your image, and somehow this one got by me." Don was actually shaking.

Mad still didn't know what Don was talking about, but for the very first time he felt a pang of real human concern for the press aide Becky had hired all those months before. Don was just so blandly polite, so unobtrusive, and such a preening Yuppie lackey that Mad had just sort of accepted his presence but given him almost no individual thought. But now Mad was moved by how deeply Don obviously cared about his job, just how much personal responsibility he took for every single bit of publicity that came Mad's way. Mad considered Don a vacuous drudge—but now he finally realized that Don was a *deeply well-intentioned* vacuous drudge. And that made all the difference.

"It's okay, Don, whatever it is can't be your fault. I'm the one who keeps putting my foot either in dog piles or in my mouth, one of the two. Now whatcha got there for me?"

Wordlessly, Don handed over the folded-up copy of *The Zodiac*. On the cover of the Los Angeles–based tabloid was a striking photograph. Until now, only a reporter's words had described Sunday's performance by the mime-cum-Lewinsky. But now here was a large color photo shot from an angle behind the mime's right ear that, combined with the distortion of a zoom lens, made it impossible to tell that the mime's head never had come closer than four or five feet from Mad's body. All the reader could see was a Lewinsky-wigged figure on its knees, head bent forward, mouth directly at the level of Mad's groin. On Mad's face was an oddly contorted grimace—in reality the result of his shock at the mime's actions, but in the context of this cover photo appearing to be the expression of a man deliberately faking orgasm.

Screaming across one side of the cover, in big letters, was this headline: "Clinton's Opponents Suck!"

Nobody in Mad's entourage knew it, but the reporter for *The Zodiac* tabloid had been trailing Mad off and on for some five months, in between devastating exposés on the sex lives of various Hollywood stars. By now he had quite a dossier on Mad, but his editor had been waiting for the right moment to publish a hit on the young Mobilian. Even with all the intermittent publicity, the editor thought (correctly) that Mad wasn't known well enough by the general public to be an attention-grabber on *The Zodiac*'s pages.

But now the time had come. The reporter always carried a device straight out of a James Bond movie: a large faux Bible with a camera hidden inside. When his editor saw the photo of the mime feigning fellatio, he knew he had struck gold.

"Jock," he had said, "you're the man; oh yes, you're the man! Now here's what I want you to do: Put together a short article on this Mad Jones guy, real quick, that I can use along with this picture as the cover photo. But don't use all your best stuff. This photo will sell the next issue big-time and introduce most of our readers to Mad. Then, once everybody knows who he is, we can follow up with another devastating exposé, using whatever else you've found on the guy—his sex life, some financial shenanigans, or whatever it is that he's got hidden in his closet that you've found out."

So Jock had dutifully thrown together a fairly vapid article that just barely covered the bases of Mad's sudden rise to prominence, with the slant that Mad was just another faker using religion as a platform for right-wing politics. And now, with the help of *The Zodiac*, Mad would become the face of the "politics of hate" that supposedly was arrayed against President Clinton.

Studying the publication in their row on the airplane, Mad, Don, and Shiloh were dumbfounded. Everything having anything to do with Mad's life seemed like a massive roller-coaster ride. Here they were coming off a trip that, after the mime/Lewinsky incident, had gone phenomenally well, and here was Mad feeling high on a newfound, exuberant peacefulness—but everywhere they turned, the reaction to the mime's event got worse and worse. In just three days Mad's preaching had moved a thematic light-year, from an emphasis on a fierce resistance to life's unfairness to a new focus on life's God-given joys. But the news cycle portraying Mad as a divisive political actor was only just beginning, and each day it became more exaggerated.

And the Lord only knew how the intensely beleaguered Becky would be back in the MMW offices in Mobile.

Before their plane landed, in fact, a phalanx of Democratic congressmen had already descended on the House and Senate TV galleries to denounce the president's opponents, suddenly embodied by Madison Lee Jones, for the supposedly increasing crudity of their viciousness.

"Nothing Mr. Clinton has done, no matter how strongly I condemn his unwise behavior, could possibly defame the presidency to even a fraction of the degree to which his persecutors are defaming it," said the unctuous "gentleman" from Michigan. "Our Republican colleagues have succumbed entirely to the hateful theocracy of the religious right—represented in this disgusting photo by angry white Southerner Madison Jones—and they don't care if their hatred rips apart the sanctity of our sacred institutions."

The lugubrious "gentleman" from Vermont chimed in: "Have they no shame?!? Oh, I ask you, have they no shame? I cry for our country when a president's few moments of weakness are turned by his political enemies into an occasion for calumny, for callousness, and for cruelty. We must fight off the ravages of these savage assaults! These attacks are un-American! We must rally around our flag by rallying around our president!"

And the oh-so-rectitudinous "gentle lady" from California used a handkerchief to dab moisture from the corner of her eyes. "Look at this photo," she said, head turned aside while holding *The Zodiac* at arm's length as if it were a pooper-scooper. "It makes me just so sad that our country has come to this. I want nothing more than to work with my Republican colleagues to find common ground, but their supposedly religious allies continue to sow discord among us. It makes my heart just weep, and then weep further still. So sad. It's just so sad."

One of the Big Three networks even led its evening news with the story, with the anchor's tone of voice and facial expression saying clearly that this was a new low for American politics.

Even the national Episcopal Church got into the act. The national church office put out a statement denouncing Mad's actions. (Oddly, there was no particular single name, such as the presiding bishop's, attached to the statement; instead, it was just a nameless screed that had the effect of seeming to be the official, corporate position of the whole denomination.) "Madison Jones may have been baptized and confirmed an Episcopalian, but he has never attended seminary, much less even been *considered* for ordination," it said. "He therefore speaks and acts with no ecclesiastical authority, and by presuming to pass judgment on our president in the president's time of need, Mr. Jones shows himself unfamiliar with the notion of Christian charity and thus unworthy of respect as a theologian, preacher, or religious sage. The Episcopal Church should not be seen in any way as being associated with Mr. Jones' enterprises or his un-Christian viewpoint."

By 6:30 that evening, somebody had thrown rotten eggs and toilet paper at the MMW offices.

So it was that when Don was informed of these developments by cell phone as soon as he, Mad, and Shiloh de-planed, he was possessed by a primitive desire for revenge unlike any emotion he had let himself feel since at least early adolescence.

"I know how to turn this story around," he told Mad through clenched teeth. "I know how to neutralize all this. Will you trust me to get it taken care of?"

Since Mad neither understood the press nor cared to understand it, he just nodded. "Sure, Don, whatever you think is right. I don't think we can undo the damage anytime quickly; I just have to stay away from politics for a long enough time that eventually this'll be forgotten. But, yeah, whatever you want to do. I trust your judgment."

Truth was, Mad had never before given a thought to Don's judgment, or to his job. But he was touched by how deeply Don obviously felt about all this, touched by how much Don seemed to care what happened to

Mad's image. So, sure, whatever Don wanted to do was fine by him. He, Mad, just wanted to hole up in his own home for the night.

As for Shiloh, he knew he would have to deal with LaShauna. They didn't agree about Bill Clinton, and she'd had four straight days now of handling the baby by herself. He didn't expect a particularly warm homecoming. But she was a fine woman, he told himself, and he loved her dearly.

The Mad Religion chat room had been broiling for three days. Thousands of notes had made the site so jammed up as to be almost inaccessible. There was no way Mad could read all the messages, so he just perused some of them at random while keeping an eye out for entries from his regulars.

"A cheap publicity stunt!" said one entry.

"A brilliant parody," said another.

"These religious people should just shut up about politics," said a third about Mad. "What an a$$h0le!"

Feelings ran very intensely. Few of the comments could be qualified as thoughtful. Mad was impressed, however, with one from Intrigued in Idaho: "I'll admit to being as offended by Clinton as anyone," she wrote. "His politics make me ill, and his immorality offends me. But this isn't about Clinton, it's about Madison Jones. I had never heard of him until today, when I saw a tiny news account of his anti-Clinton comments and pantomime at that church outside New Orleans. But I've spent the last solid hour reading and trying to make sense of his theses posted on this web site. I'm pretty strict in my faith, in fact very traditionalist, but when I take the theses as a whole, they don't offend me at all. I mean, here's a guy who was in real pain, and you can just see him working through his pain as he wrote them. Even on all those parts of the theses I don't agree with (and some I just don't understand), I am fascinated by his thought processes. If you take him on his own terms, rather than with any pre-conceived beliefs (such as my own, which I've been trying to set aside for the last hour so I could follow Jones' own arguments), then he's really found an original way to arrive at an understanding of God's grace. And now that I know he agrees with me on Clinton, I feel a kinship with him. I'll be paying a lot closer attention to him from now on!"

(To which some lunk had written: "Who unearthed the Idaho potato? It's obviously rotten. What a load of fertilizer!")

Skimming through the comments, Mad realized just what a mistake he had made by spouting off about Clinton. Mad's entire message, such as it was, was being lost in the political sniper fire. Already, he saw that by Tuesday afternoon he had lost one of his most devoted adherents.

"Dam [sic] Mad! Dam [sic] him! Just when I was starting to believe in somebody, he goes and joins the Pattersons and Falstaffs of the world and takes a cheap shot at my president. My soul is back in the desert again! I have nobody to believe in anymore. You'll never see me in this chat room again. All of you can just go to He**!!!"

It was signed "Perdicaris."

The entry broke Mad's heart. He felt guilty. He wished he knew how to reach Perdicaris, so he could explain what had happened. Mad didn't care that *he* had lost a believer, but it just killed him to think of this guy's soul being back in a "desert," especially when he had seemed so close to opening up to God.

But back to the chat room: "Mad's turned into the Scarecrow!" wrote Cowardly Lion. "He doesn't have a brain! But don't worry, because I've found enough courage to help him find the Wizard and get his senses back. Unlike Perdicaris, I ain't leaving!"

Defender was delighted with Mad's criticism of Clinton, and said maybe Mad wasn't totally misguided after all. Affirmed was more than delighted; he was ecstatic.

"So far I'm with Mad on everything!!!" he wrote. "I'm with him on religion and I'm with him on Clinton. I told you guys I understand him! That's why you guys should believe me when I say he's Moses and Luther all at once. Or maybe he's Elijah. But he's definitely one of the great prophets come back for another visit. Hear his words, people, and heed his words!"

On the other hand, there was FD Thom, who wrote with great sorrow: "I'm not ready to give up on Mad entirely, at least not just yet, but this wounds me to the heart. Mad's criticism of Clinton is inconsistent with his whole message. I'll stick around for a while guys, but I'm again dropping the 'Formerly' from my name. From henceforth, I again am Doubting Thomas. Over and out—D Thom."

And then there was this from Jezebel?, added that night after the evening news: "Look, guys, I've been biting my tongue, but I can't keep quiet anymore after watching how the media is playing this story. I wish I had some real clout with the networks, because then I'd set them all straight! You see, they are all getting all this all wrong. The reason I know is because I was there Sunday morning at Apostles of the Word Church. I was there and I saw it all. That guy in the Lewinsky suit was as much of a surprise to Mad as he was to all the rest of us. You could tell by looking at Mad's face that he was horrified and shocked. The guy just came running up the aisle out of nowhere, and totally took all the power from what Mad was trying to say!

"Now I don't like Clinton, and I don't like his Republican critics either, and I didn't like Mad using Clinton in his speech at church, but you could tell he was ad-libbing. It wasn't planned at all. I could tell he was just hitting on notes that were in the tune of the audience, so he could get his bigger message across to them. I'm still not up on all this God stuff, but I was there and I tell you Mad didn't mean it to come out the way all the reports have made it seem. And I still think that if there is anybody who can make me understand more about God, if there even is a God, then it's Mad."

Mad felt goosebumps up and down his arms. Bless that Laura! After all the suspicion he had shown her, here she was setting the record straight and defending him. And of course it was Laura; now there was no doubt. Who else would have been in the New Orleans area, and with the interest to go all the way out to Apostles of the Word even when she wasn't sure there was a God, just to hear what Mad had to say?

"Jezebel? has it right again, and I thank her for it," he wrote (with the appropriate electronic identifier). "I had no idea the mime was gonna pull that Lewinsky act, or even that he was there on Sunday morning. He's around me a lot, and he's talented and sometimes he's really funny, but this time I thought he was not in good taste. Anyway, Jez is also right that I didn't plan even to talk about Clinton. But I wasn't firing on all cylinders that morning, and I was losing my audience, so I just started to spout off on the spur of the moment about what I really thought about Clinton, since that's on everybody's minds. But I promise y'all I'll try real hard NOT to talk politics any more. That's not what I'm about. In fact, I already told Jez (hint hint) that I wouldn't talk politics, way back a couple of weeks ago, and I just slipped up.

"Oh, and if Idaho is still there, I liked and appreciated your comments. And if Perdicaris is reading this, or if anybody knows how to reach him, please tell him to forgive me and come back. Just because he doesn't agree with me on Clinton doesn't mean I don't care what he thinks. His comments are always so constructive. He's a real valuable member of this web site.

"Now, what I really want to say is, I've had a revelation in the last three days. From now on, you all will hear me talking a lot less about overcoming God's mistakes, and more about celebrating God's joy. More on that later. Thanks, as always, for reading. Mad."

Mad turned off his computer too soon to see M. Magdalene's first Mad Religion comment in ages. "I hope Mad's not confused about something," she wrote. "But Mad should know he has just as much right as anybody else to talk about politics, and if it's done right, without any surprises from a mime, it can give him some good publicity for the rest of his message. And every time he goes on TV he'll get more women followers. For instance, even in *The Zodiac* cover photo, I still think he looks like a hunk. I wish I could meet him someday!"

As for Perdicaris, he never returned.

On Thursday morning in New York, famed TV news guy Spike Walters looked at the summary review folder, prepared by his personal assistant, of the previous day's news from a host of sources. Among the items inside were the front page and Jock's story from *The Zodiac*, along with the criticisms from the Democratic congressmen and the transcript of his own network news' lead story on the subject from the night before. Walters wasn't just any news guy; he was the septuagenarian host of the granddaddy of all TV news magazines, *Hour of Truth*. In his own mind at least, he was more responsible for exposing the crookedness, hypocrisy, and other forms of venality of more skinflints, scoundrels, and scofflaws than any other living journalist. A regular crusader for justice, he was, and also so wise as to be the definer of what was and wasn't just in the first place.

And now here was some upstart Christian hatemonger bringing the presidency of the United States down into the gutter, at a time when the nation obviously needed to forgive and forget (and punish Ken Starr for prosecutorial abuse). This was more than right-thinking people should have to bear.

He buzzed his personal assistant. "Start up a file on this Madison Jones guy," Walters said. "Find out all the usual stuff. Check his finances; get Bishop Brindle and Rabbi Heintz to poke holes in his theology. I don't just want an Achilles' heel on this guy; I want his Achilles' gonads being used to feed the fishes. Let's see how fast we can build a dossier and decide whether he's worth a segment on our show. If he's worth going after at all, we'll want to do it before the Republican jihad against Clinton plays itself out. Oh—and see if we can get that aggressive producer on this. Whatshername, Martina? Yeah, Martina Bigtitsky, or whatever it is."

And so it was that the assistant, Al Bobbitt, and young producer, Martina Beritzky, began their pursuit of Mad Jones.

That same morning, the Rev. Larry Falstaff released a statement distancing himself from the Mad/mime antics: "It is unfair to paint all conservative Christians with the brush of a crude charlatan whom I have already personally denounced at every turn for months on end."

The Rev. Rob Patterson remained silent, but he personally thought the mime had performed a useful service. The more the godless liberals held up *The Zodiac* front page and the more they denounced Mad, the more the image would get planted in American minds of just how vile was the president's behavior that the mime was mocking. Patterson was surprised by how strongly Mad himself was reported to have denounced Clinton, but he figured that Mad was merely seeking publicity and hoping to piggyback on the strongly anti-Clinton sentiment the polls had shown in the first two weeks after his mid-August deposition. In Patterson's mind, it showed that the young upstart was desperate for attention—which meant that Mad's ministry must not be going well. When a man is imploding, Patterson thought, there's no need to help him do so. Just stand back and enjoy the spectacle.

As for Gladys Phillpott, the doyenne of the conservative movement, she just watched and wondered. She couldn't yet ascertain whether the young man would be a boon or a challenging enemy for her causes. He certainly had a talent for publicity. He merited close scrutiny.

Mad slept late on Thursday morning. But when he finally forced himself out of bed, he decided to take care of something that had been bugging him for more than four days. He called the police headquarters and left a message for Officer Williams to call him when he went off duty.

A dispatcher relayed the message to Williams in his patrol car (he was alone this morning, because Shiloh had desk duty until mid-afternoon), and since it was a slow day, Williams drove right over. He figured it was time he taught this young pissant a lesson.

Mad was shocked, first to hear his doorbell ring, and second to find Officer Williams there on his porch, belly thrusting angrily forward like an aggravated hippo.

"Whachu want, a-ess-hole?" said the officer. "You mighta been an ath-uh-lete in high school, but if I wudn't in uniform right now, I'd kick yer pansy faggot ass until it was as black 'n' blue as a nigger's toothache."

Mad immediately felt his bile rising, but by dint of supreme effort he kept a temperate countenance.

"I didn't expect you so soon," he said, opening the door wider and making a gesture of welcome. "Can you come in for a minute?"

The officer looked at him suspiciously. "Last time I was here, you shut the door in my face, a-ess-hole. What makes ya think I want to contaminate my uniform by entering yer pansy-ass premises?"

Mad stared into the officer's jowl-dominated face. He felt his fists clenching and unclenching of their own accord. He forced his mouth into a half smile.

"A good cup of coffee, perhaps? It might make my apology easier to swallow."

Still scowling, but also looking a little confused, the officer lumbered inside while saying, "Ya better damn well apologize, ya two-bit punk, or else I'll be forcin' an apol'gy down yer gullet so far that ya shit it out with yer breakfast."

By now, Mad was grinding his teeth enough to give hope to a den of dentists. But he walked Williams back to the kitchen and poured him a cup.

"Here's the deal," he said, finally. "You've been making me mighty angry by the way you've been talking about Shiloh Jones, and by the way you call him a nigger and warn me away from him as if you own him or something…"

The officer sneered and started to say something, but Mad put up his hand to stop him and continued his thought: "But that's no excuse for me slamming the door in your face. That's why I apologize. I think you and I need to reach some kind of understanding."

The officer was still suspicious but slightly less belligerent. "I'll tell ya what ya need ta understand, punk, is that ya shouldn't be messing with the head of Jonesy. Yer leadin' 'im in the wrong die-reckshun, and ya damn well know it." Williams was poking his finger near Mad's chest for emphasis. "And fillin' his head with all that college garbage, as if a nigger who cain't play sports no longer has any business thinkin' about college!"

Mad tried one more time. "Officer, why don't we try something here? Here's what I want to try. Why don't you let Shiloh make his own decisions, and why don't you give me the courtesy of not offending me by calling him a nigger—and in return, I'll lay a promise on you. In return, I give you my word of honor that if college doesn't work for Shiloh—and I know it *will* work for him, but I'll pledge this anyway—then I will personally re-pay Shiloh for the amount of police pension he'll be losing by coming to work for me. And not only that, but"—Mad searched his mind for something else to say—"but, uh, if you just give *me* a chance, I'll, uh, I'll even…"

Officer Williams cut him off. "You better not be trying to bribe me, boy. You better not be about to offer me some cash to keep me from kickin' yer ass. But I'll tell you what. I'll tell you this. Maybe you're actually sincere about this. Maybe you're one of those goody-two-shoes dreamers who really think that nigg—I mean that our Negro friends have some mental abilities. Tell ya what: You promise never to shut a door in my face again, and I'll take ya up on yer offer to make up the money in Jonesy's pension. And I'll accept yer apology, fer now, and we'll both stay out of each other's way. You jes go about preachin' yer nonsense interpretation of religion, and I'll jes go about protectin' the citizens of Mobile. And I'll even tell everybody that asks that you're a good kid at heart, even if you're a little cracked. How's that? We got a deal?"

Mad forced himself to reach out his hand for a handshake. "The joy of the Lord be with you, Officer," he said.

That afternoon, Mad received a phone call from The Colonel.

"I say, I say, I say, son, you been kickin' up a mighty big fuss, son, you been kickin' up a fuss. Our Society had another phone conference about it, son, yes we did, I say, we had a conference."

"Sir, I'm sorry, sir, it's just that…"

"Hear me out, now, son, I say, hear me out. I'm not finished talkin', son."

Mad sighed. "Yes, sir."

"You gotta understand, son, that our society isn't threatening you with anything. All we do is good for the university, son; we never do anybody harm. But, I say, son, I say, you're not behaving like a gentleman, son. We have a big investment in you, son, and we want you to live up to its standards. All we can do is appeal to your conscience, son, but we *are* appealing to it, and we're appealing to it *right now*. If you're gonna go around doing this preaching and meddling, son, at least do it with dignity. Please at least promise me that, son. And if you don't promise it for the sake of the society, son, then do it for the memory of your Daddy Lee. Am I making myself clear?"

"Yes, sir, I promise this time that I'm really going to watch myself. The society has been very good to me, sir, and I am very sorry if I am letting you down."

"Well, that's good, son, that's very good. Now I don't want to have to call you again, son, I say, I don't want to have to chastise you again."

"Yes, sir." Mad's politeness had its limits, and they were fast approaching, but he managed to still stay within its bounds. Besides, he was sure this conversation was about to end.

"Oh, son, and between just you and me, son, I say, just one more thing."

"Yes, sir?"

For the first time on any of these phone calls, The Colonel chuckled. "Every one of us on the conference this morning, every one of us who knows the power of Eight, we all like the fact that you're against that draft-dodging drug-using womanizing piece of trash. Frankly, if anybody else but one of our own had pulled that stunt with the guy looking like Lewinsky, our whole society would be laughing about it over cocktails, and loving every bit of it.

"But that's jes between you and me, son. You just keep up your dignity, and you'll be okay."

The phone went dead.

The next day, the fruits of Don's damage-control labors became evident. Personally, Mad didn't really like the counter-offensive when he saw it, but for this week at least he was beyond worrying too much about what was in print. No matter what he did, the media seemed out of control, so he tried to just ignore it all.

Don's ploy was to call in some old chits he had with the other major national tabloid, *The Investigator*, produced from an office in the Hollywood Hills and delivered at all newsstands first thing every Friday morning. True to form, *The Investigator* was vicious. "Soiled White House, Dirty Tricks," read the headline. The gist of the article was not just that the mime's Lewinsky impersonation was a surprise to Mad and everybody else at Apostles of the Word (the Rev. Hebert was quoted as saying that "that nice young Jones boy was obviously horrified"), but that the whole thing had been a setup by the Clinton White House so as to make its opponents look sleazier than the president did. It quoted Mad's chat room comment that he thought the mime "was not in good taste." And it quoted "an observer in the church that day" (Don, speaking anonymously) to the effect that "that mime is obviously just a nutball."

"And sources say," concluded the article, "that proof will soon be forthcoming that the White House made him a nutball for hire."

In his tiny (500-square-foot) French Quarter apartment, the mime read the tabloid and fumed. He wasn't a nutball; he was an artist! And he didn't know a soul at the White House, and he would never sacrifice his artistic talent for dirty lucre regardless. He wished he could find out who in the church had called him a nutball. Whoever it was should pay a price.

CHAPTER SEVEN

The tabloid publicity boosted Mad from mid-level star to certifiable national phenomenon. Even when Congress released the videotape of President Clinton's Lewinsky testimony, and Mad studiously avoided all requests for comment, his very refusal drew attention. In some ways he had achieved that uniquely American status of being famous for being famous. Becky was able to jack up Mad's appearance fees, and even began following Mary's lead by charging admission to some of his speeches, and yet ever larger throngs crowded each event. It quickly became clear that at MMW Corp.'s next semi-annual board meeting, the company would have plenty of profit on hand to donate to charities. Quietly, Becky began sending out word through the non-profit network that MMW would begin taking applications for grants.

But Mad was taking only intermittent pleasure in his "success." He was lonely. Sometimes he missed Claire so much that his insides felt twisted in Gordian knots not only too tangled to untie but also too rock hard for any knife to cut. But when he wasn't missing Claire, he increasingly felt the bodily desires that had tempted him with the co-ed Mindy at Ole Miss. He had not yet succumbed (other than months ago to Laura), but the temptations were becoming more and more difficult to ignore. And when Hurricane Georges battered southern Alabama on September 27 and 28, Mad had an odd reaction. Rather then fretting much about whether his house would suffer damage, and rather than becoming agitated when his section of town lost power for nearly a day, all Mad could think about was how frustrated he was that he was holed up in the darkness without an intelligent woman to keep him company.

The first weekend of October, Justin and Becky and a few others dragged Mad out (in dark glasses) to Mobile's downtown street music festival known as Bayfest. A mix of local and national acts performing on stages spread over about 25 square blocks, Bayfest was the perfect event—busy but not overcrowded—at which to relax and just have fun.

There, at one of the stages very early on Sunday afternoon, Mad found himself entranced by a singer out of New Orleans of whom he had never heard. Leslie Smith was a fit, long-legged, dark-haired beauty with a voice so rich and expressive that even in broad daylight it evoked the deepest tragedies and triumphs of the most dramatic love stories played out in the best dark, smoky, post-midnight jazz joints. Mad had never seen and heard anything like her. She looked perhaps a few years older (at most) than his age of 25, but he wouldn't let that deter him. *This* was a woman he just had to meet.

So Mad stayed after her act, hoping he could catch her mingling afterward with the crowd so he could approach. Sure enough, she came right off the stage to a holding area just across a small police barricade from where Mad and Justin stood. But before he could try to get her attention, she was whisked away by a vibrant short-haired woman, who seemed to be a good friend of the singer's, and a man with wavy, dark hair and a mustache who seemed to be a friend of the short-haired woman.

"Damn, Justin," Mad said. "That woman has it all. I gotta find a way to hear her sing again."

For once, Justin was speechless. He, too, was enthralled.

Only later did Mad realize that this was the first time since Claire's death that he had even considered taking the initiative to meet a woman, for any reason. It was like breaking through an invisible electric fence. Henceforth, he might just begin—he might just consider—he might occasionally find himself in a mood—to actively look for female companionship.

But still he didn't act on those thoughts. Mad, the ghostwriter, and their publisher approved a final version of their book (like the web site, to be called *Mad Religion*), and Mad kept writing his newspaper columns and taking three- to four-day speaking tours every other week, constantly updating and modifying his basic message of Creator/dice-loading God as jerk-turned-joy giver. The fall elections came and went, and Speaker Newt Gingrich was deposed, and the *Mobile Register* bragged that it had the only columnist in America who had correctly predicted the electoral outcomes—but Mad's life seemed to just spin along of its own accord. (*The Zodiac* and *Hour of Truth* quietly continued to investigate Mad's life for potential use in future hit pieces, but Mad was unaware of their efforts.)

But on Friday morning, November 20, Justin gave Mad's life a jolt. He called Mad from New Orleans, where Justin was attending some seminar or other for athletic trainers.

"Hey, buddy, I'm here in New Orleans, buddy, and I'm checking out their 'Lagniappe' section of the paper, which is where they list all the musical acts and stuff. And buddy, guess what? This is your day, buddy, this is your day! Guess who's singing tonight? Just guess. No, don't guess, I'll tell you: It's that girl Leslie Smith, that gorgeous singer from Bayfest. Yeah, buddy, here's your chance. She's with some group with a weird name, The Cleminists, whatever that means, and she's at this place called Carrollton Station. Why don't you come over to New Orleans tonight? I know you got nothing going on in Mobile. Come on over here, crash in my hotel room, and come out with me to hear your dream girl."

Mad protested feebly, but Justin knew that the protests would fade. By 4 p.m. Mad was on the road to New Orleans, and by 7:30 he and Justin were finally seated (after a lengthy Friday-night wait) at the Houston's on St. Charles Avenue. Snippets from more than a few overheard conversations made clear that lots of people in New Orleans were excited that its native son and congressman, Bob Livingston, was about to become speaker of the U.S. House of Representatives. Judging from the comments, he seemed to be an unusually well-liked politician. People sounded genuinely proud of him.

But as for Justin, he didn't look very good, and he kept sniffling. "I don't know what it is, Mad, cuz I felt great this morning, but since mid-afternoon I've been sneezing and getting all congested and my eyes are itchy and it's just driving me crazy."

"Hmmm…allergy attack," Mad mumbled.

"I dunno, Mad, I've never had allergies before—but you know what? Come to think of it, last time I was in New Orleans, the same dadgummed thing happened."

Anyway, Justin's sinus problem didn't stop him from talking a light-year a minute, and by dinner's end the monologue combined with the sniffling was getting on Mad's nerves. They drove on over to the riverbend neighborhood of small shops and modest houses where the Carrollton

Station bar competed with two other nearby music clubs, with Justin insisting all the way that of course he felt good enough to stay out and listen to "that Smith babe" play. But he was wrong. Even before the music started shortly after 10, the little guy had developed a pounding sinus headache to go along with his watery nose and itchy eyes.

"Look, friend," Mad said. "You go on back to the hotel room and sleep it off. You've already given me an extra room key; I'll just catch a cab when I'm ready to call it quits for the night. Yes, I'm serious: Go on. I'll be fine here by myself. Go get some sleep, Justin."

Which was how Mad got to hear Leslie Smith and The Cleminists without having to endure Justin's running commentary. Again, he was entranced. Smith was sultry and soulful and obviously highly intelligent, all at once, with a voice that could move even a statue's emotions. She was joined by two other attractive and talented women—one on piano and the other, who looked barely out of high school, on bass. At times they sounded like they hadn't practiced together much yet, but overall the effect was stunning. And Leslie Smith was a woman Mad told himself he just had to meet.

So it was that Mad's hunting instincts were re-awakened for good. Problem was, when the first set was over and Mad made his way up to try to speak to the singer, two other guys got there first. One was a skinny, dark-haired guy with a beard; the other was heavyset and curly-haired, like a less hefty Norm from *Cheers*. Ms. Smith greeted the former like a long-lost friend, so Mad hung back to wait for a less intrusive opportunity.

Which was when he heard a voice, a fresh and soothing voice, that he recognized.

"Ohmygod, it's Mad! Gosh, Mad, what are you doing here?" It was Laura Green, and she sounded genuinely delighted to see him. And Mad was destined to never meet Leslie Smith.

Which was how, as Mad reflected much later, life seemed always to work. Led by a chance phone call from a friend, you finally decide to go after one thing, and something else entirely comes up instead that would never have arisen if you hadn't responded to the possibility of the first.

Mad could have been home in Mobile, staying out of trouble and perhaps enjoying a quick bite with Father Vignelli, or maybe with his friend Jason and Jason's fiancée, Vicki. Or Mad might just have been glued to the sofa in front of a silly rental movie like *Scream 2*. Hell, he thought Neve Campbell was cute. He would have been perfectly safe at home watching her escape a deranged killer again. But no, not Mad. He had to drive all the way to New Orleans to try to introduce himself to a singer he had heard only once in his life, and then he had to go and virtually order back to the hotel the annoying little buddy who would otherwise have kept him from doing anything he later regretted. And, Mad being Mad, he had to do it all *not* in order to meet this entrancing singer, but instead to find himself soothed again by Laura's fresh-sounding voice that always seemed to have an odd power over him. It was all as if fate were the scriptwriter for an inane TV sitcom called "Mad Life"—one of those sitcoms on which the joke was always on the main character. Which, of course, was Mad.

Before Mad really knew what was happening, he and Laura were deep in conversation. She was telling him how she had moved up to New York to work full-time for *Acute Vision*, and how the show was still languishing slightly below the middle of the ratings list, but was well above where it had been when she and he had made their debuts on it the previous spring. It was still, therefore, on the network's "bubble" of shows that might or might not be cancelled at any minute. But the good news was that the network execs were happy with her work on the show, and had already begun talking with her about changing her contract so that she would be tied not to *Acute Vision* specifically but to the overall network news operation. In other words, if the show were cancelled, she would still have a job. She was back in New Orleans only because her show's whole crew had Thanksgiving week off; she had flown into town just that evening. But she wasn't staying at her parents' small house; she was house-sitting at the apartment of a friend who had flown out that night to spend the week with family in the Atlanta suburbs. Laura was supposed to meet some other friends at Carrollton Station, but so far they hadn't shown up.

The conversation continued even when another band, called Twangorama, this one all men, took the stage. (Apparently Leslie and The Cleminists were doing only one set.) Laura forgave Mad for mistrusting her; Mad forgave Laura for failing to emphasize, in her national report on him, how reluctant he had been to be a public figure. A few times he pointedly, but laughingly, called her Jezebel, and she always shrugged off the reference with what looked like a slightly quizzical smile. "You don't mind me calling you Jezebel?" he asked at one point. "Sweetheart, you can call me just about anything you want to," she said, leaning in close to him. "Besides, wasn't Jezebel a powerful woman? I like being thought of as a powerful woman, sweetheart. And if Jezebel was bad… well, I can be bad, too, if ya know what I mean."

She was practically purring.

What she didn't tell Mad about was her network boyfriend up in New York. He hadn't proposed to her yet, so certainly she was free for a little play on the side while on vacation—wasn't she?

Mad couldn't resist. As before, Laura did have a power over him. Not only that, but this time he was on the prowl anyway. She offered to drive him back to his hotel. At her car around the corner from the music club, he found himself kissing her. Kissing her with abandon.

They never made it to Justin's hotel. They went back to her friend's apartment instead. And the next morning, Mad didn't cry. He smiled.

What they didn't notice was the young woman who had several times tried to get their attention at Carrollton Station, and who had even begun to follow them around the corner in hopes of getting a few words with them. She was a reporter for the local paper. She wrote the weekly "seen about town" social gossip column called "Hip Chick's Picks." The column was the cool younger version of the society page, and Yuppies and chic *artistes* alike usually got a kick out of being recognized in it. The Hip Chick had been out for a non-working night on the town when she recognized both Mad and Laura. As a matter of fact, she had seen and heard their surprise at running into each other and, knowing of how they had effectively helped each other reach public stardom, she had figured a few comments from each about their chance meeting might liven up her next column. But after she pulled a tiny notebook out of her purse, she could never catch their eyes. Both of them, obviously, were aware only of each other.

Now this, thought the Hip Chick, was even more interesting. Juicy stuff for her column, perhaps.

And so it was that, six days later, a special Thanksgiving Day version of "Hip Chick's Picks" contained these lines near the top of its rollicking survey of the New Orleans social scene:

> The pre-holiday weekend got off to a Mad, Mad start last Friday night at Carrollton Station, where young religious phenom **Mad Jones** was seen canoodling with local-girl-made-network-newsie **Laura Green**, whose up-close reporting helped launch Jones' career back last March. But her reporting then was nothing near as 'up-close' as the, uh, rapt attention she was paying to Mr. Jones on Friday night… and speaking of rapt, "It's a wrap." That's what the word is from the director of the latest movie to use the Crescent City as a backdrop…

The ensuing firestorm didn't exactly erupt; to mix metaphors oxymoronically, the firestorm snowballed. It started small but grew as it rolled along. Laura was at her parents' house early to help prepare Thanksgiving dinner, and had not even thought of reading the paper. Until, that is, her mom casually asked, "Darling, what does 'canoodling' mean?" She handed the paper to her daughter and watched as her normally composed baby Laura began to blush.

The news director for the local affiliate of a competing network did know what "canoodling" was. Truth be told, he was less interested in knowing whether the canoodling had led anywhere that night than he was in knowing if the canoodling was the continuation of similar activity from as far back as March. He remembered when Mad's theses first were discovered, and remembered the race among the news shows to try to track Mad down—and he remembered thinking then how odd it was that a second-rate assistant producer had been the one to get the scoop. "So who is this Laura Green girl?" he had asked his news staff back then.

"Oh, I've run across her before," said one of his cub reporters. "She's a little vamp on the make. I wouldn't put it past her to screw her way into a scoop." (The cub reporter hadn't mentioned that Laura had turned him down cold when he had asked her for a date.)

The news director didn't like getting scooped, not on anything, and he had the hubris to think that the only way he could get scooped was through a violation of journalistic ethics by his competitors. And sleeping with a source isn't exactly kosher. Heck, if he could bring this Green girl down, her former bosses at his competitor's newscast would surely be tarred with guilt by association. So he made a few phone calls.

Phone calls were also on the mind of nurse number three, Sue, from the Mobile psychiatric ward. Driving that morning from Mobile to her family's Baton Rouge home for Thanksgiving dinner, the nurse picked up a paper in New Orleans when she stopped for gas. That afternoon, while all the family men were in one room watching football, she escaped dishwashing duty by sneaking into her old childhood bedroom with the paper. The column entitled "Hip Chick's Picks" caught her eye. She thought it sounded like a fun read. And when she saw the item about Mad and Laura, it made her think back to that weird incident in the hospital room when Mad had grabbed her breast. (Okay, she had actually taken the initiative in placing his hand there, but nobody would ever know that.) She pulled out a scrap of paper she had carried in her wallet for two months now. It was a parenthetical note, including a contact phone number, that had run at the bottom of Jock's story in *The Zodiac*: "*The Zodiac* is offering a $50,000 reward for anybody with information, and proof, of where Mad Jones spent his week in hiding after his wife's tragic death."

Hospital records were, of course, confidential. She could lose her job if she released them without permission. To her, $50,000 was a lot of money, but not enough to make it worth losing her job. But these tabloids loved stories with a sexual angle. This "canoodling" stuff with Laura gave her an idea. Maybe if she played her cards right, she could get *The Zodiac* to jack up its reward money. For $100,000 she probably would be willing to give up her job. Heck, she figured she was smart enough to parlay a nest egg that large into something really special.

She called an old high school friend, now a lawyer, and he used three-way calling so together they could call the number listed in the tabloid.

Their call would make Jock the reporter very happy.

On the day after Thanksgiving, otherwise universally known as "the busiest shopping day of the year," bookstore browsers nationwide were greeted with stacks of quickly produced hardbacks titled *Mad Religion.* The cover photo showed a Redford-like 25-year-old with an engaging smile, against the backdrop of a medieval scroll with the word "Theses" barely discernible in larger type than the rest of the scroll's faded calligraphy.

Inside was a book that was an amalgam of a short (20-page) biography of Mad and a popular-religion manifesto that unpacked Mad's unique, controversial, and somewhat complicated theology in a way that could be understood by an educated ninth grader. (For mass sales to the American reading public, that was about as demanding a comprehension level as could be risked.)

Five pages were devoted to an explanation of the history behind Martin Luther's original 95 theses in 1517. Exactly 1½ pages were devoted to each of Mad's 59 theses. His St. Louis speech, in which Mad first combined his highly individual explication of the Einstein/science/religion background with his new message of God's joy, was printed in its entirety. So were reprints, each on its own page, of the 50 of Mad's daily advice columns (out of more than 200 published so far) that Mad and the ghostwriter and the publisher had determined were probably the most popular or memorable.

Padded with a series of lists ("Mad's suggested reading list of religious-themed books"; "Mad's top 20 heroes of the 20th century"; "Mad's favorite movies," etc.), along with a concluding 1,500-word essay by Mad, the whole thing barely stretched to 200 pages. It was intended by the publisher to be a mass-marketed quick read for the spiritually challenged—that year's winning Christmas entry in the "dumbed-down, self-help way to spiritual wholeness" sweepstakes.

Mad (along with Shiloh, in his inaugural service on MMW's full-time payroll) was scheduled for a brutal three-week, cross-country book tour. The publishing house would handle all the publicity, so Don would not be shadowing Mad to do whatever mysterious alchemy it is that PR folks are supposed to do. (In what should have been a blow to Don's ego, part of his duties in Mobile during those three weeks would be to run errands for LaShauna, who was not at all happy that her husband's new job would take him away from sharing parenting duties with her for three whole weeks.)

The tour was to begin in New York on Friday evening. In what was a harbinger of how controversy would dog its every step, the very first event was graced with the re-appearance, for the first time since Labor Day, of the mime. Shiloh eyed him warily, but as the mime was on his best behavior and causing no actionable disturbance, nobody could figure out reasonable grounds to ask him to leave. He was dressed like Santa Claus, with the one difference being that rather than wearing Santa's red cap, he was wearing a Lewinsky beret. He obviously wanted people to know that he was the same guy whose back had graced the photo on *The Zodiac*'s cover. (Of course, when a reporter tried to interview him, the mime wouldn't make even a sound. He was, after all, a mime.) But what his presence mainly accomplished was to change the whole focus of the event from Mad's intended message to Mad's views of the ongoing impeachment drama. The more Mad declined to comment, the more people (especially the reporters) tried to find clever ways to lure him into at least an indirect reference to the scandal. The way the elite media works, any and every story has a better chance of garnering attention if it is somehow tied in to the day's dominant story or theme.

"Listen to me!" an exasperated Mad finally said in response to the sixth or seventh question relating to President Clinton. "I'm not here to talk about politics but about faith. Faith is what's important. In fact, maybe if people paid more attention to their faith, then our politics wouldn't be so polluted with these kinds of stories. Now, as I was saying about how God respects those who wrestle with him…"

Mad went right back to his theological themes. But one of the New York papers the next day ran a small but well-placed story at the top of an inside page, headlined "'Polluted' politics." The sub-head read: "Religious author says faithlessness at root of scandal."

Other than including a short new quote from Mad, the rest of the story was a re-hash of the Labor Day weekend controversy, along with a passing mention that Mad was in town to plug his new book. Alongside the story ran a photo of the mime as beret-clad Santa.

That same morning, Mad's advice column, now running in 71 papers, added more grist for the unintentional-publicity mill. The letter writer had asked a question concerning divorce. Mad responded that although he didn't personally condemn those who got divorced, the Bible and especially Christ himself spoke rather explicitly against the practice.

"I think it's safe to say," Mad wrote, "that there are three absolutely legitimate grounds for divorce: abuse, adultery, and abandonment. Beyond that, divorce is hard for me to justify, based on my understanding both of my faith and of my moral belief that a promise made should be a promise kept. And he or she who is not faithful to that promise will have to answer, in some way, to God—who may well forgive, but that's for God alone to know. As for third-party witnesses to an act of faithlessness, such as adultery, I think our vows as members of a Christian community require that we quietly but firmly let it be known, in private conversations with the adulterer, that we urge him or her not to forget that he (or she) made a vow before God's altar. Nobody should ever give the impression that adultery is acceptable, or that abandonment or abuse is acceptable either. And if believers abjure all three of those betrayals, divorce should diminish as well."

It was a fairly orthodox, Anglo-Catholic response. But in the following days it would be juxtaposed with the New York paper's sub-head—both spoke of a condemnation of "faithlessness"—in a way that made it seem, during such a mono-maniacal news focus on the Lewinsky scandal, as if Mad were taking another shot at the president.

And then there was a slowly but surely growing buzz, fueled both by the Internet and by quiet efforts of the New Orleans news director, about the report of Mad's canoodling with the very reporter who had helped make him famous. His book, marketed brilliantly by the publishing house, was already flying off the shelves. The sense that Mad was controversial further fueled its success. And as his book tour moved from New York to Philadelphia to Washington, D.C., he was met everywhere by excited, burbling crowds.

Then Wednesday afternoon rolled around, and *The Zodiac* hit the newsstands.

It was the kind of story that, if its subject survived it, would guarantee the subject's ensconcement in the realm of superstardom. But survival of such a story was a decidedly dicey proposition.

Here was the headline:

Clinton Hater: Nutty, slutty, rich men's putty

It ran across the cover, bracketing a photo of Mad from one of his appearances months earlier, when Jock the reporter had caught him with an odd and highly unflattering expression.

The story inside, a massive one, ran as follows:

> *Mad Jones, the newest religion phenomenon and* fakir *who grabbed some free publicity several months back by jumping on what then seemed like an anti-Clinton bandwagon—with a vile mock act of fellatio in a right-wing "church," no less—is now revealed, in a* Zodiac *exclusive, to be not just "Mad" by nickname but actually mentally unstable.*
>
> *Mr. Jones also has a history as a sex addict—possibly turning that to his advantage by using sex to help launch his so-called ministry in the first place—and, in another twist worthy of suspicion, may have long benefited from the support of a shadowy cabal, a "secret society," based at the University of Virginia.*
>
> *Put all these strands together, and it may well be that Mad Jones is at the vanguard of the actual "vast right-wing conspiracy" that Hillary Clinton was ridiculed for warning the nation about late last winter.*
>
> *These revelations come courtesy of an exhaustive eight-month investigation by* The Zodiac.
>
> *First things first: Three new developments in the past week have again put Jones in the spotlight. First,* The Zodiac *has discovered that Jones has a history of mental illness (see related story beginning on this same page). Second, a "social scene" column in a New Orleans paper reported on Thanksgiving Day that Jones had been seen "canoodling" the weekend before with Laura Green, one of the top reporters for the network news show* Acute Vision. *Green was a mere assistant producer at a local New Orleans TV station when Jones first posted his religious "theses," or propositions, around which he has built his entire ministry. But, with no prior experience as an investigative*

reporter, Green somehow beat a host of other reporters trying to track down Jones, who had been in hiding for more than a week after his wife died unexpectedly of a mysterious "hemorrhage."

The question naturally arises, if Jones was "canoodling" with Green two weekends ago, is there a history there? Did Jones and Green mutually sleep their way to stardom? The Zodiac has uncovered evidence that makes this speculation sound less far-fetched.

But more on that in a moment.

The third new development in the growing brouhaha over Jones occurred last weekend, when, as the New York Informer reported, Jones began a new book tour by accusing President Clinton of "faithlessness," on the same day that his syndicated newspaper column equated marital "faithlessness" with spousal abuse (otherwise known as "wife beating").

Jones' Clinton-bashing is in line with his earlier remarks at a right-wing New Orleans-area "church," when he said the president had turned the White House into a "brothel" and that the Oval Office had become an "oral orifice." Right after he said so, an accomplice wearing a Lewinsky wig and blue dress rushed the platform and simulated oral sex on Mr. Jones as a way to dramatize the president's supposed transgressions.

And as early as the interview Ms. Green did with Mr. Jones for her Acute Vision debut last March, Mr. Jones was criticizing Mr. Clinton.

All of which, The Zodiac has learned, leaves Jones wide open to potential charges of rank hypocrisy. Not only is his relationship with Laura Green in question—after all, this is still less than nine months after his supposedly beloved wife suddenly died, and his original interview with Green was barely more than a week after the mysterious and tragic demise—but, as The Zodiac's investigations long ago discovered, Jones has a history as a "lady's man" that Bill Clinton could only hope to emulate.

Ironically, Jones is a graduate of Clinton's own alma mater, Georgetown University. A former Georgetown classmate of Jones', now a Democratic staffer on Capitol Hill who asked to remain unnamed, said that Jones' sexual exploits were legendary on the campus.

"Mad wasn't a one-night-stand guy," said the classmate, "but he was the king of the three-night stands. Find a girl and con her into bed on the very first night, jump her bones again a few nights later, then give her the old horizontal mambo one more night for good measure—and then, after the girl was hopelessly in love with him, dump her like a ton of bricks."

And Jake Murphy, a teammate of Jones' on the Georgetown baseball team, called Jones "a regular babe magnet. I mean, most of the guys on the team did okay with the ladies, if you know what I mean, but Mad was the kind who got so much action that we were all in awe of him."

Also, the chief operating officer of Mad Mad World (Jones' supposedly non-profit corporation), Becky Matthews, has been identified by several former Georgetown classmates as an old flame of Jones'. "She's a slut through and through," said one former classmate who wished to remain unidentified. "I remember when she and Mad hooked up in the first place. She couldn't stop bragging about it."

Matthews, still single, is now living in Mobile, Alabama, just a few miles from where the also-single Jones maintains his bachelor pad.

And in the crowning blow to Jones' standing as a legitimate critic on sexual issues, he was reported for sexual misconduct while a patient at a Mobile hospital (see related story).

Finally, there is the matter of the secret cabal that may have been financing Jones' efforts as early as his days as an undergraduate at Georgetown. Oddly, the shadowy organization at issue is not affiliated with Georgetown, but with the University of Virginia, which has numerous "secret societies" running around on campus. Most of them are known for pulling harmless, funny pranks, but the granddaddy of them all, the Crazy Eights, is more serious.

While nobody has ever offered proof of any nefarious doing by the Eights, as they are commonly known, they have an aura of mystery and power. The Eights are known for donating large gifts to the university, making them obviously a gathering of the wealthy elite of Virginia society. But on a more sinister note, powerful secret societies have long been associated with elitist tendencies and sometimes bizarre, even Satanic, rituals, and those in the South have sometimes been suspected of virulently racist activities. Few doubt that such cabals are a hotbed of right-wing thought and action.

Two factors make it likely that Jones has some connection with the Eights. First is his family history. As a member of the famous Lee family of Virginia (on his mother's side), Jones had a great-uncle, Jackson Lee, who was a prominent financier and graduate of UVA and who was widely suspected of being a member of the Eights. And Jones' late father, Ben, received not one but three different degrees from Virginia.

The second factor was an odd ritual Jones performed each semester while at Georgetown. Once per semester, Jones would recruit eight new Georgetown students to make a pilgrimage two hours south from Washington, D.C. to Monticello, the home of UVA founder Thomas Jefferson.

Yes, eight students. A crazy eight, perhaps?

On each of those trips, Jones paid for all the gasoline and for light snacks for the ride. In fact, fellow classmates said Jones always seemed to be (by student standards) "rolling in dough," in the words of one Hoya—which was odd considering that Jones had been orphaned by his middle-class father when Jones was only 16.

Apprised of all these facts, U.S. Rep. Rusty O'Sullivan (D-Mass.) said he was not surprised.

"It all adds up," he said. "This is just more evidence that the forces arrayed against our president are both reactionary and dangerous. This young man appears to me to be a hater of the first order—and, if what you say of his sex life is true, he's also a hypocrite of the first order as well. Of course, the right-wing elite has long been known for wanting to apply draconian *standards to others while allowing themselves to behave like Mount Olympians in heat."*

And Democratic consultant Carney "The Gorgeous Georgian" James had this to say: "It jes' goes to show that the president's enemies are rotten to the core. But the war this Jones guy is fighting along with all his right-wing nutcake friends is a war that will turn against them and obliterate them all."

Along with that article ran this shorter sidebar, headlined "Jones' secret psychiatric retreat."

A nurse at a prominent Mobile hospital has finally cleared up the mystery of Mad Jones' whereabouts during the first week after his wife, Claire, died, immediately after which interlude Jones posted the 59 religious propositions that first made him famous.

The nurse showed The Zodiac *copies of hospital records that prove that Jones spent the week in a psychiatric ward. There, not only was Jones prone to "insane-sounding outbursts," as the nurse put it (and as the records confirm), but he was recorded as having made aggressive, inappropriate sexual advances against the nurses.*

(The nurse who is The Zodiac's *source asked to remain nameless, for fear of losing her job—and because of the same possibility, was reimbursed by this newspaper for her cooperation with our investigation.)*

According to the hospital records, the nurse reported an incident in which Jones suddenly placed his hand under her uniform and grabbed her breast.

"Not only that," she told The Zodiac, *"but as he did it, he said one of the most insane things I've ever heard—and since I work on a psychiatric ward, I've heard some crazy stuff. He almost shouted it. He called me Esmerelda, even though he was looking right at my name tag that showed my name to be nothing like that, and then he said, 'Esmerelda, your eyes are like stars in a chuck wagon soup.' It was so bizarre it scared me. I felt lucky to have escaped his room without any further harm."*

146

The nurse said that she had good reason, based on cryptic comments from two of her colleagues, to believe that at least those two other nurses also experienced uncomfortable, sexually charged incidents with Mr. Jones.

The records show that Mr. Jones checked himself into the psychiatric ward on the morning of Sunday, March 1 of this year—just one day after the mysterious death of his wife. He checked himself out during the evening of Saturday, March 7. In the interim, he was diagnosed with severe depression bordering on dementia, highly passive-aggressive behavior, and sexual dysfunction, and he was reported to see imaginary visions and to carry on loud "conversations with God" in his empty room.

Nevertheless, a psychiatrist on duty the next weekend, Dr. Theodore Theodore—who had not overseen Jones' care at all during the week—signed Jones' release papers. Four days later, Jones was videotaped hurling a golf club at a TV reporter and a cameraman while yelling: "A plague on both your houses!"

Since that incident, Mr. Jones has not been seen in public engaged in behavior that, according to several psychiatrists consulted by The Zodiac, *could be characterized as psychotic. But he has at times seemed to experience what observers have called "somewhat volatile mood swings."*

Mr. Jones could not be reached for comments on these reports.

CHAPTER EIGHT

Late that afternoon, all the usual suspects in Congress paraded before the microphones. The unctuous Democratic "gentleman from Michigan" said this was just one more case in which "the president's accusers are themselves unclean. Mr. Clinton's sins are a speck compared to the log in his accusers' eyes. Can any of them stand the scrutiny? Let those who have not sinned cast stones, but let the rest of these hypocrites be warned that they have opened themselves up for stoning." He paused, as if thinking deep thoughts. Then he added: "Let it be clear that the mentally ill are to be pitied and not condemned, but I do think it's instructive to learn that some of this anti-Clinton hysteria and hate comes straight out of the loony bin."

Added the rectitudinous Democratic "gentle lady from California": "This is all so sad. Rather than wallowing in the mire of hate and lunacy that our Republican colleagues have been sucked into, I think we need to elevate our conversation and go back to doing the nation's business."

Shortly afterward, the four most prominent "moderate" Republicans on Capitol Hill issued a joint statement. Hailing from Maine, Connecticut, Illinois, and Oregon, the three male representatives and one female senator were widely known by the moniker "The Mod Squad."

"We have long been troubled by the intemperate tendencies of some of our more conservative Republican colleagues," they said. "Now we see that they are taking their lead from a charlatan who may well be mentally unstable. Our country needs healing, so this impeachment saga must be stopped. Regretfully, we urge adoption of a resolution of censure for our troubled president—and then we should move on to saving Social Security and providing better healthcare for all Americans."

On the congressional right, reactions were mixed. Some immediately distanced themselves from Mad. A mid-level member of the Senate leadership blasted the left-wing media for trying to link all Republicans with "a confused young man who not a single one of us even knows," and said that the latest "tempest in a tabloid" should not stop the House from "doing its duty by the Constitution to see that the laws be faithfully executed." But the libertarian Republican representative from Florida jumped to Mad's defense, urging a full-scale investigation of how Mad's hospital records had been made public. "This is an egregious violation of his civil rights by the nexus of the left-wing media and the allies of the Big Brother in the White House who has done the same thing many times before, ranging from the pilfered FBI files to the threats made against so many of the other women who were victims of Bill Clinton's libidinous exploits."

As a guest on CNN that night, Gladys Phillpott said empathetically that the media should "leave that poor boy [Madison] alone, and concentrate on the constitutional crimes of the president." But on MSNBC, the Rev. Larry Patterson said that "the sinner from Mobile should repent, just as our criminally perjurious president must be made to pay the piper. We who favor impeachment as a simple matter of justice do not deserve to be branded with the mark of a sexual deviant we have long condemned. We stand with the Lord against sinners of both the left and the right. And by the way, speaking of the Lord's justice, I think it's interesting that the biggest hurricane to strike the United States this year went straight for Mobile, which is Madison Jones' hometown."

Justin, calling on Mad's cell phone, was apoplectic. "They're not gonna get away with it, buddy! We'll sue them all, buddy, we'll sue! And how dare they say those things about Becky? If I get my hands on that *Zodiac* reporter, I'll rip his nuts off! I swear I'll rip his nuts off!"

For her part, Becky passed out, dead drunk, under her desk at the office.

That same night, The Colonel somehow tracked down Mad on the road. (How The Colonel always managed to know how to reach him was more than a little unnerving, to say the least.) But this time The Colonel wasn't calling to chew Mad out.

"I say, I say, I say, son, this is one fine mess we're in. These evil bastards have used you to attack us, and they've used us to attack you, all at the same time. This won't stand, I say, this won't stand. We're in this together, son, we're in this together."

"But sir, I thought you would be furious at me," Mad said.

"I say, son, you are one of our own by adoption, son, and you've been wronged by those bastards. Our disappointments with you in the past are jes' between you and us, but we stand up for our own. We're like the Crazy Eight Musketeers, son, 'all for one' and all that good stuff. And I jes' want to make some things clear, son, before we talk about what we're gwoin tuh do to respond to this outrage.

"First, son, I say, first I want to reassure you that the Crazy Eights have never done anything to hurt anybody, not in all the long, long history of our organization. We have no Satanic rituals, and while we are proud of the old South, we aren't the slightest bit racist. Not only do we have Negro members, but back when the university was integrated, we played a role in making sure it was integrated without any of the unseemly problems that were seen in places like Mississippi and Alabama and Arkansas. All we ever do is provide anonymous gifts and services to our beloved Jefferson's university, son, and that's all we will ever do. I say, that's all we'll ever do."

Mad was a bit dumbfounded. He had grown to heartily dislike and even slightly fear The Colonel, even while he was grateful for the financial support the Eights had provided him. But here was The Colonel entirely on his side.

"Aren't you disappointed in me, sir?"

"I say, son, now is not the time for us to worry about the past. So you took a little vacation in a hospital when you lost your lovely bride so soon after losing your daddy Lee. So what? And so you sowed wild oats in college. So what? And even if you're back to your old tricks of playing around with the ladies, well, so what? As long as you keep your vows when you're married, what does the rest of it matter when you're fancy-free? If having a way with the ladies were a crime, your Daddy Lee woulda been cut off from contact with the society ages and ages ago. We sure as heck wouldna' provided all that money to his grandson if we were embarrassed by him doin' what any red-blooded man woulda done once his wife departed this earth."

The Colonel went on to give Mad "instructions" on how Mad should respond to the *Zodiac* article. Mad should issue a statement, every word of it true, to the effect that he was not now, nor had he ever been, a member of the Crazy Eights. He should say that his MMW Corp. had "never received a dime" in support from the Eights, nor was it affiliated with the Eights in any way. He should say further that he had never knowingly even laid eyes on a living member of the Crazy Eights, and that his father, Ben, had never even said a word about the Eights to him. And, based on the implication that Mad, his father, or his great-uncle had any connection with any group that took racist actions or performed Satanic rituals, Mad should say that he was having lawyers investigate the possibility of suing *The Zodiac* for libel.

Meanwhile, The Colonel told Mad that a former governor of Virginia would call a press conference on behalf of the secret society during which the governor would relay the message that the Eights themselves were considering a libel suit against the tabloid. The governor would note that while he wasn't himself a member of the Eights, he knew them to be of excellent character and a "progressive" force in the state. The potential libel suit would be based on the implication that the Eights did harm to people, that they were racist and Satanic, that they were politically active or right wing, or that they had in any way donated money to MMW Corp. in order to promulgate an anti-Clinton agenda. He also was to relay the message that Madison Jones was not now, nor had he ever been, a member of the Crazy Eights.

"The idea, son, I say, the idea is to give our message heft and weight by threatening legal action. That'll get the news stories we want. But of course neither of us will actually follow up with a lawsuit, because that would open the Eights up to discovery during depositions. The whole point of doing anonymous good deeds for a university is so that the individuals involved will do the good deeds for the sake of the school and not for public credit and self-aggrandizement. If they do discovery and publish our membership, then that whole point will be defeated.

"Meanwhile, son, I got one more message for you: Keep on preaching *your* message that Christ is a redeemer and that God's goal for us is joy. None of us quite understands all your theology, son, but we've been noticing that you are emphasizing those two constructive ideas. So jes' keep it up, son. Now that we've been attacked together, we'll make sure you have all the support you need. All for one and one for Eight."

The line went dead.

The next morning in New York, Spike Walters looked through the packet that assistant Al Bobbitt had prepared for him. It included *The Zodiac*'s hit piece on Mad. Walters buzzed Bobbitt on the intercom.

"Hey, Al, I see where this trashy tabloid took young Mr. Jones to the cleaners. They really did a number on him. Could not have happened to a more deserving little punk. But, look, I don't want *Hour of Truth* to look like we're following in the footsteps of a trashy tabloid. Besides, as far as the Clinton fight goes, Jones has been totally discredited now, so there's no use for us to go ahead with a show on him. So I know this might disappoint you and Martina, but this project is now on hold. But I'll tell you what: I don't think we've heard the last of this punk, so keep your file on him. Keep it active. We won't blast him now, but if he raises his punk head to cause any more trouble later on, we'll be ready for him."

Mad's publisher didn't know whether *The Zodiac* story would be a disaster for book sales or a boon. He suspected that, if the publicist did his job right, it would be the latter. Controversy creates buzz, and buzz sells books. He decided to play the story up. Mad was due in Atlanta the next afternoon; the publicist made sure all the appropriate Atlanta radio stations talked up the arrival of the "controversial, sometimes outrageous, and sometimes, yes, *mad*, Mad Jones."

It worked. The crowds in Atlanta that evening were bigger than ever. And Mad, hyped up on angry adrenaline, wowed them all. It took him hours to sign all the books that sold at the bookstore that hosted him.

But when the adrenaline wore off that night, Mad had another of his "episodes." Shiloh found Mad sitting at the base of the ice machine at the end of their hotel hallway. Mad was holding his hands together in a cupped position, staring intently into them. In his hands was a tiny pool of water with a few tiny pieces of not-quite-yet-melted ice. Mad's stare was so intense, it looked as if he were trying to divine some mysteries from the melting ice the same way a fortune teller uses a crystal ball.

"Hey, Mad, you okay?" Shiloh asked.

Mad stared at him rather blankly. "This, too, shall melt away," he said.

Shiloh reached down and shook Mad gently by the shoulder. This was really weird, he thought.

With the shake, Mad jerked his head a little and his eyes lost their glaze. "Oh, Shiloh, were you saying something? I must've fallen asleep. I better get back to my room and go to bed."

The next day, Mad's tour took him to Savannah. While the publicist took care of some business, Mad and Shiloh visited some of the city's historic homes, ate lunch at the Pirate's House restaurant, and relaxed for a while, unrecognized, in the lovely Trustees' Garden. It really did seem like a charming place. They saw two plaques there, dedicated to the husband-and-wife team who apparently had started the city's whole historic renovation movement a good half century earlier. "If only all of us could leave as pleasant a legacy as these two folks," Mad said to his bodyguard.

Shiloh was happy to see that Mad showed no signs whatsoever of the weirdness he had demonstrated the night before.

When they checked in at their hotel that afternoon before the evening book signing, Mad was greeted by a FedEx-ed letter along with a copy of the newest weekly *Investigator*, just out on the newsstands that morning. Again, Don had planted a hit piece of his own to counter *The Zodiac's* article. The story in *The Investigator* essentially accused Carney "The Gorgeous Georgian" James of orchestrating the entirety of *The Zodiac's* coverage of Mad. The press questions that had goaded Mad into the quick-veiled reference to "faithlessness" in politics? The Georgian's doing, said the article. The "bribe" paid to the nurse to release records of Mad's psych-ward stay? Financed by Carney James. The false accusation that Mad was a member of the Crazy Eights, and that the Eights were racist and Satanic? Again, a Clinton hit job funneled through Mr. James. And so on and so forth. And the story quoted an "associate of Madison Jones" as saying that "there's every reason to believe the mime is actually a paid political hack."

Inside the FedEx-ed letter were two pieces of paper and a videotape. One paper was a copy of the press release put out the previous afternoon, from Mobile, by Don. Two paragraphs of the release followed The Colonel's instructions (as relayed through Mad) to a T, with the libel suit explicitly threatened but no mention of which law firm was looking into the case. Another paragraph contained a quote from Mad: "Again, a wholly random comment of mine has been blown way out of proportion. Yes—when asked again and again about my opinion on the current impeachment crisis—I reluctantly expressed my disapproval of the president's actions. But I have never tried to emphasize that subject. In fact, I consider myself fairly apolitical. And, far from being right wing, my personal political beliefs (when I even think about politics, which isn't all that often) are only slightly to the right of center: moderate by national standards, and perhaps even liberal by the standards of the average Alabamian."

A final paragraph gave information on the next stops of Mad's book tour, and referred all questions concerning it to the publishing house in New York.

The second paper was a letter to Mad from Don. It was Don's resignation from MMW Corp., effective immediately.

"You will see, Mad, that I have responded professionally to the latest controversy. I have followed all your instructions, and I also took the initiative to again plant a story in *The Investigator* to provide cover for you. But I can no longer allow my reputation to be sullied by association with somebody who has spent time in a nuthouse and who has ties to a sinister secret society at a university that is not even our own alma mater. You should have told me of these flaws of yours before I agreed to join your employ. Anyway, as a professional I will certainly leave your employment quietly, with no public notice. But I leave, nevertheless, with some bitterness. As a close personal friend of yours, I believe I was owed full disclosure from you before you allowed me to put my own reputation on the line on your behalf. I think I will go back to work on Capitol Hill, where the politicians have more character than you do."

Mad was not overly disturbed to see Don go. "Close personal friend?" Where had that come from? And Mad was distinctly uncomfortable with the retaliatory hit piece in *The Investigator*. That just wasn't Mad's style.

Nevertheless, Mad felt a little guilty. Don was a cipher and a drone, but Mad realized that Don had put himself on the line for him, for whatever reason. And Mad had never extended himself in the slightest on Don's behalf. Mad thought of himself as a more considerate person than the one who had taken Don so much for granted. How, he wondered, had he allowed himself to become so oblivious to the feelings of another person?

Finally, there was the videotape. Scotch-taped to the top of it was a hand-written note from Don: "Did you give your approval for this? As your press secretary, I should have known about this. Your failure to inform me about it is just one more example of why I can no longer work for you."

From somewhere or other, the publisher's publicist conjured up a VCR. When they plopped in the videotape, Steve Matheson's face and voice filled the screen.

"And as our last guest of the night, we have Buzz Buskirk, distinguished history professor and also godfather of Madison Lee Jones, the young armchair theologian who has caused such a stir not only in the religious community this year but also in politics through his pithy criticisms of our priapic president. Mr. Jones, as some of you know, was recently revealed by *The Zodiac*—if you can believe *The Zodiac*, of course, when it's not writing about Martians landing in Mayberry—anyway, Mr. Jones apparently spent a week in a psychiatric ward earlier this year after his wife died.

"Buzz, you're a military historian. What would Sun Tzu have said in his famous *Art of War* writings about somebody who takes on the president just a few months after creating a sexual storm with the nurses at a loony bin? I mean, I just love the style of your godson, but isn't there some good advice somewhere about not attacking from a position of weakness?"

"Well, Steve, not even I knew where he had been during that week when he was incommunicado, so I still don't know if the tabloid report is true. But I'll tell you what, Steve, Madison is a fine young man, and even if he went haywire there for a week you've gotta understand what a lovely bride he had just lost. Not only that, but—"

Matheson interrupted: "So you're saying Mad is not mad? Not even a little looped? I mean, dontcha have to be a little loopy to take on a president who critics say is surrounded by thugs who threaten to break the kneecaps of his amorous conquests? I mean, you're a friend of mine, you know I'm just joshing with you a little, but after this *Zodiac* article don't you think your godson oughtta lie low for a while? Or is this his *Gut Check* time when he stands up for what he believes, no matter how his own past makes him look?"

"Well, uh…"

"I know you'll say, and I believe, too, that perjury by a president is worse than a little nookie in a loony bin, but dontcha think Mad is getting into some pretty tough company when he tries to match epithets with Carney James, "The Gorgeous Georgian," who is so often a guest here on *Gut Check*?"

"Well, you know, Steve that compared to Mad I'm just a wise old owl past my best hooting days, but you know how young people can ignore the advice of their elders. I might advise him to cool it, you know, but when you're young it can be awfully fun to be rash."

"Well," Matheson said, "*I* say more power to him. If he's got a gripe with the president, good for him for going for it with gusto. But meanwhile, Buzz, if *I* need any wisdom over a few workingman's brews, I'll turn to you even if your godson won't. Thanks a lot for being on *Gut Check*, and come back soon. Bye, folks!"

Mad covered his eyes and groaned.

Why had nobody asked him if it was okay for Buzz to go on the air? Mad thought the result of his godfather's appearance was that he, Mad, sounded like a circus freak. Who had given Buzz permission to go on the air? If it wasn't Don, it must've been Becky. Damn her—how could she do this without asking *him*?

Mad grabbed his cell phone and began to call Becky at the Mobile office, but then changed his mind and instead dialed the number of Buzz's university office. Maybe Buzz would be done with classes for the day.

"Y'ello?" said Buzz.

"Dammit, Buzz, this is Mad. Did Becky tell you to go on last night with Steve Matheson? How could you go on the show without checking with me?!?"

"Hey, young buddy, I was just doing you a favor. It was a last-minute thing: Steve had somebody cancel on him, so he called me up and said to go over to the studio. I didn't even think of calling Becky, and I didn't know how to get in touch with you on the road for your book tour, and I figured that *some*body needed to stand up and defend you. What're you so hacked off about?"

"Dammit, Buzz, the one thing I insisted on at the very beginning of all this lunacy was that if y'all wanted me to start a so-called ministry, *nobody* could speak for me without my permission. You made me sound like a clown, Buzz!"

"Jesus, Mad, all I was doing was doing you a favor! But okay, I'll tell you what: Steve'll have me on his show again lots of times, cuz he says he needs an academic expert on military affairs, like I am. So, from now on when he wants me on his show, I'll be the star instead of making you the star. How's that sound, *young* buddy? You just get somebody else to defend your honor. *If* you can find somebody else. Jesus, you really have let all this attention go to your head, haven't you?"

Mad was therefore not in the best of moods for his book signing that evening. Even worse, the mime was there. Shiloh really was tempted to give the mime a piece of his mind, but he couldn't bring himself to do so because the mime was actually making him laugh. Dressed like a penitential altar boy, with ashes smeared on his forehead, the mime wore a sign on his back that read:

Mea culpa
…But…
Mad's a Cupid

A local reporter at the book signing tried to ask the mime a few questions, but the mime covered his own mouth and ran away.

That same night, Justin convinced Becky to let him take her to a nice dinner at a little restaurant across Mobile Bay in the quaint bayside town of Fairhope. By now, Becky considered Justin a friend, despite how much he unintentionally annoyed her. She referred to him as "my sweet little man," and when he told her that she deserved a nice night out to take her mind off *The Zodiac's* "hideously unfair slander," she didn't even try to find an excuse to decline.

Still wary of alcohol after her terrible hangover the day before, Becky had to be coaxed to accept even a single glass of wine with dinner. That's why she knew it wasn't drunkenness that led her to actually laugh at some of Justin's oddball jokes that on previous occasions would have made her cringe at his weirdness. Her "sweet little man" was still a goofball, but at least his heart was good and he made for a loyal friend. She didn't understand why she had not found a boyfriend since moving to Mobile, but a sweet little platonic companion was better than renting a movie alone at home or getting hit on by rednecks or sleazy lawyers in various bars around town.

After dinner she was too tired to go "out on the happenin' town," as Justin put it, but when he dropped her off back at her condo and showily kissed her hand in that silly little way of his, she responded for the first time ever by kissing him on the cheek.

"G'night, Justin," she said. "You're a good guy; you know that?"

That same Friday night, *Acute Vision* aired in the dead-end time slot to which it had recently been moved in a last attempt to find it a more receptive audience. Laura was the reporter for the show's first segment (an investigation of a $2,311 student loan that a local bank back in 1962 had "inexplicably" forgiven for a now leading Republican, when the Republican had been an entry-level, 23-year-old corporate sales clerk recovering from a badly broken leg). With the canoodling report and then the *Zodiac* article, the *Acute Vision* executives had wondered whether they should garner some publicity by firing Laura for supposedly compromised journalistic ethics. In the end, they decided she was the most glamorous thing going for the struggling show, so they just called her on the carpet at a meeting intended primarily to scare her and remind her (for their own ego gratification) that she served only at their pleasure. She told them the same lie she had told her network boyfriend: She had unexpectedly run into Mad after having about four drinks, and so yes, she had responded to his kiss for about 10 seconds when he opened her car door for her—and then they had both laughed and she drove him back to his hotel without further incident. *Of course* there was no history there, especially no romantic history that had anything to do with the story she had done on Mad for the show. (Her boyfriend accepted the story and forgave her, but only at the cost of making her prove her love for him by performing some new bedroom gymnastics for him.)

Anyway, what neither the network executives nor Laura expected was that the show would jump up 14 spots in the Nielsen ratings that week. The publicity about Laura's possible tryst with Mad had attracted a host of living room TV rubberneckers, eager to see for themselves what this vixen looked like and whether the stress from the attention would cause her to have an on-camera wreck.

But Laura had done fine, and although the show's real investigatory news value was nearly nil, her slimness and fresh good looks impressed a segment of the 20-something American male population. The better ratings—still not spectacular, but solidly acceptable to the network—continued the next week, and the week after that, and the week after that. And in the back of her mind, Laura made note of the career advantages that could accrue from canoodling in public.

The chat room traffic had become so heavy that the server was having trouble handling it all. Critics were having a field day calling Mad a "male slut," a "heretic," and an "orgiastic fornicator," and also a "cracked cultist," a "crazy nutbag," and a "cuckoo's nester in lust with Nurse Ratched."

Jezebel?, though, had become active again, defending Mad fervently. "He's a young man and he's gorgeous," she wrote in one entry. "Who are any of you to condemn him for doing what comes naturally?" About the psych ward visit, she wrote that "if I were the nurse, I would have jumped his bones and kept my mouth shut about it." And as for the reports about the supposedly evil secret society, she called it "nothing but innuendo that I don't believe for even a moment. But if he's involved in a ritual, I want to be the woman he ravishes. SO THERE! But on a more serious note, what does any of this other stuff matter? What's important is his message of redemption and joy that is making even this non-believer take another look at God."

Ever Faithful responded that Jezebel? obviously was a sinner who needed to repent of her sexual longings, and that Mad had now been proven "nothing more than a crackpot." Defender, despite his happiness at seeing President Clinton criticized, concurred with Ever Faithful. D Thom wrote that he wouldn't pass judgment until a "real" newspaper ("unlike *The Zodiac*") confirmed the reports about Mad.

But Affirmed was as ebullient as ever. "Okay, so maybe I STILL have my Biblical figure wrong," he wrote. "Instead of Moses (or Luther), maybe Mad is the new King David. David still did great things for God and for God's people even though he screwed around all the time on the side. Remember Bathsheba? Even after that episode where David clearly was in the wrong, God blessed him with power for decades more, because David was overall doing God's will and serving God well. Hail, King Madison!"

The book tour continued down to Florida and then across the country to Phoenix, San Diego, Los Angeles, Sacramento, and San Francisco. Then the House of Representatives impeached Clinton on two counts and the tour took nearly three weeks off for Christmas and New Year's. By that time, Mad realized that he had actually been enjoying himself. He was thriving on the attention. His continuing episodes of spacing out aside, the stress that did accrue gave him an adrenaline rush that was sort of fun. He managed to succeed at sidestepping the constant political questions, and was gratified that the majority of his audiences were more interested in asking him how a God who was a jerk could also be a God whose goal for us is that we find joy through the strength He gives us.

On Christmas Eve, Mad was delighted by a request to read the famous Christmas passage from Luke for a national radio broadcast. "Glory to God in the Highest, and on earth peace, goodwill toward men," he concluded the reading. Then he added, extemporaneously: "And if I may add, at this Christmas celebration, we should all rejoice that God's love has been poured into our hearts through the Holy Spirit that has been given to us. Have a Mad-ly Merry Christmas."

The next day would be the first Christmas Mad had ever spent without a single family member, but that was okay: Gifts and cards had come in from all over, and Mad spent much of the day at a soup kitchen doling out meals for the homeless, and he arrived back home to find on his side porch an ice chest with some casserole dishes full of leftover turkey and stuffing, along with a kind note, courtesy of LaShauna and Shiloh.

Mad tried not to think about how, just a year ago, he and a pregnant Claire had celebrated their first Christmas as a married couple, along

161

with Daddy Lee, with a joyfulness full of the hopes of a lifelong bond complete with not just the wondrous child in Claire's belly but three or four more children to come. But if life was full of pain, so too was it full of the grace he had somehow, mysteriously, begun to know.

CHAPTER NINE

After the grueling book tour schedule between Thanksgiving and Christmas, Mad and Shiloh both had insisted upon easing back into things even after the three-week break. (The "break" had still involved plenty of work, because Mad had naturally fallen a bit behind on his column writing and other projects while on the road.) The agenda in early January involved hitting smaller prestige stops rather than big media markets. In fact, part of the trip would re-trace the steps they had taken on Labor Day weekend. It began at noon on Saturday, January 9 in New Orleans, at the neighborhood Maple Street Book Shop. Maple Street's owner, Rhoda Faust, had been a second-generation friend of the great novelist Walker Percy, and also was friendly with a bevy of other New Orleans–area authors. Not much more than a converted one-story house, the bookshop featured narrow aisles where books almost seemed to be falling in on visitors—but somehow with such charm that a literate person would welcome such an avalanche. Really, the shop was too small for the crowds that Mad had been drawing—which was why a second lecture/signing was scheduled for mid-afternoon at the student center of nearby Tulane University.

But because the bookshop's cachet was so well established, it was a must-stop on his tour—and on the porch at Maple Street Mad felt immediately at home and, having relaxed so much over Christmas break, was so at ease as to charm virtually everybody in attendance. The crowd, about 50 strong, was clustered in the tiny fenced-in front yard and spilled out onto the sidewalk. A woman in her late 40s, saying she had been a high school English teacher of Claire's, asked Mad how, if at all, Claire's memory influenced his theology. Mad was surprised that being asked to talk publicly about Claire didn't rattle him. Maybe it was the pretty day and the shop's homey atmosphere, but Mad felt comfortable in being expansive. And in being expansive, he became more eloquent than he ever thought possible.

"If anything I ever do is good or right or helpful to somebody, Claire is somewhere in the endeavor," he said. "I know that people have a tendency to idolize loved ones after they are gone, but since you knew Claire, you'll know I'm not exaggerating when I say that Claire was the kindest, purest, most gracious and grace-filled person I've ever known.

"It was in response to Claire's death that I wrote my theses. To have somebody so good, so loving, so bright and pure, suddenly taken away, is to feel like you've been plunged into the deepest darkness imaginable. And I blamed God for taking her. I blamed him with all the anger and sorrow in my soul. I really thought God was a jerk for taking her away, and that's exactly what I wrote in my theses.

"But as you certainly know, Claire herself would never have believed that God is a jerk, no matter what disasters occurred or how wrenching a pain that life inflicted. Claire's faith, not just in God's existence but in His deep and unimpeachable goodness, was unmistakable, unshakable, and unbreakable. And the more I thought of Claire, the more I knew that for the sake of her memory, if for no other reason, I could not rest until I reached a point where God's apparent jerkiness was not the end of the story.

"I remember one time at Georgetown, a good friend of Claire's was jilted by the boy she thought she was going to marry. In fact, she wasn't just dumped; it was worse than that, although the details aren't important. But what happened was that this girl, this friend of Claire's, found a way to climb up on the roof of the Copley Building on campus. And there is no doubt about it: This girl was going to jump. Meanwhile, Claire and I had been at what for us was a huge event, a play at the Kennedy Center. We didn't know that any of this had happened with Claire's friend. But right in the middle of the final act, Claire stiffened next to me and told me we had to leave. She didn't know why, but she just knew she had to get back to campus. And even in the darkness of the theater, her eyes shown with an intensity and a light I had never seen before. So I didn't even question her. We rushed out, hailed a taxi, and sped to campus. Claire was just frantic.

"Anyway, when we got to campus Claire ran to the Copley Lawn and started looking around. And something made her look up, and she spotted her friend on the edge of the roof.

164

"Well, I'm making this story too long, but what happened is that Claire somehow convinced her friend, calling up to her on the roof, to wait there on the roof until she, Claire, could climb up with her. And she sent me to run for help. And by the time I got back with a couple of campus police officers, there was no sign of either one of the girls on the roof. And then, as I started to go nuts with worry, the two of them walked out of the building, Claire's arms around her friend. Apparently, Claire had crawled out on the roof with her and had talked her back to safety. And when I asked her later how she had done it, Claire wouldn't give me many details. But the one thing she kept repeating, and it has stuck with me, was that 'God is good, and if you open your heart and let him in and let him use you, he'll speak through you. I didn't do anything up there on that roof,' she said; 'God did.'

"So at some point in that week after Claire died, as I wrote those theses, I reached a point where I thought of Claire and thought of her goodness and thought of her love for God. And that's when the tenor of my writing began to change. And you'll see that at some point I wrote about guardian angels, and I was thinking about Claire when I did. Suddenly I was re-copying all the most comforting passages from the New Testament or from prayers I had heard in church, and I somehow ended up with God's love being poured into our hearts through the Holy Spirit.

"And, to finally answer your question, there's no way that, in all my grief and pain, there's no way that I would have ended up there without Claire's memory and her example to lead me back to a sense of God's love."

An agitated young man then spoke up.

"So if you end up with God's love, that leaves out in the cold all of us who think God is a jerk. Just when you give us hope because of your message that we don't have to feel guilty about being mad at God, you leave us in the lurch. What do you have to say to that?"

"Look at it this way," Mad answered. "Are you ever a jerk? Do you ever do things, even or especially to people you love, that really aren't very nice? And if you do jerky things, does that mean you don't actually love the person you do them to? Of course not."

The young man was tentatively nodding his head. Mad continued: "If you do jerky things, it doesn't mean you are always a bad person. It just means that you messed up. And if you're like me, you try to make up for messing up by loving that person even more. Well, why can't God do the same thing? Why can't He be a jerk and yet still love you? And, being God, why can't He go back and forth like that several times, all the while finding the power and goodness within Himself to make sure that He finally brings you to a place where His jerkiness is no longer apparent and where all you know, forever and evermore, is His love? And, being God, His love is so much richer, so much more joy-filled, than any love you've ever known, that when you come to the place where His love is forever, it is indeed greater than any heaven you've even imagined. At least, that's what I've come to think. And I feel sure that that is the conclusion that Claire would have wanted me to reach, no matter what circuitous path I took to get there. And my wish for you is that you reach the same conclusion, and the same place, and God's same love that Claire channeled so well into my own life. Good luck."

The young man first looked like he wanted to make some smart aleck remark. Then he looked a little puzzled. He cocked his head and stared at Mad with a slightly perplexed expression on his face.

And, suddenly, he smiled. And he nodded. And he smiled again, and then turned and walked away and disappeared down the block in the direction of P.J.'s coffeehouse.

And Claire's former teacher watched the young man, and then looked at Mad, and then back at the young man walking away—and she had big, happy tears in her eyes and a small but heartfelt smile on her countenance.

At Tulane, Mad was treated almost like a rock star. That night, he checked the paper to see if the jazz singer Leslie Smith was playing anywhere but did not see her listed—and so, at Shiloh's urging, he took it easy instead. The next morning he and Shiloh together quietly attended Trinity Episcopal Church in New Orleans—a grand old church at the very edge of the Garden District, built in 1851, with one of the most active social outreach programs in the South and a reputation for a warm and welcoming congregation. Not only that, but Trinity Episcopal

School, on the same grounds as the church, had a reputation as one of the finest elementary schools in the country. In fact, it was from Trinity's school prayer (he had come across it at an Episcopal schools conference while working at St. James in Mobile) that Mad had stolen the words to his 58th thesis: "Hold fast to that which is good; be strong and of good courage." At the communion rail, Mad saw that the rector, Hill Riddle, recognized him. When pressing the wafer into Mad's hands, the Rev. Riddle leaned over and whispered: "Welcome, Mr. Jones. I'd love to visit with you some time. Give me a call."

Mad wasn't sure when he would get back Trinity's way, but the warmth and genuineness of Riddle's words made Mad decide on the spot that if he ever moved to New Orleans, Trinity would become his church home.

Straight from church, Mad's entourage (including the publisher's publicist) drove to the airport for a flight to Memphis. Even though Mad thought Sunday night was an odd time for a book signing, Rhodes College was sponsoring one that evening. Everything went fine—except that there were a couple of cute co-eds there who were clearly, uh, impressed with him, and the attention got his blood flowing. He did, however, resist.

The next day featured a return trip to Oxford, for an early-evening book signing at Square Books (actually, its sister shop down the street) and then another dinner (this time at a gourmet pizza place) with web site founder Mark Mariasson. The secondhand bookshop event, with nice wine and cheese and crackers, featured a standing-room-only crowd. Mad went through his usual routine, being sure to credit Mark Mariasson both for starting the web site and for opening his eyes to the science/ religion nexus that now was part of Mad's standard remarks. When he finished his reading, he opened the floor for questions—and saw the old battle-axe, Ms. Jennings, with her hand raised high. Immediately he turned his gaze away and recognized another questioner. And that question over, he looked elsewhere again and recognized another. That Jennings lady had left a bad taste in his mouth.

But after he had called on a third questioner and responded to him, Ms. Jennings gave him no chance to pick a fourth. Without waiting to be recognized, she piped in, loudly: "Young Mr. Jones, Lola Jennings here. Last time you came through Oxford, I questioned you about your outlandish behavior—and now it looks like I didn't even know *how* outlandish it was. How can you go around the country putting yourself forward as some religious leader when you're tomcatting around with female reporters and God only knows who else? Oh, don't look at me like you don't know what I'm talking about, young man. Your reputation precedes you. I want you to respond to the charge that you are nothing but a bad influence on our youth."

Mad was taken aback. The truth was that, in the 10½ months since Claire's death, the only person he had strayed with was Laura. And what business was it of this old witch, anyway? He took a deep breath to try to control himself before replying.

And then he didn't have to reply at all. Another voice jumped in. It was Mindy, the blonde co-ed. And this time she was more attractive: dressed up more nicely (except for the stupid bow in her hair, which he hated) and, it seemed, at least slightly slimmer than she had been four months earlier.

"Mrs. Jenson,"—as was the case four months earlier, Mindy got the name wrong—"I just have to say something about that. Obviously, I'm one of those youths who you are talking about, and, like, I don't think Mad is a bad influence on us at all. I mean, it's like, you know, we go through college and sometimes we're not always up on God, you know, and then Mad comes along and makes it cool again to talk about God. He can, you know, like relate to us. And, like, not only that, but," she said cattily, "how would somebody your age *know* what kind of influence Mad is on somebody young like me? I mean, you're, like, so judgmental and all, and what makes you think you even know what you're talking about when it comes to relating to my generation?"

They were the rude words of a girl with a crush, rashly defending the object of her adoration from a perceived attack. Mad knew he should be appalled at her rudeness but, truth be told, he got a kick out of her outburst. Before he could think of something good to say, Mrs. Jennings chimed in again, with righteous indignation.

"Mind your manners, missy. I don't believe anybody was speaking to you. But I'll say that if you think you've been influenced by Mr. Jones here, then obviously he's not a very good influence, because if he were a good influence you'd know how to behave like a proper young lady and not like a…like an inarticulate little street hussy."

An uncomfortable and embarrassed hush fell over the whole gathering. Mad could see Mindy's face turning reddish. She looked like she was about to erupt. But then, suddenly, what seemed like anger turned into a quivering lip, and tears sprang forth, and Mindy ran from the room. Sometimes the brash confidence of youth masks a lack of self-esteem that lurks just beneath the surface.

Two of her co-ed friends followed Mindy out of the bookshop, and the audience, agitated, began murmuring.

Mad had conflicting urges: one, to somehow politely smooth things out and try to make the atmosphere more pleasant; and two, to lash out at the battle-axe. Sensing that Mindy's tearful exit had earned the sympathy of the crowd, Mad's second instinct won the day.

"Not to be too cliché about it, Mrs. Jennings, but aren't you casting stones here? Is there a mote in your own eye? What gives you the right to call that girl a hussy? And what gives you the right to assume that just because some Hollywood tabloid prints something about me, that it's the gospel truth? And what kind of influence does it have on our youth for somebody of your apparent social stature to give credence to trash like *The Zodiac*, anyway? You know what, Mrs. Jennings? I bet if you and I compared our beliefs, item for item, we might find we agree far more than we disagree. In a lot of ways, I'm pretty damned…uh, pretty *darned* traditionalist. Who are you to assume anything about me? Do you read my newspaper columns? Do you realize how often I refer my correspondents to either the 10 Commandments or Jesus' two great commandments? And who are you to judge Mindy like that?" (Mad didn't even realize that he remembered her name until it sprang from his lips.) "All I know is that I struggle with my faith every day, and if I can influence people like Mindy to struggle with their faiths, it's a lot better than if they don't even think of their faith at all. Maybe if you struggled some with your own faith, you'd be less judgmental and more generous. I mean, I really don't want to be rude, Ms. Jennings, but darn it, you just made that girl run out of here crying. I just spent a half hour reading from my book and talking about how God's love has been poured into our hearts, and you start talking like you are the very spokesman for the avenging God of the Old Testament."

Mad paused just a split second for breath, and in that instant was seized by an impulse that at once was generous and also tactically sound from the standpoint of cementing most of the audience in his corner:

"I'll tell you what, Mrs. Jennings. I think you've turned a very nice evening into a nasty one. But I'll just chalk it up to it being a bad day for you. How 'bout if you just leave now before you hurt anybody else's feelings, and in return I promise that the next time I come through Oxford, I'll treat you to a nice polite lunch where we can talk theology one-on-one? How's that sound? I think you probably have some valuable wisdom to impart to me, so why don't we give each other another chance, another time? Sound okay?"

The audience burst into applause, and an aghast Ms. Jennings was hustled out of the bookshop by two of her matronly friends before any more unpleasantness could ensue.

Over a restaurant dinner that night that was interrupted numerous times by collegiate autograph-seekers, Mad and Shiloh and Mark Mariasson had another conversation as enriching as their first meeting four months earlier. In the intervening months, Mark seemed to have come a bit out of his shell, to have re-discovered some confidence and some sense of self. And he was absolutely delighted to know that Mad had been making reference, at all his appearances, to the science/religion nexus to which he, Mark, had introduced Mad. Mark had brought with him a book called *The Cosmic Adventure*, by Georgetown theology professor John F. Haught. Oddly, Mad had never taken a course from Professor Haught, although he had heard good things about Haught's classes. With Mark leafing through Haught's pages, showing passage after passage to Mad and Shiloh, time passed quickly indeed. Three passages hit Mad so well that he grabbed some napkins and used them as paper to jot the passages down for future inclusion in his speeches:

» "Ethical concerns are an important dimension of Christian life, but they are not the ultimate horizon of faith. The ultimate horizon of faith and hope is a universal beauty."

> » "Christianity has an important role to play in the future evolution of our planet.... Christianity is intrinsically open to the possibility of further cosmic emergence.... Being a Christian is an acceptable way of endorsing and fostering the scientific discoveries of modernity."
> » "The ultimate context of our lives is a pattern of ever-widening beauty lured forward, held together and felt in its massiveness and intensity by God."

Shiloh particularly liked the third quote, although he said it sounded a little too "newfangled New Age–like" to him if it didn't also note that the original author of that beauty also was God, and that only through God could that beauty be known—and that when it came right down to it, the beauty itself was part of God's very being, non-existent without God Himself.

But Shiloh definitely did *not* like the third part of the second quote, because he said (in essence) that it made Christianity sound like a means to an end in science, whereas he said the proper sequence would be that *science* is an acceptable way to find a path to Christianity.

"The Good Book says that God is the Alpha and the Omega," Shiloh said. "This quote makes it sound like science is the omega that God is leading us toward. I never did quite get into all those Greek letters and stuff, but my pastor says that nothing should ever come before God in the beginning or after God in the end."

"You got a point there, Shiloh," Mad said. "I think Professor Haught is probably addressing that sentence, though, to more scientifically inclined people, in order to lure them into the great possibilities of Christianity. I still think it's a great line, and at times I sure will use it."

Finally back at his motel room that night, Mad took the napkins with notes out of his pants pocket. With them came a scrap of paper. Looking at the scrap, it occurred to him that the last time he had worn those same pants was the last time he was in Oxford. The paper had Mindy's phone number on it. Poor girl, he thought. She seemed so upset earlier tonight. Maybe he should call her and thank her for defending him. It would probably cheer her up.

171

This time Mad remembered to dial 9 for an outside line. Sure enough, Mindy answered. When Mad convinced her that it really was him on the line, she virtually squealed with delight. After a few back-and-forths, she said: "Hey, do you think, I mean, I just thought that, well, like, would you be interested in, like, a cup of coffee or something? I think the coffee shop is still open."

Mad wasn't at all sleepy. Hell, why not? It would probably make her day.

"What the heck," he said. "But coffee will keep me up; how about a beer instead?"

"Ohmygawd, I would *luu—uuvv* a beer," she said. "But I'm only 20 and my stash of it has run out, and the bars won't sell it to me."

"Idiotic drinking age law!" Mad said. "I'll tell you what: If you really want a beer, I'll buy a six-pack and come pick you up and we'll just go sit in the car somewhere and drink it and you can tell me what college life is like here at Ole Miss. I've only been out of grad school for about a year and a half, and I already feel like college was so long ago that I'm like an old man or something."

"Like, *awesome*," Mindy said.

Something in Mad's head told him he was making a mistake, but that's what they did. And in the rural area surrounding tiny Oxford, the drive to a secluded spot for beer and conversation took almost no time at all. And the more Mindy babbled about college, the more Mad's own college days and college habits seeped back into his way of acting. And one of those habits was girls. And sure enough, Mindy went Mad that night with passion—and Mad went Mindy.

And Mad again didn't question why the sex-conquest thing came so, *so* easily to him. Before Claire, he never had been introspective about sex; now he was reverting to bad old habits.

The next morning featured the hour-long drive back to Memphis, a short flight to Nashville for an afternoon book signing, and then a flight back to Mobile. The next two days were extremely busy with column writing and other office work Becky had piled up for him to do. Mad worked very late both nights, until he was bone-weary. (His Monday-night antics with Mindy had already put him behind on sleep.)

The point of getting so much work done was to enable Mad to take a four-day weekend for what would be, in effect, a private retreat with Father Vignelli. Mad had not told anybody other than the priest why he had been so insistent that his retreat be that particular weekend, but he had been adamant about it. His private reason was simple: Saturday would be a year to the day after Daddy Lee had been killed when unhorsed while on a fox hunt. In Mad's mind, in retrospect, that's when his life had begun to change so drastically. Daddy Lee, dashing and rakish and breezily dauntless, had been Mad's outsized living icon. A dead Daddy Lee was so unimaginable that it was Mad's first sign that the world could be flapjacked. Now, a year later, the basically apolitical, haphazardly Episcopalian Mad had become a nationally recognized religious guru and sometime political lightning rod.

More amazing was that he was starting to like it.

Celebrity could really be a bitch. But at the same time, what frightened Mad was that it also was starting to feel really cool. If he allowed it, celebrity could be a 24-hour head rush. A still-wise part of him even worried that it might become addictive. Before he forgot that wisdom, Mad figured, it was probably time to get himself grounded. Hence, a long weekend near a windswept winter beach with a Gibraltar Rock–like, spiritually centered, semi-retired Jesuit.

A friend was letting Mad have use of a comfortable three-bedroom cottage on a hillock, 75 yards off the beach east of Sandestin, Florida. The beaches on that part of the Florida Panhandle are a luxuriously soft and brilliant white, backed by towering, sparsely grassed dunes. The water is almost always a near-translucent, bluish green. The houses, very few of them full-time residences, are packed fairly tightly together, but the garish condos and touristy beach establishments are miles to the west. So, while not exactly secluded, the sands there are usually peopled with only a pleasant smattering of quiet beachgoers searching for a respite from busy lives.

The drive from Mobile took about 2½ hours, and Mad and Peter pulled up to the house a little after noon. After dumping their suitcases inside, the two quickly walked down to the beach. The temperature, as it would be all weekend, was mild: in the high 60s at its hottest (and in the high 40s overnight). On the otherwise overcast and damp (but rarely

173

rainy) weekend, a short-lived gap in the clouds let the winter sun briefly insert its light well beneath the waves. About 20 yards out, odd dark shapes glided through the surf. Mad and Peter stood silently looking out, with Mad intent on those shapes while the Jesuit gazed more toward the horizon.

"Hey, Peter, what are those things in the surf?" Mad said. "They don't exactly look like fish, but they're not just flotsam; they look alive."

Vignelli adjusted his eyes but had trouble seeing what Mad was pointing to.

"There!" Mad said. "Don't you see? Was that a fin? No…what the heck?"

Mad had been watching about three of the shapes, but suddenly they were joined by nearly a dozen more. A wave crested, limpid green, and then it all became clear. As if they were bodysurfing, their kite-like "wings" spread expertly into the current, a group of stingrays soared just barely sub-surface. The priest, too, now saw them.

"Well I'll be," he said. "I didn't know stingrays schooled together like that, much less played in the waves. I've always thought of them as dangerous creatures, but they look positively graceful out there."

Mad nodded, and kept watching in silence. But then the sun hid again behind the clouds, and took with it the light rays necessary to see the sea's rays. And Mad thought there must be a metaphor in there somewhere, but he couldn't figure out what it was.

Anyway, the plan was for a free afternoon of reading or beach-lounging or whatever, followed by a homemade-pasta-and-wine dinner (Vignelli was an amateur gourmet chef and insisted on cooking most of the meals for the whole weekend), followed only then by the introduction to a series of contemplative exercises that the Jesuit had designed specially for Mad. The exercises would continue intermittently throughout the following three days, to be interrupted by nine quick holes of golf at a nearby course beginning mid-morning on Saturday, an all-day visit by Becky on Sunday (Mad had insisted that she come relax a bit), and a tennis match against the Jesuit early on Monday afternoon.

The dinner was divine. Angel hair pasta luxuriated in a creative tomato-basil-secret-ingredient sauce with occasional visits by small pieces of Italian sausage. The Chianti pleasantly and thoughtfully loosened the tongue.

"So, Madison," said Father Vignelli suddenly, just after a debate about which teams would play their way into the upcoming Super Bowl, "What the hell are you trying to accomplish for the health of your own heartsick soul?"

"Huh?"

"The spiritual exercises have begun, Mad. Answer my question: In the midst of your high-profile new life, what are you doing for your inmost self? How are you trying to enrich your spirit? How is Madison Jones finding inner victory without Claire Victory Jones to help him find it?"

Confrontation with Claire's absence hit Mad like a hard slap in the face. It temporarily shut down his brain and made him unable to focus on the real point of Peter's questions.

"Umm, what do you mean?" Mad was stalling for time and composure.

"C'mon Mad," Peter answered. "I know it's not fair to expect immediate eloquence from you; I don't expect you to *really* be able to even start to answer these questions decently until you've wrestled with them for a whole weekend. But don't give me this 'whaddya mean?' crap. You know what I mean. You're going all over the country telling other people how to find God or how to wrestle with God, but you're giving yourself a pass. Well, I'm the hall monitor, and I say your pass is revoked. I'm gonna ride your back all weekend, Mad—and I'm also gonna kick your butt in both tennis and golf, for that matter, even though you're supposed to be the star athlete who's 40 years younger than me. So get used to it. You aren't gonna relax this weekend, not even if you're physically napping on the beach. Even your dreams are gonna be serious work. I'm gonna work your butt and work your butt, and it starts right now."

Father Vignelli was true to his word. He gave Mad some spiritual reflection exercises that kept Mad up past midnight (during which time Vignelli did two sets of 50 push-ups and read several chapters of a new biography), and then woke Mad up at 7:30 the next morning for a brisk three-mile run that, considering the three glasses of Chianti Mad had drunk the night before, left the younger man gasping for breath. Then, while the Jesuit whipped up a five-ingredient omelette along with biscuits, juice, coffee, *and* hot cereal, Mad ambled down to the beach for 20 minutes—but only with Peter's admonition that he should use the time to start considering whether he had the humility ever to follow instead of lead.

Breakfast over, Peter hustled him to the golf course. "Only nine holes?" Mad asked.

"Yeah, that's all we'll have time for, because the rest of the afternoon is all work," Peter said.

Mad was a fairly long hitter, but the older man belted his drives within 15 yards of Mad's on every hole. A nine handicap, Mad ordinarily would have been more than pleased with his performance upon reaching the ninth tee just three over par—but the Jesuit had played Mad all square to that point, and then told Mad that it was *Mad* who would need an extra boost to win the final hole and thus the match. Although the hole (445 yards uphill) was an extra-long par-four, Father Vignelli announced he would hit only a 4-wood off the tee, while Mad used his driver. Mad promptly pulled his shot into the left rough, behind a small tree, while Vignelli split the fairway. Mad advanced his ball another 125 yards, and Vignelli used a 3-wood to trickle almost to the front edge of the green. Mad, always a clutch performer, played a beautiful long wedge shot to within three feet of the cup; and then, with Vignelli's permission, rammed in that putt for a par. Vignelli faced a 35-foot putt from the fairway, over a ridge, breaking first left and then right, with a severe downslope just on the far side of the cup. A two-putt would keep the match tied, but even a small mistake could spell a three-putt and give the match to Mad.

Vignelli rapped the putt authoritatively, though, without the slightest apprehension, and watched matter-of-factly as the ball disappeared into the hole. Birdie, Vignelli, and victory in the match.

"You can't beat me, Mad, and no matter how much you wrestle with God, He'll beat you every time as well," said the priest. "Let's go grab some lunch."

Mad didn't know what to make of this aggressive attitude from a mentor who, in the nine months Mad had known him, had offered nothing but comfort and been an entirely empathetic (although far from fawning) sounding board. He also was confused. Father Vignelli was asking Mad to focus on himself and his own supposedly unmet spiritual needs, but at the same time the Jesuit was trying to break Mad's self-confidence and maybe his will. The first goal was self-centered; the second was self-abnegating.

Lunch was nothing but a stop at Wendy's. Peter passed over a burger for a cheap salad and baked potato.

Back at the cottage, Mad was so tired he wanted a nap. Vignelli said, "No way."

"This is where the real work starts, Mad," he said. "Last night was just an introduction."

What the priest wanted Mad to do was to think of the absolute worst thing that had ever happened to him, *aside* from any deaths of loved ones. He gave Mad a half hour to consider the question, and to come back not only with a brief oral explanation for it but also a rhymed couplet that summed it up.

Mad sat, sweatshirt-draped, on the porch. He came back with the story of how, at age 8, his youth basketball team had been within one point of the league championship as the clock ticked its last seconds, and Mad had the ball. He had just faked the guy guarding him out of the guy's socks and was about to put in an easy layup for the victory when the guy stuck out his leg and deliberately tripped him. Somehow the referee missed the foul, and the game ended with Mad sprawled on the ground as if he had stubbed his own toe in a spastic fit. All that effort and no championship. His couplet:

"A youth's whole world is in the glory of his game / So my trust in justice would never be the same."

Vignelli looked at him skeptically. "No wonder you're considered a pop prophet in such shallow times as these," he said dismissively.

Peter next assigned Mad the task of deciding what was the biggest mistake he had ever made in the first 20 years of his life. Again, he had a half hour, and again he should come up with a rhymed couplet.

This time Mad wandered down to the beach again. Low clouds blocked the sunlight. He saw neither stingrays nor any other sign of aquatic life. Mad came back telling of how, during the summer after his first year of college, he had driven home drunk one night from across the bay. He said it was the one and only time he had ever driven drunk. But, with a date in the car, he had zoomed down a wide street at nearly 50 miles per hour, been knocked off course by one of Mobile's ubiquitous speed bumps, rolled over the curb, and grazed a tree, all before fishtailing horribly across to the other side of the road. Both he and his date had at least been wearing seat belts, but she had been so violently jolted that she banged her temple hard enough to give her a mild concussion. He was lucky, in fact, that nothing worse had come from his idiocy.

"Driving drunk could well have caused a death / I'll ne'er repeat it, not while I draw breath."

Vignelli rolled his eyes. "Profound," he said, in a voice that made it clear he thought Mad's couplet was anything but.

Something in Mad wanted to react with rage. All Peter had done all weekend (other than provide the delicious food) was put him down. But something else in Mad hurt deeply. Vignelli had become such a touchstone for him, such a mentor, that Mad felt crushed by the Jesuit's sneers and aggression.

"Dammit, Peter, what do you want from me?"

Vignelli, standing rock straight like a Marine, looked back at Mad coldly.

"What if I told you, Mad, that Claire is coming back to you tonight for a visit? What if I told you that she is full of smiles, that she looks beatific, that indeed you can see a soft halo around her head? What if she is clearly so full of joy where she is, so blessed with God's everlasting love, that it would make your spirit soar? Can't you just see her? Can't you feel her warm intelligence? Can't you just be sure that she is so good and so pure and so wonderful that your whole world would be perfect if only you could embrace her again?

"But you can't touch her. If you reach out toward her, she floats further away. And what if, while she is full of joy, she makes clear her disappointment in you? What if she still and always loves you, but says you have gone way off track? What if she says you are too full of yourself? What if she says you have no clue what you are talking about when you talk about God? What if she says you've done nothing for the past 10½ months but screw things up?"

Mad couldn't believe his ears. He almost thought he really could feel Claire's presence, and through Peter's words it was as if she herself really were condemning him. Why she was condemning him, he didn't know, because he thought he had done alright. He wasn't preaching anger; he was preaching God's joy, just as she would have wanted. Why was Peter doing this to him? What more was he supposed to do?

Mad broke down in wordless tears. Peter kept staring coldly.

"Cry, baby, cry," said the priest. So Mad sobbed some more.

"Here's a poem by Sir Thomas Browne," Vignelli said. "I've reversed the order of the verses, because I like it better this way. Listen, and then I'll give it to you on paper for you to keep." Peter read aloud:

> "Thou are all replete with very thou
> And hast such shrewd activity
> That when He comes He says 'This is enow
> Unto itself—'twere better let it be,
> It is so small and full, there is no room for me'
>
> But if thou could'st empty all thyself of self,
> Like to a shell dishabited
> Then might He find thee on the ocean shelf,
> And say, 'This is not dead,'
> And fill thee with Himself instead."

Wordlessly, Mad took the paper and stared at the poem rather blankly. But Peter wasn't finished speaking.

"Okay, Mad, now I'm going to give you some passages from C.S. Lewis' book *A Grief Observed*. You may be familiar with the book. It's a collection of his writings in his personal journals after his wife died of cancer. He waited until very late in life to find a wife, and then he virtually worshipped her, and then, all too soon, she had a relapse of cancer and died. And he was crushed so badly that the whole world seemed dead. Certainly, his faith took a beating. Here I'm giving you just a few passages from what he wrote, the very first ones and then some from very near the end of his book. Take them to the beach, while there is still a little daylight left on this cloudy day, and study them. And then write something for me. Reach way down inside yourself and write something really good. Make it a poem, or an essay, or a song, or whatever. But ensure it comes from the deepest recesses of that soul of yours whose surface you rarely go beneath. And don't come back until

179

you have something at least halfway worthwhile. Bring a flashlight; it might take you well into darkness.

"Oh, and you can't mention Claire in what you write. And you can't mention Daddy Lee. It has to be written in such a way that it's universal. So that anybody who picked it up and read it could identify with it."

Mad looked at the priest, peered at him, trying to take in everything.

"Now *go!*" Vignelli said. "Go."

Mad took the other sheets of paper from Peter, the sheets with the C.S. Lewis passages. Shaken, he grabbed a flashlight and walked to the beach, turned right, and kept on walking. The sun was within an hour of setting, but only rarely did it faintly peek out from behind the clouds. A chill wind blew off the water. Mad's sweatshirt had a hood, so he pulled it over his head for warmth. He passed four or five houses, and then there were nothing but the huge rolling dunes that began about 25 yards inland from where the waves petered out on the shore. Mad absent-mindedly climbed up the first dune, down the other side, and up to the top of another one. Wispy grasses sprang haphazardly from its top. Mad sat and faced the water, and looked to the southwest horizon to see a few faint sunset-inspired colors that, windblown, were beginning to peek out shyly from beneath the clouds. Finally, he looked down at the papers and read from C.S. Lewis:

No one ever told me that grief felt so like fear. I am not afraid, but the sensation is like being afraid. The same fluttering in the stomach, the same restlessness, the yawning. I keep on swallowing.

There are moments, most unexpectedly, when something inside me tries to assure me that I don't really mind so much, not so very much, after all. Love is not the whole of a man's life. I was happy before I ever met H. I've plenty of what are called "resources." People get over these things. Come, I shan't do so badly. One is ashamed to listen to this voice but it seems for a little to be making out a good case. Then comes a sudden jab of red-hot memory and all this "commonsense" vanishes like an ant in the mouth of a furnace.

On the rebound one passes into tears and pathos. Maudlin tears. I almost prefer the moments of agony. These are at least clean and honest. But the bath of self-pity, the wallow, the loathsome sticky-sweet pleasure of indulging it—that disgusts me. And even while I'm doing it I know it leads me to misrepresent H. herself. Give that mood its head and in a few minutes I shall have substituted for the real woman a mere doll to be blubbered over. Thank God the memory of her is still too strong (will it always be so strong?) to let me get away with it.

For H. wasn't like that at all. Her mind was lithe and quick and muscular as a leopard. Passion, tenderness and pain were all equally unable to disarm it. It scented the first whiff of the cant of slush; then sprang, and knocked you over before you knew what was happening. How many bubbles of mine she pricked! I soon learned not to talk rot to her unless I did it for the sheer pleasure—and there's another red-hot jab—of being exposed and laughed at.

"Then, skipping to page 82 of my edition," Peter had written.

The fruition of God. Reunion with the dead. These can't figure in my thinking except as counters. Blank checks. My idea—if you can call it an idea—of the first is a huge, risky extrapolation from a very few and short experiences here on earth. Probably not such valuable experiences as I think. Perhaps even of less value than others I take no account of. My idea of the second is also an extrapolation. The reality of either—the cashing of either check—would probably blow one's ideas about both (how much more one's ideas about their relations to each other) into smithereens.

The mystical union on the one hand. The resurrection of the body, on the other. I can't reach the ghost of an image, a formula, or even a feeling, that combines them both. But the reality, we are given to understand, does. Reality the iconoclast once more. Heaven will solve our problems, but not, I think, by showing us subtle reconciliations between all our apparently contradictory notions. The notions will all be knocked from under our feet. We shall see that there never was any problem.

And, more than once, that impression which I can't describe except by saying that it's like the sound of a chuckle in the darkness. The sense that some shattering and disarming simplicity is the real answer.

It is often thought that the dead see us. And we assume, whether reasonably or not, that if they see us at all they see us more clearly than before. Does H. now see exactly how much froth or tinsel there was in what she called, and I call, my love? So be it. Look your hardest, dear. I wouldn't hide if I could. We didn't idealize each other. We tried to keep no secrets. You knew most of the rotten places in me already. If you now see anything worse, I can take it. So can you. Rebuke, explain, mock, forgive. For this is one of the miracles of love; it gives—to both, but perhaps especially to the woman—a power of seeing through its own enchantments and yet not being disenchanted.

To see, in some measure, like God. His love and His knowledge are not distinct from one another, nor from Him. We could almost say He sees because he loves, and therefore loves although He sees.

"As a post-script, here's the last line of the second-to-last chapter of Lewis' book *Surprised by Joy*," Vignelli had written.

The hardness of God is kinder than the softness of men, and His compulsion is our liberation.

Mad looked out at what, because of the clouds, was a supremely dim vista. The sun still had about another 10 or 15 minutes before it would set, but the clouds were so thick it might as well have set already. Only a few pale colors painted the horizon. The surf, Mad now heard more than saw, was up. It sounded like the kind of waves that would create a wicked undertow. In the bleakness, it sounded dangerous.

Mad realized that although he had a pen in his pocket, he had brought no paper other than the sheets on which the C.S. Lewis passages were typed and the one with the poem by Browne. Hesitantly, shivering more from a sadness within him than from the southern winter's mild chill, he began to write on the back of one of those sheets. And he wrote, and he stared at the sea, and he wrote some more, and he stared at what was becoming pitch darkness too thick to see the sea through, and he scratched out some lines and, using the flashlight, he wrote still more.

It wasn't until nearly two hours later, when his fingers were cramped and uncomfortably cold, that he finally stood up and made his way back over the dunes, along the beach, and back up to the cottage. Wordlessly, he handed his poem to Father Peter Vignelli—who, although his mien was now utterly warm and cheerful, took the paper and folded it inside his biography on the coffee table without even a look.

The whole cottage smelled delicious. Peter had cooked another feast. Chicken breasts simmered in some kind of white-wine-and-butter sauce, with a fine palette of subtle herbs and spices. A rice dish flavored with the chicken's sauce. Perfectly prepared snap beans. A wonderful salad. Italian bread. Ice water and (between the two of them) a six-pack of ice-cold Michelob. A fudge brownie pie à la mode. A cup of decaf Irish coffee with a touch of Bailey's Irish Cream for added flavor.

During the whole repast, Peter said not one word about the afternoon's exercises. He didn't explain anything, and he certainly didn't apologize for his harshness. But, with the help of the sensory bonanza on the table, he did manage to draw Mad into a conversation that, of its own momentum, somehow moved from classic movies to Tennyson to Arthurian romance to the legend of Lombardi's Green Bay Packers to (Lord only knows how) a line Vignelli had memorized from a John Cheever short story: "Then it is dark; it is a night where kings in golden suits ride elephants over the mountains."

By the time Mad retired for the night, most of the pain and confusion, the bafflement at Peter's earlier criticisms, had dissipated. With a nice buzz going but far from drunk, he quickly fell asleep.

As for the Jesuit, he did not look at Mad's poem until he was sitting, propped up by a pillow and side-lit by a bedside lamp, in bed in his own room. (This was only after his nightly two sets of 50 push-ups.) Mad's poem began:

"Waiting, expectant, hopeful, scared, / searching, determined, unaware…" **(SEE PSALMS.)**

Vignelli read it slowly. And then re-read it. And then read it yet again, and even yet a fourth time. And the rock-hard priest smiled, and then cried like a child.

The next day, an early-rising Becky arrived at the cottage, all the way from Mobile, by 9 a.m., while Mad was still sleeping. The priest welcomed her with some homemade honey-bran muffins. Even in torn blue jeans and a baggy sweatshirt, she looked sensual enough to drive a man to distraction, and Father Vignelli didn't hesitate to tell her so.

"Lotta good it does me," said Becky in disgust. "The way my dating life is going, you'd think I was a leper or something."

"Find some peace, my darling," Peter said, "and love will surely follow."

Before Mad arose, Peter warned Becky that Mad might be out of sorts that day. "I was pretty hard on him yesterday, and I know he doesn't know why. Sometimes you have to tear people down a little in order for them to build themselves up in a better way. Mad's been masking a broken spirit. And I spent all of yesterday exposing his brokenness. So please be gentle on him today."

"I'll do even better than that: I'll leave him by his own big-shot self. All I want to do today is nap on the beach with the sound of the surf. Far as I'm concerned you can tear Mad down all you want, as long as you leave him able to function well enough for him not to screw up my company."

"Peace, child," said the Jesuit.

Becky strode purposefully to the beach, glared quickly at the grayish morning tide, threw down a towel, and lay on her stomach. For a pillow, she pulled an old sweater out of her bag and placed it atop her *Iacocca* biography.

Forty-five minutes later Mad sat down beside her. Becky was sleeping. "God, she's gorgeous," Mad thought as he looked at her. "No wonder I hooked up with her back at Georgetown." But, oddly, his loins didn't give him a pull as he stared at her. And there wasn't any of her in-your-face, I-am-modern-woman-who-does-what-I-want bravado that was one part sexual come-on and another part warning that she might run you over. Instead, the sleeping Becky looked girlish and somewhat frail. And she didn't look sexy; she looked lovely. While Mad didn't exactly feel brotherly toward her at that moment, he did feel the kind of affection that one might for, say, a third or fourth cousin whom one was fond of in at least a partly disinterested way. And he felt sorry for her. He knew she wasn't happy.

She stirred and opened her eyes. "Oh, it's you," she said.

Mad just nodded. Becky closed her eyes again and lay still. Mad looked out at the sea in silence.

A few minutes later: "Becky?"

She still didn't move. "Huh?"

"Why'd you drop everything and come to Mobile last year when you saw me on the news?"

"I guess I was just stupid," she said.

"No, really. I'm serious. I want to know. I was a jerk to you in college—not that I meant to be one. But I just sort of walked away. Why'd you leave a nice life in Houston for an idiot who you only spent a couple of weeks with?"

"I don't know," she said a bit impatiently. "What do you care, anyway? I guess I had my reasons, but what's it to you?"

Her bitterness struck Mad like a slap in the face.

"Becky, I want you to know I'm sorry. I mean for everything, not just for how I acted at Georgetown. You're doing a phenomenal job here with MMW Corp., and I'm actually starting to think that our enterprise is doing good for some people despite all my screw-ups. But I know you're not happy."

"Look, Mad, if I wanted a confessor, I'd go talk to Peter. But this isn't a retreat for me; it's just a day for me to get away from that godforsaken burgh you call home. And even if it was a retreat, you're not my retreat leader. I'm not about to open my soul to you, or whatever it is you're aiming at. So just go blow."

Mad couldn't think of anything to say to that, so he fell silent. After a while he saw Becky shift uncomfortably, do a funny little stretching rotation of her left shoulder and neck, and then reach up with her left hand and rub the back of her neck.

"You sore from something?" Mad asked.

"Yeah. I don't know if it's from all the working out I've been doing, or just from the tension of running the stupid business for you while you run around making embarrassing headlines."

Mad moved closer and turned over to kneel above her. She was still lying on her stomach.

"I bet I can help with that," he said. "I'm not hitting on you or anything, but can I massage that for you? I think I can help." Becky didn't say a word. Tentatively, Mad reached down and gently used two fingers to rub the nape of her neck. She didn't argue, so he used his whole hand and massaged a little harder. She still didn't say anything, so he shifted into a better position and began using both hands to massage her whole upper back, shoulders, and neck.

"Mmmmmm," she said.

"That feel good?"

"Yes, good," she answered. So, silently, Mad continued to massage for another 15 minutes. Even through two layers of clothing, her skin felt taut and healthy. But he could feel some knots in her muscles, and he worked those extra hard while she groaned in the combination of pain and pleasure that is the usual response to having somebody working on one's sore spots.

When Mad finally stopped, he said: "Ya know, Becky, I'm serious: I want you to be happy. And I'm gonna try more often to show that I appreciate everything you've been doing."

Becky almost shot back a typically caustic line. But for once she caught herself in time.

"Well, uhh…" she said. "Thanks, I guess."

There was another uncomfortable silence, so Mad got up to leave.

"Hey, Mad," Becky said suddenly before he was out of earshot.

"Yeah?"

"Thanks for the massage."

Vignelli had gone to mass at a nearby Catholic church, and Mad was just as happy. Despite rallying that morning in his attempt to reach out to Becky, he was now feeling a little shaky from the Jesuit's tough treatment the previous day. Yes, the dinner and conversation had been delightful, but its effects had worn off while the aftertaste of Peter's calling him "shallow" and a "baby" lingered. And why in hell had Peter made him write that poem if he wasn't even going to look at it?

Eventually all three mini-vacationers found themselves back at the cottage for a lunch of leftovers from the previous two nights' meals. As they pushed their plates away, Vignelli surprisingly announced: "Alright, folks, we're going fishing."

Through some contacts he had, the Jesuit had lined up the free use of a 27-foot motorboat that was waiting for them at a nearby mini-marina. He vetoed their protests that with the dampness and the wind on the open water, the 65-degree day would feel too chilly for a boat ride. "You young people are too soft," he said. "If the wind were lower, I'd put on my full-body wet suit and make you pull me around for a while on water skis."

So they anchored about a quarter mile offshore, and Peter played classical CDs (some Bach concertos, and "Finlandia" by Sibelius, and even some Aaron Copeland, all at a low volume) on a portable jam box (with a combo of CD and cassette players) while showing them both how to play out their fishing lines with live bait.

Nothing seemed to be biting, and as they rocked with the waves there wasn't much to do but carry on an intermittent conversation about nothing in particular. Or at least it seemed to be about nothing in particular. Somehow, over the course of several hours, the Jesuit managed to work in references to a number of poems potentially pregnant with meaning. There was W.E. Henley's poem "Invictus" ("I am the master of my fate, / I am the captain of my soul"), which Peter said would have been the right message if it hadn't overshot its target just a little and veered instead into hubris. There was Hamlet's soliloquy (Peter pronounced it the weak rantings of a self-indulgent twerp). And there was a line from Gerard Manley Hopkins: "Grace rides time like a river."

187

"Grace, my ass," said Becky. "I'll dam up that stupid river and use big old turbines to produce lots of energy from it. If you wait around for grace, the rest of the world's gonna pass you by and leave you sputtering in its wake."

"Maybe so," said the priest, pulling up anchor. "But wakes are for funerals. Unless you want to provide the occasion for a wake, you might be better off waiting for grace to find you instead."

"So we're heading in?" asked Mad, changing the subject with the sullenness of somebody still smarting from a previous day's emotional thrashing. "I told you we wouldn't catch any fish today."

"Oh, so you want to catch some fish," said the priest, gunning the engine. "You shoulda said so earlier."

With that, they roared up the coast and a little farther offshore. By now it was getting dark. Abruptly, the priest killed the engine and swerved the boat into a sharp turn. "Drop anchor here," he ordered. "Now bait your hooks one more time and throw in your lines."

His two young charges, rolling their eyes, did as they were told—and Vignelli pulled out a cassette tape. Totally shocked them, too: It was a Springsteen mix tape. The Jesuit played it loudly. "The poets down here don't write nothing at all / They just stand back and let it all be," he sang along. "And in the quick of the night they reach for their moment / And try to make an honest stand / But they wind up wounded, and not even dead / Tonight in Jun-gle-land."

Suddenly, the lines of both Mad and Becky went taught. Becky squealed as they both started furiously trying to reel in their lines. The priest pushed some buttons and a different song came on, and he threw in his own line while leaving the younger people to fight their own fish. The music blared on, and Peter sang even more loudly: "I believe in the love that you gave me / I believe in the faith that can save me / I believe and I hope and I pray / That some day it may raise me / Above these badlands!" His own line went taught, and then began to play out away from the boat. As it did, the priest picked up the Springsteen words again: "It ain't no sin to be glad you're alive!"

Mad soon landed his catch: a four-pound speckled trout. Becky was cursing up a storm as she fought her fish, and cursed even more when Mad tried to help her. Finally, she landed a whopping five-pound speck.

And then both of them watched, stunned, as the Jesuit strained and played out his line and strained and reeled it in and strained some more. And finally what came to the side of the boat, and what Mad scooped up with a net as the Jesuit held his line, was a 12-pound bull red snapper.

Mad and Becky shot looks at each other as if to ask how on earth Father Vignelli managed to seem so in control of everything he put his mind to, even including control of the fish in the Gulf.

"'Never question the truth of what you fail to understand,' kids," Peter said. "'For the world is full of wonders.' That's a pearl's wisdom from *King Rinkitink in Oz*, and don't you forget it."

Mad rolled his eyes and began to throw his line out again, but the priest stopped him. "We've got our catch for the night," he said. "We're going in."

When they finally returned to the cottage, Peter expertly filleted all three fish, divided up the snapper and the four-pound speck into three equal portions and put them in the freezer, and then worked his culinary magic on the five-pounder, which the three of them shared along with some wild rice and broccoli that he conjured up.

"Is there *anything* you don't do well?" Mad asked.

"I can't do math," said the priest. "And I can't fix anything mechanical that breaks down. And I can't paint or draw to save my life. And my ego is too big. And I'm really, really pathetic at convincing young adults that *carpe diem* should take a back seat to letting grace ride time like a river. All you all ever want to do is run your race like a sprint, sow your oats, and let the devil take the hindmost of all the badly worn, metaphorical clichés I can come up with."

After dinner Becky started gathering her things for the drive home. But the priest pocketed her car keys. "Stay the night, Becky. Take tomorrow off; it's a government holiday for MLK Day. Relax here and sleep late, my darling."

Unable to bend the Jesuit's will, Becky grabbed a blanket and strode down to the nearly pitch-dark beach. Mad washed the dishes and went to his room to read. Peter did two sets of push-ups.

A while later, the priest saw the light under Mad's door go out. He knocked and said: "Mad, don't go to sleep quite yet. Mind if I open your door?"

"Whatever."

So the priest cracked the door open just enough to stick his head through. "By the way, Mad," he said. "Your poem yesterday. It was terrific. We have just one more big spiritual exercise tomorrow. You may not know it, but you've turned a corner."

Then the priest walked to the beach. Becky was curled up in her blanket. He stood about 10 feet behind her. He could see that she was shivering a little.

"Becky." His voice was avuncular but strong, like Ronald Reagan's at his best. "Becky, my child. You're a Catholic, but I know you haven't been going to church. God can't give you a break unless you give yourself one. You're a remarkable young lady, brilliant and beautiful and with a heart much bigger and more vulnerable than you let on—and you deserve to be loved. You don't have to be miserable if you don't want to be. I love you, my child. Come on back to the house and go to sleep. Let grace ride, my child. And let yourself ride on grace's back. You'll be loved if you do; I promise you that."

The Jesuit turned and walked back to the cottage, and five minutes later Becky quietly followed.

The next morning, early, Becky and Mad awoke in their respective rooms to the smell of *huevos rancheros*. Peter had already run a hard mile and a half, showered, and begun to cook.

"You guys run down to the beach real quick," he told them. "The sun is out and bright, but the clouds are supposed to come in again soon. Go take a look at the pretty water for five minutes; your eggs'll stay warm until then."

By now they were both used to following Peter's orders. And it was a good thing, too. They stood on a dune and were amazed. Where the stingrays had played on Friday afternoon, 20 yards offshore, six or maybe even seven porpoises now frolicked in the surf. Neither one of them had seen porpoises quite that close to shore before—and the mammals looked like they were having a high old time. Neither Mad nor Becky could avoid smiling. Then, suddenly, the porpoises turned tail and swam straight away from shore to deeper water.

Back at the cottage, with a leisurely and delicious breakfast over, Becky finally gathered her belongings. There was an ease about her, or at least what for her passed for an ease, that Mad had never seen before.

Before she walked out the door, she turned to them both. She was trying not to show it, but her eyes glistened with moisture. "Thank you both," she said. And then she smiled so uncharacteristically and brightly that it would have made the hardest heart go pitter-pat. "I mean it. Really, thank you both."

Once the two men let their breakfasts settle, Peter announced it was time for the tennis match then, rather than after lunch. "You're going to have to dig deep to beat me," he said as they drove to the courts to play. "You'll need to get rid of all your worst instincts, use your brain and your heart, and then work like hell."

Sure enough, the Jesuit began the match by frustrating his companion at every turn. Vignelli belted the ball on every shot with a fierce and slashing power. As the far younger man, Mad couldn't bear the thought of being overpowered. But with so much pace on the ball, he couldn't keep it in control. Sure, the Jesuit missed his fair share of shots, too, but far fewer than Mad did. And Mad kept trying to rush the net, trying to be the aggressor, only to see Peter's shots whiz past him with regularity. Before Mad knew what hit him, Peter closed out the first set 6-2 and jumped to a 2-0 lead in the second set. Mad felt his equilibrium spinning out of control.

More from disgust than anything else, he tried a drop shot all the way from the baseline on the first point of the next game. Almost by sheer luck, it came off the racket just right. Peter did manage to barely reach it, but his resulting return poofed over the net with lots of air time and no power at all. Mad, moving in, easily flicked a half lob over Peter's head for a winner. The priest just smiled.

Something clicked in Mad's mind. Forget his pride. Forget trying to overpower his opponent. Show some humility and use some guile. On the next point, he didn't try a drop shot, but he took pace off the ball and angled it wide. Peter hit it well and hard on the run, but Mad pushed it back, again at half pace, toward the other corner. Again Peter managed to reach it, but he was out of position. Without using more than half his power, Mad was able to put the next shot away. And then he was off to the races. As fit as the older man was, Peter still couldn't cover as much ground as Mad could. Mad's young legs stretched more quickly and easily. Mixing his shots, using his head, he pulled even and then ahead, and eventually closed out that set 6-4.

Mad also had the advantage in that the Jesuit had run a brisk mile and a half while Mad slept. Mad's legs were not only younger but fresher. In the third set, Mad jumped to a 4-1 lead, and he was serving. The match seemed in the bag. But in that game, Mad got sloppy. After a double fault and two unforced errors by Mad, Peter hit a winner to take the game at love and close to 4-2. Then Peter held his own serve; 4-3. Mad did manage to hold his serve for a 5-3 lead, but in the next game Peter came up with some viciously effective serves, and pulled within 5 to 4. By now both men were breathing heavily between each shot. Mad made a couple of errors, but so did Peter. Mad built a 40-30 lead—*match point*. Mad reared back and belted a zinger of a serve right down the middle. It should have been an ace—but Peter had started moving early, on a pure guess. He flung out his racket, clipped the ball on the frame, and watched as the ball fluttered to the net cord and rolled gently over it, far too short for Mad to reach. Deuce. Mad promptly double faulted, and then Peter ripped a winner to break serve and pull even at five games all.

Peter held serve easily, and Mad, frantic now, fell behind 15-40 on his own serve. Double match point for Peter, and Mad was gasping for breath. He stalled and paced around the baseline for a minute. He came up with a strategy for the point. Instead of a big serve, he put extra spin on it and the ball, landing just inside the service box, kicked out wide. Peter, stretching, got it back, but he was out of position. Mad easily put it away. Peter's shoulders sagged a little. On the next point, Mad hit another drop shot for a winner. Rejuvenated, Mad held the next two points as well, and it was tiebreaker time. The first one to seven points, with at least a two-point advantage, would win.

Peter had no legs left. Mad jumped out to a seemingly insurmountable 6-2 lead. Two sloppy errors later it was 6-4. Then Peter, grunting, smashed two straight winners. Tied again, and Mad felt like panicking. This blasted Jesuit just seemed to have an undefeatable will. And then Peter served an ace for a lead of 7 points to 6.

Mad tried to collect his thoughts. Peter's pre-match words came back to him: "Use your brain and your heart." Blowing a 6-2 tiebreaker lead would be his most embarrassing defeat since the one time he truly failed in the clutch in baseball, when he struck out for Georgetown once with two outs and the tying run on third base. The opposing pitcher, a fastball specialist, had surprisingly come in at Mad with a screwball, and he whiffed at it helplessly. A screwball. *Hmmmm.*

Mad decided, for the first time in his life, to try the tennis equivalent of a screwball. Rather than curve right to left, as most of his serves did, he would try to make it kick out to the right by twisting his wrist and shoulder counter-clockwise on the service motion. He had no idea if it would work.

It did. Perfectly. The ball landed just inside the service box and kicked out wide past the startled Jesuit's reach. Ace; 7-7. Next point, decent first serve, Peter hit his return low, into the net. Now Peter would be serving, down a match point again. For some reason, this tennis match had taken on a furious importance for Mad. Win it here, and the whole crazy past 10½ months would somehow make sense.

Well, not really, but that's how Mad felt. And he thought of Claire and wished she were there watching him. She was the real tennis player, not him. He was a baseball player who used his natural athleticism to win at other sports without any particularly practiced skill. In tennis, she had been the technician. What did she always say? "When it's clutch time in a match, I don't try to do too much. I let the point come to me and just take what it offers."

He looked across the net. This time it was Peter, looking physically whipped, who was stalling for time before serving. Mad almost decided to forget Claire's strategy. Peter was weakened; Mad could finally overpower him. That's what the pride of male ego told him to do. But then Peter, bouncing the ball before his serve, mishandled it and it rolled away. That gave Mad another few seconds extra to think some more. It provided time for a line from Saturday's C.S. Lewis reading to come, unbidden, to Mad's mind. "The sense that some shattering and disarming simplicity is the real answer."

"Let the point come to me…. Shattering and disarming simplicity…"

Now the idea came to him. Mad knew what to do. Peter's first serve, hard but safe in the center of the service box, gave Mad the chance to try the shot he wanted. It wasn't a special shot at all. He didn't swing hard, and he didn't try an acute angle, and he didn't try a drop shot, and he didn't do much of anything. Instead, he just stuck out his racket and softly blocked it back at Peter, right to the center back of the court, with a short pushing motion. Peter, long past being too tired to follow his serve to the net, had been expecting more pace on the ball. He had begun to swing too early—and then in the act of slowing his stroke to wait on the bounce, Peter himself had to push it back weakly toward Mad. With the extra second to prepare, Mad's brain was able to process the court's geometry and angle the ball short to Peter's backhand. Peter, hustling, scooped it up but again was unable to do much with it. Scrambling, he tried to return toward the center of the court—and Mad lightly pushed the next shot behind Peter to the spot the priest had just vacated. Vignelli tried to twist around and lunge backward again, but to no avail. Winner for Mad. Game, set, and match for Mad.

Take what life offers, let life come to him, keep things in play with disarming simplicity. And, another line from Peter, from a conversation over coffee months ago with him and Shiloh: We must avoid a "pride so overblown that it puts ourselves above God and says, in effect, that we are responsible for our own salvation." Forget ego; keep the ball in play and wait for opportunity to arrive.

Against all his instincts, that's what Mad had done.

Mad looked up and Peter was smiling broadly, almost laughing, as he made his way slowly, breathing heavily, to the net to shake Mad's hand.

"Well done, young friend," Peter said, with no sign whatsoever of disappointment that he had lost. "Very well done."

On the drive back to the cottage, Peter gave Mad his last assignment of the retreat. "Write one more poem for me," he said. "I'll give you no direction, but it's gotta be at least as good as the one you wrote Saturday night. Whatever topic strikes your heart. But make it good."

That afternoon, after a ham sandwich and a shower, Mad sat down on the porch to write. It took him three hours. Finally, almost shyly, he handed the paper to Peter, who put it down on the coffee table right next to the first poem. He began to read, and as he did so, his smile grew and grew. He finished, and his countenance was as bright as the sun. He then read the first poem and smiled some more. And then again he read the new one. It began:

"I crave the limelight, the fine light, the big life."

BOOK FOUR: PSALMS

(written on a windswept beach at twilight)

Lost at Sea

Waiting, expectant, hopeful, scared,
Searching, determined, unaware
Of how to get from here to—to where?

Tell me God, how to ride this wave.
From the breakers keep me safe.
I feel the wave is riding me.
If so, I might get lost at sea.

Loves I've lost or never had;
Goals I've set that have gone bad;
Dreams slip-slide away—I'm glad
They came so close, yet mad.

Tell me God, how to ride this wave.
From the breakers keep me safe.
I feel the wave is riding me.
If so, I might get lost at sea.

Every day and every hour,
Every precious we/us/our,
Every struggle side by side:
Will they help us turn the tide?

Tell me God, how to ride this wave.
From the breakers keep me safe.
I feel the wave is riding me.
If so, I might get lost at sea.

Still, friendships, care, abiding love:
They lift me, Lord.
They keep me going, conscious of

A mystic chord
Of memories of future things,
Of times when grace on sea-wind wings
Alights, and of the joy it brings.

Tell me God, how to ride this wave.
From the breakers keep me safe.
I feel the wave is riding me.
If so, I might get lo—
No, might get *found* at sea
By your harsh peace, which sets me free.

(*written on a sunlit porch*)

<u>Good Works</u>

I crave the limelight, the fine light, the big life.
I want the attention, the dimension of tension
Which, I must mention,
Lets me know that I'm known
As the one
Who alone
Got the task done.

Look at me: Can't you see
That I really, freely, have chosen to be
So noble, so giving, so loving and living
That *I* set an example
For others to sample?

Of course,
It's a farce.

Not my giving or loving, nor my coming or going,
Nor the fact that God's showing
My way every day—if I pray.

No, I say, none of that's play.
None of that fake, false, or futile.
For that done for God's sake, in his name, for his fame,
If actually helpful—delightful, not frightful—
To those affected, connected
In some sense to the deeds
I hope lead—
If only
Incidentally—
To praise for me too—Whew!—
That good cannot be done in vain.

The farce is in thinking that I am alone in doing God's work.

Or that *I* am special.

Or that God, who works through me and so many others—
Through lovers, and preachers, and teachers, and creatures,
Through friends and relations
In all of the nations—
With such a God, it's a farce to believe,
He's not the one worthy of praise and of fame.

The limelight shines not *on* me, but *through* me,
To **God**, who works in me and for me, despite me.

But I should not grieve, nor shoulder the blame,
For God has redeemed me—in Jesus' name.

BOOK FIVE:
SECOND CHRONICLES

CHAPTER ONE

Grace Feinstein Martin was worn out. Her son had celebrated his eighth birthday the previous weekend, and what had begun as a roller-skating party had turned into a fight when her son pushed another kid into the railing. The other kid sprained a wrist and bruised some ribs in the process, and his irate parents, even though they were rich as Croesus, had not only threatened to sue Grace but had even commissioned a lawyer to call her at home and repeat the threat. Saturday night, while her ex-husband kept her kids, she had met a man for a rare blind date. He was a total loser. He drank like a fish and kept touching her without invitation, and then (although they had arrived at the restaurant in separate cars) insisted on following her home—"to make sure you make it safe and sound," he said. She tried to ditch him at a stoplight that was changing, but he ran the red light. And when she got home, he screeched to a halt behind her and rushed to escort her to her door. He even made a move to follow her inside, uninvited, but she finally had had enough.

"You are *not* coming in," she said. "I did *not* invite you in. Good night." At which point he laughed and put a foot past the door jamb, as if it were a game. All she could think of to do was to kick his shin, hard, and then when he withdrew his leg, howling, she slammed the door and ran to her room, ignoring his yells through the door that she was a bitch. That night she could barely sleep, and the next day her washing machine went on the fritz while full of clothes and soap and water. And when her ex brought the kids back that night, her daughter was whining incessantly because the son had been the center of attention all weekend.

It had gone hellishly through the first two days of Grace's workweek as well. The lawyers she worked for were stressed and ornery, and a client kept doing things to screw up his own case, and she spilled coffee all over her billable-hours time sheets. Tuesday was February 2, Groundhog Day, and in light of the Bill Murray movie of the same name, she thought it sickeningly appropriate that she would have to re-do the record-keeping work she had already completed. So today, Wednesday, she was so depressed that she called in sick and lay in bed watching pointless daytime TV. Something in her life had to change, and soon.

Grace glanced at a scrap of paper she had looked at a number of times before. On it was the phone number for MMW Corp. in Mobile. Some incessant urge had been telling her for months that she should talk to Mad. Oddly enough, she thought he could give her some good counseling.

Grace had already gone a long way on an inner odyssey that began when she first saw the news about Mad's theses nearly 11 months earlier. She didn't know it, but she also had a long way yet to go.

Out of sheer curiosity, Grace had been in the Apostles of the Word church on that Good Friday morning when Mad told the story of the blackberries and the Rev. Hebert had tried to turn it into a profound metaphor. She could tell Mad hadn't meant the story metaphorically, but she was impressed with the graciousness with which he played along with the minister's interruptions. Moreover, she had seen that the grown-up Mad was a remarkably handsome young man. The attractiveness was only heightened by her sense that in some ways he seemed like an innocent, swept along by events and interpretations that he had neither planned nor anticipated. And yet, something emanated from him, something intangible, that had seemed to her that day to suggest a transcendence of sorts.

Considering how bizarre she had felt just to be in that church, it was a wonder that anything could make her conscious of transcendence. There she had been, an atheistic Jew divorced from a lapsed Catholic, standing amidst a throng of tongue-speaking worshippers in an evangelical Christian church. If the people around her had not been so genuinely friendly, she might even have been a little frightened.

Grace didn't understand this Jesus thing, though. It made no sense that someone could be fully human and fully divine at the same time. It made no sense that he could be born of a virgin. It made no sense that his death could make up for the sins of all mankind. And so on. And this bit about the "Living Word"? What was that all about? Why would a human, much less a god, be happy to be reduced to a single word, even a capital-"W" Word, as the case may be? For that matter, which Word? The whole Christian story seemed to her just like so much mumbo jumbo.

Yet Grace knew that she felt a void inside her. Maybe it was just a cultural thing. Maybe, having been born into the Jewish culture without ever seriously observing Jewish customs—much less having taken any stock in the Jewish faith—what she might be missing was the sense of community that had enabled Jews to remain an identifiable people through three millennia of wars, diaspora, pogroms, and Holocaust. Maybe her Jewishness cried out subconsciously for obeisance, for respect, or maybe even for celebration. Or so she had concluded one sleepless night late last summer. In the next few weeks, she had done a little cursory reading about Christianity and read a slightly more intensive primer on her own Jewish faith. Or, to be more accurate, not *her* Jewish faith, because she was still faithless, but the Jewish faith of her family. Maybe, she thought, if she took part in some important Jewish ceremonies, the faith might come to her of its own accord.

She was encouraged in that direction by Mad's almost gratuitous inclusion in his theses (number 44) of an exhortation that "all, of all faiths, should honor the Jews." Rosh Hashanah and Yom Kippur were coming soon, and Grace had decided on that summer night to observe both holidays not just nominally but with a seriousness she had never before afforded them.

Her family had been shocked. Her parents, nominal Jews at best, had taken it as a sign that Grace was so unhappy as to be desperate; her aunt and cousins, far more serious about their faith and culture, welcomed her participation warmly but secretly wondered if she had some ulterior motive.

On one level, everything had gone well for Grace on both of those September holidays. "*Leshanah tovah tiktavi vetichtami,*" she had said, ritually wishing all her family a good new year. Something about all the rituals of Rosh Hashanah—the bread and apple dipped in honey, the recitation of psalms, the blowing of the *shofar* (ram's horn) at the synagogue—had the feel of being so right, so appropriate, so full of a solemn but joyful hope that Grace wondered why she had ever taken the day for granted. And Yom Kippur, the Day of Atonement, marked by fasting and repentance and communal confession of sins, might seem to an outsider to be a grim observance. Truth be told, that's how Grace, too, had always regarded it. But this year it seemed different. This year it seemed a thorough but gentle purging of her system, the sort that leaves one feeling rejuvenated and healthier.

But on another level, neither Rosh Hashanah nor Yom Kippur really did the trick for Grace. The God of her people was still a God of harsh judgments and of promises of communal rewards that always remained unfulfilled. Her people were a people who, despite their reputation, were a community of amazing warmth. But their faith itself—not their culture but their faith, their theology—left her cold. She knew that it wasn't supposed to feel this way, that for many observant Jews it was a faith of deep joy and hope. But, despite two surprisingly good experiences on these September holy days, the faith didn't yet give her warmth or fill her void.

It certainly didn't both unnerve her and inspire her, and frighten her just a tad in the good way of boosting her adrenaline a little, the way that Mad's lines quoted in the newspaper had unnerved and inspired her several months earlier. She still had that newspaper article she had clipped out, the one that quoted Mad as saying: "Go out and love God today, because in the course of loving we find small but wonderful redemptions along the way." She still didn't quite comprehend what "redemptions" really meant. But in her own way, Grace had vowed to find out. One day. When she had time. When it would be easier for her to think about.

Four and a half months later, she still hadn't found time. And she had experienced four horrible days in a row, and was playing hooky from work and sulking in bed with the TV on. It was early afternoon, and she decided to check out that *Winifred* show that she had heard so much about but had never been able to watch. Winifred was the universally known one-name moniker of the host whose classy TV talk show had made her perhaps the most widely respected black woman in the country.

When Winifred opened that day's show with her usual recitation of who and what would be that day's guests and topics, Grace gasped so hard it made her chest hurt. She hadn't expected this:

"And we're thrilled to have the author of a great new book that's climbing high on all the country's bestseller lists," Winifred said to the camera. "When we return from this commercial, please welcome Mad Jones to talk about his book of spiritual rejuvenation, *Mad Religion*."

For his part, Mad was exceedingly nervous about appearing on the *Winifred* show. In the aftermath of his retreat two weeks earlier, he had at least temporarily found an equilibrium and a humble confidence that he had not known since Claire's death. The book tour had resumed with ever larger crowds that were ever more insistent on getting Mad to comment on the Senate's trial of Bill Clinton—but Mad had become ever more adept at avoiding politics and keeping the focus on his now more tightly honed theological message(s). More and more, Mad got the sense that people were leaving his book-signing/speaking sessions with a new openness to faith and a renewed sense of purpose. Shiloh agreed. He said that at the beginning of each event he had his hands full with making sure the crowds did not become unruly, but that by the end of virtually every session he had the sense that people were paying respectful, even rapt, attention to Mad's words.

But Winifred was the big time. Winifred had clout. If Mad screwed up on her show, or if she baited him or put him on the hot seat in front of millions and millions of people, he feared he could easily lose his newfound inner peace. Mad actually had the sense that he would like Winifred, but he didn't trust himself. His experiences with national media so far had been anything but pleasant.

His fears turned out to be unfounded. What Grace and millions of other viewers saw was an attractive, compelling young man with a cogent, interesting and even inspiring message, conversing pleasantly with an informed, empathetic interviewer. Winifred had done her homework; she took Mad and his writings on their own terms, and asked questions designed neither to embarrass nor to entrap Mad but rather to entice him into elucidating his theology in an approachable, comprehensible manner. The cameras, the lights, and the audience quickly seemed to recede into the background, and Mad felt as if he were engaged in a coffee table conversation at a cosmopolitan sidewalk bistro.

"Mad, please stop me if this gets too personal for you," Winifred said at one point. "But, knowing your story, I was struck by how raw the emotions seemed to be in your theses numbered 16 through 19. They seemed to me to contain the very heart of your complaints against, and anger at, God. And the depth of their pain makes it even more remarkable that you found such strong resolve to return to God in spite of the agony you went through. Let me read those theses, or parts of them, out loud:

"'The words of Jesus to the crowd of wailing women as Jesus was led on his march of death to Golgotha: "Daughters of Jerusalem, weep not for me, but weep for yourselves, and for your children. For behold, the days are coming, in which they shall say, Blessed are the barren and the wombs that never bore and the breasts that never gave suck." Luke, Chapter 23.' And then you write: 'What kind of God, except a fallible God who is a jerk, would curse innocent women whose wombs become with child?' And then you quote several verses from the letter to the Romans, 'For we know that the whole creation groaneth and travaileth in pain together,' and 'For thy sake we are killed all the day long; we are accounted as sheep for the slaughter.'

"Mad, that's pretty grim stuff. And as I understand, you wrote it in a hospital bed where you had gone for some R&R after suffering a horrible triple tragedy, with your wife and unborn child dying of a hemorrhage and your mother-in-law perishing in a car crash. In other words, there you were grieving about your wife whose womb was full, whose very pregnancy cost her her life, and you are quoting Jesus saying that it would one day seem that only the barren are blessed, because they at least would not know that kind of pain.

"Okay, I don't mean to make this a monologue, but am I right in thinking these theses grew directly and explicitly out of your own agony?"

The camera focused tightly on Mad's face. Looking stoic, he merely nodded while silently mouthing, "Yes, that's right."

"Okay," Winifred continued. "And yet you somehow found the strength to turn all that around. Instead of being sheep for the slaughter, you quickly became an advocate of being lionhearted on God's behalf. You write that 'Christ calls us all to be lions.' And you quote the Letter to the Hebrews saying that 'we are made partakers of Christ, if we hold the beginning of our confidence steadfast unto the end.' And so on and so on…. You keep meeting pain with strength, and overcoming disaster with confidence and even hope, and now in the last four or five months you've gone beyond that even to preaching about God's joy.

"So here's my question: How did you do it? Where did you do it? Where did you find a way to overcome the pain of the whole earth travailing and groaning? And, more important for those of us in today's self-centered world who always want to apply everything to ourselves, where and how do we who read your book, or who listen to you preach, where do *we* find that strength? Can all of us, Mad, find a way to overcome adversity as impressively as you have?"

"That's very kind of you, Winifred," Mad answered. "At the risk of seeming really self-absorbed by quoting myself, there's a poem I wrote just two weeks ago—and two lines from the poem are the crux of the matter:

"'The limelight shines not *on* me, but *through* me / To **God**, who works in me and for me, despite me.'

"You see, Winifred, just as I blamed God for my pain, I have to give Him credit for the strength I found to overcome that pain. I know it sounds like a paradox, Winifred, but the best way to become strong is through submission. The best way to triumph is by letting life come to you and accepting what it gives you. I'm not saying something stupid like you win by losing—not by a long shot—but I am saying that we win by being willing to lose, and by accepting losses if they come our way and not regarding them as final. And the God we put our faith in is a God who never stops offering love; even when He allows us to be ripped by pain He still offers love—and so the credit is His, not ours, when we accept that love and use it to find strength and to triumph.

"And, to close the circle, the most important step toward finding the glory of joy is to give the glory to God rather than taking it for ourselves. I miss my wife Claire every day, Winifred, but I am humbled by the knowledge that she is secure in God's love. That's the true glory, and my small job is to bear witness to it."

Another camera focused tightly on Winifred's face as she wiped a single, genuinely heartfelt tear from her eye. And all across America, people watching the show were crying. And Grace was crying, too, and vowing to herself that she would keep searching to understand and to find the love that Mad was talking about.

A full half hour of that day's *Winifred* show was devoted to Mad and his theses and his book. By the end of it, Mad seemed a heroic figure.

By the end of it, more than a hundred thousand Americans who had forsaken faith, Americans who were Catholics and mainline Protestants, evangelical Protestants and Jews and atheists, vowed to return to churches or temples or synagogues and give faith another chance. They were vows that many actually kept.

"Madison Jones, may God be with you," Winifred said in conclusion.

"Thank you so much, Winifred," he said. "No thanks to me, I think He already is."

A few weeks later, the MMW Corp. board gathered in Mobile for its semi-annual meeting. Becky announced with pride that, after salaries and expenses, MMW already had accumulated $76,427 to distribute for charitable purposes. Moreover, it was a near certainty that earnings during the next six months would dwarf that sum. For a company less than a year old, it was a stunning achievement. Nevertheless, Becky as an executive was still a tightwad: She berated both Buzz and Mary for each having the gall to make reservations, on the corporate account, at the most expensive hotel in town. "Hey, little lady, cut us some slack," Buzz responded. "You can write it all off on our corporate taxes, anyway." Across the table, Mary shot a knowing look (and an approving one) at Buzz, while Mad (playing peacemaker) suggested the group just move on to more important matters.

The board decided to set aside $25,000 as the corpus of a new, permanent foundation fund (for as-yet-unspecified purposes), and used the rest of the available revenues for grants to a wide array of causes across the country. In Mobile, MMW gave a grant to a program called GROWTH (Girls Reaching Our Womanhood Through Healing), a new program for at-risk minor offenders; and (at Peter Vignelli's request) to Catholic Charities. In New Orleans, a beneficiary was the Trinity Educational Enrichment Program, a hugely successful summer educational project run by the Episcopal Church that Mad had liked so much during his visit there the previous month. In St. Louis, MMW gave a grant to a women's shelter; in Houston, to an inner-city grocery co-op that was a favorite cause of some oil executives. A soup kitchen in Washington, D.C. also benefited, as did a prison ministries program in New York. In all, 11 organizations earned grants ranging from $1,200 to

$12,000. Justin was upset that he couldn't convince the others to become one of the major sponsors of a local 10-kilometer road race for charity, but everybody else seemed more than satisfied with the selections.

But the biggest decision ratified by the board of directors involved a major change in event-planning strategy. The *Winifred* appearance had been such a success that the publishing house had cancelled the remainder of the book tour (with the exception of one more major appearance each in New York and in Los Angeles), on the quite reasonable grounds that *Mad Religion* was selling so spectacularly that it didn't need any more boosts from Mad's appearances at bookstores. Moreover, Mad's celebrity and popularity were now so great that Becky, Mad, and Shiloh all figured that Mad could easily fill far larger venues than before. Henceforth, Mad would speak at only one major event every other weekend, at paid-admission forums as large as mid-sized college basketball arenas. Mad's speaking engagements still wouldn't be events as large as, say, Billy Graham's crusades, but on a smaller scale Mad would begin to follow the Graham model.

An added advantage of this approach was that it would keep Shiloh at home far more often. LaShauna had begun to complain vociferously about Shiloh's being away so regularly from her and their toddler, and under the new arrangement Shiloh would begin helping Becky with administrative and other duties around the MMW Mobile office when he and Mad were not on the road. Between that and his still part-time backup status with the Mobile Police Department, and one night class that he was now taking as his first stab at college, Shiloh would be a busy man indeed. But at least he would be able to be at home enough to maintain marital harmony. Well, *sort of.*

"You know, Shiloh," LaShauna had said to him, "I actually agree with what Mad says about religion more than you do, and I admit that he seems to be treating you well. But I just don't trust a white man like that; he's using you for his own reasons, I'm sure, even though I don't know what those reasons are. You just better damn well be careful, 'cuz I don't want my baby's daddy to get screwed over and ruin my baby's future."

Home wasn't the only place where Shiloh was still catching grief for working for Mad. When Shiloh reported to the police headquarters once while Officer Williams was also there, his former partner sidled up to him to give him some hell. "You better come back full-time to the force soon, Jonesy," he said. "You know that religious freak-ass you work fer is gonna start gettin' a big head with all his celebrity, dontcha? Pretty soon, young freak-ass is gonna figure he's important enough so he don't need no Negro around no more to make him look acceptable to the Yankee Jewboys who run the media. Yer gonna be out on yer ass then, Jonesy, and don't try to say I didn't tell ya so."

Shiloh somehow found the graciousness to laugh at Williams' remarks as if Shiloh were the willing brunt of a big joke. "Well, Buster, it's a good thing I've got you watching my back," he said. "It's a good thing I've got a mentor on the force who's got enough horse sense for the both of us."

Speaking of mentors, Peter Vignelli, along with both Shiloh and LaShauna, joined the five board members for a celebratory dinner at the elegant downtown restaurant Justine's—and it was a good thing that he did. The Jesuit had a way of defusing tension, and there was indeed tension to defuse. At the board meeting earlier, there had been a constant undercurrent of friction between Becky and Mary. For one thing, Becky and Mary had clashed about the new dual check-signing system they had set up after the incident with Preacher McGee. Becky had to admit that the system operated well—Mad still didn't quite understand the concept or how it worked—but the truth was that she just didn't like any situation in which she wasn't in total control. Anyway, Father Vignelli effortlessly used his wiles to guide the dinner conversation in such a way that Mary and Becky found themselves on the same side of a discussion on the merits of various movies. As for Justin and Buzz (and to Buzz's surprise), the two of them found much in common in their mutual (but quiet) denigration of a few chick flicks that the two young women adored. Somehow, the dynamic worked so well that, later on, Mary, Becky, Buzz, and Justin found themselves all happily out drinking after dinner at a neighborhood dive called The Garage, long after all the rest of the crew had gone home.

LaShauna and Mad, meanwhile, soon were engaged in a side conversation about how even God can, and does, make mistakes. As Shiloh drove home later that night, LaShauna rested her head on her husband's shoulder. "You may be right, honey," she said, contentedly.

"I think Mad really might be an okay guy, especially for a white man. You keep being careful, honey, but I think you might really be in a good situation after all."

In all, by weekend's end everything looked rosy indeed for all the principals of Mad's accidental enterprise.

Time whizzed by. Mad passed the one-year anniversary of Claire's death without sinking back into depression. With his lighter travel schedule, he began putting more time and thought into the responses he wrote for his syndicated advice column, and into more carefully crafting his remarks for the big Mad Religion rallies that Becky scheduled for him around the country twice a month. He also began auditing a theology course at Spring Hill College, and haphazardly (but not infrequently) doing volunteer work around town at a soup kitchen, at Habitat for Humanity houses, and at other social service agencies.

Becky finally began, haltingly, to find a life in Mobile outside of MMW. She went on a few dates, joined a running club, and when there was nothing better to do she more readily accepted Justin's entreaties to join him at various excursions around town. "Hey, pal," she would say when she recognized his funny-sounding voice on the phone. "Whatcha got goin'?"

The little guy, meanwhile, was feeling like a rising tycoon. His Justin Time holistic training business was going so well that he had to hire a personal secretary, and he still had enough money left over that, by late April, he was able to make a down payment on a Lamborghini.

As for Shiloh, he earned a B− on his first mid-term exam at the University of South Alabama, a C+ on his first mini-essay, and a B− on his second one—not a bad start.

MMW Corp. began running like clockwork. Mad drew large crowds and inspired them while avoiding gaffes and negative publicity. His column now was running in 86 papers. The web site was getting so many hits that advertisers were in a virtual bidding war for the right to appear on it. The book kept selling like hotcakes after a weeklong fast. Two of the three traditional network morning shows had Mad on as a guest, and both were friendly and intellectually unchallenging in a way that helped Mad appear almost preternaturally compelling and charismatic. (The network for which Laura worked on *Acute Vision* had also been ready to issue him an invitation for its morning show, but its bigwig Spike Walters of *Hour of Truth* got word of the plans and quashed them.)

As the whole Clinton impeachment-trial imbroglio faded remarkably quickly from public consciousness, so did the tendency of political actors from both the right and the left to use comments from Mad (or others) as pretexts for verbal assaults. But several of the more liberal congressmen did not forget Mad's few critical comments about the president, nor did they forget how useful a foil he had turned out to be in their never-ending quest to denigrate their opponents as right-wing haters. On the other hand, neither the Rev. Rob Patterson nor the Rev. Larry Falstaff nor the Rev. Bill White forgot how, when Mad had left himself open to the left's attacks, he had been used as a prop for an attack on the three of them and their politico-ministries as well. Even on the rare occasions when they kept *their* heads low, this young creep let himself be used as a pretext for calumnies aimed at the religious right. Moreover, what particularly galled Patterson was that many of his own followers had ignored his denunciations of Mad, and had ignored the reports about what he called Mad's "unforgivable sexual licentiousness," and instead had rallied around Mad the more the left attacked. Patterson considered Mad not only a charlatan but also a rival.

Finally, Spike Walters also didn't forget. He despised the whole lot of what he thought of as "those hypocritical Christian troublemakers," and he had in his head the idea that Mad, with his youth and attractiveness, was the gravest new threat from that source. The *Hour of Truth* hit piece on Mad had been put on hold, but it had been anything but buried.

But for now, none of that mattered. All of that was hovering underneath the radar. For all anybody else (including Mad and his associates) could see, the ministry of MMW had left all political controversies in its wake and now was skyrocketing in popularity, without any obvious remaining enemies. With Winifred's imprimatur, combined with Mad's new sunny disposition and palpable inner calm, there seemed little reason to expect anything but a continuing growth in pop stardom and respect. Mad's audiences and his readers alike were overwhelmingly receptive to Mad's messages, not to mention inspired by them.

Seemingly unchallenged pop stardom also carried with it certain rewards—or at least what some people might regard as rewards. Mad had survived the tabloid report that presented him as an out-of-control satyr, and in truth his subsequent night with Mindy had revived his old tendency toward satyriasis. In short, every time Mad traveled he turned into a horndog. As always, it was easy for him: first the eye contact, then the virtual contract sealed with merely a nod of the head or the surreptitious hand exchange of a phone number, and then, after Shiloh had retired to his own room without suspecting a thing, the final assignation and its attendant cheap-won passion. For Mad there was no real emotion involved, but merely release. And because he took these pleasures only while on the road, there was no opportunity for the awkwardness of follow-up chance meetings. In Mobile, Mad remained perfectly chaste, and thus perfectly unhindered by complications or guilt.

In fact, the only continuing troubles that seemed to plague Mad were the now regularly occurring trances of the sort that had plagued him that day on the golf course and the day with the blackberries and the night Shiloh found him with a glazed expression by the ice machine in Atlanta. Almost invariably, the episodes occurred on his first or second day back from his bi-weekly travels. But because Mad worked mostly from home, he was always alone when the episodes happened. There Mad would be, writing or reading or studying, or maybe lost in thought while on an evening run. And then, without warning, there he would find himself 45 minutes or an hour later, having no idea where the time had gone. Mad would emerge from his daze (sometimes with a clammy forehead and an elevated heart rate) and find new phone messages on his machine or random ink scrawls on his papers or books, or (if he had been running when the episodes attacked) perhaps find himself sitting heavily against some old oak tree well off his intended course.

The episodes puzzled Mad, but he tried not to worry about them too much.

The chat room remained a never-ending source of entertainment, enlightenment, and almost enraging idiocy, each aspect randomly distributed throughout the room's pages and pages of cyber-comments. There were probably about 60 or 70 regular contributors now, along with literally thousands who found reason at least once to put in their own two cents. In truth, there was no way Mad could possibly review all the entries each day before chiming in with his own daily comment. Although he tried to avoid paying undue attention to the regulars who had been with the site almost from the start, he still was naturally drawn to a closer reading of their wisdom and wisecracks than he was to the remarks of even the more active regulars of more recent vintage. When Affirmed or Cowardly Lion or D Thom or Ever Faithful or Defender joined the conversation, Mad almost always read every word. And he kept a special eye out, without much satisfaction, for any word at all from Jezebel? or M. Magdalene.

Not often, yet less and less infrequently as time went by, Mark Mariasson also took part. His handle (which he had told Mad) was No Dice, in reference to Einstein's comment about how God interacted with His universe. One day in late May of 1999, No Dice wrote that he very respectfully disagreed with a recent bit of Mad's newspaper-column advice. A letter writer had asked Mad whether God had been complicit in the death of her son by way of a lightning bolt that had struck him the summer before, when his sailboat had been caught in a sudden squall. "Only in the sense that God did not intervene to stop the lightning bolt," Mad had written, before launching into some boilerplate (he had been lazy while writing that column) about how what now mattered was not how much loss the woman still felt but rather how she chose, with God's help, to work through the loss.

"Mad's usually right, but he's wrong this time," wrote No Dice. "Of course God is complicit in ways other than a mere failure to intervene. God is a God of science, too, and it was God who created the natural processes that cause lightning. And God knew when he created lightning that lightning could be deadly, and that lightning would kill people like this woman's son. God does not play dice with the universe. His universe is a purposive universe, a universe always working its way toward a loving goal that God has set for it. And as a purposive universe, it is a universe whose every instant and whose every occurrence is continually used by God, through the natural laws He Himself created, to achieve an ultimate purpose that is His alone to comprehend. So, yes, God IS to blame for her son's death by lightning, even if only by mistake, and Mad's own other writings teach us that our role is to accept God's complicity and yet still love God and work with Him in the furtherance of a better creation."

"Hmmmm…" wrote D Thom. "No Dice is making some sense here, I think. I think he has applied Mad's own theology better than Mad himself did in this morning's column."

"Balderdash!" wrote Ever Faithful. "The pain this woman is feeling, due to her son's death, is a manifestation of the work of the Evil One. God never causes pain; He only causes joy. But Satan takes advantage of man's own sinfulness to unleash evil and pain on the world. All of these other theories, whether they come from Mad's idiotic brain or from you other New Age nincompoops, are nothing but pseudo-religion. Why don't y'all spend less time reading Mad's claptrap and more time reading the Bible?"

"You're *all* wrong," opined Cowardly Lion. "The lady's son hasn't suffered evil; he's been blessed. And it wasn't a mistake by God; it was a deliberate act as surely as God meant to send that tornado that took Dorothy to Oz. The lady's son is in the everlasting Emerald City now, and that's cause for celebration!"

Mad enjoyed the debate. For his daily entry, he typed: "First, I must say that I am awed by the Lion's never-ending ability, day after day, to find Oz-related metaphors. Frank Baum would be proud of you, my courage-seeking friend. But, more seriously, I stand corrected. My good friend No Dice is correct (as is D Thom's concurrence): The logical conclusion from everything I've been saying since my wife Claire died is that God IS complicit and yet that He still merits our love. I think I must've just been lazy when I wrote this morning's column. I'll issue a corrected answer in my column in the next few weeks.

"As for Ever Faithful, I should have said this long ago: You and your cyber-pal Defender have my utmost respect. Here you are in total disagreement with my whole theological outlook, and yet you continue consistently to engage in the dialogue on my web site. That kind of persistence is commendable, and it adds immeasurably to the richness of these chat room conversations. Please keep it up!

"G'night, y'all!"

CHAPTER TWO

Chet Matthews was livid. That SOB Spike Walters had really done a job on him. Or to be more accurate, Walters had demonized a small, privately held oil company whose majority owners were close associates of Chet's. Chet himself owned 20 percent of the company, and knew from a recent geological survey that one of its oil field leases was soon to produce a fair-sized jackpot. Chet already had plans to take his share of the earnings and leverage it for an even bigger deal he was putting together with a subsidiary of a major oil company. And what nobody else knew was that if all the pieces fell into place—and for the astute Chet Matthews, the financial pieces *always* fit together—then Chet eventually wanted to parlay his riches into a self-financed run for high political office. Not that Chet wasn't already plenty rich, mind you. Yet all of Chet's other holdings were tied up in long-term enterprises. Only with this side deal he had working could Chet find the short-term liquidity he needed to fund the political race on his own, without having to ask others for contributions. And that was the only way Chet would attempt the race, because Chet Matthews would never allow himself to be beholden to anybody. Just like his daughter, Becky, Chet liked to be in control.

But now the *Hour of Truth* had come in and done a real number on the company that was the key to Chet's plans.

There had been a little environmental mishap. It was small in scope but at least temporarily disastrous for a small nearby Indian reservation. Walters and his gang had gotten wind of the story, and by the time they finished massaging it into yet another of their stock morality plays, the small oil company had come out looking like a corporate version of Pol Pot. The core of the report, of course, was true: The mishap had indeed occurred, and the Indians did suffer. But the truth was that the mini-disaster was entirely an accident: A worker had mistakenly left some valve open when he rushed off to the hospital after hearing that his wife had gone into premature labor. The company had offered a more-than-generous settlement to the Indians, a huge majority of whom accepted the offer with alacrity. Nevertheless, *Hour of Truth* found one victim who wasn't satisfied—a victim who retained the services of a rich plaintiffs' attorney married to the daughter of the CFO of one of the biggest sponsors of *Hour of Truth*.

The little oil company's goose was torched. None of the mitigating circumstances were aired. Interview tapes were spliced in such a way that Chet's associates, in reality rather decent corporate citizens, came out looking heartless and even deliberately cruel. Within a week after the show aired, credit lines were pulled right and left, and eco-freak activists overran the company's major oil field and used their bodies as human shields to block production. Within another two weeks, the company filed a preliminary motion in bankruptcy court.

And Chet Matthews' secret political plans were effectively aborted.

In her Mobile office, Becky Matthews pored over the latest numbers. It was late June, and she was preparing for MMW Corp.'s semi-annual board meeting, which would be held two weeks hence. In one sense, the numbers looked spectacular. Royalties from the Mad Religion book had been pouring in, and paid attendance at Mad's speaking engagements around the country had exceeded all earlier expectations. On July 1, the 99th, 100th, and 101st newspapers would begin running Mad's daily spiritual advice columns. It looked as if the corporation would be able to distribute close to $400,000 to charities this go-round.

But Becky had inherited her business acumen from her father. She saw things in the numbers that others would not notice. She saw the numbers beginning to flatten. Book sales, still strong, were nevertheless beginning to drop. While attendance at Mad's last two rallies—most recently in Madison, Wisconsin, and before that in Berkeley, California—had been substantial, it had not quite reached the newly heightened expectations. And Shiloh reported that Mad's speeches (or, as Shiloh called it, Mad's preaching) were becoming more and more intellectual and even esoteric. The preaching also had lost much of its edginess. No longer was Mad saying that in the long run it didn't matter that God could sometimes be a jerk; now he had begun leaving out all mention of God's jerkiness. The speeches were all joy with little anger or sorrow, all redemption with almost no suffering to be redeemed. The tone was verging on the vanilla of elevator music, but the concepts sometimes became as abstruse as avant-garde jazz. Mad's charisma still helped keep his audiences enthralled, but they were no longer responding as viscerally as they once had.

"I wrote down some of the words he's been using," Shiloh told her. "He's using words like 'noosphere,' whatever that means, and 'cosmogenesis,' and quoting some guy named Teilhard de Chardin. It's like he thinks he's Confucius or something. Sometimes nobody even knows what he's talking about. But then he cracks a joke, or tells some really moving story about Claire, or something like that, and so the audience can relate again, if you know what I mean. So he still thinks he's doing just great."

Becky figured that Mad, and the non-profit company she had built around him, could coast along for a while. But because Mad was still so new on the national scene, he had not had enough time to be an iconic figure so enmeshed in the popular heart and mind that his name alone could command attention. A little controversy every so often—as long as it didn't get out of hand—might actually be desirable. Otherwise Mad risked fading like so many other flashes in the pan.

Just as Becky mulled over these things, her secretary put through a call. "There's a woman on the line, name of Martina Beritzky," said the secretary. "Says she's calling on behalf of Spike Walters of *Hour of Truth*. Sounds important."

Spike Walters wasn't one to rest on his laurels. Three weeks before Beritzky's phone call to Becky, Walters had ended the 1998–1999 TV season with a splash by crucifying a couple of those asinine oil barons who were despoiling the environment and making poor people sick. But he was already thinking ahead to how his show would open its 22nd season in September. He knew the show's staff would come up with a hot current topic for one of the three segments, and some other corporate villain for another. But for the third segment, *his* segment, he wanted something unique. He wanted to expose hypocrisy, pop somebody's balloon, nip some noxious weed in the bud. He had just returned from San Francisco, where he had picked up yet another public service award from yet another foundation, and he had seen a small article in the paper there about an appearance at Berkeley by this Mad Jones creep. Walters still regretted that he had not found a good enough reason to spank that young jackass on the air. And now, according to the news article, Mad was going great guns in front of a crowd of 4,300, talking about how the upcoming millennial celebration really shouldn't be seen as important at all.

"First of all," Mad was quoted as saying, "the real millennium, mathematically, won't happen until 2001—and chronologically, if you date it from Jesus' real birth year of approximately 4 B.C., the millennium actually has passed already. And nothing much happened.

"People, don't you see that God isn't bound by human time? Don't you see that in the greater scheme of things, the cosmogenesis that is occurring all around us will not be the slightest bit affected just because a human calendar changes to a number with three zeros at the end? What we should be talking about here is the ultimate will of God, not some dumb computer bug and not how many women's shoes full of champagne you can drink from around midnight on December 31."

"Cosmogenesis?" Walters had thought to himself. "What is this flake talking about?"

Walters had put the article aside an hour ago. This Mad Jones kid might be a fruitcake, but Walters didn't see how *Hour of Truth* could develop a storyline about him that would grab the public's attention. Jones had briefly become a moderate pop phenomenon, but Walters had bigger fish to fry.

But then his aide, Al Bobbitt, poked his head in to say that the Rev. Rob Patterson was on the phone demanding to speak to Walters. This should be interesting. Spike Walters actually was in Patterson's debt. Two years earlier, *Hour of Truth* had done a hit piece on Patterson, but had demonstrably screwed up the facts on a major allegation. Not only that, but Patterson somehow had assumed possession of a recording that could be embarrassing to Walters. The tape featured a stray comment of Walters' that a boom microphone had picked up, at one of those black-tie dinners Walters always was emceeing. "I hate those Christian assholes," Walters had said to the dinner's host, during a private side conversation about an anti-abortion demonstration in that day's news, "and I'll do whatever it takes to hang them from their own holier-than-thou cross."

In short, Patterson held in his hands some reasonably good materials for a high-profile libel suit.

To Walters' surprise, Patterson had been willing to cut a deal. If *Hour of Truth* ran a retraction of some of the disputed "facts" from its report, *and* if Walters promised that Patterson could call in a chit one day, then Patterson would hold off on a messy libel suit. But if Walters failed to do a return favor for Patterson whenever the televangelist called in his chit, Patterson would release the damning audiotape of Walters seeming to slander all Christians.

"Hiya, Spike," Patterson said on the phone now, his voice oozing false sincerity. "I got a story I want you to do, yes indeed I do. Time for both of us to settle old scores, both with each other and with a piddly upstart who's blaspheming his way to the top."

"Do tell," Walters said, his curiosity piqued.

The truth, which Patterson didn't mention, was that the preacher feared his empire might be falling apart. His TV show was having trouble finding enough advertisers. The dues-paying membership of his organization was well down from its peak. Sales of videotapes and religious-themed lapel pins and bumper stickers were declining. And Patterson's big investment of time and money into millennial-themed merchandise was not paying dividends. He thought that, especially with the Y2K bug scaring everybody, he would be able to attract a flood of new converts to his version of that old-time religion. But for some reason it just wasn't working out that way. And since the Rev. Patterson couldn't figure out anybody else to blame, he blamed Mad. Mad's blasphemous messages were proving popular. And last year's attacks against Mad from the lefties in Congress had made Mad a hero among Patterson's natural constituency. Good people of the Lord always rallied to the defense of whoever was under assault from the enemy. Patterson had always taught that the enemy of an enemy is one's friend. Now, that teaching was coming back to haunt him.

Not only that, but Mad was now going around the country belittling the importance of the millennium. Mad was saying that despite the year, God's ultimate judgment was *not* necessarily at hand. Even worse, that idiotic Rev. Hebert down in Louisiana kept giving Mad cover by vouching for Mad's bona fides to any evangelical Christian who would listen.

Hence, Patterson's call to his former nemesis, Spike Walters. If anybody had the power to destroy the young upstart, it was Walters.

On the phone, of course, Patterson didn't mention any of his empire's weaknesses. Instead, he focused on how horribly worried he was that a blasphemer, a heretic, was leading his flock astray. "He's one of those false prophets the Bible warns about," he said to Walters, "and he needs to be crushed. It took Winifred to make him a hero; now you can make him back into the villain he really is. I need you to find the dirt on him and bury him with it by year's end, Spike, or else I'll… well, you know what I mean, my good friend. I need a favor, if you know what I mean. Mad Jones says that God is a jerk; I need you to show the world who the jerk really is!"

Spike Walters really hadn't paid much attention to Mad's past preaching. He had only skimmed through the voluminous dossier that Al Bobbitt and Martina Beritzky had prepared for him. All he knew was that Mad had criticized the president and arranged for some guy dressed as Lewinsky to give him a mock blow job, plus what Walters had read in *The Zodiac*'s big hit piece (which had *not* mentioned Mad's earlier infamy for calling God a jerk).

"What do you mean that Jones called God a jerk?" Walters asked. "Did he really say that? If I play that remark right, that's enough to rip him to shreds right there! None of you preacher guys can survive by cursing God, can you?"

Patterson tried to explain that just about everybody who knew anything about Mad knew that Mad had called God a jerk, but Walters was not to be deterred. In his mind, that was red meat to exploit.

"Not only that, but you're in luck totally aside from that," he told the televangelist. "I've already got a file going on this guy. We'll nail him to a tree, mark my words. If you're sure that us nailing this little shithead will make you and I all even, then it's a go. You sure this is the favor you want? Promise me it'll make bygones by bygones?"

So the deal was sealed, and Walters told Bobbitt and Beritzky to make the Mad Jones file active again pronto, and within two weeks his team was ready to roll.

As for Becky, she was delighted to receive Martina Beritzky's call. What a lucky break! Here she was, just now thinking that Mad needed

226

a new burst of publicity to give him (and *her* non-profit company) some oomph, and lo and behold, somebody calls from the most popular TV news magazine in the country. Bingo!

Becky's guard was down. Ever since Winifred had given Mad such a sympathetic hearing, it seemed like nobody much was out to tear Mad down anymore. And with the new peacefulness Mad had shown since their January retreat with Father Vignelli, Mad seemed far less prone to major foot-in-mouth-itis. Even when the mime showed up, which was far less frequently, the mysterious silent actor also behaved himself.

So Becky saw no downside to the interest from *Hour of Truth*. She figured that if they played their cards right, MMW Corp. could jack up the admission prices for Mad's rallies *and* hold out for an ever bigger advance than the substantial sum the publisher was already offering for a second book. Besides, didn't the great Spike Walters have a reputation for always siding with the underdog? He was probably tickled pink that a young guy like Mad had made good in response to personal tragedy, and that Mad was shaking up the worlds of all the holy rollers who posed as evangelists.

Martina Beritzky played right into Becky's preconceptions. Martina was well practiced in the misdirectional arts of a TV news magazine producer. Most subjects, she had found, were so awed by the interest of a celebrity such as Spike Walters that his name was all the bait needed to hook them right through the gills and reel them in.

"Yeah, Spike wants to do a segment on Mr. Jones," she said, as friendly as could be. "He thinks Mr. Jones is a breath of fresh air on the religious scene. He wants to get into Mad's—can I call him Mad, instead of Mr. Jones?—anyway, to get into Mad's theology, and even to give Mad a chance to put to rest all that controversy last year about the impeachment stuff. D'ya think we can set up an interview?"

"That sounds cool to me," Becky said. "Could we do it down here in Mobile? I'd love to meet Mr. Walters; it seems like I've been watching him all my life."

Martina was more than agreeable. "Oh, and one more thing," she said. "Mr. Walters will probably want to interview a bunch of people who have known Mad for a long time, maybe see some of his college records, talk to the professors who taught him theology, that kind of stuff. We usually find that people are more than willing to talk for a friendly interview if they know that the subject of the story doesn't mind. Any problem with signing one of our standard blanket waivers to give everybody permission to help us, so we won't have to bother you every time somebody balks at helping us out without your specific go-ahead?"

Becky, usually so practical, had stars in her eyes. Her mind was racing ahead triumphantly. Sure, Mad had been a hit with Winifred, but to businessmen such as her father that was just "women's stuff." Once Mad got a boost from Spike Walters and *Hour of Truth*, she could really rub her success in her daddy's face.

Because she avoided talking to her father, she was unaware of her father's own animus against that particular TV show.

"Sure, just fax the waiver to us and I'll sign it and send it back," Becky said. "I know it'll be okay with Mad, and he's already given me power of attorney to handle these kinds of details for him. When do y'all wanna come down for the interview?"

Four days later, it was Becky's birthday. As usual, her mother had a family flunkie send Becky another pair of pearl earrings. As usual, her father deposited more stock options in Becky's account. And as usual, her father also called her on the phone to wish his little girl a happy birthday.

"Yeah, Daddy, I've gone another year without nabbing you a son-in-law you can talk football with in the hunting blind," Becky sneered as soon as she heard his voice. "Don't even pretend that's not the real reason you're calling, so you can make me feel guilty for screwing up for another whole year."

Chet Matthews sighed. Why couldn't he have a decent relationship with his little girl?

Becky continued: "But I'm doing you one better this year, Daddy Dearest. We're gonna be featured on the show *of 'Hour of Truth*. I know you thought your stupid little girl was wasting her time on this religion business, but we're raking in money hand over fist and now we're gonna really hit the big time. Spike Walters' producer called me just a few days ago; I'm gonna leave you and your oil business in the dust."

Chet nearly gagged. He smelled disaster.

He tried to tell Becky the story of how Walters had cheap-shotted and killed the little oil company in which he owned 20 percent interest. He tried to tell her that Walters didn't play fair. He tried to warn her that she was being set up for a kill. All of which, of course, only made her resentful. She thought he was competing with her, belittling her, refusing to give her the credit she was due. Nothing was ever good enough for him, she thought. Nothing.

Voices were raised. Old wounds were rubbed raw. Stilettos slashed along hundreds of miles of fiber-optic phone lines. But before hanging up, Chet Matthews tried one more time to make his point clear and set things right.

"Dammit, Becky, you never listen to me! But if you ever calm down, remember this: I want to help. At some point you're gonna realize that Spike Walters has an agenda to make you look bad. I guarantee it. And when you realize it, if it's not too late, call me. I've got some folks here who want revenge on that SOB, and I want to keep you from getting hurt. Call me, and we'll figure out some way to beat this bastard."

"As if I'm gonna run to *you* for help!" she said. "You just can't stand the thought that I'm a success without you. Just go blow, Daddy, just go blow."

Mad wasn't so sure that cooperating with *Hour of Truth* was a good idea. Yes, *Winifred* had gone well, but she specialized in human-interest stuff. Laura's intermittent kindnesses notwithstanding, he had learned to distrust these big-time national media folks. He saw Spike Walters as a "gotcha journalist," always out to make somebody look bad. Yes, Becky said that this Beritzky woman sounded friendly on the phone, but Mad still had a hard time believing the program would open its fall season with a story complimentary to *anybody*. As he saw it, *Hour of Truth* lived for controversy and for taking scalps. He wanted his own scalp protected.

On the other hand, he didn't see how they could back out now. Becky had promised that Mad would do an interview, and a lack of cooperation now would surely just invite trouble. The interview was scheduled for late July, at the studios of the network's Mobile affiliate. Between now and then, Mad had plenty of time to prepare. Besides, the MMW board's next semi-annual meeting would take place in just over a week, and he felt sure his friends would be good at advising him about how to put his best foot forward.

For now, Mad was most worried about his recurring episodes of spaciness. Another had happened again just last week, the day he returned from Madison. The night before that, he had enjoyed the company of one of those pretty, fair-skinned, healthy Teutonic Midwestern girls. She had had lots of energy. She was one of those young women intent on discovering how many times it could happen in one night. Mad had done his best to help her find the answer.

But the next day, back home in Mobile, he had fallen into his longest trance yet. More than three hours just disappeared. He didn't understand what was happening, and it was starting to bother him. A few more trances, he told himself, and maybe he really should see a doctor.

Then again, maybe not. He otherwise felt perfectly fine. And life was good: Nobody was hounding him, audiences seemed to love him, young women swooned, and he had a pleasant routine at home and friends of enough varying ages, interests, and outlooks to keep things interesting. He still missed Claire, of course, and deeply, but other than that he had no complaints. Maybe Candide's Dr. Pangloss wasn't too far off: If this wasn't "the best of all possible worlds," then at least it was a pretty darned good one.

From St. Louis, Mary was due to fly into Mobile on a Friday night for Saturday's board meeting. Buzz was due to arrive from D.C. at about the same time. Don't bother picking them up, they told Becky; they would share a rental car to the (this time inexpensive) motel where Becky had insisted they both stay. As it turned out, it was a good thing that nobody had to pick them up. Becky probably would have forgotten. She was dealing with a crisis.

Late that afternoon, a certain Dr. Theodore Theodore had called the MMW offices in West Mobile. He was distraught. He thought that Mad ought to know what was happening. Just that morning, he had been interviewed by phone by Martina Beritzky. And he had the overwhelming feeling that she was up to no good.

Ted Theodore was the sympathetic psychiatrist whom *The Zodiac* had identified as the one who'd signed the papers 16 months earlier that released Mad from the psych ward. He said he had tried to avoid Beritzky for days, but that she had faxed him the waiver Becky had signed. Among other things (in a clause Becky had not noticed), the waiver released all medical and legal personnel from confidentiality requirements concerning Mad. The producer also had left phone messages for Dr. Theodore at his home, sounding sweet as honey, explaining that *of course* Mad wanted him to talk to them, because the doctor obviously had been impressed enough with Mad to let him out of the hospital.

But Dr. Theodore still avoided her calls until once, just as he was arriving home, he heard the phone ringing and raced to pick it up before his machine kicked in. He had been a second too late—and then had to let the machine run as he spoke to Beritzky (for the first time, a real dialogue, rather than just machine messages), to try to get her off his back. His interrogator, though, seemed to think he had turned the machine off when he picked up the phone.

"Did you really think Mr. Jones was, you know, *all together*, if you know what I mean," she had asked, "or did you just think that even if he was a little loopy, he was no threat to himself or others, and thus could not be kept in the hospital against his will? I mean, letting somebody go is different from pronouncing him totally sane, isn't it?"

"I thought he was a nice young man having a perfectly understandable reaction to tragedy," Dr. Theodore had said. "To tell the truth, I was very impressed with him. Frankly, I thought Dr. Roberts, who had seen him earlier in the week, had been too hard on him."

"But what about all those nurses he made inappropriate advances to?" she had asked. "I mean, from what I've heard, the guy could act like a total menace. I mean, seems to me you'd look awfully good if you could say how reluctant you were to let him leave the hospital. You could be an advocate for reforming the whole system if you explain how little choice doctors really have when dealing with self-admitted patients. Our show could really give you a megaphone for reform. You'd be famous."

"Look, I don't care about any old confidentiality waiver," he had responded. "I'm not talking about a patient to an outsider."

But before Beritzky had hung up, she had wheeled out of Dr. Theodore the fact that Dr. Richard Roberts now was practicing in

Tallahassee, Florida, and she left the distinct impression she soon would be following up with Dr. Roberts—*very* soon.

"I got the overwhelming sensation she was trying to find ways to make Madison Jones look bad," Dr. Theodore said to Becky. "I mean, you can just hear it in the tone of her voice. I've played the tape over again to listen, and it's obvious she's up to no good."

"So you've still got the tape?" Becky asked.

"Yep. And it's all yours, if you want it," he said.

Becky said yes, please, she'd like the tape. But it didn't give her any comfort. If this doctor was right, she had made a *huge* mistake. Not only that, but it would mean her father had been right and she wrong, a thought that made her nearly apoplectic. If *Hour of Truth* were able to destroy Mad and the non-profit company she had built around him, her father would, for the rest of her life, be able to remind her about how much wiser she would be to just take advice (or orders) from him.

And tomorrow she would have to tell the board that she might have made a mistake so grievous that it could obliterate all the company's gains. This was an utter disaster.

It was a disaster Becky couldn't figure out how to fix. So, despite some of the personal strides she had made since the retreat with Father Vignelli, Becky reverted to her usual method of dealing with looming failure that she couldn't control. She rushed home, opened an extra-large bottle of wine, and started guzzling it like grape juice.

The next day, Becky ran the board meeting with a fierce hangover. The others couldn't figure out why she seemed so unenthusiastic, so lifeless, when the numbers she reported all looked so good. Together the board enjoyed deciding which charities would be the worthiest recipients of the $397,438 that MMW had available for distribution. ("This just rocks, dudes; this absolutely rocks!" enthused Justin.) But they didn't understand why Becky refused to accept the pay raise that Mad offered her, as he gave her ample and eloquent credit for the company's successes. "Stupid slut-whores don't deserve any more pay," she replied in a dead voice, as the rest of the board tried to figure if she was somehow attempting to sound facetious. After not too much longer, Becky's odd, downbeat mood began to wear on them.

Finally, Buzz could stand it no longer: "Lookit, what in God's name is eating you?!"

Becky sighed. And steeled herself. And then she finally launched into an explanation of Spike Walters' interest in Mad, and her own signing of the confidentiality waiver (Mad blanched), and her father's warning, and Dr. Theodore's report of Martina Beritzky's apparently unfriendly agenda. "And now Spike Walters is due down here to interview Mad in 11 days," Becky said, "and if Walters is out to get you, you're pretty much a goner."

Becky said this while staring relentlessly down at the tabletop in front of her and rubbing her palms repeatedly across her temples and down around the back of her neck. Her strawberry-blonde hair, usually so lustrous, had taken on an aspect of wilted hay. She was taking this as hard as if her whole self-worth were tied up in her immunity from bad decisions concerning the corporation. She looked positively ill.

As usual, Mary was the implacable one. As she had done at other meetings, she quietly took charge.

"Now, Becky, what's that you said about your father wanting revenge on Spike Walters?" Mary asked. "He's got lots of money and power; why don't we see what *he* can do to bail us out?"

"I'd rather die," said Becky, without much conviction.

But the others all warmed to the suggestion.

"Look, Becky, even though I've been against this *Hour of Truth* thing ever since you mentioned it to me, I don't think it's the disaster you're making it out to be," Mad finally said. "I think I can handle Spike Walters okay. I'll take whatever he dishes out. But what's the harm in us calling your dad and seeing what he can do to make it easier on us? Hell, I'll be glad to call him myself and tell him what a wonderful job you're doing and how incredibly talented you are. I'll make it so that asking him for help here won't sound like some kind of panic move, but like—oh, I don't know, like a mutually beneficial business deal or something. How's that sound, Beck? I promise you won't be embarrassed."

In the end, Becky gave in. That day, she didn't have much fight in her to start with, anyway. She tracked down her father coming home from his favorite Houston golf course, and put him on speakerphone so all five board members could kibitz.

"That sumbitch Walters is always up to no good!" Chet exclaimed when he was apprised of the situation. "He's a nasty, cheap-shot-artist sumbitch and the turd of all turds. We need to flush him down the crapper, and flush him *but good!*"

Becky wasn't up for saying much, so Mad jumped in: "Becky said, Mr. Matthews, that you might have some ideas about how to block Walters. Said that you knew some people who could hurt him, or something like that?"

"No specific ideas, son, just me and some other bidnessmen with a desire to slap that sumbitch so silly that he thinks he's Jerry Lewis. But I'll tell you what: How reliable do you think that doctor is, the one who warned you about the tone of that interview? Do you think he'd be believable on camera if he said that the producer lady was clearly out to nail your hide?"

"Hey, Daddy, it's me again," Becky said into the speaker. "I was the one who spoke to the doctor, and he sounded like a good guy. But nobody would have to just take his word for it; he says he's got the whole thing on tape. His answering machine recorded the whole conversation. He dropped the tape off to me this morning. I haven't had time to listen to it yet, but I've got it right here in my purse."

"Hot damn, little girl, you got game! Mr. Hidden Microphone gets caught by a hidden microphone! This is bee-you-tiful! This gives us sumthin' good to start with. That's my girl! Let's hear this tape right now. You got a machine can play it for us?"

Never mind that Becky had lucked into the tape; Chet Matthews was giving his daughter the credit as if she herself had deliberately sucked Walters (or, actually, Martina Beritzky) into a ruse.

Everybody assembled listened intently to the tape of Beritzky's voice: "Letting somebody go is a different thing from pronouncing him totally sane, isn't it...? From what I've heard, the guy could act like a total menace..."

"That sure as hell ain't no objective reporter," Chet said from his car phone. "If we could get Walters himself sounding so biased ahead of time, maybe we'd have a fightin' chance to put his sorry ass in a noose." (Chet Matthews didn't mind mixing metaphors.)

This time it was Buzz who spoke up: "You know, my friend Steve Matheson doesn't like Spike Walters, either. Steve's an up-front guy; he doesn't like all those hidden agendas and that 'gotcha journalism' stuff with edited remarks and all that. He said over a beer one night that he'd like to put a hidden camera on Walters the way Walters does to everybody else—and, come to think of it, the same way that doctor in effect had a hidden microphone taping the phone call with that producer lady. Wouldn't that be pretty sweet? I bet I could even get Steve to play it on his show if we caught ol' Spike on camera deliberately screwing us over."

"Cool, dude!" chimed in Justin, high-pitched voice climbing even more than normal. "Screw the screwer and make him the screwee instead! A sting operation! Redford and Newman stuff! That'd be just the coolest!"

Both Buzz's and Justin's voices were unfamiliar to Chet, and Justin's threw him off a little. But Chet warmed very quickly to the idea.

"I'll tell you what, folks. Why don't we just set a trap for this turd? No reason we can't pull off a hidden camera. How much time we got before he interviews you, Madison?"

"Eleven days from now, Daddy—but I don't see how we can set up a camera," Becky said. "The interview is at the local network studio. They'll be totally in control."

"Christ, little girl, that's what negotiatin' is for! Come up with some reason—any cockamamie excuse'll do—for insisting that the interview be conducted there in your offices, or at Madison's house, or someplace like that. Don't take no for an answer! And between now and then, I'll pay for whatever technician you hire to go set up a camera in a wall or in a bookshelf or, or, uh, through a mirror, or however the crap these things are done. But damn, if we get him on camera doing somethin' crooked in the interview, we'll have some damn good leverage. We can figure out what to do with the film later, but the first step is catching this bastard in the first place. Just go to it, girl, and send me the bill! I'll be damned if ol' Spike is gonna mess with my daughter. Before I let him bust up your business, Becky, I'll stick that turd where the sun don't shine!"

Matthews' take-no-prisoners attitude was so infectious that even Becky forgot for a moment to keep hating him. She resented his "little girl"-ing her, but when she thought back on the conversation later she would find herself touched by the fact that, however much of an ogre she tried to make him, her father seemed to genuinely care what happened to her. As for the rest of the board, by the time Chet hung up, they were ready for battle.

As it turned out, Spike Walters was delighted with the invitation to film at the MMW offices. "As we're going in, be on the lookout for any good little details," he told Beritzky, "You know, anything that shows ostentatious wealth that makes him look like one of those people using religion to make a quick buck, or anything that shows him to have a big ego, like pictures of him with celebrities…that kind of thing. Get that stuff on video, and we'll show what a fraud he is."

"Oh, we'll have no trouble blowing him out of the water," said the producer. "The shrink in Tallahassee, Dr. Roberts, gave us all kinds of good stuff to use. He said this Jones kid showed a hostile streak a mile wide, and some severe sexual hang-ups. As a matter of fact, when he saw Jones on the news just a few days after the other doctor let Jones out of the hospital, he Xeroxed the written records of his analyses of Jones. As long as we don't say that we got the records from him, we're free to use them however we want. For a little fee, of course."

Walters chuckled. "Good, good, good. But don't stop there. Any good pics we can take of his house or office, to make him look like the profiteer charlatan he is, don't hold back. I'll never forget seeing that little pissant pretending to be President Clinton getting a blow job! If we don't pick off these right-wing jackasses one by one, they'll be taking over the country. But not while Spike Walters can do anything about it! I'll tell you that: not while Spike's around."

Five days before the interview, Laura Green called Mad on his cell phone. It was the first time they had spoken since their canoodling (and its aftermath) the previous November.

"Hey, sweetheart," she said. "I wish I were calling for something fun like a rendezvous or something, but there's no time for that right now. Mad, I've just found out that you're up shit's creek. Word around the network offices up here is that Spike Walters is out to castrate you. I don't know what you did to get on his bad side, but he's aiming to make you his first big scalp of the news season. Or not a scalp, actually, but a eunuch. He's going after your balls, Mad. This is serious."

Since her mini-flurry of publicity last fall, Laura had continued to attract a high enough percentage of male TV viewers that *Acute Vision* had again been renewed for at least the first half of another season. That moderate success, combined with Laura's talent for internal politics, had kept her near the top of the network's short list of rising young stars. In addition to her main duties with *Acute Vision* and an infrequent cameo on the nightly news, she now was slated for one segment of *Hour of Truth* (subject yet to be determined) in the coming season, so the network brass could see if she could handle the big time.

The only problem was that she and Martina Beritzky flat-out didn't like each other. It was one of those situations in which when young women clash, they *really* clash. In the network's pecking order, they were approximately equal: Laura had a leg up because she was on-air talent, but Martina had the plum assignment of working for the network's only perennial, money-in-the-bank, Nielsen-ratings heavyweight. Laura had an added advantage in that her hotshot network boyfriend had hinted that a marriage proposal would finally be in the offing by summer's end. But Martina wasn't far behind: She was sleeping with a high-profile, artsy-social A-list consumer advocate attorney.

In short, Laura wanted Martina to fail. And when she heard the talk about Mad's being the target of Spike Walters and Martina (and Walters' creepy assistant, Al Bobbitt), she had even more reason for wanting to see a project blow up in Martina's face.

Hence, the phone call.

For the most part, Mad now trusted Laura. He still had a tiny spot of doubt about her in the back of his mind, but he made a spur-of-the-moment decision to bring her at least partly into his confidence on this. After all, she *was* being kind enough to call, out of the blue, with this warning.

Mad told Laura about the answering machine tape of Martina Beritzky's call to Dr. Theodore, and about how he and his friends were now aware that Spike Walters meant them harm. (He did not yet tell her about their plans to install a secret camera in his office.)

"God, it's good to hear from you, Laura!" he concluded.

Laura asked Mad if there was anything she could do (*very* quietly, obviously) to help.

"I dunno, Laura. Thanks for offering. I guess if there's any way to find out exactly how he intends to hit me, what kinds of questions he's gonna try to trip me up with…that'd help. In fact, any intelligence you can give us about his plans would help. The more we know, the better. For that matter, I don't even know why he's after me. What did I ever do to Spike Walters?"

"Dunno," Laura said. "But this producer Beritzky is a bitch and a half. I have no idea what else exactly I can learn for you, but anything I find out I'll be glad to pass along. But, sweetheart…?"

"Yeah?"

"Please be careful. These people can really ruin you if you give them the slightest opening."

"Believe me, Laura, I'm not taking this lightly. But you're really sweet to call, and anything else you can find out, please lemme know…. But anyway, girl, how've you been doing? You're looking mighty good on your show when I get a chance to check you out."

So the two of them talked pleasantries for about seven or eight minutes more, and then Laura again promised to keep an ear to the ground for him. And after they hung up, Mad called Becky to give her the news.

Two days before the interview, The Colonel called. He said he had received word that some lowlifes named Bobbitt and Bitchkey had been snooping around the University of Virginia, asking questions about the Crazy Eights. "They won't find anything bad about us, of course, or at least nothing bad that's true," he said, "'cuz there's nothin' bad to find, I say, there's nothin' bad there to find. But I say, son, I say, I just want to ask you that whatever's going on, you keep your nose clean and watch the society's back. We're all behind you, son, I say, we're all behind you. You been keeping your nose clean and staying out of controversy, and our wives are all saying you come across as a nice young man. But now these reporter creeps from some highfalutin' TV show are asking lotsa questions, and we don't want either you, or us, to get hurt."

The Colonel paused for breath. "Now what the heck's going on with these snoops, anyway? You got any idea what they're up to?"

The Colonel always made Mad nervous. Mad always suspected that because The Colonel was part of a secret society, he had a hidden agenda as well. But because Mad's father and great-uncle had been members, and because Daddy Lee had been loosely affiliated with the group, Mad always gave the Eights the benefit of the doubt. He filled in The Colonel on everything he knew about Spike Walters' agenda, and about the plans the MMW board (and Chet) had cooked up to surreptitiously videotape the interview. What they would do with the tape, Mad still didn't know.

"That's rich, son, I say, that's really rich! Videotape the videotapers! I love it! And you say Chet Matthews is involved? I've heard of him before. Tough-as-nails businessman, he is. But honest, I've heard. He'll run you over like he's a tank, but no dirty deals. He'll always have an angle, but he'll never cheat. Or so I've heard. Maybe I can have some of my people get in touch with him. Maybe together we can teach a lesson to old Spike Walters. I say, son, maybe we can make old Spike lose his toupee—and that lump the toupee's attached to, if you know what I mean, son."

Abruptly as always, the line went dead.

The day before the scheduled interview, technicians finished installing the hidden videotaping system in the MMW offices, and taught Shiloh how to operate it from inside a closet. (Becky would be sitting in the interview room, off camera but close enough to provide any factual assistance needed.) That night, Shiloh and LaShauna (their toddler in tow) joined Mad and Father Vignelli at a little chapel on the Spring Hill campus.

"Let us pray," said the Jesuit. "Tonight, Lord, we pray for wisdom and courage, for patience and for insight. Tomorrow our friend Madison will be accosted by people who mean to do him harm. Tomorrow Madison will be tested. Tomorrow, Madison's very ministry may be at stake. It is not an orthodox ministry, Lord, and his is not a theology fully consonant with the One True Faith to which I have devoted my life—but Mad is nevertheless bringing sheep back into the fold, Lord. Mad is bringing people back to You who have long utterly rejected You. I have seen them come back to You, Lord, and I have seen their lives transformed in Your love because of his ministry. Madison Jones is doing good work, Lord, and we pray tonight that his work not be destroyed. So, therefore, in tomorrow's interview, we pray that You give him the mental acuity and the spiritual grace to turn an intended attack into an opportunity. Whatever happens tomorrow will be part of a broadcast seen by 25 million Americans, Lord. Please let Madison parry whatever thrusts come his way, not with anger but with love. Please let him be a vessel for Your love, and let his words be a vessel for Your truth, so that those 25 million Americans are not enraged by Madison's weaknesses, but inspired by his ultimate dedication to You and by the redemptions he has found despite his pain.

"And Lord, finally we pray that those who interview Mad tomorrow will themselves have their hearts transformed, so that when they craft their story for broadcast, they will be moved to fairly and responsibly and sympathetically represent our friend Madison Jones. All of this we pray, Lord, in the name of and through your Son, our Savior, Jesus Christ, and through the Holy Ghost. Amen."

"Amen," said the other three, in unison. "Amen!" merrily shouted the nearly two-year-old Gloria Jones from a hiding place underneath a pew. Shiloh had begun to add a "Praise the Lord" but instead began chuckling at his daughter's timing.

"Thanks, y'all," said Mad. "I'm really nervous about tomorrow. This little session has helped. Really. Thanks. Have a good night. And Shiloh, I'll see you in the morning."

As scheduled, the *Hour of Truth* crew arrived at the MMW offices at 9 a.m. sharp to begin setting up. Shiloh, equipped with some water and even a small makeshift pissoir, already was ensconced in the hidden closet. Martina Beritzky and Al Bobbitt acted oh so benevolently, as if their highest calling were to give a positive forum to a young, unordained preacher. And Becky and Mad (and MMW's grandmotherly secretary) all acted slightly starstruck, as if they were honored and thrilled that *Hour of Truth* found them worthy of attention. (Justin, too, was there, having taken the morning off, and he kept flitting around nervously, getting in the way.) The technical crew, seven people strong, unraveled lots of electrical cord, and moved chairs around and moved them around again, and fiddled with their huge light stands, and whispered back and forth with Martina in conspiratorial tones. But one cameraman, a bearded Hispanic in his 30s, did find the opportunity to pull Mad aside and whisper, apropos of apparently nothing: "I don't care what my bosses think; I think you're onto something. No matter what happens, don't give up, okay?"

As for Spike Walters, he didn't arrive until nearly 10:30. He was muttering some complaint, inaudible to Becky, about the lack of some amenity or other in "this pathetic little burgh" of Mobile. (Oddly, Becky bristled when she heard this, even though she had until recently regarded Mobile with the same contempt.) Crankily, he ignored Becky as somebody wholly unimportant. But, as if turning on his personality with the flick of a switch, he immediately assumed an ingratiating manner when he was introduced to Mad.

"You're all the rage, young man," Walters said, so convincingly jovial that Mad might not have noticed the smarm if his antennae hadn't already been attuned to it. "Here you are, just beginning your little career, and already you've made a wave or two. Well, Spike here is gonna make you a household name beyond your wildest imagination, young man. Yes, Spike here knows what power is, and believe me, Spike can guarantee that Mr. and Mrs. Six-Pack will be talking about you once Spike's done making you famous."

Mad made sure to beam like an ingénue. "You're awfully kind to come down here, sir," he said. "I'm incredibly flattered that you are interested in anything I have to say."

So all appeared to be sweetness and light as the two men, following Martina's stage directions, took their respective seats. And when the camera lights finally shone red, Spike Walters had the inquisitive smile on his face of an ever reasonable interlocutor.

"So, you've got yourself a wonderfully redemptive story, Mr. Jones, don't you?"

"Well, sir..."

"No need to 'sir' me; we're all friends here."

"Well, sir, I mean not 'sir,' but you know, anyway, I don't know if anybody should see *me* as some redemptive example, or anything like that. I mean, I'd rather not have had the dire straits in the first place that you're saying I was redeemed from. The important thing is…"

Again, Walters interrupted. He was a master at this business of pretending to be so kind that he looked like the good guy on camera while at the same time throwing his interviewees off their message by cutting them off just before they made the point *they* wanted made.

"Those dire straits you mention," he said. "I guess anybody would sympathize, now wouldn't they? There you were with a beautiful young wife, still newlyweds, and she was pregnant, and then, mysteriously, she died alone next to you in your bloody bed. It would make anybody just sick with grief, now, wouldn't it?"

"Oh, I can't even begin to tell you," Mad said. "I mean, the shock of that is just so great that you have trouble even thinking straight, and…"

(Becky blanched. She saw that Mad had given Walters a perfect setup line.)

"Thinking straight is really the nub of it, isn't it, Mr. Jones? There you were, grief-stricken, and so you ended up in a psychiatric ward. Tell us about that, Mr. Jones."

Walters still had empathy painted all over his face. Mad knew that even with advance warning, he already had stepped right into the quicksand he had been determined to avoid. It was one thing to go into an interview expecting to be set up; it was a far tougher thing, even when supposedly prepared, to actually keep one's wits when being interviewed by such a master.

In the closet next door, Shiloh watched his tiny video feed and felt queasy in the pit of his stomach.

The good news was that Mad knew this topic would come up, and had prepared extensively for it. The bad news was that Spike Walters somehow was already in total control of the interview. Mad had a prop ready in his pocket—a prop he had not intended on relying upon quite so soon—but, feeling defensive, he pulled it out now.

"Well, I want to make clear that this was always a matter of my own choice, of me just wanting a place to hide from the world, not of me being committed or anything like that. I checked myself in of my own free will, and when I was ready to leave, this is what the doctor wrote…" Mad looked down as if to begin reading from his prop, which was Dr.

Theodore's exit evaluation of him that, among other things, called Mad "grieving but well-adjusted. A thoroughly charming young man, bereaved but neither beaten nor bereft of his full faculties." But Mad never got to read it. Spike Walters, reading from a similar hospital evaluation form that magically appeared in his hand, said:

"Oh, yes, the doctor. Here's what the attending physician wrote, man by the name of Dr. Richard Roberts. He wrote that you were belligerent. He also wrote, and I quote, that you were 'full of unresolved sexual angst, even to the point of obsessing about bestiality, and full of rage, and highly emotionally unstable.' Now some would say this suggests that you…"

This time it was Mad who interrupted.

"Wrong doctor, Mr. Walters. That's not fair! What Dr. Theodore wrote was…"

"This is all part of the record, Mr. Jones. If you'll just calm down"— Walters smiled reassuringly for the camera—"you'll see how we're just establishing a context for you that lets you explain your unique religious views. We're trying to understand you, Mr. Jones, trying to be genderous to you…"

Walters screwed up his face and turned to Martina. "Damn, that came out 'genderous' instead of 'generous.' Cut that; let's do it over."

Mad, incredulous, watched as the camera light went off, and then Walters caught a breath, and then Walters nodded to the cameraman and the light went on again. As if it was part of an uninterrupted train of thought, Walters repeated: "We're trying to understand you, Mr. Jones, just trying to be as generous to you as we can be."

"But Mr. Walters! I…"

"Context is everything in your line of work, isn't it, Mr. Jones? That's why we want to give you the benefit of every doubt. Mental illness these days isn't as much of a stigma as it once was, so we want to let you establish your prior mental illness in case you need it to explain anything else we cover. For instance, in the light of this bit about bestiality, it's almost a relief to know that, if other published reports are right, that you're a rather randy young ladies' man. Now isn't that right?"

The rout was on.

If Mad left an obvious opening, Walters dived in. If Mad seemed to have a good answer prepared, Walters interrupted and changed the subject. If Walters messed up, they stopped the tape and re-started it. If Mad said something that sounded the least bit charismatic or wise, Spike found a way to turn the statement on its head.

For instance, in talking about the Crazy Eights (of which Mad said, truthfully, he was not a member), Mad said this: "I know nothing about how they operate, but I've heard they are famous for giving anonymous gifts to their university. You're wrong to condemn them for secrecy, because they are merely following the advice of Christ himself. Jesus said that when you give alms, do it in secret, and beware of practicing piety in front of men, but do it in secret instead, so that you'll be doing good deeds for the sake of the good itself and not for the sake of having others praise you for your generosity."

It was one of the longest uninterrupted statements Mad had been allowed to make all morning, partly because Walters had been sipping a glass of water. But Walters' mind had not a bit of the slowness of some of his septuagenarian contemporaries. He came right back at Mad by pulling out of thin air a biblical quote, even though he himself disdained most religion.

"But didn't Jesus also say something about how you shouldn't hide your light under a bushel?" Walters asked. "Any clever young Bible-thumper can quote the Good Book out of context to justify all sorts of nefarious action, now isn't that true? That's been the favorite trick of evil men throughout the centuries, to quote the Bible wrongly when cornered by their own immorality."

Walters was taking Mad apart, piece by piece. He covered the gamut, from Mad's reported Clinton-bashing to his supposed anti-Catholic bias (based on the old press release from Gladys Phillpott). "You've even been condemned by the national office of your own Episcopal Church," he noted. All that was left was the subject that Walters thought was his ace in the hole. ("That's old hat, and we've got enough to hang him with, anyway," Martina had told Walters the day before, but Walters wouldn't listen.) This was what he thought would most permanently drive a wedge between Mad and everybody who was the slightest bit devout. "For one final topic," he said to Mad, "I bet a lot of your newest followers don't know this about you, because you haven't stressed it much all year, from what I can tell. But you are on record multiple times as saying that God is a jerk. You can't deny you've said that. Isn't that an obnoxious position to take, and an arrogant one, and one that throws into doubt whether you are a man of God at all?"

Mad had had enough.

"Well, God's nowhere near as much of a jerk as you are, Spike. And the other difference is that God really *is* God, while you just like to *pretend* that *you* are."

Walters' face turned red. He was so used to rolling over people that the last thing he expected, this late in an interview in which he had so repeatedly worn down his subject's defenses, was for his subject to come back at him with an insult.

"*Cut!*" he yelled at Martina. "Cut this crap right now!" And then, with the camera off, he said to Mad: "You think you're very clever, don't you, you nutcake son of a bitch? You must not know who you're dealing with. This is Spike Walters you're talking to. I have the power to make you a hero or to ruin your life, whichever I choose. And you just signed your own death warrant."

Spike took a deep breath, and then took a few swallows of water. Then, to Mad: "Okay, cocksucker, let's try this again."

Mad, smiling nervously, nodded.

"For a final topic, here's your own words coming back to haunt you. I bet a lot of your newer followers don't know that you spent time last year babbling that God is a jerk. Doesn't that throw into question the very idea that you're somehow a man of God?"

"You must not have done your homework, Spike. I've answered that question a million times, and in the context of all of the religious theses I published, you'd have to admit that my message is one of both thanks and praise to God."

"So you're denying that you said God is a jerk?"

"Holy cow, you're thickheaded! Of course I don't deny it. Can't your pea-brain get around the fact that thinking can evolve? Can't you see that me writing about God being a jerk was, quite openly, just one stage of a longer process of understanding God?"

"The fact is, then, that you've said God is a jerk. In fact, you've gone even farther than that: You've also said that God is, quote, a 'flawed SOB.' Whose side are you on, anyway, God's or the devil's?"

"Spike, old man, you must have never taken a class in formal logic. If you start with a hypothesis at step one, and by step 59 you're reached an entirely different conclusion, then the hypothesis no longer stands. My hypothesis was that God is a flawed SOB. That was thesis number one. My conclusion is that…"

"Oh, cut the crap! You know you're cornered, Mr. Jones. Do you or do you not believe that God is a jerk?"

"If you would stop interrupting me, Spike, my man…"

"Don't 'Spike, my man' me, you cocksucker. I can cut this videotape anyplace I want it. Nobody'll ever see anything but me giving you all the time in the world to answer a reasonable question. Now give me an answer: Is God a jerk?"

"Not according to my final thesis, Mr. Walters, and I quote: 'God's love has been poured into our hearts through the Holy Spirit which has been given to us.' What's important, Mr. Walters, is the redemption."

"So you're denying that you've said God is a jerk? How can you deny what you yourself put down on paper?"

"The same way you can edit the videotape so that nobody will see you using the word 'cocksucker,' Mr. Walters."

"Mr. Jones, do you realize the trouble you're in now? Do you even know what you're getting into?"

"I don't know, Mr. Walters. I can't rightly remember. You may have mentioned that to me a few moments ago." Mad's voice was full of disdain and sarcasm.

Spike Walters turned to Martina and the technicians: "It's a wrap. Let's go home and crucify this bastard."

The interview, including all the stops and starts, had lasted more than an hour. And it would prove to be more than an hour of truth.

"Jesus Christ, we're screwed," said Becky once the TV crew had left. "What the hell was that bestiality stuff?"

Mad explained how, when Dr. Roberts had accused him of a sexual obsession with his mother-in-law, he had shot back an angry, sarcastic line about giving blow jobs to rhinoceri. Dr. Theodore had even asked him about the reference, in Dr. Roberts' report, to that outburst, and had chuckled appreciatively when Mad told him why he'd said it.

Becky didn't think it was funny. Again she said: "Jesus, we're screwed."

But Justin, bless his heart, always saw the positive side of things. "We're not screwed! We're all set! We got all we need to blow them outta the water! Don't you see? We have our own videotape. We've got a tape of him saying 'cocksucker.' We've got a tape of him bragging about how powerful he is. We've got a tape of him being totally unfair. He's the one gonna get screwed, not us!"

Becky had for months been far kinder to Justin, but this time she couldn't hold back. "I don't care what we have, you stupid little shit," she snapped. "They've got a report saying Mad was into bestiality. There's nothing we can do to overcome that!"

"And we've got Dr. Theodore on our side," countered Justin, trying to hide the hurt over Becky's calling him a little shit. "He'll tell the truth! He'll explain it!"

Becky started arguing back, but Mad wasn't saying anything. He was looking through his copy of Dr. Theodore's report. As it turned out, Dr. Theodore had filed an addendum with an unusually thorough explanation for his decision to release Mad from the hospital, on the off chance that Dr. Roberts, as the prior attending physician, ever asked for a formal review of the dismissal.

"Here it is," he said suddenly, and then began to quote from the paper. "Mr. Jones also complained that Dr. Roberts accused him, for no reason, of a sexual attraction to his mother-in-law. Said he responded sarcastically with a joke about also lusting after a rhinoceros. Said he wished he could file a formal complaint about Dr. Roberts' conduct. Said it with good humor, though. Seemed pretty funny to me. No problem there at all."

"What good does that do us?" Becky said. "Spike Walters never let you say anything about that on the air. We can't even prove that he has a copy of that addendum from Dr. Theodore. And even if we have the videotape of how unfair Walters was, what good does that do us? What are we ever gonna do with the videotape that can possibly match the 30 million people who'll see the version that runs on *Hour of Truth*?"

And there matters stood for about 12 days, spilling into August. Chet Matthews called several times to discuss how to respond to the September airing of the show, and The Colonel called Mad at odd hours of the night for the same reason. Indeed, Chet reported that some guy named The Colonel also called him in Houston, out of the blue, to say he wanted to help.

"Guy won't say exactly who he is or what his connection is to you, Madison," said Chet on the phone. "But said he and some mysterious colleagues had some money to spend, and that they are hatching a plan. He says he knows how to pull lots of strings. And I've got some money to spend, too. Some of my oil buddies, guys on the board of a big conglomerate that often advertises on *Hour of Truth*, they hate Walters as much as I do. Seems ol' Spike has made a habit of making some oilmen look bad. We're all up for hitting back at this asshole, if we can only figure out how."

"Sweetheart, it's Laura! I'm so excited, sweetheart, I've got big news!"

Laura reported that she had been given access to the videotape library of *Hour of Truth*. She said the network execs wanted her to study old shows, to get a perfect feel for the formula the show used in crafting its reports. "It's a highly evolved reporting style," she said. "They just keep using the same tricks of the trade, and the same storytelling techniques, over and over again. They said that once I master their techniques, they'll give me an assignment on a segment to air right after New Year's."

Mad wasn't catching on. "That's great Laura; so you get to watch a lot of old shows," he said. "And you'll be on the air with those same shitheads who are out to destroy me. I guess I'm happy for you, but right now I'm about to get my scalp taken off."

"Mad, don't you see? I have unrestricted access to their library and their offices! I can make copies of tapes! As long as I put the original tape back where it goes, I'm sure I can get away with smuggling out a copy without anybody knowing."

Mad still didn't see the point.

"C'mon Mad!" Laura said. "It's so obvious! They'll have their report on you ready to go probably 10 full days before it airs. But if I smuggle a copy out to you, you'll know in advance exactly what they're gonna do and you can have a response all prepared."

Laura smelled Martina Beritzky's blood in the water. If a Beritzky project blew up in Walters' face, Laura knew that somehow the blame would be foisted onto her rival.

That night, Becky arranged a five-way conference call with her father at one end, The Colonel dialing in from an undisclosed location, Buzz calling from D.C., Mary phoning from St. Louis, and her, Mad, Justin, Shiloh, and a highly cooperative Dr. Theodore at the MMW offices in Mobile. For once, everything came together in a wonderful synthesis. Together, the conspirators hatched a superbly clever plan.

CHAPTER THREE

Two days later, Shiloh and Dr. Theodore flew together to New York, with tickets paid for by The Colonel. Shiloh had called ahead, from the Mobile police headquarters to a private parking lot at network headquarters in New York, for advance permission to enter the lot with an amateur video camera and a partner. One of those "hush-hush" drug investigations, dontcha know? Trying to nail the New York source for a Mobile drug runner, he said. Won't even have a firearm, he said. Just need about a half hour of surveillance.

At the expected time, a limo driver pulled into the lot and Spike Walters emerged from the back seat. "Excuse me, Mr. Walters," said Dr. Theodore, emerging from the shadows. "Sorry to bother you like this; I just want you to have these papers. They'll clear up something about that young guy in Mobile, Madison Jones. I know you're after him; this'll help."

Startled but reassured by Dr. Theodore's friendly manner, Walters took the papers. He never saw Shiloh, sitting quietly in a nearby car with the video rolling. Dr. Theodore then turned and began walking away, full of nonchalance. Spike Walters went on up to his office, and Shiloh caught up with the doctor a while later.

During the editing sessions to prepare the final version of Walters' report, Walters was as meticulous as ever. Even when he seemed to have gotten the best of Mad, he wanted to look better still. "See that bit where I pull out the line about a 'light under a bushel'?" he said to Martina and the technician. "I sound a little like I'm guessing, because I said Jesus said *something like* not hiding our light. Why don't you insert in there one of those scenes we have of the Jones kid looking like he's been caught in a lie, one of those stricken looks we caught him in, and let me do a voiceover there before I resume my question? I looked it up: The bushel bullshit in the Bible came *right before*, just a few verses before, the crap he quoted about giving alms in secret. So let's record my voiceover citing the exact location of that passage in the book of Matthew. It'll emphasize that even a layman like me knows more about the Bible than this faker."

On that, and on everything else in the report, what Walters wanted, Walters got.

The night arrived for the season opener of *Hour of Truth*. With a big football game as a lead-in, the national audience was particularly large. The first two segments did not disappoint. And then came the final story, reported by the venerable Spike Walters. As an unparalleled morality play, it was boffo. Here was a young high school history teacher who in just a year and a half had conned an entire country into thinking he was a religious sage. But the charlatan did not entirely refute the evidence of a connection to a shadowy secret cabal at a university that once was a bastion of Southern whiteness. And he had taken cheap shots at President Clinton. And he was certifiably a psychiatric case, so messed up that he fantasized about bestiality. And not only that, but his theology, such as it was, amounted at heart to a rant against God. God was both a jerk and a flawed SOB, he had said. And when asked point-blank, "Whose side are you on anyway, God's or the devil's?" Mad's apparent answer (with tape expertly and cleverly spliced on Spike Walters' orders) was this: "I don't know, Mr. Walters. I can't rightly remember."

All throughout, Spike Walters looked like he was doing his level best to be "generous" with Mad. "We want to give you the benefit of every doubt," Walters told him quite clearly. "We're trying to understand you, Mr. Jones."

And every time, Mad was forced to admit, uncomfortably, that Walters was right. "The shock of that is just so great that you have trouble even thinking straight," Mad said, in acknowledging that he was a nutcase. "My hypothesis was that God is a flawed SOB," he confirmed.

Walters also culled the usual outside sources. Charles Brindle, the radical Episcopalian bishop who denied the divinity of Christ but who nevertheless was always held up by the media as a bulwark of mainstream Christianity, said that Mad obviously didn't know what he was talking about. Brindle said God is not a jerk, but rather pure love that forgives all sins and is comfortable with all lifestyle choices. Rabbi Ehud Heintz added that because Bill Clinton obviously was a King David–like figure, the president could have as many women as he wanted and that Mad had thus been small-minded to criticize him. (Left on the cutting room floor, of course, were Mad's protestations that, first, he had never made a habit of criticizing the president and, second, his rare comments on the situation had focused less on sex than on obstruction of justice.) Finally, to hurt Mad with more conservative viewers, Spike Walters quoted the Rev. Patterson (off camera) as saying that Mad was "a dangerous charlatan and a false prophet."

By the time the report was over, there seemed no doubt that Mad was utterly finished, destroyed, kaput. Nobody could survive such a thrashing.

And yet.... *And yet.* Something funny happened right after the report ended, when *Hour of Truth* cut to its last commercial break before returning to advertise the topics of the next week's show. The commercial began with the familiar figure of the executive for a corporate conglomerate that often advertised on *Hour of Truth.* The executive had a folksy manner, and had excelled as a TV pitchman as well as a brass-knuckles corporate czar. But it wasn't the same commercial. A new one had somehow been smuggled in.

"By now, you out there in American TV-land are probably used to seeing my ugly mug," said the executive. "But I'm just here in this ad to introduce my friend Madison Jones."

Then the camera panned back far enough to see Mad sitting next to the exec.

"The show you just saw was entirely fraudulent," Mad said to the camera. "If you'll now turn to the American Heritage Network on most of your cable systems, you'll not only see the real Madison Jones but also the real Spike Walters. We have caught him red-handed, with proof that he's a scam artist. Go ahead, change the channel now. You'll never think the same way again about Spike Walters."

And then Mad was gone from the screen.

The American Heritage Network was a fairly new outfit that had only recently negotiated a spot on most of the nation's cable lineups. Advertising on it was still relatively inexpensive. And between Chet and his oil friends, and the mysterious Colonel and his ability to "pull lots of strings," Mad's team had arranged to buy an entire half hour of airtime.

The effect was devastating. With the videotape that Laura had smuggled out, Mad and his team (including some Mobile-area film editors hired by Chet) had interspersed segments from Spike's report with sections of the wide-angle, uncut recording of the interview that Shiloh had secretly taped.

"There are lots of serious breaches of trust in the *Hour of Truth*, Mad said at the beginning. "But first, let's take a silly little example to show the kinds of techniques that Spike Walters used throughout. Watch how Mr. Walters is so vain that he even does a new take to hide that he mispronounced the word 'generous.'"

He then played, from Shiloh's version, this uncut portion of the interview:

"This is all part of the record, Mr. Jones. If you'll just calm down"—Walters smiled reassuringly for the camera—"you'll see how we're just establishing a context for you that lets you explain your unique religious views. We're trying to understand you, Mr. Jones, trying to be genderous to you..."

Walters screws up his face and turns to Martina. "Damn, that came out 'genderous' instead of 'generous.' Cut that; let's do it over."

Walters catches a breath and then nods to the cameraman, and the light goes on again. As if it's part of an uninterrupted train of thought, Walters repeats: "We're trying to understand you, Mr. Jones, just trying to be as generous to you as we can be."

Mad continued: "Now here's an even sillier example. Note how Mr. Walters actually does a voice-over, added later, to make it look as if he, purely from his own knowledge, had come up with the reference to the Gospel of Matthew."

Mad then showed Shiloh's unedited version of this full exchange, beginning with Mad speaking:

"Jesus said that when you give alms, do it in secret, and beware of practicing piety in front of men, but do it in secret instead, so that you'll be doing good deeds for the sake of the good itself and not for the sake of having others praise you for your generosity."

"But didn't Jesus also say something about how you shouldn't hide your light under a bushel?" Walters asks. "Any clever young Bible-thumper can

quote the *Good Book* out of context to justify all sorts of nefarious action, now isn't that true?"

Then came the final version from the just-completed airing of the show, in which, between "bushel" and "Any clever…" Walters was heard saying: "Matter of fact, if memory serves, the bit about not hiding your light was in the Gospel of Matthew—and it was just a *few verses* before the passage about giving alms in secret that you just quoted out of context."

Mad now looked at the camera: "Let's watch that again. First, here's the original interview." (Again, the scene with the Matthew-less dialogue.) "Now, here's the part with a voice-over added later, to make it appear that Mr. Walters knew the Gospel of Matthews off the top of his head." (Again, the voice-over with a close-up of Mad looking stricken.)

Mad again to the camera: "Now if Spike Walters will go to all that trouble on a relatively unimportant point, imagine how dishonest the rest of the report was."

The rest of the MMW-produced half hour was a series of comparisons between the original interview's reality and the Walters-edited version. Particularly damaging to Walters was this exchange from the actual interview, at a point where a discomfited Mad had begun trying to talk tough to make up for being so obviously cornered:

"The fact is, then, that you've said God is a jerk. In fact, you've gone even farther than that: You've also said that God is, quote, a 'flawed SOB.' Whose side are you on, anyway, God's or the devil's?"

"Spike, old man, you must have never taken a class in formal logic. If you start with a hypothesis at step one, and by step 59 you're reached an entirely different conclusion, then the hypothesis no longer stands. My hypothesis was that God is a flawed SOB. That was thesis number one. My conclusion is that…"

"Oh, cut the crap! You know you're cornered, Mr. Jones. Do you or do you not believe that God is a jerk?"

"If you would stop interrupting me, Spike, my man…"

"Don't 'Spike, my man' me, you cocksucker. I can cut this videotape anyplace I want it. Nobody'll ever see anything but me giving you all the time in the world to answer a reasonable question. Now give me an answer: Is God a jerk?"

"Not according to my final thesis, Mr. Walters, and I quote: 'God's love has been poured into our hearts through the Holy Spirit which has been given to us.' What's important, Mr. Walters, is the redemption."

"So you're denying that you've said God is a jerk? How can you deny what you yourself put down on paper?"

"The same way you can edit the videotape so that nobody will see you using the word 'cocksucker,' Mr. Walters."

Of that, of course, the only part that had made it onto *Hour of Truth* was the question about whose side Mad was on, God's or the devil's. It was followed on *Hour of Truth* by Mad's later comment, *"I don't know, Mr. Walters. I can't rightly remember."*

Now, to the camera, Mad said: "My comment about not remembering something had nothing to do with God or the devil. It came from an entirely later section of the original interview."

Mad continued: "But the worst distortion of reality, the single slimiest and sleaziest, was that Mr. Walters effectively accused me of bestiality. Here's the tape." Mad then ran the appropriate segment from *Hour of Truth*, with Spike talking:

"Here's what the attending physician wrote, man by the name of Dr. Richard Roberts. He wrote that you were belligerent. He also wrote, and I quote, that you were 'full of unresolved sexual angst, even to the point of obsessing about bestiality, and full of rage, and highly emotionally unstable.'"

Mad again: "To explain not just how unfair that was, but how Spike Walters knew that it was unfair, here's Dr. Ted Theodore, the physician who did my exit interview at the hospital where I had checked myself in, *by my own choice*, as a way for me to grieve the death of my wife and unborn child without interruption."

Dr. Theodore came on the screen. He showed a video clip of Mad trying to quote from his exit analysis, but with Spike not letting Mad do so. He then read from his own glowing analysis of Mad. He then explained that Mad himself had told him about the rhinoceros remark, and its context, and that he thought it was a humorous and perfectly appropriate response to an out-of-line comment from the other doctor.

"What's worse," Dr. Theodore said, "was that from the very start, it was obvious that *Hour of Truth* was biased against young Mr. Jones.

Here's a tape from my answering machine at home, with Spike Walters' producer, Martina Beritzky, weeks before Mr. Walters even interviewed Mr. Jones, showing clearly what their agenda was:

"Letting somebody go is a different thing from pronouncing him totally sane, isn't it…? From what I've heard, the guy could act like a total menace…"

"My report on Mr. Jones refuted all their charges, specifically including the rhinoceros part," the psychiatrist continued. "And what's amazing is that Spike Walters himself had my report in his hand, but he ignored it."

He then ran the videotape from the parking lot of him personally handing the report to Walters.

"I'm appalled," said the doctor to the camera. "Spike Walters knows that Mad Jones is a bright, engaging, and perfectly sane young man, but he deliberately made Mr. Jones out to be some sort of wacko. In his hands was my contemporary analysis that Mr. Jones was 'grieving but well-adjusted. A thoroughly charming young man.' But Spike Walters bent the truth to his own will. And that's despicable."

Mad came on camera again:

"To this day, I don't know why Spike Walters decided to do a hatchet job on me. I don't know what he has against me. But it's clear that he detests me, and that his entire goal was to distort reality in whatever way he could, solely to make me look bad. As my final proof, here are two more exchanges from the actual interview. For obvious reasons, Mr. Walters never put *these* verbal exchanges on TV."

Then Mad played this segment from Shiloh's tape, beginning with Walters talking:

"'God is a jerk.' You can't deny you've said that. Isn't that an obnoxious position to take, and an arrogant one, and one that throws into doubt whether you are a man of God at all?"

Mad: "Well, God's nowhere near as much of a jerk as you are, Spike. And the other difference is that God really is God, while you just like to pretend that you are."

Walters' face turns red. "Cut!!" he yells at Martina. "Cut this crap right now!" And then, with the camera off, he says to Mad: "You think you're very clever, don't you, you nutcake son of a bitch? You must not know who you're dealing with. This is Spike Walters you're talking to. I have the power to make

257

you a hero or to ruin your life, whichever I choose. And you just signed your own death warrant."

Then came this segment: *"Mr. Jones, do you realize the trouble you're in now? Do you even know what you're getting into?"*

"I don't know, Mr. Walters. I can't rightly remember. You may have mentioned that to me a few moments ago." Mad's voice is full of disdain and sarcasm.

Spike Walters turns to Martina and the technicians: "It's a wrap. Let's go home and crucify this bastard."

Mad, again to the TV audience: "Let's play that again."

"Let's go home and crucify this bastard." And again: "Let's go home and crucify this bastard."

Mad spoke one more time to the TV audience: "Well, my friends, I'm still standing. No crucifixion here; not even a cross. But if Spike Walters even *had* a conscience, then his utterly dishonest and unfair treatment of me tonight would be an incredibly heavy cross for *his* conscience to bear for the rest of his life. As for me, I'll stick with the same message of redemption and hope that is my 59th and final thesis, a thesis that Mr. Walters would not let me say on his show. It's a direct quotation from the Letter of St. Paul to the Romans. I quote: 'Suffering produces endurance, and endurance produces character, and character produces hope, and hope does not disappoint us, because God's love has been poured into our hearts through the Holy Spirit which has been given to us.'

"Thank you very much for watching."

The fallout from Mad's sting operation was immediate. The very next night, Steve Matheson finally featured Mad (not just Buzz) as a guest on his show, and for a full half hour at that. Matheson's criticism of *Hour of Truth* was withering. The late-night TV comedians all made fun of Spike Walters all week, and one of them even shoehorned Mad into the show's schedule for the Monday a week later. Cable TV and the two other traditional networks all had field days with the story. Newspaper columnists, especially conservative ones, went bonkers. Editorial boards weighed in, almost uniformly lambasting *Hour of Truth*. (The one exception was *The Metropolitan Daily*—motto: The Newspaper of Record—which cluck-clucked awhile about Walters' ethical lapses before

258

arguing that this one episode shouldn't obscure Walters' "distinguished record of journalistic service," especially considering that "Madison Jones is, after all, a brazenly cheeky young hothead with a flair for self-promotion but not a single relevant academic degree. Almost anybody could be excused for finding Mr. Jones distasteful; Mr. Walters' sole error was succumbing to the understandable temptation to dramatize Mr. Jones' obvious shortcomings.")

Republican politicians jumped eagerly on the anti-Walters bandwagon. "He's a perfect example of why the scourge of the left-wing media must be destroyed," said one. "The evil underbelly of the liberal New York media has been exposed," said another.

Not to be tarred with the same brush, the unctuous Democratic "gentleman" from Michigan said, "Spike Walters has shown that when you wrestle with dogs, you get fleas. Rather than wasting time on a right-wing hater, Mr. Walters should be examining why so many of our citizens don't have health care and why the Republicans have kept the minimum wage so low."

At *Hour of Truth*, the network execs made Martina Beritzky the primary scapegoat. She was easy to blame for supposedly being careless with the show's videotape: She was the only one who had signed out a copy before it aired, and the assumption was that somehow, somebody had "borrowed" it from her when she wasn't looking. (Laura, of course, had been careful to smuggle her copy out under separate cover. Besides, she had spent the better part of a year denigrating Mad for having had the gall to try to kiss her that night in New Orleans, thus almost ruining her career. Everybody at the network thought that she legitimately despised him.) Walters blamed Martina, too, for doing the "flawed" research that misled him into a "poor understanding" of Mad's ideas. He also claimed that when Dr. Theodore handed him Mad's medical file, he had merely passed it on to Martina without examining it himself. Clearly, he said, it was her fault that they misrepresented "the bestiality stuff." Result: Martina Beritzky found herself out of a job.

Network execs also put out a statement noting the "stress" Walters had been under because of high blood pressure combined with the recent diagnosis that his wife "might" be suffering from the early stages of Parkinson's disease. The statement said that Walters had "magnanimously" tried to assume some of the blame that belonged at Martina's feet, and that because of all these factors combined, the network would "regretfully" accept the "venerable newsman's offer" to take a one-year leave of absence from full-time duty with *Hour of Truth*.

The chat room, of course, went nuts. D Thom pronounced himself again to be FD (Formerly Doubting) Thom and firmly in Mad's camp. New participants wrote that Mad was "an inspiration" and "a hero." Even usual critics Ever Faithful and Defender wrote that Mad had been unfairly treated.

And Affirmed was over-the-top: "Spike Walters is like the Roman emperors and Mad like the Christian martyrs fed to the lions for sport! Mad is surely now a candidate for sainthood. He should be canonized while he's still alive!"

Amazingly, M. Magdalene also broke her silence. "This episode clearly shows that programs like *Hour of Truth* need new blood. It's a credit to Mad, both his guile and his essential decency, that he survived. But others may not be so lucky. So let's everybody pay tribute to Mad, but agitate for change from the networks!"

Mad was now a certifiable superstar. His bi-monthly rallies began attracting up to 20,000 attendees per event. He signed a hugely lucrative contract for another book, with a small part of the advance going to him and to Becky personally (she had insisted on the former, he on the latter) in the form of tax-protected personal savings accounts, rather than to MMW Corp. He signed a deal to do a weekly national radio call-in show (an hour each Sunday), to begin just after New Year's. And by November 1 the list of newspapers subscribing to his daily column had grown from 101 to 153, and the column's allowable length, 300 words on weekdays, was expanded to 400 words on Sundays.

And through all that autumn's hoopla, Mad tried (not always successfully) to keep a level head and keep his focus on refining his theological message.

Later in November, he chose as his column's subject letter one written to him by G.F. Martin. (He did not recognize the name.) "Dear Madison," it began. "In the Christmas story, as read by Linus in *A Charlie*

Brown Christmas, there is a great line about shepherds' being 'sore afraid.' That captures my own feelings perfectly, although for a different reason. I'm a Jew by birth, but always more of an atheist than anything. And recently, largely because of what I've read and seen from you, I've been recognizing a big void in my life and trying to see if God can fill it. I just don't 'get' Christianity, though, and my own Jewish tradition leaves me cold. I'm haunted by a God who has abandoned His promise and allowed the Holocaust to happen, and I don't see any real hope in 'God' no matter how hard I look. That's why I'm sore afraid—afraid that this emptiness inside will never leave me. In my situation, what do you think I should do?"

"Dear G.F.," Mad answered. "I wrote in my theses that those who keep the Jewish rules of Leviticus 'are to be honored' and that 'all, of all faiths, should honor the Jews.' You belong to a faith tradition that is an inspiration to all people of goodwill. While I myself am a Christian because I believe that God's redemptive promise has been made incarnate, along with God's very being, in the person of Jesus Christ, I am always eager to reassure Jews that even without Christ, God's redemptive kindness, and promise for more of the same, is manifest throughout the history of your people. At the end of Second Chronicles, and again repeated almost word for word in the beginning of Ezra, there's the story of what happens after Jerusalem has been destroyed and its people butchered in what for those days was a holocaust. But the Lord did not forsake his people. He raised up a Gentile king, Cyrus, and moved his heart to compassion. And Cyrus ordered that a new house, a new temple, be rebuilt for 'the Lord, the God of Israel.... And let each survivor, in whatever place he sojourns, be assisted by the men of his place with silver and gold.'

"God does not forsake you, G.F. I urge you to try again to understand Christianity, but if not that, take pride and take heart and find your spiritual center in your Jewish heritage, which is noble and good. May God be with you—and may He be with all of us as we struggle to build, and ceaselessly rebuild, the edifice of our faith."

EPILOGUE

Alas, for those who enjoy the limelight, the psalmist offers warnings.... In this trilogy's third book, *Mad Jones, Agonistes,* what goes up must come down. Mad cannot escape the laws of physics or of human nature. Spike Walters will not be the only one eager to topple Mad's pedestal, nor will even his most loyal supporters keep silent witness as Mad's own weaknesses emerge. But the question remains, and demands again and again to be answered: Is there redemption, and from whence does it come?

APPENDIX:
59 THESES BY MAD JONES

Would you believe...

1. God is a flawed sonuvabitch, just like the humans he created.

2. "So God created man in his own image, in the image of God created He him; male and female created He them." Genesis 1:27

3. "I, the Lord thy God, am a *jealous* God, visiting the iniquity of the fathers upon the children unto the third and fourth generation." Exodus 20:5 "For the Lord thy God is a consuming fire, even a *jealous* God." Deuteronomy 4:24

4. "For thus saith the Lord God of Israel unto me: 'Take from my hand this cup filled with the wine of my *wrath*, and cause all the nations, to whom I send thee, to drink it. And they shall drink, and be moved, and be *mad*, because of the sword that I will send among them.'" Jeremiah 25:15-16

5. God is arrogant, and mad with power, as when he tortures Job. God says: "Who then is able to stand before me? Who hath prevented me, that I should repay him? Whatsoever is under the whole heaven is mine." Job 41:10-11

6. Christ said: "And his lord was wroth, and delivered him to the tormentors, till he should pay all that was due unto him. So likewise shall my heavenly Father do also unto you, if ye from your hearts forgive not every one his brother their trespasses." Matthew 18:34-35

7. It therefore follows that when God created man in God's image, or "likeness" (Genesis 5:1), it was a spiritual and emotional likeness—an interior image—intended, not a physical likeness (which is abundantly made clear throughout the Bible). So we see that God is jealous and wrathful and unfair (as He was to Job), and arrogant and prone to going mad with His own power, and that He punishes mankind overly harshly, even unto torture, when man acts imperfectly, even though it was He, God, who created man as an imperfect being because man is in God's own image—which, of necessity, means that God Himself is imperfect. QED.

8. As God is imperfect, therefore He is inconsistent—yea, even mercurial.

9. As God is mercurial, therefore His mercy, at least here on earth, is dependent on God's mood swings, or, i.e., contingent rather than unconditional.

10. As God's mercy is contingent, and as God is imperfect, so therefore may His mercy be contingent on something other than man's own merit, but rather, at times, on circumstances beyond the ken of man.

11. God's mercy is therefore entirely unpredictable and unreliable, at least within man's temporal existence.

12. *For all intents and purposes, then, to man's way of knowing, God is a jerk.*

13. Because God is a jerk, mankind cannot count on God for comfort during this life.

14. Therefore, men and women must rely on other men and women for comfort on earth. (For what it's worth, safe sex can be heap big comfort.)

15. When human turns to human for comfort, which man often does because God cannot be counted on to provide it, God may become jealous (for He is a jealous God), and in His jealousy God may

deliberately cause *dis*comfort to man—for no good reason, not even for good reason according to the unknowable lights of God.

16. This reality helps explain the words of Jesus to the crowd of wailing women, as Jesus was led on his march of death to Golgotha: "Daughters of Jerusalem, weep not for me, but weep for yourselves, and for your children. For behold, the days are coming in which they shall say, Blessed are the barren, and the wombs that never bore and the breasts which never gave suck." Luke 23:28-29

17. Yea, verily do I ask of you: What kind of God, except a fallible God who is a jerk, would curse innocent women whose wombs become with child according to the life-creating union sanctified by God himself through Holy Matrimony?

18. "For we know that the whole creation groaneth and travaileth in pain together until now." Romans 8:22

19. "As it is written, For thy sake we are killed all the day long; we are accounted as sheep for the slaughter." Romans 8:36

20. If we are in pain, and are counted as sheep for the slaughter, shall we then bleat like sheep? Nay, we are sheep only insofar as we acquiesce to sheep-hood.

21. To acquiesce in sheep-hood is to sin greatly, for it puts us in the position of trying to become Christ, who is the only Lamb of God. Christ Himself commanded us, not to *be* lambs, but rather to consume Him, the only Lamb, by partaking of the Eucharist. Lambs do not eat Lamb; lions do.

22. Therefore, Christ calls us all to be lions.

23. No wonder, then, that the first of God's worshipful seraphim was like a lion (Revelation 4:7) and that the being found worthy to open the book of God was "the Lion of the tribe of Judah" (Revelation 5:5).

24. As we are called to be lions, and to honor the Lamb by consuming the Lamb, therefore let us also devour life with both reverence and gusto, or else God's great but imperfect creation will devour us who are unworthy, timid souls whose existence rebukes God by reminding Him that what He created can be weak.

25. "For we are made partakers of Christ, if we hold the beginning of our confidence steadfast unto the end." Hebrews 3:1

26. "Cast not away therefore your confidence, which hath great recompense of reward...but if any man draw back, my soul shall have no pleasure in him. But we are not of them who draw back unto perdition, but of them that believe to the saving of the soul." Hebrews 10:35, 38-39

27. "The Lord loves winners." —Gene Hackman, in *The Poseidon Adventure*

28. Winners and lions. *The Wind and the Lion.* Perdicaris alive. And God said: Yes, we can survive even in the desert of our souls. Yes.

29. Jesus survived the wilderness of the desert for 40 days, and withstood the temptations of Satan, all on God's account; yet God repaid Jesus' loyalty by requiring that Jesus suffer on the cross. Jesus did not forsake God, yet Jesus on the cross was moved to ask, and ask rightly, "*Eloi, Eloi, lama sabachthani?*"—which means "My God, my God, why have you forsaken me?" (Matthew 27:46; Mark 15:34) They were His last words.

30. Christ, God the Son, was forsaken by God the Father. It is said that Christ suffered in order to take upon himself the sins of the world— but God the Father created the world, and created it flawed, so the world had sin. Therefore, God is the original author of the sins of the world, sins which we, mankind, who are not omnipotent, have therefore not only committed but also suffered from due to the sins not of our own commission, but of God's.

31. As in: "Hath not the potter power over the clay, of the same lump to make one vessel unto honour, and another unto dishonour?" Romans 9:21

32. Christ's suffering therefore not only redeemed *us*, for our sins against God, but also redeemed God for his sins against we humans who mightily suffer.

33. Christ died, and was raised through the ultimate grace and glory of God, to save sinners; so, therefore, Christ died to save God, whose mercy grew in strength because Christ allowed Himself to be forsaken and thus gave God a new birth in man's hearts just as he gave man a new birth in the Holy Spirit.

34. In prayer we call Jesus Christ "our only mediator and advocate." A mediator, by nature, mediates *between* two (or more) entities, and so therefore both entities are equally beneficiaries of the mediation. God, therefore, is a beneficiary of Christ's mediation with us just as we are beneficiaries of Christ's mediation with God.

35. "As it is written, There is none righteous, no not one." Romans 3:10

36. God, too, is among those who aren't righteous. Jesus withstood Satan's temptation, but God did not withstand Satan's temptation when Satan challenged God to prove His power over Job. "Then Satan answered the Lord, and said, Doth Job fear God for nought?" Job 1:9

37. God also cruelly tested Abraham: "And He said, Take now thine only son Isaac, whom thou lovest, and…offer him thee for a burnt offering." Genesis 22:2

38. What kind of God is it who requires that his chosen patriarch be willing to sacrifice the son who is most dear to him, and that his righteous follower Job suffer, and that His only Son be crucified, all to demonstrate His own power and glory (amen)?

39. Yes, until Christ Jesus transcended the Law so that man might be justified by faith in God's grace, God was consistently a jerk—and He continues frequently in such jerkiness, which is part of His flawed nature, with the distinction that, post-Christ, God allows us eventual union with God's better self, by means of our spiritual resurrection after death, which is given us through our faith by means of God's grace.

40. Because God sent Christ to redeem man to God and God to man, and because God's ultimate will is grace (even when His temporal will is inconstant and jealous and wrathful, and causes us to suffer for no good reason), therefore "whatsoever ye do, do all to the glory of God." (Corinthians 10:31)

Would you believe?

41. Abide by the Ten Commandments, as Christ explained.

42. Abide by the two Great Commandments identified by Christ Jesus. (Love the Lord with all thy heart, etc., and the second is like unto it, etc.)

43. Ignore (if you must) all those other rules in Leviticus, which were for a particular people at a particular time, for Paul said (in effect) that the Law was superseded by Christ—although those who keep the rules still are to be honored for keeping their faith through the centuries.

44. All, of all faiths, should honor the Jews, "chiefly, because that unto them were committed the oracles of God." Romans 3:2

45. Do all such good works as the Lord hast prepared for us to walk in.

46. It is very meet, right, and our bounden duty that we should at all times, and in all places, give thanks unto...everlasting God.

47. Yet the greatest thanks we can give God is our honesty, which means we should curse Him mightily (though fearfully and with love—not hate) when He does us wrong.

48. *God respects and ultimately blesses those who wrestle with Him honestly,* as Jacob did at Penuel. Wrestle with God for that which is good, however, not to give license for sin.

49. The Twelve Commandments are to be observed because they are right and just and good in and of themselves, not because we want to gain God's favor.

50. Just as the Law (12 Commandments) condemns us when we break it (though we are not eternally condemned if we accept God's grace), so too does the Law condemn God when we faithfully observe the Law and God does not reward us in this life for our doing so.

51. God is condemned by the Saints who He allows or forces to suffer even though they abide by the 12 Commandments.

52. God is redeemed by offering the grace of eternal life in propitiation for the sins He and we commit against each other.

53. There is a special place in Heaven for the saints, who become Guardian Angels and thus find the special joys of helping future generations abide and find some triumph over the pains of earthly life. (For reference, see angels throughout the Bible.)

54. "Blessed are they that do his commandments, that they may have right to the tree of life." Revelation 22:14

55. Despite his temporal jerkiness, "For God so loved the world, that he gave his only begotten Son, that whosoever believeth in him should not perish, but have everlasting life." John 3:16

56. Said Jesus Christ: "Come unto me, all ye that travail and are heavy laden, and I will refresh you." Matthew 11:28

57. Forgive God the Father, take comfort and joy in God the Son, and honor both by striving to be lions and winners.

58. Therefore, hold fast to that which is good; be strong and of good courage.

59. As Paul wrote (Romans 5:3-4): "Suffering produces endurance, and endurance produces character, and character produces hope, and hope does not disappoint us, because God's love has been poured into our hearts through the Holy Spirit which has been given to us."

Amen.
Here I shout; I cannot do otherwise.
Madison Lee Jones

ACKNOWLEDGMENT

The phrase "God is a jerk" originally came from one of the opening lines of a sermon in the mid-1990s by the Rev. James Adams, the (now deceased) rector of St. Mark's Episcopal Church in Washington, D.C. I was not at church that day to hear the sermon, and am still not sure what Adams' ultimate point was, but his parishioners were still talking among themselves about that particular sermon for well over a year. *Mad Jones* appropriates the phrase from the Rev. Adams but for different purposes.

NOTES

NOTES

NOTES